FLEETING IMAGES

Caroline emerged from her meeting with Images' newly appointed PR company, well pleased with what she had accomplished.

Now that Images was solidly in business, she meant to see that its name became a household word, and the sooner the better. Already it was being picked up in the trade magazines, and talked of on Seventh Avenue, as well as the Madison Avenue gossip. With the clinching of the Avlon Cosmetics deal the time was exactly right for the big PR push.

It was Jessie-Ann who'd initiated the Avlon deal, but it was Caroline who had brought it to final triumphant completion. And Danae's work had been examined – practically under a microscope – by Avlon's advertising agency execs.

The new photographs she'd taken of Jessie-Ann – casting her in a different, softer, more mature, and gentle role, sort of a cross between Grace Kelly and Catherine Deneuve instead of the young, healthy-animal Jessie-Ann – had flipped their minds. Danae had the Avlon Cosmetics job in *her* pocket and Images had one of advertising's most lucrative contracts of the year in *theirs*.

About the Author

Elizabeth Adler was born in Yorkshire. She is married to an American lawyer and has one daughter. They have lived in Brazil, the USA, England, France, Canada and Ireland.

Fleeting Images

Elizabeth Adler

CORONET BOOKS
Hodder and Stoughton

Copyright © 1987 by Elizabeth Adler

The right of Elizabeth Adler to be identified as the Author of
the Work has been asserted by her in accordance with the
Copyright, Designs and Patents Act 1988.

First published under the pseudonym Ariana Scott in Great Britain
in 1987 by Hodder and Stoughton
A division of Hodder Headline PLC
First published in paperback in 1988 by Hodder and Stoughton
A Coronet Paperback

10 9 8 7

A CIP catalogue record for this book is available from
the British Library

ISBN 0 340 41551 7

Printed and bound in Great Britain by
Caledonian International Book Manufacturing Ltd, Glasgow

Hodder and Stoughton
A division of Hodder Headline PLC
338 Euston Road
London NW1 3BH

For
Liz, Peter and Jonah Adler,
with much love

Prologue

The television screen flickered brightly in Laurinda's shadowy room as Jessie-Ann Parker, all swinging corn-blonde hair and legs that went on for ever, patrolled the catwalks of the Paris fashion collections. She paused for a moment, smiling disarmingly at the TV cameras, before continuing on her way.

Nobody would ever guess what lurked behind that Miss All-American smile, thought Laurinda, peering closer at her prey; no one would ever believe that this oh-so-innocent success-symbol was evil. But she, Laurinda, knew what it was to suffer because of Jessie-Ann's depravity . . . even when they were just kids in school . . .

'Isn't it great,' commented the Spring Falls TV station presenter, 'to see how our very own local girl has made it big in that tough international fashion scene? Jessie-Ann has been up there at the top for some years now and we still haven't managed to get an interview with her. I guess she's just having too much fun racing around the world, modelling all those luxury couture clothes you and I can only dream about. Nobody can wear them better than our Jessie-Ann – and that's exactly what Monsieur Yves Saint-Laurent thinks – and Karl Lagerfeld and Ungaro . . . Jessie-Ann could even make a sack look sexy. But the word from her folks here in Spring Falls is that Jessie-Ann's still the same sweet Montana girl she always was . . .'

Laurinda Mendosa switched off the TV, leaving her alone in a silent and colourless world. Her room was as bare as a laboratory. The vinyl-tiled floor was scrubbed clean and polished to a waxy shine and it smelled of disinfectant. A cheap wooden desk held an ancient typewriter and a glass jar crammed with ballpoint pens. A sheaf of papers was placed with meticulous precision in the exact centre. There was no comforting cushion on her upright brown wooden chair and no soft rug for Laurinda's bare toes when she stepped from her bed – the same old bunk beds she'd had since she was a kid. She'd thought when she first got those beds she'd be able to invite other kids to stay. But no child had *ever* been invited to sleep over at the Mendosas' house.

Laurinda lay back against the pillows, her eyes closed, thinking about Jessie-Ann. She could re-run whole scenes from memory, just as though it were a roll of movie-film . . . Jessie-Ann was the most popular girl in both Junior High and at High School. Of course Jessie-Ann had had sleep-over parties for her friends all the time, but Laurinda had never been invited to her sprawling, sunny house on the corner lot, where the Parkers' two dogs barked joyously as they bounded across the neighbours' lawns. Laurinda could still see the three older brothers who treated their sister like a little princess, and the smiling Mom who baked great cakes and saw to it that Jessie-Ann's teeth were straightened and that her daughter always had pretty clothes – including the cutest jeans that somehow always fitted Jessie-Ann like a second skin. And Jessie-Ann had a wonderful father, a tall, blond giant of a man, who loved his daughter – the way a father should.

Laurinda's eyes flew open as a faint noise disturbed the silence. She stared balefully at the locked bedroom door as her mother's shuffling footsteps came closer.

'Laurinda?' The sound of her mother's stertorous breathing echoed through the door. Then the doorknob rattled angrily. 'Laurinda? I know you're in there. Why won't you answer me?' Her mother's voice rose an octave, but already it sounded uncertain and blurred. Laurinda smiled. She had left the usual brown-paper parcel on the kitchen table when she came home from the office, and whatever magic it worked was already happening. Mrs Mendosa was on her way to her nightly oblivion.

Grumbling angrily, her mother shuffled back along the corridor and Laurinda heard her curse as she stumbled on the stairs. One day she would just tumble head over heels down those stairs and into *permanent* oblivion – and that day couldn't come soon enough for Laurinda.

She never allowed her mother into her room. *No one* ever came there – not for years now. Sometimes it seemed her room had always been like this, grey and silent and solitary, but then the memories would come back to torture her. She'd thought she had found a way to rid herself of them long ago. The old typewriter, waiting on her desk, had served its purpose – so far. But lately the past kept crowding into her mind even when she was at work, disturbing the one thing she really enjoyed, the only thing she was good at. Being a book-keeper was not everyone's idea of fun but after her mother's 'illness' had forced her to abandon her plans for college, it was the closest Laurinda could come to the one pure passion in her life. There was a cool logic to mathematics that didn't exist in the complexities of her daily existence – because she was sure she would have been one of the world's acknowledged mathematical geniuses if she'd been able to continue her maths studies . . . But she hadn't. And it was all because of Jessie-Ann.

She'd been laying her plans carefully this past year, preparing the way. Not that she was sure how it would all work out, but at least she had made a start by taking the job with Jessie-Ann's father at the *Spring Falls Gazette* and making herself indispensable – because she was *very* good at her job. And when Mrs Parker had invited her over for coffee she'd done her 'poor, heroic Laurinda struggling and sacrificing to keep her invalid mother' act that had worked a treat, and now Mary Parker was helpful and sympathetic and often asked her to stop by for coffee. Laurinda thought that Mrs Parker was an angel . . . she wondered how different her life might have been if she'd had a mother and father like the Parkers? But she didn't – And that bitch Jessie-Ann did! And it was Jessie-Ann who had brought Laurinda's whole world crashing in nightmare ruins around her.

She sat up in bed and stared around her grey, twilit room. It was stripped to the bare essentials, a room that left no soft corners to ease away the pain, a room that offered no diversion to soothe her wounds. Her father's old pruning knife, honed to gleaming sharpness, waited on the shelf, reminding her of her purpose . . . and now only that knife would satisfy her need for revenge on Jessie-Ann.

Laurinda smiled, imagining that local television presenter as she talked about Jessie-Ann again, only this time it would be *she* who would be 'the local heroine', *she* would be famous. Laurinda would be the Spring Falls girl who'd made it big. And Jessie-Ann would be dead – and all the terrible memories would disappear – just like magic.

1

Jessie-Ann Parker paused on her way through the mirrored lobby of her apartment building, giving her appearance a quick final check before heading for the Madison Avenue offices of the Nicholls Marshall Advertising Agency. It was important that she looked exactly right because the 'Royle Girl' job was one of those lucrative plums that only occasionally fell into a model's lap, and she wanted that job desperately.

Her agent had called yesterday to tell her that Harrison Royle, owner and President of Royle's nationwide department stores was convinced that the only chance for them to penetrate the enormous, affluent youth-market was to feature clothes specially for that age group, under a 'name' designer label. They had decided to pull out all the stops and attack the market in a big way. It was Harrison who had suggested that Jessie-Ann would be the perfect model for the 'Royle' label. Everybody knew and admired her . . . if Jessie-Ann wore it, then so would the rest of the country!

Pulling a bright yellow daisy from the lobby's flower display, she tucked it into the ornate silver Scottish plaid-pin at the neck of her ochre-wool shirt, smiling as its petals reflected yellow under her chin. Jessie-Ann was twenty-four years old and six feet one inch tall, with a mane of silken, wheat-blonde hair that just skimmed her shoulders. She was wearing a Ralph Lauren denim skirt belted with Barry Kieselstein-Cord's expensive leather and silver tassels, mahogany-colour cowboy boots and an oversize steamer-coat in sheared beaver, dyed a deep sapphire blue.

Satisfied that she looked the part, she hurried across the hall, picking up her mail en route, and checking it while the doorman prowled the sidewalk in search of a taxi. There were the usual bills . . . God, had she really spent that much at Bloomingdales last month? A letter from her Mom and Dad in Spring Falls,

Montana . . . great, she'd read that in the taxi. And a familiar square white envelope with her name neatly typed in small red letters.

Jessie-Ann's heart lurched as she stared at it. It had been months since she'd had one of these anonymous notes and she'd hoped that whoever it was had forgotten about her at last; or, after eight years, had grown tired of her and latched on to some other celebrity to be the recipient of his nastiness. There was no need to open it, she knew only too well what it would say . . . but it was upsetting – today of all days – to get that filthy letter. Come to think of it, the letters always seemed to coincide with key moments in her life, almost as if the person knew what was happening . . . She could still remember the first one, vividly. It had come just after she'd won the model contest and her picture had appeared in the national press and on TV, and the local papers were heralding her as being 'on her way to fame and fortune'. Of course they'd shown photographs of her in a bathing suit, quite innocent ones, she'd thought – but obviously not to this perverted mind. Scott Parker had raged helplessly against what he called 'some cowardly, ignorant, vicious-minded madman who was threatening his schoolgirl daughter'. He'd called in the police and they'd advised him it wasn't unusual for something like this to happen, just to forget about it – odds were it wouldn't happen again. But it did – three more letters had arrived – each one becoming more explicit in its language and threats and for a few weeks Jessie-Ann had never gone out alone. Her brothers had escorted her to school – and either they or her friends had walked her home. Even the girls at school she wasn't close with, the ones she and her friends called 'the outsiders', had rallied round. Some had made a point of telling her, sympathetically, how awful they thought it was, offering to keep her company when she needed to stay late at school to finish up a project. 'They're just basking in your reflected glory,' her boyfriend, the high school football star, Ace McClaren, had told her, and though Jessie-Ann had dismissed it as nonsense, she'd had an uneasy feeling that Ace was right. Some people did seem to enjoy the attention she was getting more than she did herself, and the mystery of the threatening letters, the shadowing police cars and the extra cops lingering around the High School – just keeping an eye on things, had seemed exciting. But not to her.

She had been the centre of attention for a few months, then the letters had stopped and the crisis appeared to be over. She hadn't given it another thought until her first big job in New York a year later – when her pictures filled the April issue of *Glamour* and she was being escorted here, there and everywhere by photographers and movie-actors and rock-stars and just having a ball. The letter, typed in red, had used the crudest sexual terms, and this time it said:

> YOU ARE A CORRUPTER. I AM WATCHING YOU, WITH YOUR MILKMAID FACE AND YOUR FILTHY MIND, USING YOUR SEX TO MANIPULATE MEN, MAKING OTHERS SUFFER FOR YOUR OWN PLEASURE, SPREADING EVIL . . .

She'd read the rest in a blur of tears; it was a graphic description of the sex act, with her and some unknown man . . . stabbing her with his body . . . The words were filthy, depraved, so disgusting she'd felt sick. And the letter was signed, 'A friend'.

Her father had employed private detectives this time, but again, with no luck, and after a few months the letters had stopped. Over the years they had arrived sporadically, sometimes three or four a week, then a gap of several months, and Jessie-Ann had grown to dread the sight of that square white envelope in her mailbox.

In the opinion of the detectives and the police, it was just some crank. 'It happens to most celebrities,' they'd told her, 'these kinky guys fix on someone in the public eye and pour out all their own secret perversions on them – it's probably some respectable-looking family man with a wife and kids and a nine to five job, just working out his fantasies on you. He'll lose interest sooner or later.' But somehow, thought Jessie-Ann worriedly, he hadn't.

Well, damn it, she wasn't going to be brought down by this! The Royle job meant too much to her . . . it held the final financial key to all her dreams.

Tossing the unopened envelope into the waste-bin, she hunched her shoulders against the icy wind sweeping down Central Park West, watching the first early snowflakes of winter settle like drifts of orange-blossom petals on the grey sidewalk. They brought a thrill of nostalgia for the cosy, snowbound, middle-western winters of her childhood and her three tall, blond, older brothers; of their house, always full of friends; of Hallowe'en pumpkins and Thanksgiving turkeys with sweet potatoes cooked as only Mom could; and of testing new sleds on Christmas morning on the snowy hill behind the house. She remembered how her father would bring out his special Christmas bottle of vintage port and decant it carefully over a candle, letting her admire its ruby colour and allowing her a sip in that mellow afterglow of Christmas day. For her father, that annual treat had been something special, but she supposed for someone like Harrison Royle it would merely be what he expected. Because Mr Royle would never have been used to anything but the best.

'Sorry Miss Parker,' the doorman told her, 'but as soon as it starts to snow New York cabbies seem to go into hibernation.'

'That's OK Michael, I'll start walking. I'll pick one up on the way.'

The walk would do her good, get her circulation going, and give her time to think about the Royle job and what it would mean to her. All the while she had been 'teenage model of the year' and 'the face of the year'; all the while she had posed for the glossy covers of *Glamour* and *Mademoiselle*, criss-crossing the world in pursuit of the ideal location to show off ever-more-youthful American fashions, Jessie-Ann had longed for two things. A sprawling ranch in bluegrass country where she could escape the city's pressures, breathe fresh air again – and breed beautiful Arabian horses; and to have her own cool, businesslike model agency, running just like clockwork and ticking over the money in her bank account – without her forever having to *smile* goddamnit!

She hovered at the traffic-lights sticking out a blue-fur arm and scowling as the cab drove past. Dodging the traffic she crossed Sixty-sixth and headed for Columbus Circle.

Sure, she'd earned a lot of money as a top teenage model – those years had been good ones and she had invested wisely. But it hadn't taken long for the gloss to wear off, and the reality of the hard work – as well as the effort of always looking her best –

was tough for someone as basically lazy as she. It might have been different if she'd had the *bones* – the long, lean, aloof *Vogue*-look, but she was 'Miss Youth of America' – with the thick blonde hair that hung, heavy and straight to her shoulders and swung delightfully as she walked. She had the long slender legs, wide shoulders and small breasts of the athletic outdoors girl – with the greatest wide, white smile and the always-suntanned glow. And of course, a sprinkling of freckles! Jessie-Ann had smiled at America from a thousand billboards and sold them cosmetics from a million ads. And enough was enough. There was nowhere to go when a great teenage model hit twenty-four. Sixteen-year-olds were already taking her place.

Pouncing on the empty cab, she elbowed an executive in a black double-breasted overcoat carrying an umbrella out of the way, smiling apologetically as the cab pulled into the traffic. 'Madison and Fifty-seventh,' she told the driver, settling back in the cracked plastic seat and wrinkling her nose at the stale cigarette smell.

The Royle Girl job would be her chance to parlay all she had worked for since she was fifteen and a cheerleader in Montana who'd won a national magazine model contest. This, at last, was the way she could earn the extra money for that horse ranch and her own model agency. If they chose her, her agent had said Royle's would be willing to pay her a fortune, not just for doing the ads, but for using *her* name on the clothes. She would get royalties, commissions, advertising money, expense-paid promotional trips. 'JESSIE-ANN' would become an industry! And then in a couple of years when it was over, she would open *Images*.

Jessie-Ann wanted to be a success in a field she knew backwards and she wanted to be acknowledged as more than 'just a pretty face'. She wanted her model agency, *Images*, to be the talk of New York's fashion world. After all, didn't she know every model, photographer, make-up artist, stylist and designer in the business? If she got the Royle job, it should be a breeze.

Paying off the cab, she strode through the soaring glass atrium of the smart office building and took the elevator to the thirtieth floor. A cheerful dark-haired receptionist smiled good morning and escorted her to where Mr Royle and the account executives were waiting. Pulling herself even taller and lifting her chin high, Jessie-Ann took a deep breath and went in.

Harrison Royle sat at the top of an immense, highly polished boardroom table, flanked by the entire upper echelon of the Nicholls Marshall Advertising Agency. An untouched coffee tray waited in front of him and as Jessie-Ann walked across the room, he continued his telephone conversation with merely the briefest glance in her direction. Stu Stansfield, in charge of the Royle account, greeted her, seating her in a throne-like chair to the left of the table where the light filtering through Madison Avenue's canyons fell directly on to her face. Harrison replaced the receiver and pushed back his chair. Walking towards her, he held out his hand.

'Miss Parker,' he said unsmiling, 'I'm happy you could take the time to meet us. I know how busy you must be.'

Harrison Royle was forty-one, tall, greying at the temples, immaculate in a dark business suit, with that special gloss of the very rich. And he had dark, intense eyes that, as they looked into hers, seemed to Jessie-Ann to see into her soul. She gazed back at him, her heart pounding so loudly she feared they could hear it. She hadn't felt like this since she was sixteen and Ace McClaren undid her buttons on the back seat of the Ford Mustang after the big high school game where he'd scored three times – four if you counted her . . . that's what he'd *claimed* anyway – though of course, it wasn't true.

Harrison returned to the table. 'Please bring coffee for Miss Parker,' he ordered, 'or perhaps you would prefer tea?' A secretary hurried to do his bidding.

'Coffee is fine, thank you,' she replied as his gaze returned to the pages of notes in front of him on the glossy table.

Jessie-Ann sat demurely while for half an hour Stu Stansfield and his account executives discussed her photographs, her merits, her looks, her style – as though she weren't there. Harrison Royle, in the big chair at the top of the table, listened – indifferently it seemed.

Then, with a glance at his watch he stood up. 'Thank you, gentlemen,' he said, 'I think I've heard enough.' They shuffled their papers and pictures, gazing at him expectantly, anticipating his acceptance. 'Jessie-Ann,' he said, and her name sounded somehow softer on his lips, 'Jessie-Ann, it seems everyone has discussed your work and talked about your talent. Would you please have lunch with me? Maybe that way, one of us will get to know you.'

Her smile flashed across the room. She was up from her chair in a minute, pocketbook under her arm, skirt smoothed over her stylish hips, and with Harrison Royle guiding her she exited from that boardroom leaving the most surprised and influential ad-men in New York gasping in astonishment.

They lunched at '21' and his eyes never left her face as he fed her her staple diet of salad and chicken – nothing ever fazed her appetite, not even Harrison Royle's unwavering brown eyes. And his questions had nothing to do with 'Jessie-Ann Clothes for Royle's' – he wanted to know about *her*; where she was from, how she'd coped with being a teenage model and with fame, and about her life away from her family. Now that she thought about it, few people had ever really wanted to know *about* her – they just wanted what she *looked* like. Even her lovers. Sometimes Jessie-Ann had suspected that the buzz of being seen in public with her was greater than the charge of being alone in bed with her. Then she was just herself, Jessie-Ann looking for love – one more time!

After lunch they walked through the cold grey streets of Manhattan that seemed to her to be suddenly golden and glowing. Outside the Plaza Harrison paused by the waiting line of carriages. Patting a calm black horse on the neck he held out a hand to her, 'Shall we?' he asked, laughing. And, wrapped warmly in a fur rug, they took that same old ride around Central Park that lovers always took – except, of course, they weren't lovers. But he did hold her hand. Jessie-Ann couldn't decide whether he were just being friendly or whether he thought it was a prerogative of the 'boss' – if in fact he really was going to choose her as the Royle Girl. And somehow the moment didn't seem right to raise that question.

That night they went to the theatre together and then for dinner afterwards in a delightful, dimly lit, sophisticated French restaurant, and this time Jessie-Ann asked the questions. Like her, Harrison didn't seem used to talking about himself, but he told her he was the grandson of the founder of Royle's. They now had thirty stores nationwide, as well as a mail-order catalogue that did more business than all the stores put together.

'I can remember my Mom ordering kitchen curtains from your catalogue,' she told him with a smile, 'café-curtains, they were called. They were red and white gingham and they hung on special brass rings half-way up the kitchen window with a ruffle across the top – My Mom's a great cook,' she added, 'I can still recall how good our kitchen smelled when we got home from school – home-baked cookies and bread, and always something delicious sizzling in the stove for supper. And your curtains.'

Harrison's dark brown eyes met hers a little sadly. 'Our kitchen was never like that,' he said, 'it was too big and tiled and white, and always clean. There was a chef from France who cooked wonderful dinners for my parents' guests but he had no time to be bothered baking cookies for small boys.'

Jessie-Ann tried to imagine the coolly powerful Mr Royle as a small boy and failed.

'It didn't matter that much,' he admitted as she smiled sympathetically, 'I was away at school most of the time. And summers we went to the Cape, or later, abroad.'

He'd been educated at prep school and Princeton, followed by a business degree at Harvard. He told her that he was Jewish, that he'd been married once but his wife had died young and that he had a son almost Jessie-Ann's age (actually Marcus was only eighteen). There had been other relationships off and on but no one serious enough to replace Michelle, his childhood sweetheart and mother of his son. Now he shared a vast penthouse on Park Avenue with his mother, and, when he was home from school, his son Marcus. 'There,' he said finally, 'you know it all.'

'All?' asked Jessie-Ann, surprised.

'All about me – my past, who I am . . .'

'Oh no. I don't think you've told me that,' she said thoughtfully, 'but maybe I'll find out for myself.' Sipping the delicious champagne he'd ordered, she cursed herself for being so attracted to him. He was seriously rich, he was Jewish – and he lived with his mother! What chance could she possibly stand? She should be

18

concentrating on getting the job, not on his smouldering brown eyes, his smoothly shaven cheeks with the faintest blue shadow, the arrogant curve of his mouth . . . 'Mr Royle,' she said firmly, though she'd called him Harrison earlier, 'we should really be talking about business. After all, I came to the agency to audition for the "Royle Girl". I think I should ask you if there is a chance that I've got the job? It's important to me, you see. Very important.'

'Jessie-Ann,' Harrison said quietly, taking her hand, 'will you consider marrying me instead?'

The champagne slopped from her glass to her skirt and he leaned across, smiling, dabbing at her thigh with his napkin. 'Of course there's no hurry,' he reassured her, 'we have time. Lots of time for you to think about it, and to get to know me better.' His hand gripped hers and she felt a blush burn her cheeks as she met his dark gaze. 'And you know Jessie-Ann,' he said, 'you can still have the "Royle Girl" job – even if you say no to becoming Mrs Royle.'

'And if I say yes?' she asked dazzled.

'No more modelling, no Royle Girl . . . you'll be my wife.'

They saw each other every night for two weeks. Just his touch on her arm, his silent presence beside her in the chauffeured car, his sidelong glance at her in the darkened theatre turned her legs to jelly. And it was his light goodnight kiss on her lips as he left her at her door – a kiss with a tremor of restrained passion behind it – that left her gasping, wondering what it would be like if he *really* kissed her, if he went further . . . if he made love to her.

Harrison Royle wasn't usually a man who acted on impulse, but when Jessie-Ann had walked through the door of that boardroom, blonde hair swinging like sunlight on a gloomy afternoon, he'd felt uplifted from his jaded routine. The flicker of her youth had touched his heart and it was contagious. Just looking at her, being with her, hearing her talk made him feel young again in a way he hadn't since Michelle died. For the past ten years he'd lived and breathed work. Jessie-Ann was *life* – and she was down-to-earth, down-home-style life. He told her that despite her glamour and her gloss she was still as fresh as if she'd never left Montana – and he loved her for it.

Harrison told her everything about his life, he talked about his business, his homes on Park Avenue and in Cape Cod and in the Bahamas. He told her about his mother and his son – but he never, ever mentioned his dead wife, Michelle. He told her he wanted her, that he'd love her, cherish her, that she need never work again – he would look after her. And of course – they would have children.

Every morning Jessie-Ann's agency called and left messages on her answering service which she never returned and for the first time in her life she forgot all about work. At the end of three weeks, when she should have been in Paris modelling the collections, they flew down to Florida in his private jet, stopping off long enough to be married by a Justice of the Peace in a small-town courthouse where no one knew them and no one cared, except the nice man and his beaming secretary who acted as witnesses. And then they went on to Harrison's island home in Eleuthera to begin their honeymoon.

The big white hacienda by the sea was the perfect place for two people in love – a long, low white house on a talcum-soft beach, with an endless vista of blue-green sea and flawless sky. The gardens were filled with jewel-coloured blossoms, oleander, hibiscus, bougainvillaea and sweet-scented jasmine and shaded by tall palms. There was a Riva speedboat for dashing across the bay to the Windermere Island Club for a lunch of fresh crayfish and crisp white wine or simply for waterskiing and exploring tiny uninhabited little coves. And there was a fifty-foot cruiser equipped for deep-sea fishing where Harrison spent serious hours sipping Scotch and waiting for his massive prey to take the bait. Wearing Harrison's plaid shirt and a white visored cap to protect her from the sun, Jessie-Ann learned how to cast a reel and fight for her catch – only one very small tunnyfish – but at least it was a catch. Then there was a forty-foot yacht where Harrison demonstrated the rudiments of sailing, grabbing her out of the way, terrified that she might get hurt as the boom swung across in the wind and lecturing her on the need to be careful. Three cars, polished to gleaming perfection, stood in the garage – a white Aston Martin with soft blue leather seats, a bright scarlet Porsche 928S, and a long, silver, Mercedes station wagon. A shiny yellow helicopter sat on a pad in front of the house and a private eight-seater jet awaited Harrison's command at Governor's Harbour Airport. 'Rich men's toys,' he explained with a boyish grin.

Eleuthera's nights were warm and soft, and they sat on the verandah with the breeze from the ceiling-fans stirring her hair, sipping cooling drinks in the ruby light of the setting sun. A white-jacketed manservant served their supper, and afterwards they strolled barefoot in the moonlight along the cool silver beach, tossing pebbles into the smooth dark swell of the ocean and pausing every few yards, to kiss. Later, naked in the vast, many-pillowed bed, they exhausted their passion for each other. Jessie-Ann thought that Harrison was the most perfect lover, tender and passionate and with a hard, firm body that he controlled until the very moment she needed his great burst of passion so desperately. She begged him for it . . . and then for a few perfect moments they were truly one. Still wrapped in each other's arms they would fall asleep as dawn crept coolly through the open windows.

Harrison wanted to know everything about her and she talked about her youth, and school and her friends – but she didn't tell him about the vile hate letters that she had been subjected to all these years, because, in her happiness, she simply didn't think about it. But she did tell him about her lovers.

Foolishly, Jessie-Ann hid nothing, confessing her girlish crush on Ace McLaren, as well as more serious relationships that had ended either in friendship or in tears. When Harrison turned away, his face dark with anger, she stared at him puzzled. 'But I didn't know you then,' she exclaimed, as he strode angrily down the path to the beach.

She hadn't expected him to be jealous, after all he'd asked her to tell him, and she watched anxiously from the shade of the verandah as he paced the curve of white sand below the house. He was gazing straight ahead, oblivious to the beauty around him, and when he finally turned back to the house she rushed down the sandy path to meet him, afraid that he no longer loved her. He grabbed her to him, his hooded brown eyes staring intently into hers. 'I love you, Jessie-Ann,' he said fiercely, 'I don't care about anyone else, I just love you.'

'And I love you,' she cried, feeling weak with relief. 'That's why I married *you* and not the others.'

Harrison picked her up in his arms and carried her back along the verandah to their room, placing her gently on their big bed. His lean, tanned body trembled with passion as he caressed her, curbing his desires to satisfy hers. Her small coral nipples hardened under his touch, as his lips moved down the smooth slope of her belly, and the long length of her soft thighs, and then further down to her smooth pink-painted toes, until she was crying out for him, waiting for his touch on that warm, damp place. She arched her back to meet him as Harrison thrust himself into her at last, crying out with passion as his love spilled into her. 'You're mine, Jessie-Ann,' he murmured as they lay still entwined, 'you belong to *me* now.'

He hadn't told her about his first wife, and it worried her; it was as though Michelle were some dark secret.

Finally, unable to keep back the question any longer, she said, 'Won't you please tell me about Michelle?'

Harrison had never talked to anyone about what had happened, not even his son, keeping his memories locked away in a private area because they had always been too painful. In the beginning he had thought of Michelle every minute of every day, and even as the years passed she was still the woman he measured others by. But it had been eighteen years and suddenly it seemed such a relief to talk about it.

Jessie-Ann listened, enthralled, as Harrison told her how Michelle had been his friend from childhood. Her parents were neighbours and good friends of the family. He had adored her from the moment he had first seen her as a new baby in her mother's arms, when he was just four years old and already in school. Michelle had grown into a sweetly smiling, timid child and somehow Harrison had always looked after her. It was *he* who came to her aid in her childish battles, *he* who helped her with her schoolwork; he went to her birthday parties and she came to his, and their families often shared vacations together. Harrison had missed her like crazy when he went away, first to prep school and later to college, and they had written to each other all the time.

The summer he was nineteen he'd come home from Princeton to find that Michelle had a boyfriend, and he was sick with jealousy. She was still only in Junior High but the guy was older – seventeen he guessed, and a real jock – he was on the baseball team, he ran track, he was a champion swimmer – you name it, this kid did it – and did it well. The only thing Harrison had over him was that he was two years older and already in Princeton.

He'd invited Michelle to the football games at college, outmanoeuvring her high school athlete, and at a Princeton party that Christmas he had found a little golden ring in his crackerjack box, a small fake emerald flanked by two tiny glittering 'diamonds'. As he put the ring on Michelle's finger she'd gazed at him solemnly with eyes as dark as his own. 'I'll keep it always,' she'd promised.

Harrison had had that ring copied at Tiffany, waiting impatiently until she was seventeen to declare his love and offer her his real ring. 'Now I can wear both,' Michelle had said laughing. 'One on each hand.'

Their parents had been delighted, they could want nothing better than their children should love each other and marry. The wedding had taken place on Michelle's eighteenth birthday. Harrison was twenty-two, just graduated from Princeton and planning on taking a business degree course at Harvard. They had rented a small apartment overlooking the Charles River and were madly happy. She was all he had ever really wanted, his friend, his love, his companion . . . and soon she would be the mother of his child.

Michelle pregnant had been almost ethereally beautiful, her slender body bearing the burden of her large baby proudly. Her pale complexion had been lit with a new pink glow and there was a contented gleam in her eyes. Their son, Marcus, weighed in at a heavy nine pounds two ounces and suddenly it seemed that all Michelle's strength had gone to him. She was happy with her baby, but she was tired and listless. They'd moved into a house in the country with wide lawns for their child to play on and shady trees to protect him from the sun. A nurse was employed to take care of his needs because Michelle complained that she was too tired. 'I guess I'm just lazy,' she'd protested, when Harrison insisted that she see a doctor. But it wasn't laziness. It was leukaemia. Michelle was dead within a year. She was buried with his two rings on her fingers, the one from the crackerjack box and the one from Tiffany.

At first Harrison had blamed himself. He should have taken better care of her, not got her pregnant, she was too young, too delicate . . . then he'd blamed Marcus for draining her, guzzling her strength the way he'd guzzled her milk. But in the end he'd realised that it was nothing to do with either of them. Michelle had suffered from a disease and she had died. It happened to people every day . . . *but why to Michelle? Why Michelle – and him?*

Leaving the boy with his grandmother, Rachel Royle, he'd fled to Europe, trying to escape his misery. At first he'd just bummed around in London and Paris but after a few months he'd discovered a peaceful old French château in the middle of a forest where, surprisingly, courses were offered in European and International business. The peace of the surroundings and the stimulation of the courses had brought him back to reality and he'd felt able to face life again. He'd finally gone home and taken an interest in work again, finding he could bury his emotions in the cold realities of facts and figures. And then he rediscovered his son.

As a small baby Marcus had been neglected by Harrison because he reminded him of Michelle's illness and death. For a while, even after he'd returned from Europe, Harrison couldn't even bear to be near him. At three Marcus was a tall, steady-eyed kid with a shock of blond hair – though where it came from was a mystery since both Harrison and Michelle were dark. He had this engaging way of just hanging around when Harrison was busy, hovering near the window at first and working his way slowly towards the desk until Harrison would glance up suddenly and find him at his elbow. His son would look at him with his trusting dark eyes and wide unchildlike grin, like they were buddies and Marcus was there helping him and trying to share in his life. Harrison's frozen heart had melted. They had been friends ever since, as well as father and son.

Jessie-Ann thought Harrison's hand felt cold in hers, even though it was a warm, sultry night. Getting up, she padded, naked, from the bed to the sitting room and poured him a shot of brandy, warming the balloon glass in her hands before handing it to him. Harrison's dark eyes were still clouded with memories, as they met hers. 'I've never talked to anyone about Michelle,' he admitted, 'just like that. The whole painful truth.'

'Then I'm glad it was me you told,' she whispered, feeling somehow even closer to him than when they had made love. He had allowed her to see the other side of him, the vulnerable man behind the cool authoritative business tycoon. The man who had everything knew what it was to lose something precious. Harrison had felt the sort of pain she had never had to go through, and her heart ached for him.

Kneeling by the side of the bed, still holding on to his hand, she kissed his fingers and he smiled at her, ruffling her silken blonde hair. 'It's all a long time ago. Michelle and I were just kids. It's so different now. We're together you and I, Jessie-Ann. And I want you to know that I've never been happier in my life.'

The next morning as they swam naked from their private beach, Harrison clasped her to his hard body, kissing her smiling wet face as the waves foamed around them. 'You're so beautiful,' he said, 'I can't stop watching you, the way you move, the curve of your cheek, your smile . . . you're like a favourite painting come to life . . .'

'You should have seen me when I was a child,' she laughed, 'until I was fourteen I was just a long skinny kid with braces. It never occurred to me that I might ever be pretty – besides I was too busy having fun. It was my friends who were pretty. *They* were short and cute, and *they* had curves where I had angles, *their* teeth didn't need braces and *their* hair had waves and behaved itself. God, we had such great fun though. The boys called us "the Centrefolds" though *I* surely didn't qualify. But I guess we were kind of the élite group of the high school. We were the cheerleaders, and in charge of organising the dances and social events. We decided who was "in" and who was "out" . . . not that it really mattered because we had our own little circle and it was the only one that counted. We did everything as a group – slept over at each other's houses, did our homework together, went out on Saturday night dates together – always with the best-looking guys. We went swimming together in the summer and skiing in winter. It was our own warm, private little world within a world. But you know something? I always felt a little sorry for the others – the kids who seemed to have no friends and no real lives. The *real outsiders*.'

'Like me,' he said, 'you would have felt sorry for me because I was outside your magic circle.'

'This was just small-town stuff,' she scoffed. 'Even at seventeen you would have been a sophisticated man-of-the-world compared to the guys I knew.' She stared at him. 'I can't imagine you ever being "the outsider" Harrison – you're a born leader, always in control . . .'

'Not true,' he whispered, kissing her wet face again, 'not true my darling Jess. I long to share your small-town memories; I'd like to meet your family, your friends . . . I *envy* your childhood.'

'Envy? But you had *everything*,' she exclaimed.

'My family had *money*, but they didn't have everything Jess. I never had what you had.'

'Of course I'll take you home,' she promised, 'but you know something, every time I go back it seems a little bit further away. It's different – and yet everything *looks* the same.' She frowned, remembering how she'd felt on that last visit home. Hadn't she found it difficult to step back into the rhythm of the daily lives of her family and friends? Wasn't she faster-paced now? Harder? More used to living on New York's sharp edges and her wits? But now she was married all that would change. She would be exactly the sort of wife Harrison wanted her to be.

Two months later Jessie-Ann paced the immaculate drawing room of the triplex, twenty-eight roomed Manhattan penthouse that she now called home – with ten working fireplaces and walls panelled in oak and Fortuny silk, a gymnasium and a swimming pool and an unmatched collection of Old Masters. She wondered anxiously if they had talked so much that first month that they'd said all they had to say to each other? Now Harrison was up at six and downing a cup of coffee before she even had her eyes open. He'd drop a hasty kiss on her forehead and in a black tracksuit he'd be off for his first run of the day; then he'd go on to the gymnasium for a workout and from there to the office. He called her once in the morning and once in the afternoon and then later from the car to let her know he was on his way home. At first she'd been pleased that he was thinking of her, but lately she found it irritating. She wondered if he was checking on her? Making sure she was where she was supposed to be, and not off on her own doing something she shouldn't. Like what, she wondered moodily? Modelling? Taking lovers . . .? But she had no need to take a lover, Harrison must be certain of that. Their nights were still filled with passion . . . it was just that her days were filled with nothing . . . except boredom. Now she knew what Harrison had meant when he'd said 'we had money – but not everything'.

She thought wistfully of the way her life might have been as the Royle Girl, filled with action, travel, personal appearances, new faces. *People!* Goddamnit, that was what was wrong. Harrison thought her friends frivolous – she found his boring. When he came home late and tired ready for a quiet supper and a bit of peace, she was ready to go out on the town – almost always they compromised by going out to dinner in some smart restaurant together.

She had a sneaking suspicion that Harrison saw her differently from the way she saw herself. Of course she was Mrs Harrison Royle – but she dressed like Jessie-Ann in a mixture of whatever took her fancy, ignoring the pearls and lavish furs he'd bought her. She'd thought Harrison found it amusing, but he'd been embarrassed when she'd shown up at his party for the Royle department store chiefs, wrapped in a big-shouldered, white-leather flying jacket and red satin pants, with a huge fake scarlet jewel pinned on her bosom. She had looked terrific and she knew it – but all the other wives were in safe and expensive dresses – and they all wore pearls.

She never met anyone *interesting* these days. They rarely entertained because Harrison preferred to be alone with her – which was OK, except that his day had been busy and filled with people, while hers had been lonely. They went to the theatre often – but alone. And occasionally, they had dinner with his mother.

Rachel Royle was a petite, bird-like woman – though Jessie-Ann thought she resembled a raven rather than a sparrow! Rachel had jet black hair streaked with two wings of silver at the temples, that she wore pulled back into a chignon, usually adorned with a silk or velvet Chanel bow. Her fine, dark eyes, so like Harrison's, bore the lines of her sixty-five years proudly though the rest of her face was as smooth as a teenager's, and it gave her an oddly compelling look of wisdom. Jessie-Ann felt sure that Rachel's smooth complexion was entirely natural, and had not been helped by the surgeon's scapel, but the contrast between her knowing old-woman eyes and her young face was intimidating.

Rachel Royle wore Chanel as easily as a second skin. The clothes suited her small figure and neat style, and she could still wear the suits she had bought when she was just thirty years old. She had taken Lagerfeld's 'new look' for Chanel in her stride, adjusting to the larger shoulders and new shaped jackets and she was, without doubt, the most pulled-together woman Jessie-Ann had ever seen. She just knew that you would never drop in unexpectedly on Rachel and find her lazing in front of the fire in an old sweater, eating chocolates and reading a magazine. Rachel would always be correctly dressed in neat tweed skirt and silk shirt, with the pale two-tone Chanel pumps she favoured. There was very definitely nothing casual about the elder Mrs Royle and after their first traumatic meeting Jessie-Ann said gloomily to Harrison, 'I'll bet if there were a fire and we all had to dash from the building, she'd be wearing her pearls and her hair bow, and those goddamn shoes and her jacket would be buttoned properly!'

Harrison just laughed, 'Don't let her bother you,' he replied, 'my mother's always been like that. She's a terrific organiser – works for a half dozen charities and keeps them all on their toes.'

'I'll bet she does!' commented Jessie-Ann, still stinging from Rachel's appraisal of her.

Their first meeting had been polite – Rachel would never be *rude* to anyone, but there had been barbs behind her charming greeting.

'So,' she said, holding out her hand to Jessie-Ann (no kiss, thought Jessie-Ann, for the new bride?) 'so this is who Harrison married!' (*Who* he married? Not 'the girl' . . . or even 'the lovely girl' he married?) Jessie-Ann knew at once she was on treacherous ground. Rachel's hand was cool and firm as her piercing dark gaze swept her new daughter-in-law from top to toe. Golden and glowing from love and their month in the sun, wearing casual black linen pants cropped at the ankle, and a long loose white T-shirt, Jessie-Ann felt suddenly badly underdressed for the occasion.

'Well there's certainly a lot of you,' commented Rachel, with a steely smile, 'you are very tall my dear.' Turning away she kissed her son. 'What a surprise Harrison, to spring on your old mother.'

Harrison grinned. 'Since when have you been old?'

'Surprises like this can be very ageing,' she replied, taking a seat on the blue silk sofa and pouring tea from a large silver pot. 'Lemon or milk?' she asked, offering Jessie-Ann a fragile blue-flowered cup. Not daring to mention that she never drank anything containing caffeine, she took the cup and a slice of lemon.

'Well now, Jessie-Ann, tell me about yourself.'

Fixed with Rachel's raven gaze she slopped the tea carelessly into her saucer, feeling like the country-cousin from Montana visiting the Queen. Damn it, she told herself, glancing quickly at Harrison, you're twenty-four years old, you've travelled the world and you're successful in your own right. You've even met the *real* Queen once, at a reception in London years ago. So why the hell should you be intimidated by this woman? What has Rachel ever done in life – except marry Harrison's father? Putting down her tea she said, 'I think we'd better get this out of the way, Mrs Royle, because I can see that it's on your mind. I didn't marry your son for his money. I'm pretty successful at what I do and Harrison isn't the first rich man to ask me to marry him. I don't need money – not even as much as the Royles have . . . Besides,' she added with a grin at Harrison, 'I'm not the sort to be content to be a rich man's toy.' Harrison laughed and she smiled at him gratefully.

Mrs Royle's creamy complexion turned faintly pink – the only sign of her anger. 'Well!' she exclaimed, 'you certainly are frank, though of course what you say remains to be proven. I can assure you that many girls have chased after Harrison since his beautiful Michelle died, but he was always faithful to her memory. I only hope – for your sake – you can live up to that.'

'Nonsense Mother,' objected Harrison, 'you make me sound like Max de Wynter in Rebecca! I love Jess and she loves me – it's as simple as that. It's time to put away all your old prejudices and worries; when you get to know her better you'll soon see why I married her.' He glanced at his wife, who seemed to tower over Rachel on the sofa, 'Besides, I can't live without her,' he added simply.

Rachel knew she was beaten – temporarily. 'There then, I'm glad that's all settled,' she said smiling. 'Jessie-Ann dear, come and sit here by me and tell me all about your work. It sounds most interesting.'

Jessie-Ann couldn't really say that their relationship had progressed much from that point. Rachel Royle maintained her privilege to object to her son's marriage through a façade of polite displeasure – though she had, at Harrison's firm suggestion, moved into a separate apartment on a lower floor of the same building – which Harrison just happened to own. But Marcus Royle was a different matter.

'I surely can't call you "Mom",' he'd said when they first met, grinning at her cheerfully, 'I confess I used to keep that famous poster of you in tennis shorts on my wall at prep school. Gosh!' he exclaimed throwing his arms around her and beaming, 'I can't tell you how great it is to see Dad this happy at last. I've always been worried about him being lonely – and you know somehow I think rich men can be lonelier than most.'

For his nineteen years, Jessie-Ann thought Marcus was the most perceptive and sensitive young man she'd ever met. He was as tall as she, with a shock of thick, straight, blond hair, his father's arrogant nose and firm mouth, and the Royle brown eyes, only Marcus's were three shades lighter. He was wearing a plaid shirt, Levi 501's and white Reebok sneakers. He was a champion rower with the muscular torso of an athlete, and he had a straightforward open friendliness that made her instantly his buddy.

After their first meeting Marcus called her often from college, just to see how she was and if she'd come to terms with 'the old battleaxe' – his grandmother; and he cheered up her lonely afternoons with his chat. He asked her advice about his girl-friends and talked about school and how hard it was to keep on top of the work and fit in enough time for rowing practice and athletics which he loved, as well as the football games and the parties and the in-and-out love affairs. She felt as though they had been friends for years and sometimes, because he was closer to her own age, she found Marcus easier to talk to than Harrison.

The exquisite apartment with its endless rooms filled with art treasures and flowers seemed more and more like a luxurious cage, trapping her youth and vitality in its too-rich silk and velvet folds. Jessie-Ann was going quietly crazy, waking later and later each morning, killing a few extra hours in sleep and dreams, ringing for the maid to bring her her tea and toast in bed and lingering there reading papers and magazines. She dawdled in the bath and spent an hour dressing. Then maybe she'd go to the hairdresser or meet a girlfriend for lunch and gossip, but everyone else was working and had to rush back to their jobs, leaving her sitting over yet another cup of decaffeinated coffee and wondering sadly how to fill in the rest of the afternoon.

The highlight of the day was when she heard Harrison's foot-steps in the marble hall. She would hear him say, 'Good evening' to Warren, the houseman, as he handed him his briefcase, and then his light eager tread on the stairs. She'd fling open the door and rush to meet him and they'd hug each other, and only then did life seem exciting and wonderful.

It was Marcus who advised her to tell Harrison that she was bored and needed to work. She had brains and talent and she needed desperately to use them. 'Dad's a jealous man,' he warned her, 'he wants to keep you all to himself. I can't blame him, but it's just not fair. You're not the sort to want to spend your days at the hairdresser and shopping.'

Finally, she plucked up the courage to tell Harrison that she wanted to work.

'But you promised me – no modelling!' he exclaimed,

31

worriedly. 'Besides, the Royle Girl job has gone to Meredith McCall.'

Jessie-Ann felt a pang of jealousy. Merry McCall was younger than she, tall and long-limbed with glossy chestnut hair. 'It's a good choice,' she admitted, trying to stay calm and not think of the fun Merry would have in her place. 'But what I mean is that I'd like to open a small, exclusive model agency – just a few really great girls and boys . . . I know *everyone* in this business, I've worked for them all!' Her blue eyes sparkled with eagerness and Harrison's heart sank as he watched her. 'And I'm friends with *all* the top models – they're always grumbling that their agents don't understand them. But you see *I'm one of them* – I know what they mean. It will be different when they are with my agency. Don't you see? I can sympathise with all their problems, help them from an insider's point of view, *I know what they need!* Of course I realise how greedy account executives and magazines are for something different and I'm going to find new faces as well.'

Looking into her eager face, Harrison knew he couldn't refuse. 'I guess it was too good to be true, keeping you here all to myself,' he said a little sadly. 'Why don't we have dinner and talk it over?'

Jessie-Ann grabbed her coat and headed for the door, 'I'm ready,' she cried.

'Wait, wait, where are you going?' he protested.

'To dinner – I made reservations at "21" . . .'

'But Jess, I thought we might have dinner here at home, after all it's raining out. There's a nice fire in the study, couldn't we have supper in there – just the two of us – alone?'

She stared at him repentantly, she was so forgetful, so uncaring . . . Harrison had been working hard all day . . . but she was just so excited about her plans . . . Over dinner she explained in detail what she would need. 'I shall call my agency *Images*,' she said finally, 'because that's really what it's all about.'

'And are you prepared to begin at the bottom Jess?' he asked, 'or do you expect to start your business at the top in a penthouse-suite on Madison?'

She knew that if she said the penthouse was what she wanted, he would give it to her. 'I've always been a hard worker,' she said proudly, '*Images* doesn't need a penthouse to make it a success, it needs *faces*! But you are the kindest most generous man,' she cried, leaping to her feet and hugging him, 'as well as being the handsomest and sexiest husband in the whole entire world!'

She thought their lovemaking that night reached new dimensions in tenderness and passion. Jessie-Ann felt as though she couldn't get enough of him, she wanted to touch him, to entwine herself around him; she wanted to straddle him and kiss him all over, she wanted him in her mouth and in her body, and she never wanted to let him go.

Two days later she left with Harrison for a whirlwind Far-East business trip and when they returned she realised that she was pregnant. *Images* would have to wait.

2

The nine a.m. flight, Los Angeles to New York, was still on the tarmac at nine twenty and Danae Lawrence bit her nails anxiously, wondering why there were always so many delays. Economy-class was full and she'd been forced to accept a seat in the smoking section, and she could tell that the guy next to her would light up as soon as they were airborne and the 'No Smoking' sign was switched off. She thought gloomily that it served her right for leaving the decision until the last minute, and even now she still wasn't sure whether she was ready to return to New York. Yet if she didn't go back she might lose all she had worked for, all she'd learned . . . it was now or never.

As the plane rolled down the runway at last, she glanced at the pile of magazines in her lap, *Harpers*, *Vogue* and *Town & Country*, all fresh on the stands today. Jessie-Ann Parker decorated the cover of *Town & Country* – only now, of course, she was 'the glamorous Mrs Harrison Royle photographed at her sumptuous Park Avenue apartment . . .' Danae examined the picture closely. It certainly wasn't Brachman's. Then who? None of the American photographers surely, not with that special softness, that gentle kind of appeal. It must be Snowdon! She could always recognise the small details that gave each of the great photographers their own personal style. *Vogue* had that new Asiatic-looking model on their cover, and this time she *knew* the photograph was Brachman's because she was there when he took it! She could remember the scene he'd caused because the stylist had lost the model's shoes on her way to the session; Brachman had thrown one of his tantrums, running his hands through his already wild hair as he hurled insults at the stylist and the model and Danae, and in the end it hadn't mattered because he'd photographed the girl with her feet up on an elegant Empire chaise-longue and the delicate folds of her silk organza gown hitched above her knees, looking like a tired beauty after the

34

ball. And only Danae knew that that smouldering look in her eyes was not sex, but anger.

But it was what was *inside* the covers of *Vogue* that interested Danae more. This was the 'New Collections' issue, and if Brachman had shown the editors her London photographs – and if she were lucky and *Vogue* had *liked* them – then they would be in this issue. And if they were, it would make all the difference to what would happen next in her life. She stared at the magazine, unwilling to open it and face the disillusionment of not seeing her pictures inside, remembering Brachman and how it had all begun – and ended.

Danae's transformation from mail girl, tea-maker and Girl Friday for 'Brachman' – the internationally famous photographer – into 'Danae Lawrence, *Second Assistant* to Brachman', had happened quite suddenly – though she'd already worked for him for nine months. And in a way she thought, it was like being re-born.

Brachman's studio in a smartly remodelled brownstone on East Twenty-sixth Street held a passing parade of glamorous international celebrities, the famous and the soon-to-be-famous models, the jet-setters and rock-stars, fringe-royalty, designers and artists. Danae knew them all, though of course they would probably not have recognised the tall, skinny, red-haired girl out on the street. Still, she knew them. She'd made them endless cups of the Earl Grey tea to which Brachman was addicted, she'd offered them a hairbrush or a lipgloss and run for boxes of tissues to blot their make-up or to mop-up their spilt tea. She'd opened endless bottles of the cheap white wine Brachman claimed was a discovery from his ancestral land of Hungary, and which everyone swore was so acid it took the enamel from their teeth. Danae had lent his famous clients quarters for their phone calls and dollars for cabs, but she had refused to cash any cheques (on Brachman's orders). At the end of each session it was Danae who'd tidied the studios, removing the litter of make-up stained tissues and forgotten powders and shadows, straightening the beautiful clothes on the metal racks for pick-up by the stylist from the magazine or fashion house. And, at the end of her long day she'd lingered lovingly over the expensive photographic equipment, replacing exquisitely refined lenses into their velvet-lined leather cases, putting away the wonderful Hasselblad, the super-fast Nikon, the Rollei and the Leica – an artist's ransom of the very best equipment – none of which could she afford to buy herself.

It had only been a couple of months earlier that Brachman had even begun to notice that she was there. The Hungarian photographer's fiery dark eyes that always seemed to flash with anger or impatience, subduing his sitters into instant obedience, had lit on her for a second as she offered him a white Limoges porcelain cup and saucer. A wafer-thin slice of lemon floated on the amber surface of the fragrant tea and as he took a sip, Brachman had nodded approvingly, examining her with a gleam of interest this time. 'What's your name again?' he asked though he must have seen her every day for months. He'd nodded when she'd told him. 'Danae,' he'd repeated. 'That's pretty.'

Her eyes had followed the famous photographer as he walked across the vaulted white-walled studio. Brachman was tall and thin, with the wiry, emaciated look of a starving artist – though nothing could have been further from the truth. His face was pale with strong lines from nose to mouth and his deepset black eyes were restless, constantly searching out angles and light and shade, even when he wasn't working. His shock of thick, dark hair was always messy because he had a habit of running his hands through it when he bullied his sitters or his assistants into doing exactly what he wanted. Brachman was notoriously selfish and egotistical. He threw tantrums in the studio like a spoiled child but was always forgiven because his work was so brilliant. His photographs of celebrities were sometimes tender and sometimes cruel, and years ago his revolutionary fashion pictures had moved photography from static posed shots to leaping movement that revealed clothes and their relationship to the models' bodies with a new reality. Brachman travelled frequently, he knew everybody who was anybody and he had an awesome reputation for being a monumental lover. Danae idolised him.

Once he'd noticed her, he'd begun to let her help more. 'Where's Danae?' he'd demand. 'She'll find it – she's the only one who'll know where it is . . .' or, 'Danae will do it.' And then one wonderful day he'd cried impatiently, 'Let Danae hold that flash, she's the only one I can trust around here!' Suddenly, she'd found herself indispensable.

Danae was always the first there in the morning and always the last to leave. She lugged the strobe lamps around happily, arranging them to Brachman's instructions, grinning at his surprise when he discovered she knew what he was talking about – and what's more, she knew what *she* was talking about! And she'd held Brachman's cups of tea, while he held the camera.

After a late-night session, when they were the last two left in the studio, Brachman had invited her to a neighbourhood restaurant. He was notoriously stingy and – over a shared small pizza – she'd told him how happy she was to be working for him – though she'd had the instinctive good sense not to mention her ambitions.

Brachman's dark eyes had gleamed with interest making Danae feel as though only she existed on this whole planet and causing little tremors of shock to run up and down her spine. He'd poured red wine with a lavish hand, stroking her fingers sympathetically, as she talked. 'Such white skin,' he'd murmured approvingly, 'none of this suntan nonsense that leaves a girl's body looking one-dimensional. The best lovers in history have always had white skin like yours Danae.'

Gazing into his dark eyes, she'd felt like a roadbound rabbit mesmerised by car headlamps . . . 'I . . . it goes with my red hair, you see,' she'd murmured, blushing.

'Tell me more about yourself,' he'd demanded, 'let me live your youth vicariously . . . mine was so sad, *tragic* even . . .' Brachman had several versions of his youth in Hungary ranging from 'the illegitimate son of an exiled count and a Hapsburg princess', to a 'father who was a man of the soil toiling all his life to give his son an education'. It all depended on the company he was in and his mood. But his emotion was always the same. His eyes had glimmered with a hint of tears and Danae had held her breath, staring nervously around the restaurant. What would she do if Brachman burst into tears? 'Continue Danae!' he'd ordered, slicing the pizza Quattro Stagioni (his choice) and taking a large bite, his tragic childhood presumably forgotten.

'I'm twenty-two now,' she began.

'*Twenty-two!* Oh God . . .' he cried loudly, raising his eyes to heaven, 'why is everyone so *young* these days! And how old do you think I am?' he'd demanded, fixing her with his piercing gaze.

Danae knew perfectly well he was fifty-one years old. 'I guess about forty,' she'd replied cautiously, staring at her plate.

'Hmmm . . . not far off,' he'd muttered, satisfied. 'Well, go on then . . .'

Swallowing a gulp of red wine, she'd told him that as a child she had wanted to be an artist, but those early years at school, struggling to find line and form had made her despair of ever being anything but an amateur. Then, as a fifteenth birthday present her father had given her her first 35mm camera, and she'd suddenly discovered another medium. With her camera she could capture all the colours and lines and movement she had been unable to achieve with a brush or pencil.

Danae's home was in the San Fernando Valley, Los Angeles. Her father worked on the fringes of LA's show-biz world in Accounting at CBS Television, while her mother filled her days doing macrame and taking courses in creative writing at Valley College.

'My Mom was always *busy*,' she'd said bitterly, taking another gulp of red wine. 'She always gave my brother and me elaborate birthday parties – but she invited kids with parents *she* wanted to impress. She organised Easter-egg hunts that were really excuses for social climbing, and she even arranged the Hallowe'en Trick-or-Treat so we never got to go around the neighbourhood with the other kids . . . we went with *her*! *She* knocked on the doors of people she wanted to meet!'

As Brachman bit into a second slice of pizza she'd told him that Mrs Lawrence was always the last mother to pick them up at school. 'Danae's Mom' was notorious for always being late and sometimes she just never showed up at all and then someone else's mother would have to bring her home. Brachman's fingers gripped hers sympathetically across the table as she admitted that it was then that she had learned not to cry, forcing back the tears as she'd waited in the lonely school yard for her Mom.

'I always had this terrible feeling that she had abandoned me for ever,' she'd told him, her low voice trembling at the memory, 'and all she was doing was trying on furs she couldn't afford in I. Magnin or buying dresses for special occasions that never happened. My mother's life seemed to consist of endless shopping, endless tennis lessons, endless lunches . . .'

She'd progressed from High School to USC film school, where she'd absorbed everything they could teach her about the art of cinematography and the techniques of movie-making. But what she'd liked most was still-photography – the art of capturing a single fleeting image on a tiny frame of film, then adding new dimensions to it in the darkroom by under or over-exposing, superimposing image on image. And most of all she had liked peering with her camera into people's lives and revealing their emotions.

Brachman had stared at her approvingly, his eyes assessing the fineness of her pale skin against the electric shock of coppery-lit red hair, and her wide, pale grey eyes with their fringe of dark bronze lashes. He'd noted the slenderness of her frame, her long-fingered over-large hands that expressed a sureness and capability, even as they lay softly in his. He took in her old grey sweatshirt and faded jeans, her worn leather sneakers and her lack of any make-up.

'Your face is as naked as your soul,' he'd said, smiling. 'You have confessed everything young Danae.'

Then he'd turned away from her, calling for the bill and Danae had felt guilty because of course she hadn't told Brachman *everything*. She hadn't told him that she wanted to be a better – more famous – *greater* photographer than he was. She hadn't told him that she was consumed with ambition . . . that she was determined to 'make it'. And she hadn't told him that when she looked at a successful picture where she'd caught a revealing expression in her subject's eyes or a moment of vulnerability, or sometimes their fear of what the camera might reveal that could destroy their own self-image – it gave her a feeling of *power* over them. And it was a feeling she enjoyed.

Brachman rested his arm companionably across her shoulders as they'd strolled through the chilly night towards his studio. 'So what happened after you left film school?' he said. 'How did you find *me*?'

Thrusting her hands into the pockets of her old jeans, Danae had matched her step to his long stride, feeling as though she must be in some sort of waking dream. Brachman had his arm around her . . . he really wanted to know about *her* – *Brachman* – who knew everybody and went everywhere, had chosen to spend this evening with her! She'd felt as elated as if her worn leather sneakers were walking on air instead of Manhattan's grimy streets. But at the same time she'd suddenly wanted to look prettier for Brachman . . . she'd wished she'd had time to change, worrying that her hair might be curling into frizz in the humid night air. But she'd kept on talking, making him laugh with her description of the ageing, once-eminent Hollywood photographer with whom she'd taken a job as an assistant.

He had specialised in eight-by-ten glossies of would-be movie-startlets, because the real Hollywood stars had long since forsaken his like for the Brachmans and Avedons of the photographic world. For months Danae had lugged heavy equipment around afraid that her boss was too fragile even to lift the camera. Occasionally she was allowed to take the preliminary polaroids, and every lunch time she'd run to Mai-Ling's on Sunset for Chinese take-out. She'd held the mirror while Hollywood beauties applied yet another coat of lipstick to their pouting mouths; she'd made endless cups of coffee and run countless errands to the labs. She wrote hundreds of invoices and rushed to the post office to mail them. *And she learned!*

After a year she'd realised that there was no future in it and that what she needed couldn't be found in Hollywood. She must go to New York.

'Getting a job with a top photographer isn't easy,' she'd admitted to Brachman with a smile, 'and I wanted the best. And that meant *you*. I knew every one of your photographs – but it was those pictures you took of Jessie-Ann Parker – not the 'America's most famous model girl' ones – but the ones of her on horseback near her home in Montana. *They* are what made me want to work for you. Somehow you'd caught the clean fresh look of the *real* Jessie-Ann Parker – the small-town girl made good, happy to be back home for the weekend with her folks. Except that revealing look you caught in Jessie-Ann's eyes told the world 'you can't go home again'; that it can never be the same as it was. You gave that blonde All-American success-story *pathos*, Brachman. It was then I decided I'd rather take the lowliest position in your studio than the title of assistant to anyone else. And that's how you ended up with me to fix your Earl Grey. As you see,' she'd added grinning, 'I'm quite expert at it. I've surely had enough practice.'

He'd thrown back his head, laughing delightedly, 'You're the best yet,' he'd said, squeezing her slender shoulder, 'you always cut the slice of lemon exactly right. *You understand me.*' He'd stopped in front of the tall thin brownstone that housed his studio, groaning as he straightened up. 'Goddamn, my back's acting up again and I'm off to London tomorrow, and then Paris. I've got to get some sleep and hope it works itself out . . . good night Danae.' Dropping a light kiss on top of her red curls, he'd limped stiffly up the steps and disappeared through the big double doors.

Danae had hovered uncertainly on the edge of the sidewalk. She hadn't known quite what she'd expected, but it wasn't this. They'd been into such an intimate mood, just the two of them, talking about life . . . or rather about *her* life. And then he'd just left, without mentioning anything . . .?

Flagging down a taxi she'd climbed in dispiritedly. Brachman had just used her to fill in a blank couple of hours in his evening . . . he would fly off on Concorde for a week or so and she guessed he'd have forgotten all about tonight when he got back.

She was wrong. When Brachman had returned he ordered that a new girl Friday be hired to take Danae's place and he allowed her to help more and more with his work. He'd even let her stand near him to observe how he constructed his shots. But he'd never mentioned the evening they'd spent together.

When Brachman's first and second assistant had had the final in their series of violent rows, the second assistant left and Danae took his place. It was then she decided that it was time also to do something about her appearance.

A long critical look in the mirror reflected a tired twenty-two-year-old, too thin at five foot seven with the pale translucent skin that went with her red hair. Red didn't quite describe it though, perhaps it was closer to copper? Whatever, the colour wasn't quite right . . . and it curled too much. Later, after a chestnut

41

rinse, her long hair glowed with subdued copper highlights and when she was working she kept it from falling into her eyes with a tennis player's headband. She hadn't been around all those models and starlets for two years without acquiring some of the tricks of the trade, and now she applied yellow and amber eye shadow, and disguised the dark circles of tiredness with a lighter shade of foundation. She applied terracotta blusher discreetly and added a touch of clear lipgloss.

Up to now she had always worn just jeans and a sweatshirt and she knew it wouldn't be easy, competing for attention with all the models and celebrities in their exciting and expensive clothes. She spent weeks hunting through Manhattan's small boutiques before she decided that discretion was her best bet. She would have a 'uniform' – black trousers, white shirt, black sweater, and a big, soft, black leather jacket for the cold days when she went on location. She allowed herself just one concession to femininity – her white shirt would always be of satin.

She'd inspected her new image in the mirror with satisfaction. This time the reflection showed a tallish girl – but looking rangier because of her extreme slenderness and long legs. The slick, white shirt made her skin look even paler and her eyes looked cloud-grey under their pattern of shadows. Her strong straight nose showed a faint dust of freckles, and she'd smiled, pleased with herself. She felt now she had definitely arrived. This was Danae Lawrence, photographer. This was who she was.

Though Brachman had made no comment on her new appearance, Danae knew he'd noticed. In the next months he'd given her more and more to do around the studio and his clients had begun to recognise her, greeting her in a friendly fashion when they came to the studio.

Rick Valmont, who was Brachman's first assistant, had been watching Danae like a jealous hawk, ready to pounce. He resented Danae's progress and Brachman's approval of her, and he did his best to make her life unpleasant. He would rush to greet the clients as they came into the studio, whisking them away from Danae, whose job it was supposed to be to bring them to meet Brachman. He'd take them to the changing rooms and make sure their make-up person and hair stylists were waiting. Valmont was keeping the clients away from her and she'd realised that he was making sure it was *him* they remembered when they left. Valmont was stocking up points for the future. And when he had the chance he would sabotage her relationship with Brachman.

It was the day before he was due to leave for Europe to photograph the collections with Brachman that Valmont had the accident. He was rushing across town from the camera supplies shop when his cab slammed into another at the intersection of Fifth Avenue and Fourteenth Street. The new dual-voltage lamps were smashed, along with Valmont's nose and his right arm. Danae wasn't quite sure which break had upset Brachman more – though she suspected it was the lamps. And of course she understood, because Brachman was a perfectionist and he depended upon his equipment to give him tip-top technical results.

Brachman had sent the new tea-girl Friday off on a string of errands and then he'd stormed around the studio, shouting commands at Danae. She'd made endless calls for replacement equipment and taken care of all the hundred and one details that were Valmont's responsibility. And Brachman had been impossible! 'Call Paris,' he'd ordered, 'make sure I've got my usual suite at the Crillon. And get them to make a reservation for six on Tuesday night at Voltaire. And while you're at it, check the hotel reservations in Milan – I've never trusted that travel agent since he got mixed up with the time change and booked me into a room for the night before I arrived, and left *me* – *Brachman* – roomless in fashion week in a town filled to the rafters with buyers and journalists! And Danae, get onto my shirtmaker in Paris – the number's in the book right there – tell him I'll be in to choose some fabrics on the tenth . . . might as well call Lobbs in London too, about my shoes . . . And get on to my chiropractor for an urgent appointment. I must see him *now*! My back's acting up again . . .'

By four thirty that afternoon, Danae's ear burned from being pressed to the telephone and she was exhausted from trying to express herself in French and Italian to impatient telephone operators and foreign concierges. Then Brachman had yelled from his studio . . . 'Where's my tea Danae . . . it's way past

43

teatime . . .' No mention of how hard *she'd* worked. No word of thanks or praise for sorting out all his arrangements . . .

Seething with anger, she'd fixed the tea and carried the tray carefully up the stairs to the studio on the top floor. 'There you are at last,' he'd cried impatiently, 'what have you been doing all this time?'

Danae had glared at him, resisting an impulse to hurl the tea in his face. She'd simply put down the tray and retreated to the door.

'And where are you going now?' he'd demanded.

'As a matter of fact, I was going to get myself a sandwich,' retorted Danae angrily, 'there was no time for lunch since I've had to do all Valmont's work – and *you've* kept me pretty busy on the phone.'

He'd glared back at her and then suddenly his thin, attractive face had broken into a grin. 'Why don't you wait a while,' he suggested, 'have a cup of tea and relax. Then maybe we could go for a pizza – I'm hungry too.'

She was so exhausted she didn't know whether to laugh or cry . . . Brachman was *impossible*. He bullied her and treated her like a slave and then he suddenly turned human and came down to her level, treating her as his friend. If he weren't such a goddamned genius she wouldn't have put up with him . . . but she might as well admit it, she was crazy about him.

Brachman stretched out in the big black leather chair, his tea forgotten, his broad brow furrowed in thought. 'Call British Airways,' he barked at her, 'tell them to change Valmont's ticket into your name.'

The hot tea burned Danae's throat as she'd gasped. 'Me? But how can I . . . I mean it's tomorrow . . . why me?'

'Who else knows how to work with me? You can do the job, can't you? Better tell me now if you think you're not up to it Danae. It's a free-for-all at those showings. I'll expect you to rush and push and elbow your way through the crowds to get what I want, and we might not get the models and the clothes from the designers together in the same room until two in the morning. It's hard work, and it's madness . . . *and I need you to help me*.'

His dark eyes defied her to let him down as she'd thought

frantically about passports and packing. It was the chance of a lifetime – to go to Europe's top fashion shows as Brachman's first assistant! And it meant she'd be alone with him, in the world's most romantic city . . . Paris. She almost wasn't sure which she wanted most.

'Well,' he demanded, 'what do you say, yes or no?'

'Oh yes,' she whispered. *'Yes, please!'*

Of course, she'd imagined the two of them on the plane to Milan, winging their way across the Atlantic, absorbed in each other's brilliant conversation as they sipped champagne, but Brachman had simply stretched out across two first-class seats, covered his eyes with a black silk mask and fallen asleep. She'd drunk two glasses of champagne, her eyes fixed on his pale, impassive face, willing him to wake up. But he didn't and the champagne seemed as much a let down as if it were flat.

As the plane touched down at Milan's Malpensa Airport and taxied towards the terminal, Brachman ran his hands through his rumpled hair, removed his black mask and said, 'I'll go directly to the hotel. Take care of everything here and be as quick as possible.'

It had taken her a frantic hour to locate their equipment which had somehow got 'mislaid' as it came off the plane, and another two hours of heated, arm-waving Italian argument to get it released from customs.

'Goddamnit Danae, where have you been?' he'd thundered, his black eyes flashing angrily, when she'd finally shown up at the Hotel Principe e Savoia. Wearily she'd explained what had happened. 'You silly girl, of course you should have offered them a fistful of lire,' he stormed, 'you'd have had the equipment out in ten minutes.'

Danae had stared at him doubtfully, tears pricking at her eyelids, sure that if she'd have done as he said she would have ended up in an Italian jail!

'Let's get moving,' he'd commanded, picking up the Nikon and heading for the door.

Her dreams of romance were disappearing rapidly . . . she hadn't even had time to catch her breath, let alone go to her room and wash her hands . . . 'Where are we going?' she asked.

He was already striding along the red-carpeted corridor towards the elevator, 'Bring the polaroid,' he yelled over his shoulder, 'we're going to Armani's rehearsal.'

Giorgio Armani was one of Italy's great designers and the sound of his name cleared Danae's head of trivia like nerves and fatigue, and a longing for a hot soothing bath and a soft bed. Grabbing the camera, she dashed after him, her tiredness dispersed by a surge of excitement. Who needed rest when they could go to a rehearsal for Armani's show?

All that week she trailed after Brachman, carrying cameras and light meters, always the girl in the background amid the swirl of pre-show hysteria and flashing displays of Latin temperament. With the leggy, stylish models they moved from designer to designer, working each show. She loaded cameras and she checked light meters, and spent hours on the telephone in her lofty scarlet and gilt hotel room, organising studios and limousines as well as dinner reservations at already over-crowded restaurants, because every top international buyer, every important fashion editor, every feature-journalist and every well-known photographer had converged upon the old city, and Milan was bursting at its fashionable seams.

Sleep became a thing of the past and she spent early-morning and late-night hours in cafés in the Galeria or the via Montenapoleone, gulping thick black espresso coffee loaded with three spoons of sugar to lift her flagging energy, and at the same time drinking in the fashion-gossip from the neighbouring café tables. She worked late into the night in overheated studios, trying to calm Brachman while he paced the floor, running his hands through his hair and raving about dresses the designer had promised him first that had been sent to a rival photographer, or clothes being delivered late or not at all; and the weary models sulked and smoked in the corner, already exhausted from the show they'd just done and anticipating another the following day.

Of course, it was still Danae who'd had to soothe the models' splintering nerves on cold misty-morning locations as they shivered in evening chiffon, and it was she who dried their tears – careful not to smudge make-up that had taken an hour to perfect

– when they strode from Brachman's camera in treacherous high heels along rain-slicked cobbled streets and turned an ankle. Then of course the tears made the mascara run and the beautiful face had to be repaired by the tired make-up artist who just knew he was going to be late for the show that afternoon.

But Danae saw fashion in a way she had never dreamed existed. She saw the life force that flowed from the designer to his models in the excitement of the live show. The magical runway and the salon crowded with hundreds of blasé fashion editors and super-critical buyers ready to acclaim the designer an astonishing success or to put down the collection as 'tired' or 'safe', the music and the clash of personalities, the bouncing light and the body heat and the tempers, were far more exciting than any studio session.

She would never forget the day Brachman had handed her the camera and said, 'Okay it's all yours – let's see what you get, Danae.' And suddenly she was photographing Krizia's show, trying to catch the rhythm and the movement and the sheer energy of it all on her film. When they got the negatives back from the lab later that evening – motor-cycle courier-expressed through the busy city – Danae had examined Brachman's pictures and then her own, and truly wasn't sure that anyone would have known the difference. And it was one of *her* shots that appeared in *Women's Wear Daily* that week, with Brachman's name under it, of course. But the thrill was still there.

They'd flown to Rome for the Fashion Celebration party to be attended by Italy's top designers as well as more than five hundred celebrities from around the world and Danae had lurked in her hotel room feeling like Cinderella left home from the ball, hoping against hope that Brachman might ask her to go with him. For once she'd had no crisis to deal with; there was no mad dash to be made by taxi to pick up forgotten shoes, no fight in halting Italian about overbooked studios, and she was feeling let down, missing the action. Tomorrow they would be on their way to Paris and it would all begin over again, but meanwhile she was alone in her hotel room while all of Rome went to the party.

'Danae,' Brachman yelled, thudding on her door, 'Danae are you ready?'

Her heart skipping a beat she ran to the door. Brachman looked very handsome in his white dinner jacket, in his own special world-weary way. He grinned as he brushed past her into her room. 'You didn't think I was going to let my poor, hard-working little Danae stay at home did you?' he said, handing her a white card. 'There'll be more famous faces together in one room tonight than you or I might ever see again. Here's a Press Pass. Take your camera Danae and get over there . . .'

'But Brachman . . . I don't have anything to wear,' she protested.

'Wear what you usually wear,' he called as he headed back down the corridor, 'you always look good to me.'

Dizzy with happiness at his unexpected compliment, she'd rushed to the wardrobe. The new pure silk creamy satin shirt from the heavenly little shop on the via Montenapoleone, that had cost her three weeks' salary, would have its début tonight, along with the black suède trousers she'd bought in an incredibly inexpensive little boutique and that fitted her like a second skin.

An hour later she was ready. She'd brushed her freshly-washed hair back smoothly from her forehead, but even so it was already beginning to curl; she'd filled the low neckline of her collarless satin shirt with a chunky golden necklace and clipped matching earrings into her small ears. Slipping her feet into low black suède pumps, she grabbed her leather jacket and her camera and headed for the door. Danae Lawrence, photo-journalist was on her way to the ball.

The Palazzo Venezia's elaborate forty-foot ceilings dwarfed even the glittering international crowd, culled from the jet-set who flitted from the beaches of Sardinia to the slopes of Gstaad, circling from Rome to Paris, London to New York as their fancy – and invitations – took them. With her camera slung around her neck, Danae peered through the smoke from the burning *torchères* at the dozens of blossom-covered tables gleaming with crystal and silver and at the garlands of flowers looped around the lofty pillars and the sweeping staircase. The room was crowded with glamorous, sophisticated women and sun-tanned handsome men and blue-liveried waiters were pouring pink champagne in an endless flow. She felt as though she had stumbled onto an Italian movie-set! She recognised the attractive Fendi sisters, charming in scarlet, chatting with Karl Lagerfeld; and wasn't that Paloma Picasso, so elegant in deep blue? – and surely that was Catherine Deneuve wearing Saint-Laurent . . . And the Americans were here too . . .. Diane von Furstenberg sexy in black and Lynn Wyatt looking wonderful in a romantic ruffled yellow ballgown. Clutching her camera Danae had edged her way through the crowd, snapping madly. It was all too good to lose . . . but where was Brachman?

Tomaso Alieri leaned against the wall, arms folded, coughing as smoke from the burning *torchères* wafted his way and not listening to the conversation going on around him. At thirty, Tomaso was one of Italy's most up-and-coming designers, and he'd already created an international name for himself with a style that was both youthful and chic. His restless hazel-brown eyes focused idly on Danae as she circled the crowd, camera at the ready . . . noting the way her soft silk-satin shirt clung to her breasts, the excited flush on her cheeks and her wildly curling red hair . . .

Pushing her way through the crowd Danae finally spotted Brachman. The girl he was with was about nineteen years old and very beautiful, with long black hair and eyes as dark as his. She was wearing a strapless red velvet top with a skirt of flounced organza that Danae had recognised as Valentino. And she also wore what looked like Bulgari's entire window-display of cabochon-rubies draped around her neck, dangling from her ears, and spiralling around her slender arms.

As Brachman slid his arm around the girl's delicate shoulders Danae aimed her camera and took a few quick shots. Burning with jealousy she slipped back into the crowd wishing she hadn't seen them but still unable to tear herself away. She'd told herself angrily that she had no right to feel this way . . . she hadn't come here as Brachman's lover, she was merely his assistant . . . and in the time they'd been in Italy together he hadn't once given her any reason to believe otherwise. She had hoped it was just because they were so busy – there had been no time for small attentions and intimate conversations, no time for romance. But oh, *damn*

Brachman, *damn him*. Edging back towards his table, she lurked in the shadow of the stairs, snapping shot after shot of Brachman and the girl . . .

'*Perdoni carina*, but surely after all that photography you must need a glass of champagne?' She glanced up at the lean, dark young man smiling at her. 'Tomaso Alieri,' he said. His light hazel-brown eyes smiled at her from beneath heavy brows and automatically she held out her hand and took the glass he offered. With a photographer's attention to detail she noted his wide brow, his strong nose and full sensuous mouth, his firm jaw and smooth dark hair. It was a face Danae recognised from *Oggi* and *Paris-Match* and *People*, a face from the international gossip magazines!

'*You* are quite different,' Tomaso had murmured, ignoring the noisy crowd, 'like a magpie – a rare bird in quiet plumage, amidst an array of parakeets and cockatoos . . . Ah, yes of course! *Now* I know who you are – they say you are Brachman's little pet.' He leaned one hand on the wall behind her, inclining his head towards hers. 'Tell me, *carina*,' he'd murmured, 'is that true?'

Brachman's little pet? she thought, aghast. What had he been saying about her? 'I'm Brachman's assistant. I've worked with him for almost two years,' she replied icily, 'my name is Danae Lawrence.'

'I see. Well then, if what they say is *not* true – I'm in luck. Tell me something else, *carina*,' taking her arm, he'd guided her through the big double doors that led to a marble hallway, 'have you ever felt terribly lonely in the middle of a crowd?'

She glanced at him puzzled – could he have been watching *her* watching Brachman? Could he have read her mind? Or perhaps her true feelings had simply shown on her face?

'Have you ever suddenly felt tired of it all? Tired of the glitz and the gossip, tired of the champagne and too-rich food?'

From the corner of her eye Danae caught a glimpse of Brachman with the girl in red. He turned and glared at her angrily and she glared back. Two could play his game, she thought, and if he didn't like her talking to the good-looking young Italian designer whose romantic reputation was as formidable as his design talents, then it was tough! *The hell with you Brachman,* she thought angrily, *you don't own me* . . .

'Have you ever longed for pasta and cool wine,' continued Tomaso, 'in a simple trattoria, where the woman in the kitchen *understands* that food is meant to nourish you, and is not merely for display?'

He paused, capturing both her hands in his and she gazed at him astonished, wondering what he would say next.

'If you have, my little magpie Danae – then you will take pity and escape with me from this too-hot, too-smoky room and these too-busy people, away from this world of fashion and fakery. We'll go together back to where my roots are – to a quarter of this city I know well. I can promise you a dinner you will never forget.'

Turning her back triumphantly on the glowering Brachman, Danae tucked her arm into Tomaso's. 'Oh yes,' she said breathlessly, 'yes, I'd love to. It sounds just wonderful.'

'But why?' she asked in bewilderment as they sped through the fountained, floodlit Roman squares in his white Ferrari. 'Why did you want to leave the party? And why with me?'

'I just realised I was starving,' admitted Tomaso glancing sideways at her and grinning. 'I don't remember eating at all this week, except for that endless party food . . . I've just been too busy. And, little magpie, I adore food – good hearty northern-Italian food. I also hate to eat alone – a good meal needs to be discussed. It should be chosen carefully, tastes should be given and taken between the company . . . a good meal is a sensual experience and one that must be shared. Besides, what other woman could I possibly persuade to leave the party and go to a neighbourhood restaurant with me, wearing her ten-thousand-dollar dress and her best diamonds?'

Despite her jealous gloom about Brachman, Danae laughed. 'If I hadn't finished my work for tonight, I would have turned you down,' she told him firmly.

'Your work?'

'My photographs.' Holding up her camera she snapped a quick shot of him at the wheel.

'Surely, little magpie, you have enough pictures of Brachman?'

Danáe slumped back in the leather seat of the Ferrari trying to hide her blushes. Then he *had* been watching her!

'So you really do *work* for Brachman?'

'I work *with* Brachman,' she corrected him, 'for the moment. But I warn you Tomaso Alieri, that before too long I shall be one of those ladies you can't take to your little trattoria – not because I'll be wearing my best diamonds – but because I shall be far too much in demand as a photographer. But maybe I'll be wearing your wonderful clothes,' she added, her spirits rising. Somehow it was a relief to be away from Brachman and his angry dark gaze and his constant demands.

'Well then Danae, let's make the most of our night together, playing "hookey" from the top-people's party.'

Parking the Ferrari in a swirl of gravel, Tomaso led the way across an ancient courtyard and into a tiny rustic restaurant. A log fire glowed in the big brick hearth and delicious smells wafted from the kitchen as they took a seat in a quiet alcove. The smiling *patrone* bustled towards them, a bottle of Tomaso's favourite wine in his hand.

'You must sit here,' Tomaso placed Danae's chair beside him, 'so that the lamplight brings out the colour of your hair . . . such beautiful hair . . . dark copper with a hint of terracotta.'

She'd looked away, embarrassed as his expert eye appraised her. 'You know why I noticed you at the party Danae? It was because you were different. No, it wasn't just your clothes, I noticed a gleam of something else in your eyes. You weren't envying those women their jewels when you took their pictures; you weren't envying them their furs or their rich husbands. I suspect that what you really coveted, young Danae, was their success. I detect a burning flame of *ambition* in you, *carina*. Tell me, am I right?'

'One word of warning,' he added, taking her hand in his smooth bronzed one, 'never let Brachman know your ambitions – that man is an egomaniac.' He frowned, trying to summon up the proper English phrase, 'He would throw you out on your ear, little Danae, in one second flat!'

They'd laughed delightedly, as though the idea of Danae being out on her ear were the most amusing thing in the world, but she'd known it was the truth.

'Still,' he'd continued, 'you mustn't let the grass grow under your toes.' Danae giggled, choking on the delicious straw-coloured wine. 'You must start right away if you are to become next year's success. Take out your camera now, my darling magpie, and begin taking my photograph . . . Tomaso Alieri eating, Tomaso drinking, Tomaso chatting with the proprietors at his favourite trattoria – Tomaso with the new young photographer Danae Lawrence . . . is romance in the air?' Laughing, he conjured up captions for her photographs. 'I'll tell you Danae, you could sell those pictures tomorrow, to *Oggi* and *People* and *Paris-Match* – and the byline would be *yours* this time.'

'Do you mean it?' she gasped, 'would you really let me take pictures of you and sell them?'

'The paparazzi do it all the time,' he shrugged, 'why shouldn't you – my new friend?'

He closed his eyes groaning with pleasure as the proprietor placed a steaming truffle-scattered dish in front of him and Danae grabbed her camera, hardly believing her luck. 'We could go back to my apartment later,' he said. 'You could be the first to take pictures of Italy's new young designer "at home". That would surely get you a feature in any Italian magazine.'

She put down her camera again, deflated. Was that what he'd been working up to all along? 'Your apartment?' she asked in a small voice.

'Why not *carina?*' He smiled as if it were the most natural suggestion in the world.

Danae considered her moves as she ate. If Tomaso were on the level it was an opportunity not to be passed up . . . though of course she wouldn't tell Brachman about it. And if he weren't? Well, she'd deal with that when the moment arrived – and she wouldn't tell Brachman about that either.

Tomaso's apartment was the top two floors of an old palazzo way up on a hill overlooking the lights of Rome, and it seemed just a few short steps from admiring the view from his terrace with a glass of champagne in her hand to the big velvet-covered sofa and his arms. As his mouth covered hers Danae wondered if Brachman were kissing the scarlet-bejewelled girl and if she were sharing his big double bed in his grand hotel suite at the Hassler?

'I didn't bring you here under false pretences little magpie,' Tomaso whispered, 'you must take your photographs, first.'

Pulling her dazzled emotions together and clutching her Nikon, Danae prowled his apartment, posing Tomaso in arrogant profile in front of the Pompeian-style wall frescoes which he informed her proudly, he had painted himself. She snapped his narrow bronze steel bed covered, military style, with just a blanket – only this blanket was terracotta cashmere. 'To match your hair,' Tomaso whispered, kissing her neck as she leaned forward to take her pictures . . . 'you were designed for this room, colour-coordinated for my bed . . .'

Ignoring the lure of his eyes she arranged him against a battery of equipment in his high-tech, burnished-black kitchen, and then in his wood-panelled library. She took photographs of his study, zooming in on a worktable littered with scraps of fabric, fashion sketches and notes. His 'atelier' and showroom was in town, but he told her that most of his best ideas came to him at night and he often worked here alone, until, just as it was then, dawn broke over Rome's beautiful rooftops.

They'd leaned companionably over the terrace, watching as the sky turned from pale pink to gold and the sun's first rays gilded Rome's pastel spires and iridescent domes. 'Well *carina?*' he said kissing her fingers, 'do you have enough photographs now?'

'You've been very generous with your time,' Danae murmured, wondering how she could get out of this gracefully. His kisses had felt wonderful last night but in the sober light of dawn they didn't seem like such a good idea. 'I've a flight to Paris at eight o'clock . . . I must get back and pack . . .'

'Of course,' he agreed with a sigh, 'magpies must always return to their nests, mustn't they?' He kissed her lightly on the lips and added, 'It's been fun Danae Lawrence, great photographer, much more fun than the party . . . of course it could have been better,' he shrugged, 'but maybe next time?'

His white Ferrari glided effortlessly through the quiet early-morning Roman streets and Tomaso left her at the hotel after a lingering goodbye kiss. She watched his car disappear around the corner feeling as though she had been taking part in a dream. But then she remembered she would have her photographs of Tomaso to prove it was real.

As the Air France Tristar circled over Paris, Danae fought her way through woolly grey layers of fatigue. Brachman was calling her and she opened her eyes and gazed at him blankly.

'Just look at you!' he exclaimed, 'You are so tired you don't even know where you are. That's what you get for stopping out all night – with Tomaso Alieri!'

'Who I was with is my business,' she snapped, glaring at the other passengers who were staring at them. How dare Brachman yell at her in public – and anyhow her private life was her own. 'Besides,' she added, shrugging on her black leather jacket as the plane touched down on the tarmac, 'you seemed pretty busy yourself.'

'Enough!' exclaimed Brachman coldly. 'We are going to be very busy – and I'd appreciate it if you would keep your mind on your work.'

It was Danae's first time in Paris and because Brachman adored early-morning locations she got to know the city when it was quiet and still, just uncurling from its night's sleep and clearing away its make-up from the face of the previous night's revels. In an entourage of taxis and vans they made four a.m. sorties to the river Seine, waiting for the misty grey light of dawn that Brachman loved; and they lingered in early-morning fog in a traffic-free Place de la Concorde while somehow Brachman managed to arrange his model so that the wisps of fog fitted perfectly into his shot, covering the girl's face like a veil. They took pictures outside the Beaux Arts and on the terrace of the Café Flore, and at the Beaubourg, the Bois and the Gare du Nord; and they attended *all* the collections.

Danae rose before dawn to go out on location and when they'd finished it was time for the next showing – sometimes two in one day. Brachman was never satisfied just to have the studio shots – he thrived on locations, he said they inspired him. By the time

Danae had finished it would usually be after midnight or even later and, with the prospect of another pre-dawn wake-up call, she'd find a café and grab a bite to eat and then simply fall into bed and snatch whatever few minutes were hers to sleep. A buzz of excitement carried her through the week, and even Brachman's impatience seemed to wear off in the embrace of his beloved city.

'Come on Danae,' he said amiably, late one night after the models had gone home and she'd packed up the cameras, 'let's get a bite to eat, I'm starving.'

Over a tiny table in his favourite Bofinger's Brasserie, on the Place de la Bastille, Brachman finally apologised. 'You've worked hard this week Danae,' he'd said, 'I want you to know I appreciate it.'

'That's what I'm here for – as you reminded me so loudly on the plane,' she replied surprised.

Throwing back his head he gave a great guffaw of laughter, 'I was mad at you for running off with Tomaso Alieri – I don't like my girls running off with other men.'

She'd looked at him warily; it was hard to keep up with Brachman's wild swings in mood. 'I'm not *your girl*, Brachman. Remember me? I'm Danae Lawrence – I work for you.'

'That's even better,' he'd retorted, summoning the waiter and ordering a bottle of Dom Perignon, 'because as you know, my work means everything to me. The clients,' he shrugged, 'they know nothing about my work. To them I'm a man who takes pictures that make them look better than they've ever looked in their lives . . . better than they really are! I give them a new image of themselves – and it's always one they prefer. *But you know how I work that magic* – and you see what it takes out of me. At the end of the day I'm drained – wrung out like an old rag!'

Of course it wasn't quite true, but she'd smiled sympathetically because Brachman was a great artist.

'We'll have oysters – the specials,' he ordered, sipping his champagne, 'and then some langoustines – and then the turbot. We've got to keep your strength up,' he'd added seriously. 'There's still London to conquer next week!'

The oysters were briny and delicious and the langoustines

firm and sweet, and Brachman ordered a second bottle of Dom Perignon while Danae stared at him in amazement remembering the meagre shared pizza in New York, until she realised it was probably all being added to his expenses and paid for by the client.

'I like that,' he said, waving his glass at her white satin shirt.

'Via Montenapoleone, Milan,' she replied, 'it cost me a month's salary!'

'Worth every lire – and anyway remind me to give you a raise when we return. You've earned it – you're every bit as good as Valmont.' He leaned across the table and ran his hand along her jaw, touching the hollow beneath the cheekbone. 'The bone reflects pale light just here, and here . . . it makes your skin look wonderful, translucent almost . . .'

She had gazed at him, scarcely daring to breathe as his long sensitive fingers etched the shape of her face. What she had hoped for was finally happening . . . Brachman was seeing her as a woman, not merely as Danae Lawrence, his assistant, there only to do his bidding . . .

'We must go,' he said suddenly, slamming his glass onto the table and waving to the waiter for the bill.

Brachman slumped in his corner in the taxi, not touching her, gazing out of the window, apparently lost in his thoughts. She wondered bewildered what had happened? One minute they were enjoying a leisurely dinner together – and the next Brachman was submerged in one of his sulks.

But it turned out he wasn't sulking – he was merely planning out his shots for the next day. 'You've inspired me Danae,' he told her back in his hotel suite, 'I want to try some ideas with you. Tonight you are my model!'

But she was stiff and awkward on the wrong side of the camera lens and he'd yelled at her for God's sake to relax!

'You've put on weight!' he'd cried accusingly, examining the polaroids.

'I can afford to eat every day now,' she grinned, 'since you promoted me to your assistant.' But her head drooped with fatigue and she couldn't hide a huge yawn.

'Goddamnit Danae,' he'd complained, 'how can I take photo-

57

graphs of you with your mouth wide open! Can't you control yourself for a few moments?'

'Brachman, it's four thirty,' she'd pleaded, 'we've been up twenty-four hours – and you have another session this afternoon.'

Tossing the sheaf of polaroids onto a table he thrust his hands in his pockets, glaring at her as she walked away wearily. 'Valmont wouldn't have quit,' he yelled as she closed the door, 'he'd have kept going as long as I wanted him.'

Flinging open the door again she'd glared furiously at him, 'Then take pictures of Valmont in a white satin shirt next time,' she yelled, 'see what a help that is to you! *I hate you Brachman!*'

His delighted laughter had followed her along the corridor as she waited for the elevator to take her back to her own room and blessed oblivion – for a few hours.

When she arrived at the studio the next morning for their final shoot, she'd gasped in amazement at the sight of yards and yards of white satin draping the walls. Brachman was fussing about arranging the expensive folds just so. 'Your inspiration,' he'd explained, 'the white satin cast just the right icy reflections for the Chanel evening dresses we're shooting today . . . it's pure thirties.' He'd hovered on the perimeter admiring his handiwork. 'Brilliant!' he muttered happily, 'just brilliant. And you'll notice Danae, that I did it all myself. I did not wake you from your so-precious slumbers to carry out this menial task. As the son of a farmer – a man of the soil who laboured all his life to educate his sons, *I understand* what hard work is.'

They'd gone in a noisy crowd to Brasserie Lipp for dinner to celebrate their final Paris shoot and were given a place of honour because everyone knew and revered the famous photographer who had been going there for years. Brachman kept Danae next to him, telling her how pleased he'd been with the session and that *she* had been his inspiration. Occasionally he took her hand, whispering odd comments on the busy scene in her ear. Alone afterwards, they drove down to the Seine and gazed at Notre Dame by moonlight, strolling across the little Pont Marie and finding themselves a cosy bar where they sipped more champagne and Brachman began to tell her of his early days in Paris as a struggling young photographer. She listened, hypnotised by his anecdotes of the artists and writers, models and designers who, like him, had all been trying hard to 'make it' in the city of light, love, and inspiration. And then suddenly Brachman kissed her cheek – and Danae kissed him back – and they took a cab ride back to the hotel, hands clasped tightly.

Brachman's vast suite at the George Cinq was typically untidy – he'd forbidden the chambermaids to remove a single one of the scattered prints, contact sheets and carefully labelled negatives. Only his precious photographic equipment, neatly stacked in one corner by Danae, was away from the clutter. Sweeping a sheaf of aloof model faces from his vast bed, he took her in his arms and told her that this was what Paris was all about. And of course she believed him. Hadn't they always said Paris was for lovers?

Then Brachman's mouth was on hers and he was holding her close, so close she could hardly breathe . . . 'Take off your clothes,' he commanded, letting go of her abruptly and stripping off his shirt. Danae stared at him in surprise. Wasn't he supposed to help her? Wasn't that how it was done at the beginning of a love affair? Brachman was already out of his trousers, and flinging them on the floor he frowned as he saw her standing there. 'Hurry up Danae,' he cried, 'what are we waiting for?'

Unbuttoning her blouse, Danae peeked at him from under her lashes, surprised by how thin Brachman was, and how pale. His body had surely never seen sunlight in a dozen years. Of course, now she remembered him telling her that he hated sweaty climates and anyway he never went on holiday – only working trips. Brachman lay on the bed, his arms folded behind his head and his eyes closed. Even now there was still a furrow between his brows and a look of anguished impatience in the tightness of his jaw and mouth. Naked, she hovered nervously by the bed.

'For God's sake Danae, get in will you,' he cried. Then he smiled, his dark eyes gleaming with appreciation, 'Lovely,' he'd murmured, 'quite lovely Danae – as delicate as a ballerina, and with skin as translucent as a pearl. Come here my beautiful girl.'

He held out his hand and she slid into bed beside him, curling against his warmth as he pulled her closer. Brachman kissed her and Danae closed her eyes, still hardly believing that this could be happening to her. Running her hands across his back she counted his ribs, God he was thin . . . but it wasn't the thinness of a weakling – Brachman's body was as lean and wiry as a starving panther . . .

'Beautiful,' murmured Brachman in between kisses, *'tell me I'm beautiful* Danae . . .'

Danae giggled, just a small giggle at first but then she could hold it back no longer. 'You're beautiful Brachman!' she gasped.

'Jesus!' said Brachman, puzzled, 'what's so funny?'

'Ho, hoo . . . haah . . .' shrieked Danae. 'Oh Brachman it's nothing, just my silly sense of humour, oh dear, haha hah ha . . .'

'Damn it be quiet!' thundered Brachman, 'You're supposed to be making love – not watching *Saturday Night Live!'* Rolling on top of her, he put a hand over her mouth, but it only made her laugh even more. His passion fading, he stared at her uneasily. 'What is it?' he asked, bewildered, 'whatever is so funny Danae?'

'It's just . . . when you asked me to tell you you were beautiful,' she gasped, 'that's all Brachman . . .'

'Am I not beautiful?' he asked, puzzled. 'Other women have told me so. And no one has ever laughed at Brachman before!'

'I'm not laughing *at you,*' she replied, 'it was just the way you said it, I suppose.'

'Well then, tell me I'm beautiful Danae. It pleases me to hear you say it.' He leaned over her as she repeated the words solemnly, and then, satisfied, he grabbed her to him. 'Aagghh,' he yelled suddenly. 'Aaghhh . . . oh my God . . .'

Trapped beneath his weight Danae lay rigid, wondering if these Tarzan calls were some new form of Hungarian passion.

'Aaghh,' yelled Brachman . . . 'Help me Danae, help me . . .'

'What is it?' she cried. 'What's the matter?'

'It's my back! It's slipped out again – it's pinching the nerve . . . Jesus, Danae, *get up,* will you. Do something! *Call a doctor!'*

Sliding awkwardly from beneath him, she stared at him anxiously. Brachman's face was even paler than usual. His dark eyes glittered and there was a faint film of sweat across his brow. There was no doubt that he was in pain.

'A doctor,' he moaned, 'summon a doctor.'

Hurrying to the phone Danae asked for a doctor to be sent

immediately to Brachman's suite. Back by his side, she wiped his forehead with a corner of the sheet.

'It's all your fault,' he muttered glaring at her, 'if you hadn't laughed this would never have happened! Well? Where is the doctor?'

'He'll be here in fifteen minutes Brachman.'

'*Fifteen minutes?* I'll be lucky if I last that long!' He closed his eyes and she hovered uncertainly by the side of the bed. 'Well, what are you waiting for? Don't just stand there,' he said suddenly, 'get yourself packed and organised. You'd better catch an early flight – the 6.30 a.m. You will have to go to London without me. *You* will have to take the photographs.'

'Me?' Her voice came out in a squeak of excitement.

'Don't let's go through that routine again,' Brachman snarled wearily. 'You are my assistant, aren't you? Well then, get your ass over to London.'

Danae was close to tears. One minute he was accusing her of causing him pain, and the next he was offering her the chance of a lifetime. *She – Danae Lawrence was going to photograph the London collections!* It was a pity that her romance with Brachman had proven so short-lived – but there would be another time. If he ever forgave her for laughing at him! It was only as she walked across to the door and saw her clothes lying on the floor that she remembered she was completely naked.

'And Danae,' called Brachman from the bed, 'it's a very *pretty* ass!'

Everything was so different in London – the clothes, the colours, the models, the designers . . . it was full of youth and craziness. There was none of the sleek tailoring of Milan and the elegance of Paris here; this was for the young and daring, for those who wanted to make an impact in a different way. These were clothes for rockstars, for punks on the King's Road, for the young in heart, and Danae fitted into the scene as easily as if it had been waiting for her all her life.

She decided that she would need an assistant, someone who knew the scene and who could show her the ropes, because, as a new girl in town on her first big assignment, she knew she couldn't afford to fail. Brachman had given her a sheaf of telephone numbers and on her first call – to Dino Marley, one of the top photographers, she got lucky, because Dino lent her one of his apprentices, Cameron Mace, for the week.

Cameron was a whirlwind of energy and Danae relaxed, enjoying playing Brachman's role, amused that now it was she who gave the orders and someone else who leapt to obey. But along with it went the responsibility – Brachman expected nothing but the best from her.

She and Cam dashed frenziedly between the shows in the big, barracks-like hall at Olympia and those of some very top designers who chose to show privately in restaurants like Langans, or at smart hotels like the Ritz.

She chose young models with classy looks to offset the outrageous garments they wore, photographing them on horseback in Katherine Hamnett's linen jodhpurs outside a stately home; she took pictures of models in a steamy sauna, naked but for various pieces of Body Map's vivid clinging tops and leggings and minis; and she photographed dazzling evening dresses on sexy girls in London taxis – clasped in the arms of much younger good-looking boys recruited from Britain's top school.

Danae flew back to New York with the precious contact sheets and negatives in a large brown envelope clutched safely in her arms, and she peered nervously over Brachman's shoulder as he placed the negatives on the lightbox and inspected her work.

'Mmnn,' he murmured non-committally, and, 'mmn, yes, this one's not bad . . .'

Biting her lip nervously, Danae wondered which one it was that he liked. She'd thought they were all great – but maybe they were really terrible? Damn it – they were good, she knew they were – and so must Brachman. He was just playing games with her . . .

Brachman winced as he straightened and the trapped nerve in his back jabbed painfully. 'I'll think about them,' he said, 'maybe we'll go with this Body Map shot and the Hamnett. I'll see what *Vogue* says. You did OK Danae. I'm glad it was you rather than me. I went through all this "youth revolution" stuff once, in the sixties, and I've no wish to experience it again. Still, good work Danae, very good.'

Danae expelled the breath she'd been holding in a sigh of relief. 'Really?' she cried joyfully, 'you really like them Brachman?'

'They're OK,' he admitted cautiously, running his hands through his hair, 'but let's not dwell on it. We've got work to do!'

'Slave driver!' she called happily, hurrying to collect the negatives to be printed. It was only then that she remembered her photographs of Tomaso Alieri – of course, she would have them printed at the same time.

At the studio a few days later she got a call from California. 'Danae,' her mother said, 'is that you?'

Julie Lawrence's voice sounded muffled, as though she were crying, and Danae frowned; her mother never called her at work. 'Mom? What is it? What's the matter?'

'Danae . . . it's your father . . . he's had a heart attack – out jogging. Oh Danae I always told him he was overdoing it but he insisted . . .'

'Mom,' cried Danae urgently, 'how is he? Is he all right?'

'All right?' Her mother sounded puzzled. 'Oh no, Danae, no. Your father is dead.'

The funeral on a hot, sunny California afternoon had been painful and her mother genuinely grief-stricken and afterwards Danae and her brother Rick, who was now a neurologist with a busy practice in the Valley Medical Centre, were left to sort out the estate. They were relieved to find that their father was quite well off and that money would not be a problem. Danae and Rick knew that once she was over the shock, Julie Lawrence dressed charmingly in black, would be back on her committees, busy once again with her good works. And Frank Lawrence had left Danae and her brother the sum of $20,000 each!

She stared tearfully at the cheque handed to her by the lawyer in the sober grey suit and bright yellow tie, wishing with all her might that her father might be alive, not wanting to take the money, only wanting him back again. When she returned home to the immaculate house in Encino with the pastel peach and pink and green living room, with the chrome and glass étagères and the pretty needlepoint carpets, there was a letter waiting for her from Brachman. He had seen her pictures of Tomaso Alieri in *People* magazine this week, he said, and in *Oggi* – and no doubt there would be others – since she seemed to have taken so many and managed to place them all over the world! As she had done this at a time when she was supposed to be working for him, and disloyalty was not a characteristic he could tolerate, there was no way he could condone her actions. Therefore he would no longer need her services as his assistant.

Danae stared at the letter disbelievingly. *Brachman had fired her!* How *dare* he? How *could* he?

'Forget him,' her brother Rick advised, 'you've learned a lot from him, haven't you? Why don't you start up your own? "Danae Lawrence – famous photographer" – isn't that what you've always longed to be?'

It was true, she had learned from him – how else would she have been able to take those pictures in London – not that it was all him, but the technique and some of the angles owed a lot to Brachman – yet the *joie-de-vivre* and the models and the special young look were hers – because she was young and in tune with London's craziness and she'd been able to capture it perfectly.

'Take Dad's twenty thousand,' counselled Rick, 'buy your own Nikon and Rollei or Hasselblad. This is your chance Danae. Take it!'

The future seemed blank and uncertain without the security of being Brachman's assistant – after all she had been with him for two years. But she knew her brother was right, it was time to make her move. 'OK,' she'd said finally, taking a deep breath, 'this is it then. Danae Lawrence – ace photographer – ready for commissions.'

So, here she was on the plane on her way back to New York. And a credit in *Vogue* would be the golden key to her future, opening a thousand doors. Picking up the magazine she riffled through its pages searching for the familiar shots, gasping as she saw them . . . Yes, oh yes . . . there they were! Her girls were spread across four pages of the magazine – laughing as they tumbled out of taxis, cavorting in the sauna, riding aristocratic horses . . . The pictures looked wonderful, better than she could ever have hoped . . . And across the top of her work was written in bold white letters – '*Brachman photographs the new young London.*' Danae flicked back through the previous pages, disbelievingly – they all had similar captions – 'Brachman adores Milan' – 'Brachman captures the essence of Rome', 'Brachman's Paris' . . . The blurb ran on about Brachman's new discoveries in London, about his brilliant sauna pictures and his fun approach to British elegance, about his ability to tune in to the tempo of each city. *Vogue had lauded Brachman's brilliance and Brachman had used her pictures!*

Dropping the magazine, Danae stumbled past the man in the neighbouring seat and hurried down the aisle to the bathroom. Locked in the tiny airless space, she sobbed away the pain of disillusionment. Finally, her anger took over from pain, she washed her face, pressing cold compresses onto her swollen eyes, vowing never to let this happen to her again. She knew now she was good enough to make it all the way to the top – those photographs in *Vogue* proved it, even though no one else would ever know they were hers. But now she knew that she'd have to be just as ruthless as the Brachmans of this world. Staring at her tear-stained face in the tiny mirror she made a vow – she, Danae Lawrence, would push and elbow and jostle her way to the top – no matter what – or who – she had to sacrifice on the way.

3

Whenever she looked in the mirror Caroline Courtney could find a dozen things wrong with her – the shape of her short, but admittedly arrogant nose, the dense brown of her hair which she would have preferred to be a dazzling blonde, with a pink and white English complexion to match – though her own slightly olive-toned skin had the advantage of always tanning an even gold without her having to bake for hours under the sun's dangerous rays. It would have been nice to be tall and commanding too, she thought with a sigh, instead of just five feet four. Still, the yellow Sonia Rykiel outfit was cut so cleverly it seemed to add inches to her slim but not-too-long legs and the bright colour suited her dark hair and greenish-brown eyes. She wondered whether the expression in those eyes should be a little more tragic – considering she was a newly-discarded mistress? But somehow tragedy didn't suit her personality.

Turning despondently from the small mirror in the washroom of British Airways 747 Flight London to New York, she returned to her seat. At least Pericles had not sent her 'steerage'; Cabin Class was comfortable, though of course it would have been a much grander final gesture to send her away First Class. But Pericles was a man who was careful with his money, especially it seemed when it came to departing mistresses!

Let's face it, she thought gloomily, this sudden idea of sending her to New York on 'business' for his gallery was just a pretext to get her out of the way so that he could patch things up with Evita. Now that she was thinking about things sensibly instead of trying to make excuses for Pericles and delude herself into believing that everything would work out all right, she could see that the writing had been on the wall for months – maybe even from the very beginning.

Staring out at the blank blueness of the mid-Atlantic sky at thirty-five thousand feet, Caroline thought that if anyone were to blame, then it was her Aunt Catriona.

The day her aunt had phoned was a stormy one. Dodging the first heavy raindrops that threatened a downpour, Caroline had hurried along South Molton Street into Maudie's, shaking her curls like a wet poodle as the polished steel door slid closed behind her.

'Late again Caroline!' Jacynth Michaels had called, smiling. Caroline was chronically late but she was so good in the shop that Mrs Michaels would forgive her practically anything. It was worth every penny of the thirty-five per cent discount she allowed her because though Caroline didn't have a model-girl height and figure, she had *style*. She wore the boutique's avant-garde clothes with a panache that tempted customers into believing that they too could get away with the latest look. Caroline persuaded customers to try on dresses they would normally have shied away from as being too 'difficult' by showing them exactly how they should be worn, adding the right belt and finding the right neck-lace, earrings, shoes . . . Caroline *organised* them, minimising their fears until they floated out of Maudie's, bolstered with a new confidence and feeling in tune with the world.

'Sorry, Mrs Michaels, it won't happen again!' Caroline had replied, grinning, because they both knew that of course it would – and probably tomorrow.

Caroline had loved Maudie's from the beginning. She'd liked its intimate bustle and she'd enjoyed meeting the customers, quite a lot of whom she knew as friends. She loved the chic little shop's high-tech theatrical décor with its brushed steel shelves and the spotlights illuminating colourful shoes, sweaters and jewellery like exhibits on an ever-changing stage. Long steel racks blossomed with Azzadine Alaia's dazzling slinky clothes, and Ungaro's bright, alluring feminine dresses as well as the cool tailored look from Basile and Soprani and a subtle collection from the latest Japanese designers – Cinderella garments waiting for a body to turn them magically into stylish outfits. But Caroline also had a good business brain and it always bothered her that though Maudie's was successful, it wasn't profitable – it simply ticked over without actually losing money – and that suited Mrs Michaels just fine. Owning a boutique had really started out just as a hobby for Jacynth Michaels – a little thing of her own, quite separate from her wealthy husband's international business activities. It kept her busy and happy and the prestige was enormous and of course, socially she now knew everybody in London. Mrs Michaels flew to fashion shows around the world, from Paris and Milan, to Tokyo and New York, where she was welcomed with open arms and the best champagne. She asked no more – but it *annoyed* Caroline. A business *should* make money – otherwise it was a waste of time. Because of her business training, Caroline had seen endless possibilities to expand the concept of Maudie's, to make it an international name – and even take it 'public'. But no one had been interested in her ideas – to most people she had seemed just another well-bred, attractive girl, filling in her time until she met and married the 'right' young man.

Of course, her father was right, she couldn't stay at Maudie's for ever. And she couldn't really blame him for grumbling that he hadn't spent all that money on her education to have her end up working as a shop-girl! There she was, twenty-four years old, product of a good English public school with a degree from Cambridge in Art History, as well as a business course at the LSE, behind her, and still – as her father put it – 'wasting her time in some silly shop in South Molton Street'. It was just that those qualifications she had gained didn't seem to equip her for what she really wanted to do – but the problem was that she hadn't been sure exactly *what would*.

She was then twenty-four years old, the only daughter of a well-connected, but rather down-at-heel Scottish family who owned a smallish, turreted Gothic castle on a windswept loch in the Highlands, and – since her grandfather had been foolish enough to sell the big, double-fronted house in London's smart Belgravia fifty years back in order to pay his gambling debts – a small flat just off Sloane Square. Her father's constant complaint was that if only his father had held on to the Belgravia house, with the way property values were accelerating they could have sold it for a cool million and they would be living in luxury today. But Caroline simply shrugged off his familiar complaints and looked forward confidently to what life might have to offer *her* – or at least what she could help herself to from life. Because it surely was not going to march up and say, 'Here you are – all you've ever dreamed of on a golden plate, Caroline.'

She'd breezed through school on exceptional brains and a willingness to contribute hard work to anything that interested her – especially the drama group. She knew that she had no talent for acting or singing and dancing – nor could she sew a fine seam or even design scenery, though she did enjoy splashing on great washes of paint and never minded cleaning the brushes and the mess afterwards. But where she really shone was her amazing ability to create order from chaos. Caroline could organise.

It was always Caroline who would take control of those first meetings of the school Drama Group, and somehow it was always she who made the final decision as to what play would be performed. It was Caroline who sent for the scripts and obtained playwrights' permissions; it was she who sorted out the bickering contenders for the leading roles, and it was Caroline who 'got the show on the road'. She drew up schedules of rehearsals and badgered reluctant girls into abandoning the evening comforts of a cosy common room and TV's *Top of the Pops*, persuading them to paint and sew or to play the piano for the heavy-limbed uncoordinated chorines to dance to.

Sometimes she'd thought longingly of training at the Royal Academy of Dramatic Art or the Guildhall School of Drama, but how could she 'train' to become a Broadway Producer – because *that* was what she really wanted. In the end, she'd gone up to Cambridge to read Art History.

The Cambridge years had been fun as well as hard work. Of course, she had been one of the many willing helpers in the college Drama Society's annual presentations as well as one of the leading organisers of the academic year's greatest social event – the May Ball.

When the final exams were over, Caroline forgot about work and plunged into festivity. Brightly striped marquees appeared on the ancient greensward and the serene grey cloisters rang to the night-long sounds of rock and roll and the popping of champagne corks. And as dawn had risen over the beautiful leafy campus, hundreds of students had taken to the river. In a long full-skirted aqua-taffeta dress that complemented her flecked greenish eyes, Caroline had rested her tired head against the punt's cushions, trailing a lazy hand in the chilly water and feeling like a character in a Seurat painting as she was poled down the fern-fronded river by a good-looking young man with whom she was half-in-love. Romance had blossomed several times at Cambridge, but nothing serious, and nothing that had lasted.

When she remembered those years, Caroline always thought of herself as being constantly busy. She had dashed between London and Cambridge, trying to cram everything she could into her already crowded life, with a scattered troupe of life-long friends and cousins and assorted affectionate relatives. Caroline's family was vast and very close and there were summer weekend houseparties and winter chalet ski trips. But she'd still squashed in time to concentrate on her studies.

It had come as a shock to leave the academic world that had sheltered her since she was five years old and emerge, age twenty-two, into the harsher realities of workaday life. Her older brother Angus was doing brilliantly in his career as a barrister and it seemed likely that he would be chosen as a candidate for a seat at the next election; while her younger brother Patrick was chasing happily around the world's motor-racing circuits as one of a team of mechanics, hoping one day to race for Jaguar or Lotus. But nowhere in the theatre was there an opening for a bright and pretty girl with a degree in Art History who spoke quite good French and a little German. So where, Caroline had wondered, was fate? Wasn't this the moment it was supposed to take a hand and with one stroke change her whole life?

When it did, it was the wrong way. The job she had tentatively lined up at one of the big art auction houses fell through, and she'd been forced to succumb to parental pressure and sign up for the Business Studies course.

After she had completed the course, Caroline had sent off applications for jobs she didn't really want, turning them down because she couldn't bear the thought of being shut away in some dreary office or attending meetings about products that bored her. She'd moped around home becoming more and more miserable and depressed, searching for a job in the theatre as a secretary or third-scene-shifter's assistant – anything to get her through those exciting portals – but it seemed every girl in London was chasing the same thing.

In the end, because money was short and she still needed time to come to a decision in her career – or for elusive fate to lend a hand – Caroline had taken a temporary job selling shoes at a shop on South Molton Street, drifting from there across the road to the high-tech smartly expensive boutique that sold extraordinary clothes by young French and Japanese designers to the golden youth of London. And somehow Maudie's had absorbed her life – it was like a too-comfortable bed – too enjoyable to leave but getting her exactly nowhere!

That fateful Monday business was slow – it seemed that no one wanted to brave the rain – and Caroline flicked idly through the pages of a fashion magazine, stopping to admire the pictures of Jessie-Ann Parker stalking down the catwalk at the Paris fashion shows, spectacular in Lagerfeld's clinging split-skirted cashmere evening dress. She had thought enviously how fantastic she looked – but of course that girl would look good in a sheet – and oh, for legs that long! And oh, too, to be as *successful* as Jessie-Ann Parker! They were almost exactly the same age, but look what Jessie-Ann had achieved – why, she must have been working since she was fifteen! Not only that, she seemed to have started right at the top. All-American Miss Parker could certainly have given *her* a few lessons in how to achieve her dreams . . . yes, Jessie-Ann had it all . . .

'Caroline,' Mrs Michaels had called, 'telephone. It's your Aunt Catriona.'

Caroline groaned. If her aunt were calling her at the shop, it could mean only one thing – one of her aunt's 'emergencies'.

Aunt Catriona's voice was always loud and high-pitched on the telephone as though she never understood that she didn't need to shout in order to be heard across the distance. 'Caroline my dear, could you possibly help me out?' she'd yelled. 'I'm giving a dinner party tomorrow night and silly old Mary Anderson has let me down – says she's got the 'flu but I'm sure it's just that

71

she's been drinking too much gin again . . . her liver must be playing her up . . .'

'Oh Aunt Catriona, it'll be all your old cronies,' wailed Caroline, 'can't you get someone older?'

'Now don't be silly, dear, my friends are not *all* old fogies you know . . . as a matter of fact I've invited some charming people. I'll expect you at eight then, and do try to look *normal*, Caroline dear . . .'

'What do you mean – "normal"?' she'd demanded, holding the phone away from her aching ear.

'You *know* . . . wear something reasonably resembling a dress – not like that Japanese potato sack you wore the last time . . .'

She could hear her aunt cackling with laughter at her own little joke as she put down the receiver. Of course she hadn't wanted in the least little bit to go to the dinner party. She knew there wouldn't be anyone under the age of fifty and her aunt would be stingy with the drinks because she still thought of Caroline as a 'wee gel'. But Aunt Catriona was her godmother and she had been a caring and conscientious one, she'd written regularly to her at school, often enclosing a five-pound note that had come in very handy on Caroline's Saturday afternoon forays into the local town for 'supplies' to keep her through the school-starved week. Caroline heaved an exasperated sigh, obviously she would have to go to the party.

It had seemed to Caroline then that fate, in one of her most smiling and beneficial moods, had finally taken a hand in her life! She'd spotted Pericles as soon as she came through the door. He was backed up against the pond-green wall that Aunt Catriona favoured as 'her' colour for interior décor, regardless of the fact that it made the spacious Cadogan Square drawing room look like a rather chilly aquarium. Pericles was being talked to by two eager and ageing ladies, and his desperate eyes had met hers across the room.

Glancing around swiftly, Caroline had decided he must be with the tall, willowy blonde with the swooping cheekbones and enormous and very bored eyes, who certainly wasn't one of her aunt's regular guests. She was being chatted-up admiringly by a portly and very sweet little man whom Caroline recognised as one of her aunt's hunting friends. Aunt Catriona patronised the horsey set in the country and the artistic set in town – the great mistake she made was in trying to mix the two socially.

Before Caroline had a chance to obey the appeal in Pericles' dark blue eyes, Aunt Catriona had appeared, kissed her and passed her on – drinkless – to Bunty Sotwell, whom Caroline had known since she was four – or maybe even younger . . . anyway, he was old enough to be her father. She'd found her gaze returing to the blue-eyed stranger, and then back to the blonde . . . wondering who *he* was . . . who *she* was . . . and how she could possibly meet him before her aunt spirited them all to the dinner table where she'd be stuck for the rest of the night with Bunty or someone else like him . . .

She'd grabbed her aunt's arm as she'd floated by, 'I want to sit next to *that* man at dinner,' she'd whispered urgently, staring at the stranger.

'You mean Pericles Jago . . . yes, well I think every woman here would like to sit next to him . . . he's an expert on modern art you know . . .'

'Aunt Catrionia! I *must* sit next to him, if I don't I'll never come here again!'

'There's no need to threaten me, child, of course you're sitting next to him.' She'd beamed at Caroline, 'See how your old Auntie looks after you,' she'd added, threading her way through her guests and leaving Caroline smiling happily.

Pericles Jago ran a successful Art Gallery in Mayfair. He was in his middle thirties, tall and noble-browed – though his critics would have said this was because of his perceptibly thinning hair. But as he'd taken a seat next to her, Caroline only noticed his beautiful deep blue eyes. He'd stared at her silently for a few moments, as though assessing her authenticity and value, the way he might a painting attributed to Caravaggio and about whose provenance he wasn't quite certain. At last he smiled at her. 'You're Caroline,' he'd said, 'I wanted to meet you as soon as I saw you come through the door. Tell me, do you know the early Goya portrait of a woman with a little black dog on her lap? You remind me of her, with your dark eyes and hair . . . surely you have Spanish ancestors?' Caroline had smiled at him shyly, explaining that in fact all her ancestors were Scottish, but yes, she did know the painting.

They'd talked about 'Art' and she had found his opinions almost as interesting as his eyes. They'd talked about Venice – his favourite city, and now certainly hers too. He'd admired her dress, one of Maudie's latest slinky Alaias that clung to her like a second silken skin and which she had thought would be wasted on her aunt's old fogies, but which she was now pleased she had chosen. And what, Pericles had asked, was she doing working at Maudie's when she knew so much about art? As it happened, he was looking for someone to help in his Gallery . . . perhaps Caroline might be interested?

Pericles had departed soon after dinner to escort the beauty to her lair, but with a last, lingering glance over his shoulder at Caroline. On the way home in the taxi she'd studied his business card over and over . . . 'The Jago Gallery, Hill Street, London, W.1., PERICLES JAGO.' Crisp, thick, heavily embossed – he was obviously a man of few words – and a lot of taste. She couldn't wait to see him again.

A few days later she'd waited nervously in a cluttered office behind Pericles' gallery to find out about her new job. She had dressed carefully, discarding three outfits before finally deciding on the bright yellow Lagerfeld duffel coat with the wide shoulders and black passementerie-fastenings, and a simple black cashmere sweater and skirt. She'd felt crushed with disappointment when another man emerged from the inner sanctum to tell her that Pericles was too busy with a client to see her himself, but could she please start as soon as possible and he would pay her whatever she was earning at Maudie's plus an extra two hundred pounds a month. It had sounded like a fortune to Caroline and it was with high expectations that she'd made her way back to Maudie's to break the news to Mrs Michaels.

She'd felt a bit in limbo her first week at the gallery. Pericles was barely there – he'd flown off to New York on Concorde on Tuesday and back again on Wednesday and then to Paris on Friday for a long weekend and Caroline had been left pretty much to work on her own. But the paintings were interesting, especially those by the new young artists that Pericles was beginning to take an interest in. The Jago Gallery was well-known internationally and there was a constant stream of people in and out – collectors, browsers, dealers – and she'd been able to pursue her urge to organise by compiling details for the next catalogue and tracking down authenticity certificates.

The next Friday Pericles had asked her out to lunch and they'd lingered late at the Caprice, tucked away in their own quiet corner, ignoring all the busy business-lunchers. She'd told him about school and Cambridge and how she felt about the theatre while he sat back, gazing at her intently with that piercing blue look that had made her feel warm all over – as though he were thinking *other* things while she talked.

A few days later he'd asked her to dinner at a surprisingly off-beat Japanese restaurant with astonishingly good food, where they'd sat on mats with their shoes off and been served delicately by a Japanese maiden. The Sake was warm and the food delicious and there was something about being shoeless on a mat together behind tatami screens that had caused Pericles to unbend to the point of unbuttoning his waistcoat and loosening his tie. He'd kissed her gently on the cheek as the taxi dropped her at her door, and she couldn't wait to get into bed and close her eyes so she could dream of him – so cool and correct, so aloof, and so attractive. The very next week Pericles had asked if she would like to go to an auction at Sotheby's with him and of course she'd accepted eagerly, expecting to stroll around the corner to Bond Street, only to jump with surprise when he'd asked her to pick up the tickets at Swissair. They would leave for Geneva the next day at eleven.

At the auction, Pericles had been furious when the small Manet on which he was bidding for a client was sold to an American museum for an unexpectedly astronomical sum that, in his opinion, contained a couple of zeros too many! He'd stalked impatiently from the saleroom and Caroline had hurried after him, watching anxiously as he paused in front of a large Venetian gilt mirror to smooth back his hair. For a moment she'd wondered whether he was angry because he'd lost the painting or because he was losing his hair. Of course what she hadn't known then was that he was really angry with Evita who'd gone off to Mustique leaving him in the lurch.

Catching her eye in the mirror, he'd smiled suddenly. 'Tell you what,' he'd exclaimed with a sudden charming boyish eagerness, 'there's a marvellous exhibition of young painters in Basle I'd like to catch. Would you like to come along?'

Caroline's worried face had lit up and Pericles had laughed, kissing her cheek lightly. Glancing around the foyer to make sure they were unobserved, he'd kissed her again – properly – on the mouth.

Even now, in the darkened cabin class of the BA flight to New York with a movie flickering on the screen and the businessman in the seat next to her sipping Scotch and writing notes in his Filofax, Caroline could remember that kiss. She could feel the intimate pressure of his mouth on hers and the faint roughness of his skin . . . Fool! she told herself angrily, clicking her seat into the upright position . . . you weren't supposed to remember that . . .

They arranged to rent a car and drive to Basle, with a little detour or two on the way to take in the wonderful scenery. Caroline was packing her bags when Pericles had tapped on her door. 'Almost ready?' he'd asked, loosening his tie as he walked in. Then he'd thrown his arms around her taking her by surprise, and somehow she'd lost her footing and tumbled backwards onto the bed, and she was pressed against the pillows, her heart racing and her mouth bruised and with Pericles on top of her. It was all a bit sudden! she'd thought, as he kissed her passionately. Not that she didn't want him – but she'd prefer it to be after an intimate candlelit dinner or romantic stroll by the lake, not just squashed between the Auction and packing! She'd sounded like a foolish heroine in a Victorian novel, explaining to him how she felt, but of course he'd apologised. 'I'm afraid I just got carried away,' he'd said, straightening his tie and smoothing back his hair again, 'you are so damned attractive Caroline – I couldn't resist you.' And he'd looked so handsome and smiled at her so charmingly, she'd wondered why on earth she'd pushed him away.

The sun had been high in a clear blue sky, sparkling on snow-capped mountain peaks as they'd driven along the perimeter of the steel-blue lake in a rented white Mercedes. Pericles had opened the sun-roof and the air was so fresh and crisp Caroline had felt sure it contained more oxygen than plain London air. Exhilarated, she'd sung along to the tunes on the radio, until Pericles suddenly switched to a tape and they were wafting along to the strains of Elgar.

'I don't blame you for not liking my singing,' she'd laughed, 'but *Elgar*!'

'Elgar represents musically all that is best about Britain,' he'd replied stiffly, and she'd glanced at him, with surprise, realising that he was serious. Was Pericles just a little bit pompous?

They'd found a small inn, exactly like a picture-postcard chalet on the banks of the lake, half-shuttered in its out-of-season calm, its little boats captured by ropes to the shore for their winter hibernation. And there was a smiling, efficient proprietor whose wife made the best coffee and baked the best pastries Caroline had ever tasted.

Pericles had gone to make a telephone call while she unpacked, and she'd arranged her black lace nightdress carefully on the big fluffy bed. After a leisurely bath she'd dressed carefully in a soft, grey cashmere shift, fastening enormous glittering Butler & Wilson 'diamond' earrings into her pretty ears. A splash of Givenchy's Ysatis, and she was ready.

Pericles was drinking at the bar. 'There you are,' he commented snappily as Caroline came towards him, making her wonder if she'd done something wrong, but she had the feeling that maybe it was the lengthy phone call that had disturbed him.

The carved pine-panelled dining room basked in the rosy glow of a crackling log fire. There were no other diners and their table was set with flowers and candles and it was just as romantic as Caroline could have wished. The innkeeper acted as waiter while his wife cooked, and they ate delicious lake trout with crisp feathery rosti and drank quantities of an unlabelled white wine from their host's own cellar which made Caroline's head whirl pleasantly.

She remembered gazing blissfully into Pericles' blue eyes as he told her about the price rises in the world art-market over the past three years; he could have talked about the complexities of diesel engines or the irrigation system along the Upper Nile Valley and she would had been enchanted to listen. She was totally and helplessly in love.

There had been a lot of laughter as the innkeeper's wife carried in a steaming plum soufflé, beaming with pride, and Caroline and Pericles had applauded. And then they toasted her health and that of her husband in fiery eau-de-vie and she and her husband toasted them, and all in all a good deal of the bottle of eau-de-vie was drunk.

She could picture their room now, with the warm red glow of the fire softening the panelled walls, and the open shutters allowing a glimpse of a silver moon over the lake. As they'd sunk onto the bed, Pericles had taken her in his arms, kissing her passionately, roughly . . .

It was exactly the romantic setting Caroline had wished – even though there seemed to be no time to put on the black lace nightdress because Pericles was so eager and passionate.

She'd struggled from her dress and he'd gazed at her in her sexy black underwear, still wearing her high-heeled shoes and black stockings, as though she were the sensual vision of his erotic fantasies. Then he'd turned away and begun to undress.

Snuggled under the soft, weightless eiderdown, Caroline had watched as Pericles folded his trousers neatly and hung them in the armoire, smoothing back his dark hair in the mirror, before he came to bed. It was odd, she'd thought, how a man's image changed once he was naked. Stripped of his clothes, Pericles had lost all the labels that identified his status in the game of life . . . without his correct dark blue pinstripe suit, his striped blue and white shirt with the plain white collar, his red silk tie and his scarlet braces, Pericles was no longer the enigmatic gallery-owner and smart man-about-town. As he came towards her she wondered fleetingly if she didn't perhaps prefer him dressed, rather than in only blue cashmere socks and an erection . . . but when he took her roughly in his arms, crushing her to him, all that existed was the moment, and that big soft bed – and each other. Pericles' mouth had demanded hers, and his body had covered her and she was drowning in his kisses and sinking under his weight, pressed against the mattress by the force of his passion.

The only trouble, she'd thought dejectedly, a few minutes later, was that his passion had been so short-lived! But he *had* drunk a vast amount of eau-de-vie and it *was* the first time. Pericles had fallen asleep right away, and she'd stroked his dark hair back from his brow tenderly, pushing her dissatisfaction to the back of her mind as unworthy. She loved Pericles, and he loved her, and things could only get better.

The next morning he'd had the urge to press on to Basle and the exhibition where, he told her, he had many friends, and somehow they lost track of their original plan to find small, out-of-the-way hotels where they could be alone. When they reached Basle, he made more lengthy private phone calls and then announced that they would leave for Paris the next day.

In Paris he always stayed at the beautiful Hotel Crillon, with its lavish new décor, but this time instead of sharing a room, he'd had a suite on the fifth floor and Caroline had a room of her own on the second. 'I'm here on business,' he told her when she looked at him questioningly, 'and we don't want to damage your reputation young Caroline, do we?'

Caroline didn't mind at all damaging her reputation with Pericles and she'd waited, disappointed as he bustled off for hours at a time – on business – he told her. Caroline had longed to go with him but he didn't ask her, so instead she browsed through the shops on the rue Saint Honoré and lingered over afternoon tea in Angelina's on the rue de Rivoli, munching on mouth-watering cakes and worrying about gaining weight and whether Pericles were falling out of love with her – although to be truthful, she couldn't remember him ever telling her that he loved her.

It was in Angelina's that she ran into Paulette Villiers, an old school friend and now a fashion journalist, in Paris for the collections.

Paulette was tall and not in the least bit pretty, with short sculptured black hair and a strong nose; but she was madly chic in Rei Kawakubo's layers of black and grey wrappings that made her look like an eager young hawk. Paulette also knew everybody – and all the gossip.

'Pericles Jago!' she'd exclaimed in between bites of chestnut meringue. 'I thought he was already spoken for?'

'You mean the blonde?' asked Caroline, her heart sinking.

'I can't remember her name but she's incredibly beautiful, though no one seems to know much about her background. Still, she seems to get invited everywhere. I could be wrong Caroline,' she said glancing sharply at her friend, 'but I had the impression that it was permanent between them . . . are you serious about Pericles? Or is this just a Paris fling?'

'Oh dear,' whispered Caroline, tears stinging her eyes, 'I'm afraid it's serious . . .'

'God, I'm sorry,' Paulette had cried, dismayed, 'I always did have a big mouth! Still, better you know now Caroline – at least you can do something about it.'

'Like what?'

Caroline looked so miserable and so unlike her usual vivacious self that Paulette wished she'd never said anything. 'Look, I'm pretty sure I'm wrong,' she replied comfortingly, 'it was probably all over between them months ago, that's why he's here with you. After all, how could he not fall in love with you? Half the boys at Cambridge did . . . you've no idea how we all used to envy your success with men Caroline!'

'But I'm *in love* with him Paulette!' cried Caroline tragically, taking another bite of her chocolate cake.

Paulette shrugged. 'I'm half French,' she said, 'maybe that's why I'm more philosophical about "love". You should use your head as well as your emotions Caroline; never let love *take over* – it's only a recipe for disaster. You must retain control. Promise me you'll try?'

'I promise,' replied Caroline, miserably.

'Good. Now look here – I have an extra ticket for Saint-Laurent's show tomorrow – how would you like to go?'

Caroline still loved fashion, even though she no longer worked at Maudie's and she cheered up immediately . . . 'I'd love it,' she'd replied, 'but maybe Pericles will want me to go somewhere with him . . .'

With a sigh, Paulette had fished the invitation from her capacious black leather purse. 'Take my advice,' she'd said bluntly, 'let Pericles wait . . . tell him you have other things to do and you can't see him . . . let him wonder what you're up to. It'll do him good! I'll see you tomorrow then.' Flinging her black bag over her shoulder she kissed Caroline on both cheeks, adding, 'and remember what I said about love!'

The weather had turned quite cold and Caroline had drifted aimlessly through the boutiques feeling lonely and trying to assuage her doubts. Pericles had never once mentioned the blonde woman to her – at that point she didn't even know her name. And if he *were* serious about the blonde, then why was he here in Paris with her? There had been no mistaking the look of longing in his eyes that first night at Aunt Catriona's party . . . but nor was there any mistaking the fact that he had pursued *her*; he'd invited her to work for him, asked her out to lunches and dinners, asked her to go with him to the Auction in Switzerland. Surely Paulette was mistaken. Everything was wonderful between them; they would have dinner tonight – admittedly with a crowd of people because Pericles had many friends in Paris, but then they'd be alone together in her quiet room, just the two of them – and that was all that mattered.

Pericles was entertaining a group of friends and business acquaintances at his favourite restaurant, L'Archistrate. 'In Ancient Greek history,' he told Caroline in the taxi on the way there, 'from which my name and some of my ancestors derive – as no doubt you are aware from Burke's Peerage,' he added pompously, 'the Greek Pericles was not only a famous statesman, but also the major cultural influence of the era. I like to think I've inherited a few of those qualities. Of course, Archistrate was Pericles' chef . . . so in a way I feel I have a personal interest in the restaurant. Naturally I told the chef and he was quite amused. And of course, the food's sublime.'

Caroline had noticed that Pericles didn't enjoy the small, off the track bistros that she knew and liked; he always preferred to go to places where doormen and barmen greeted him by name – and he tipped lavishly for that service.

There was no doubt, she remembered thinking later, as she sat in the beautiful fin-de-siècle restaurant, nibbling moodily on Senderens exquisite chocolates at the end of another delicately perfect meal, that Pericles was definitely Right Bank and she was definitely Left. She would much rather have spent the evening with some of the young artists he'd told her about than with the pompous bunch of guests he'd invited tonight. But she pricked up her ears when Claude d'Amboise asked Pericles where 'La belle Evita' was tonight. At first Caroline thought he meant the musical but when Pericles replied that 'Evita was busy this week,' she realised that he was talking about *the blonde beauty!*

'Evita is more than a girlfriend,' he'd told her later that night, pacing the length of the Crillon's blue-patterned carpet clad only in a paisley silk nightshirt, a large glass of brandy in his hand, and looking, thought Caroline disloyally, slightly ridiculous. 'Evita has been my mistress for three years,' he went on, 'she's half Brazilian, half French. And she was brought up here in Paris,' he sipped his brandy, 'that's why my friends were asking about her. Evita knows everyone.'

'Then what about me?' cried Caroline. 'If you are in love with Evita, why am I here?' Suddenly she was afraid of the answer . . .

'Of course I'm not in love with Evita,' he'd told her soothingly, 'and I'm here with you because you are young and lovely and charming, and you make me feel good – and maybe I'm even a little bit in love with you . . .'

Caroline's face had lit with relief as he'd grabbed her to him and carried her towards the bed, pulling down the straps of her new peach satin nightdress and kissing her breasts, and she'd quite forgotten the questions about Evita that had trembled on the tip of her tongue.

A short time later she slid from beneath Pericles' already somnolent weight, trailing despondently into the white-tiled bathroom, blinking in the strong light. She was beginning to believe that their quick couplings were just another manifestation of the pace at which Pericles took life – he did everything at the gallop. Hurrying off here, there and everywhere – never still for a minute. But as she soaped herself under the warm shower, she wished wistfully that he wouldn't fall asleep right away, thinking how nice it would have been to linger in each other's arms the way true lovers did.

Remembering Paulette's advice the next day when Pericles suggested lunch, she'd told him firmly that she had other plans. Perched on a brittle chair amid a throng of fraught-looking female journalists and fashion buyers waiting for Saint-Laurent's show to begin, Caroline suddenly felt her spirits begin to rise. The lofty salon bristled with tension and excitement and she'd watched interestedly as photographers jockeyed for position at the edge of the catwalk. Surely that dark attractive man was the famous Brachman, and the red-haired girl must be his assistant – though the poor girl must need nerves of steel, the way he was ordering her about! Everyone knew Brachman's high-handed reputation.

'Hi!' Stark in a grey turban, pale make-up and bright scarlet lipstick, Paulette waved as she pushed her way along the row of chairs towards Caroline, apologising as she stepped on toes and tripped over chair legs. 'Sorry I'm late, but there's chaos back there – Jessie-Ann Parker hasn't arrived – and no one knows where she is! If it were anyone else but Jessie-Ann you might expect it, but she's the *complete* professional. Her agency hasn't heard from her for three weeks, but the rumour is she's run off and got married . . . but no one knows who the lucky man is. So, how are things with Pericles?'

'I had it out with him – about Evita. He's not in love with her, Paulette – and he thinks he's in love with me . . .'

Paulette glanced shrewdly at her friend's glowing face, unwilling to burst Caroline's bubble of happiness . . . that would come soon enough, she felt sure.

'I took your advice though, I told him I was busy this afternoon – that I had other plans . . .' She laughed happily, 'Isn't it crazy Paulette? I never *ever* thought I'd feel like this about a man.'

'None of us ever do, dear,' Paulette had commented as the lights dimmed and the music started up.

Then the curtains parted and with a clash of cymbals a troupe of near-naked fire-eaters catapulted along the runway, tossing blazing torches into the air, forming a living line of statues as the models swarmed on stage parading the first of Saint-Laurent's breathtaking spring clothes.

It was sheer magic, thought Caroline, as wave after wave of models swept disdainfully past in ravishing evening dresses. They drifted lazily across the catwalk in elegant day dresses that would grace Ascot or a smart wedding, and posed coquettishly in black lace, sequins and feathers for cocktail time . . . This was better than Broadway, Caroline realised suddenly, six months of sheer hard work and genius had gone to make this single show and it commanded an audience of the world's top professionals! Photographers crowded the edge of the runway, snatching shots as the models swooped above them and Caroline noticed that Brachman bided his time, waiting for just the right model in exactly the right dress, before taking a picture. When you were as good a photographer as he was, she supposed you needn't grab all the pictures you could and hope that one or two would be good. Brachman knew exactly what he was doing.

The show ended with a ravishing bride in petalled organza and gardenias. Caroline had watched enviously as the rest of the models crowded onto the catwalk around their 'maestro' – the slender, bespectacled Yves Saint-Laurent – amid a wave of applause and a shower of kisses, wishing she could have been a part of the excitement.

She'd floated back to the Crillon on a wave of exhilaration, still dreaming of the clothes, the glamour, the sheer excitement of it all! Back in her room she'd read the little note Pericles had left for her, with a sinking heart. 'Sorry Caroline,' it said, 'but I've been called back on urgent business – an American client in London only for one day. Unfortunately I did not know where you were so I was unable to contact you. The hotel is charged to my account so please feel free to stay a few days longer if you wish. It's been fun – Pericles.'

Caroline had re-read the note, hardly believing what it said. Pericles was gone! He must already be in London . . . Was it really business? Or was it Evita? Had she called and given him an ultimatum?

Tears had trickled down her cheeks as she slumped back into the chair, the note still clutched in her hand. Couldn't he at least have waited until she got back to the hotel? There were planes every hour to London – surely an hour or two wouldn't have made that much difference? Or maybe it would? Pericles might have missed his client and she knew that business always came first with him. She'd gazed sadly at the note, analysing his large looped handwriting as though it might give her some clue to his intentions. He hadn't signed it 'love' she thought dismally; and surely it would have been easy to write 'Love Pericles' – even if he didn't mean it. Because suddenly, despite what he'd said the night before, she wasn't at all sure that Pericles did love her – and she was so very sure she was in love with him.

She'd taken the nine o'clock flight to London the following morning and after dropping her luggage back at the flat, she went straight to the Jago Gallery. The other members of the staff eyed her curiously, their conversation stopping abruptly as she entered the room.

A large cream-coloured envelope had been waiting on her desk. 'Dear Caroline,' Pericles had written, 'I suddenly find myself awfully busy with clients and won't be in the office for a few weeks. I had intended to go to New York next week, but as I've had to change my plans, I wondered whether you might like to go over there and check some of the new galleries and generally see what the scene is? I know I can trust your judgement. My secretary will arrange everything. I can't tell you what fun it's all been. Thanks for everything. Pericles.'

On the BA New York flight, the movie came to an end. As the credits began to roll and the lights went up Caroline brushed away a surreptitious tear, remembering how angry she'd felt with Pericles – and with herself at her naïveté. She'd stalked out of the office without glancing at the curious faces of her fellow workers, heading back to the security of her apartment like a wounded animal. For a week she'd tried to get Pericles on the phone, leaving endless terse messages on his answering machine. But he'd never called her back. When the pictures of his wedding to the glamorous blonde Evita had appeared in the newspapers a few days later, she'd been swept with anger at herself for being such a little fool, and then with anger at *him*. She'd cried for two solid days and then she'd sat up in bed with the morning sunshine flooding in, feeling suddenly better. The hell with men, she'd decided suddenly, she would take up Pericles' offer – even though she knew it was just an excuse to get rid of her. She'd always wanted to go to New York.

'Ladies and gentlemen, the Captain is now beginning his final descent into New York's John F. Kennedy Airport. Would you kindly make sure that your seatbelts are securely fastened . . .'

Caroline cinched her seatbelt tighter, peering through the window at a tilted version of the New Jersey coast, searching for that magical Manhattan skyline . . . Pericles was behind her – and somehow Broadway still beckoned . . .

4

Gala waved goodbye from the train window, waiting until Debbie's smart figure had disappeared completely and all that was left of Leeds was a grimy grey blur of warehouses and factories, gradually giving way to the rolling green fields of West Yorkshire. Then she sat down and took a deep breath. She was on her own now. London, and a tiny bed-sit in some mysterious part of it called Earl's Court awaited her. Nervously she contemplated what she would do when the train arrived at King's Cross station . . . she must keep an eye on her luggage because she'd heard how quickly thieves spirited away your baggage even if you only glanced away for a second; she must keep her handbag close to her at all times, even though she was only carrying enough money in it to take care of her taxi fare and a sandwich on the train – she had the rest of her cash in a moneybelt, strapped uncomfortably beneath the waistband of her skirt, and the new chequebook – her first – was in her purse.

Biting her lips nervously Gala stole a glance at her travelling companions. The train seemed to her to be full of bored business-men reading *The Times*, all looking as though they went to London on Monday morning every week, and students with backpacks, chewing nonchalantly on apples and potato crisps while they read the *Sun* or the *Guardian*. No one cast a glance her way and she checked her appearance anxiously. She had shopped for her new clothes with care, after all it was going to be the big city's first glance of 'Gala-Rose' as well as *her* first glimpse of London. She thought she'd got it exactly right. A grey pleated skirt, a loose grey sweater and flat-heeled red shoes. A matching grey jacket lay neatly folded in the rack over her head, and she had tied a bright little scarf around her neck, rolling it and letting the ends dangle the way they'd taught her at modelling school. Her streaked blonde hair was brushed back and held with a big red clip and her face was carefully, but discreetly made-up.

But it seemed she needn't have bothered for all the attention she got. Nobody even glanced her way. Nobody cared. She was invisible, just as she had always been.

Gala quashed the sudden feeling of fear that threatened to overcome her . . . she wasn't going to get upset – she would ignore them just the way they ignored her. Because she was 'Gala-Rose' the soon to be famous international model, just like her idol Jessie-Ann Parker, and she was on her way to London – and success.

Photographs of Jessie-Ann cut from magazines and newspapers had covered one wall of her sparse little bedroom at home and every night before she'd gone to sleep Gala had gazed at the tall rangy blonde who looked as beautiful in simple shorts and shirt as she did in black velvet and diamonds. 'Glamorous' was the word Gala used to describe Jessie-Ann – a word so remote from her home town of Garthwaite that it belonged to people who lived on another planet. Yet in her dreams she had seen visions of herself as a famous model, travelling the world just like Jessie-Ann, adored by everyone – invisible no longer.

Of course Gala wasn't her real name. It was the name she had always called herself in those childhood fantasies when she was free to be anyone she liked and not just a plump, plain child burdened with the name Hilda Mirfield. *Hilda!* All the other girls had pretty names, like Tracy and Angela and Sharon. Not that her fantasies were restricted to childhood – they still continued even though Gala was now seventeen. The difference was that when she was a child there had been nothing she could do to make them come true. She'd been trapped by that name 'Hilda' – and trapped in the grim backstreet house with two-rooms-up and two-down, and a grey cement extension that accommodated a cold little bathroom.

She had always felt that a terraced cottage in a little Yorkshire mining town was not a suitable environment for a soul as different as hers. She knew that she was different by the way the others laughed at her. Not just for her name, though heaven knows she'd taken enough stick for that thanks to her Mam who'd gone uncharacteristically sentimental and named her for a sister who'd died young.

Gala's mother had always been busy with her own social activities – usually at the pubs in town, so their house had never been like the others on the street – bustling with warm Yorkshire goodwill and hospitality. The other kids were always in and out of each other's houses, skipping rope or rollerskating in the road, dodging the cars and shrieking with laughter, or whispering secrets to each other with furtive glances over their shoulders and loud giggles. Locked into silence by her shyness and insecurity, Hilda was never asked to join in and she had begun to live more and more in her own fantasy world, fuelling her imagination and flights of fancy with magazines and American soap operas on television, when she would escape for an hour at a time into a rich sumptuous world where somehow, strangely, she felt certain she belonged.

She'd taken quite a lot of harassment at school about her Mam's romances too. There was always a lot of guffawing from the boys in the spear-tipped, iron-railinged, concrete schoolyard – the spears were there to prevent them climbing, but they didn't succeed because one day Wayne Bracewell had clambered up . . . Gala usually tried to push the memory of what had happened next from her mind, letting it dwell in a sort of quivering jelly of fear somewhere at the bottom of her brain . . . But today she was being brave and facing up to things.

She'd searched her face afterwards in the mirror for traces of guilt, recalling how small Wayne's crumpled body had looked, and how the other children had gathered round, gazing in silent wonder as the red blood poured down his cold winter-white nine-year-old face. She could even remember his expression of surprise, and how shocked she had been when he hadn't even screamed as he slid down the roof of the infants' block and over the edge . . . onto the cruel, spiky railings that were meant to stop them from climbing. But *she* had screamed and screamed, still clinging to that roof. No one had taken any notice of her, they'd just kept on gazing at Wayne until the teachers came running. Even then, no one had seemed to notice her . . . she had been the invisible person . . . a ghost at the scene of the crime . . .

The funny thing was that she still couldn't remember exactly what had happened and it wasn't until a few months after the accident that she started to have the dreams. They came most often when her Mam stayed out all night and she was alone in the house, stealing up on her sleep-darkened eyes like a red mist swirling around her until she realised it was not fog but blood – scarlet and wet and sticky! In the dream the smell of blood filled her nostrils – dank and warm – and she was all alone on a high precipice. Wayne's face would be miles below her on the ground and she would gaze silently at him from her lofty pinnacle. Wayne's eyes were open and there was so much blood and she was so high up, teetering on the brink . . . fear would rip through her like the iron spikes had ripped through Wayne and she'd hear herself screaming, again and again . . . but there was no one to hear, no one to stop the blood . . . and no one to take away the look in dead Wayne's eyes . . . Her own thin screams would awaken her and she'd lie there, her heart pounding and her body filmed in the clammy sweat of fear, back in her tiny room with its Jessie-Ann pictures and the splotches of damp climbing the walls.

If people hadn't noticed ` ¨ilda, they certainly had noticed her Mam. At school there was always a lot of sniggering when the name of the local pub, the Cock and Bull, was mentioned – always coupled with her Mam's name.

Her mother, Sandra Mirfield, was still only in her late thirties and liked what she called euphemistically 'a good time'. Wayne Bracewell had been one of the worst for teasing her about her Mam . . . even at nine he'd been full of sexual innuendo. He knew what it was all about, Wayne did – from his three older brothers, she supposed. Anyway, *they* should talk – *their* father was *always* drunk on Friday nights. And so what if her Mam did like the pub? After her Dad had died in the pit she and her Mam had been distraught for weeks, but eventually they began to enjoy the comfort of the small pension and the relief from her Dad's continual nagging at her Mam because she dyed her hair blonde and liked silky dresses and high-heeled sandals. He hadn't wanted his wife to look different from all the other women in their street who went around in plain jumpers and mud-coloured skirts and a clean apron – even when they weren't working in the kitchen.

But her Mam just used to laugh at him and say, 'Well lad, that's why you married me, y'liked me satin knickers!'

Anyway, it was after Dad died that the real teasing started at school and it had been hard for her. Especially on Monday mornings when everybody knew just *who* her Mam had been with. In a place as small as Garthwaite there were only a half-dozen pubs and most of the regular customers did a 'grand tour' of them all on weekends and naturally, her Mam kept up with the best. Sometimes for a change, Sandra took the bus twenty miles into Leeds and had a real 'fling', but most Saturday nights she didn't come home.

Gala could still remember how awful it had been that first time. As darkness closed in, the house had seemed to fall eerily silent and she'd turned up the volume on the television, trying to fill the small room with music and people. Later when the programmes were all finished, the house had settled into even deeper silence and she had peered anxiously outside, hoping to see her Mam hurrying along the street, straining her ears for the tap-tap of her sandalled high-heels on the flagstone pavement. She'd huddled in the big chair with her knees under her chin, staring into the fire until the red embers in the old-fashioned coal-grate had turned grey and died. As a chill grey dawn brought reality back to Garthwaite's unlovely streets, Hilda had fallen into an uneasy doze only to be startled back into life by her Mam's sharp voice exclaiming over the fact that she'd gone to sleep leaving the light on, and complaining that the fire had gone out! When Sandra Mirfield had snapped off the lightswitch, without an explanation as to where she'd been, or any question as to whether her eight-year-old daughter had been worried or afraid – Hilda Mirfield's real life at number 27 Balaclava Terrace, Garthwaite, had snapped off too. It was then that Gala took over.

She had chosen her new name after watching a 'Gala Night' of ballet from Covent Garden Theatre on television. For her it had been a magical hour of escape into a world of beauty, where breathtakingly slender graceful girls were pursued by romantically handsome male dancers. Poor Hilda, plump and ordinary, had longed to be one of those dancers, and longed to be a part of the colourful exciting life that she knew existed outside Garthwaite and its drab surroundings. She had looked up the word 'Gala' in Collins' dictionary and to her surprise it was the same word she had always pronounced, Yorkshire-style, as 'gayler'. Somehow it sounded so much prettier as 'Gahla' – and so did she. And the word meant 'a celebration, suitable for a festive occasion . . .' 'Gala' was what she would become – and she added the hyphen and the 'Rose' to make the new name sound like Jessie-Ann's.

'*Hilda*' at eight had been just a plump, frightened child with stringy mouse-brown hair and round blue eyes, spaced wide apart beneath fine, surprised brows. *Hilda* had a straight nose whose nostrils seemed too wide and a mouth that was too small for the roundness of her pink-cheeked face. *Hilda* ate too many chips, hated school and had the broadest of Yorkshire accents. But as she grew older 'Gala' began to take over. When Gala was thirteen, she was clever enough to realise that to have any chance she would not only have to lose weight, she would also have to do something about her Yorkshire accent and her voice.

Her Mam didn't know about her secret plan, nor did any of the girls at school. But, as Gala-Rose (Rose because the white rose was the symbol of Yorkshire), she was going to take London by storm. As a start, she persuaded her Mam to send her to Miss Gladys Forster in Leeds for elocution lessons and while she didn't quite learn to talk like Miss Forster, she persevered until at least she had learned to sound her consonants as well as all her endings – think*ing*, and not think*in*, gra*t*itude and not gra-itude, with what Miss Forster called her 'glottal stops' in the middle. 'Gala', at fourteen, had *no* 'glottal stops'. Gala had one more year of school and then that was-it – she'd be off to London. She knew her Mam wouldn't even miss her – she'd have missed her chain-smoked cigarettes and gin and tonics in the Cock and Bull on a Saturday night a lot more than she would her daughter!

Gala had quit eating chips and chocolate that year and, surprisingly, the weight had begun to melt away. In a sudden spurt of growth she'd reached a lofty five foot ten so that she'd towered over all the other girls, and the chubby flesh that had plumped out her knees and expanded her thighs disappeared, revealing long slim legs, slender hips and a small bosom. Her face though, had never quite lost its soft roundness.

She'd been saving a bit of money every week earned as a checkout-girl at the local supermarket on weekends and as an assistant in the cloakroom of a disco in Leeds on Friday and Saturday nights, plus the money she'd earned working in Woolworth's over Christmas. She had saved all her school-dinner money too – which was another reason she'd lost weight so quickly, since she ate nothing from breakfast at seven in the morning until her tea at five in the evening when she got home from school. And every now and again – on the principle that all it meant to her mother was another round of gin and tonics, she'd helped herself to a fiver from her purse. It was all for a good cause, she'd told herself guiltily, and anyway, it couldn't really be stealing – not from your Mam – could it?

But when she was fifteen and had just left school, her Mam got ill. Sandra Mirfield had been complaining of weakness and dizziness and then she'd been rushed into hospital for an emergency hysterectomy. Of course Gala had had to stay home and look after her. It had been really frightening, because she had realised that if anything happened to her Mam she would be completely alone. Nervously she'd put off her plans to go to London and instead when her mother recovered, she'd gotten herself a job as a receptionist at 'Figure It Out', the new 'fitness studio' in Leeds. Using her new, more refined accent she answered the telephone and made appointments for large urban ladies wishing to reduce their bulk and tone their muscles. After work she was allowed to join in the evening classes held specially for the working girls unable to make it during the day. She'd pranced her way through the aerobics and tackled the weights and exercise equipment enthusiastically. Those exercise classes tightened her already slender body until it felt as supple and elastic as a kitten's and a new glow of health and satisfaction had coloured her cheeks. Her only disappointment came when the lights were finally turned out in the studio at ten o'clock, and she had to catch her last bus back to Garthwaite.

She'd almost forgotten about London and her ambitions in the excitement of being 'Gala', the receptionist at 'Figure It Out'. Her hair was highlighted in Sassoon's Leeds salon, and trimmed into a long tousled mop that she stiffened with gel so that it looked a bit like an angel's halo although she hoped it looked daring and sexy. But the boys didn't seem to find her attractive, they went for the big, firm-fleshed Yorkshire girls with temptingly obvious bosoms under fluffy sweaters. Gala told herself she didn't care, but still it had undermined her always tremulous self-confidence and she'd stopped going to the disco.

Her mother had surprised her last Christmas when she told her that she was getting married again and going to live in Leeds with her new husband, and that there would be no room for Gala in his one-bedroomed council flat. 'You'll have to get a room of your own,' she'd said unfeelingly, 'or share with some other girls. You're sixteen now and grown-up.'

Gala had spent a long lonely night, hunched in the old rocker, gazing into the dying embers of the coal fire and trying to sort out her life. She loved her job and enjoyed the companionship she found at the studio – it was the first place in her life where she felt she was 'someone', where people called on the phone and said, 'Hi Gala' – where they smiled and waved as they hurried in and out. It was a place where, for once, she didn't feel invisible. Torn between the security of the world she knew and the question of the future, Gala had taken a long look at herself in the mirror seeing her new slender, blonde image. She'd thought of Jessie-Ann Parker and of her old dreams. She knew it was now or never!

In the end she told Debbie Blacker, who owned and ran the studio, of her dilemma. Debbie was thirty-nine, thin and flashy, with a native Yorkshire shrewdness. She liked Gala, finding her reticence and shyness a change from all the pushy, demanding clients – besides the girl was a willing worker, and she was attractive, polite and pleasant.

'I've only been to London once in my life,' confessed Gala, 'I went on a Miners' Outing with my Dad when I was just six – all I remember about it was the bus.'

'But what would you *do* in London?' Debbie had asked, straightening the line of exercise mats.

Gala had taken a deep breath, she'd never admitted this to anyone in her whole life . . . 'I'd like to be a model,' she'd blurted. Trying to ignore Debbie's look of surprise, she'd added hurriedly, 'I've watched those girls in Schofield's department store at lunchtime – you know the ones I mean, they stroll around the restaurant showing you the price tag on their frock as you drink your coffee. I expect you think I'm daft,' she added, twisting her hands together nervously, and watching Debbie for a reaction.

Debbie had given her a long assessing look. 'I don't see why you shouldn't be a model Gala,' she'd replied at last, 'but why go to London? You'll have to take a modelling course and Leeds will be a lot cheaper – and they'll do just as good a job of training you. That way you can stay home and save money too.' Remembering Gala's mother's marriage and the new too-small council flat with no room for an unwanted daughter, she'd added comfortingly, 'Don't worry, I'm sure we can find a nice room for you somewhere near here.'

'Then you think I could do it? I could really be a model?' Gala had demanded, excitedly.

Debbie certainly didn't want to encourage the girl to run off to London and the 'big time'. Gala was too naïve and innocent to be alone in the big city, and anyway she wasn't sure she could be a really good model. 'I wouldn't say you're the ideal model-type Gala,' she'd admitted, 'but you are *different*. I don't see any reason why you can't be as good as any of those models you've seen in Schofield's.'

Images of her new self parading down catwalks at fashion shows and posing for fashion shots beside fountains in Paris had flickered through Gala's mind. 'I'll go this very afternoon and enroll at the Model School in Harrogate,' she'd decided happily.

It was harder work than she had imagined learning to walk properly with the required model slouch, shoulders swinging, long legs striding as far as they could. Gala twirled and spun, she sat and unsat gracefully, she spent rapturous hours creating a new face on her own, learning how to shade those too-round cheeks, how to emphasise her soft, pouting mouth, and how to make those wide-spaced grey eyes look wider, deeper – and more mysterious. She learned about accessories and how to smile from beneath a wide hat brim, how to unfurl a glove casually and to toss a scarf along with a glance. And when she had finally completed the course, Gala had felt she was ready for London, at last.

Her Mam had folded a twenty-pound note into her hand as she kissed her goodbye, but her new husband kept in the background, saying nothing. As the door closed Gala almost felt their sigh of relief. They were rid of her at last.

Her Mam hadn't come to the station to see her off, though Debbie Blacker had.

'Here Gala,' she'd said, thrusting a little white pot of flowering African violets at her, along with a mysterious, gaily wrapped parcel. 'The flowers are for your room,' she'd said, 'to make it feel more like home. And you can open the present later . . . when you arrive.' She'd handed Gala a list of names and addresses. 'I asked around some people in the fashion trade,' she said, 'and these are the names of some wholesale houses who might need house-models – after all you can't expect to start at the top, can you?'

As the train began to slow down, wending its way through London's grimy outskirts, Gala's heart pounded with a mixture of fear and excitement. Clutching her little pot of violets in one hand and her suitcase firmly in the other she stepped from the train with Debbie's words still ringing in her head. She stopped for a moment to take in the scene – the hordes of hurrying people, the noise of the trains and the smell of diesel oil and exhaust fumes and hamburgers and chips, the sunlight filtering through the grimy steel and glass station roof. *This* was London, the city where anything was possible and dreams came true. And despite what Debbie Blacker had said she just knew she was destined to start right at the top – the way Jessie-Ann had.

A week later Gala sat in the chrome and glass thirties-style reception of the Kline Model Agency on Old Brompton Road, resisting the impulse to get up from her deep chair and run. Instead she pulled herself more erect, straightening her spine and holding her head high. She had been there for forty-five minutes, she'd given the receptionist her name and been told to 'wait', she'd check if Barry would see her. Barry Kline *was* Kline Models – party-goer, bon vivant, and driver of a black Lamborghini.

And Kline Models was the best agency in London with branches in Paris and New York and the very names of those far-off cities conjured exciting visions in Gala's mind of French couturiers in elegant dove-grey salons on the Right Bank, and of Manhattan skyscrapers pointing ever-upwards to success.

It had taken her a week to summon up enough courage to come here, and each day she had found yet another reason to delay – a rare pimple on her smooth cheek; a cold that gave her a headache and red-rimmed eyes; the loss of one of the large pearl earrings that were the only ones she thought right to wear with her new suit. And now that she was here, she was invisible again.

Sitting anxiously upright in the slouchy black leather chair Gala watched models dashing in and out, tote bags clutched in their hands, calling 'hi' to the busy receptionists as they barged their way through to the inner sanctum where Gala knew Barry was. Occasionally, as the door swung open or shut, she heard his voice talking on the telephone or his laugh when one of the cute young models greeted him. Gala bit her lips nervously, feeling out of place, almost wishing she hadn't come. But how else was she to get started? She checked her watch again. An hour and fifteen minutes had gone by. Taking a deep breath she pulled herself from the chair and walked over to the desk.

'Excuse me?' she asked. 'But is Mr Kline free yet?'

The chic black receptionist – who looked good enough to be modelling for Saint-Laurent – glanced up at her in surprise. 'Oh, are you still here? Sorry I forgot. Mr Kline says he's too busy to see anyone today. Can you leave your pictures for him to see?'

'Pictures?'

'You know – your portfolio, or your model card . . . have you done anything before?'

'Oh no. I'm new. I'm just down from Yorkshire . . .'

'Aren't they all!' sighed the girl. 'Well, listen, you're not going to get anywhere without pictures . . . you'll have to get some taken.' She looked at Gala curiously, 'Let me give you a word of advice though – don't wear that suit.'

Gala glanced down at her new outfit, bought after much heart-searching and at great expense from a smart up-tight little shop in Leeds, wondering where she'd gone wrong. It had looked so chic in the shop and with the high-heeled pumps and the shiny wide-brimmed straw hat and matching gloves, she'd felt very elegant.

'Ask around the other models where to get your photos taken,' advised the beautiful receptionist, turning back to the busy switchboard, 'they know where to go.'

The trouble was Gala didn't know any other models. Her bed-sitter with its blank walls and her small pot of violets, and the pink satin cushion appliqué'd with her name, 'Gala-Rose', in lilac lace, Debbie's present to her, became both her refuge and her prison. In the next few weeks she sat alone at night in its strange solitude, with the whole of London bustling outside, worrying about her clothes and her hair and her photographs, and how to summon up enough courage to tackle the next day's agency – for one a day was her limit. But she made her rounds and scoured the ads in newspapers as well as in *Time Out* and *What's On in London*. She wandered lonely, through the streets, anonymous in her grey skirt and sweater, occasionally stopping off for a hamburger in McDonald's as a treat but mostly she was trying to save money and ate small salads of lettuce and tomato and tuna, or just beans on toast.

She sat in the waiting rooms of 'in' agencies, shrivelling beneath the dismissive gaze of strange-looking young models, un-made-up and spike-haired, long-limbed in loose pants, brogues and baggy sweaters. They seemed to know everyone by their first names and hung over the reception desks to make quick personal phone calls, pushing buttons with authority, giggling intimately with each other. In her smart suit with its carefully toning silk blouse and her neat, small-heeled pumps appropriate for a provincial department-store fashion show, Gala felt she might as well live on another planet. Garthwaite was further away than she had thought.

After a month and more than a dozen agencies, Gala abandoned her beautiful expensive suit, took off the make-up and bought herself a baggy sweater and pleated pants from a shop on the King's Road. She found a pair of black lace-up brogues that were a cheap copy of those she'd seen in Rossetti on her daily prowl of the smart shop windows of Bond Street. She examined again the advertising leaflet for a hairdresser thrust into her hand by a girl on the Earl's Court Road as she was shopping and noted that the hairstyles shown were very much like those she had seen on the young models at the agencies.

Taking her courage and her money in both hands, Gala ventured into the jazzy salon and in a whirl of loud music and fast chat her hair was cropped short as a boy's.

'There you are, love,' said Nico, the young stylist, whisking off the towel from around her neck, and holding a mirror so she could inspect the back of her head. 'Looks terrific, don't you think?'

Gala stared at the new her in dismay. Shorn of her long hair, her jaw looked wide, her eyes bigger, and her neat ears that lay flat against her skull seemed suddenly prominent. She looked a lean, young and boyish Gala – someone she didn't recognise.

Nico stared at her in concern, 'It's a bit late now love, to decide you don't like it. You did ask for it you know. Besides, it's the latest look . . . it just takes time to get used to it, especially when you've had long hair like yours.' He stood back to get a different perspective. 'Tell you what I think love, you could be a model with that hair-cut – it changes your whole personality.'

Gala's face lit up as her eyes met his in the mirror. 'But I am a model, or at least I trained as one – I've not actually had any work yet.'

'Trained?' Nico threw back his head and laughed. 'None of the models I know have trained – they just got asked to do it – picked up waiting at a bus stop on the King's Road, or shopping in Hyper-Hyper. Seriously though love – you are different-looking, but it's that kind of difference that could really make it.' Helping her to her feet he took her to stand in front of the long mirror. 'You've got that great boyish look. They should love you – if you photograph well that is. You should get some new photos done – take 'em round the agencies – I'll bet you'll be taken on right away.'

Gala sighed, they were back to the photos again.

Thrusting her fears and shyness into the background, she haunted the agencies, discovering that the models she'd thought so intimidating weren't really – they were just too involved in their own ultra-busy lives even to notice her; yet one of them took the time to give her a bit of advice.

'Of course you'll need photos if you're going to get through the doors,' she said, 'but be careful. Don't go to those places that advertise – they'll rip you off and take your money and you'll never see that *or* a photograph – again.' She told Gala that occasionally photographers let their assistants practise after hours. The trick was to find a young guy who had the use of the studio for an hour or so at night. Gala could model for him free, and he'd give her some of the prints. 'You might have to pay for the film and processing but,' she winked at Gala, 'there are ways around that too – if necessary.'

Gala stared at her wide-eyed – she'd thought that kind of thing went out with Hollywood starlets! Nevertheless, back in the pleated pants and baggy sweater, unmade-up and thinner, she went the rounds of photographers' studios. Finally at Marley's, she met Cam.

Cameron Mace had been working as an assistant to Dino Marley for a year and was learning fast. He was twenty-two, had a quick mind, a good eye and was a fast talker. Cam anticipated Dino's wants before he knew them himself, he now shot all Dino's preliminary polaroids to check the lighting and the angles, and Dino let him practise at night when their studio wasn't in use. When this odd-looking girl showed up, the timing was just right.

Cam's girlfriend, a make-up artist who also acted as his model, had phoned that afternoon to say she'd be working late on a session, and he was pissed off because he'd got the studio for the night. He'd thought they'd do the photographs first and then have a little privacy with a bottle of Dino's wine to keep things moving.

Cam walked around her silently as Gala waited, her list of photographers still clutched in her hand. Marley's had been the fifth on that list she tried today and her eyes followed Cam anxiously. He was quite good-looking, in a rugged out-doorsy sort of way – dark and strong with muscular arms – not at all what she'd expected from a photographer. He was young though and that made it easier, but still, having a man look at her that way made her feel uncomfortable.

'What's your name again?' asked Cam, lighting a cigarette and studying her through narrowed eyes. She was surely a challenge, with that wide-boned face and the scrubby haircut . . . fantastic eyes though and a long, long neck . . . well, at least the evening wouldn't be a total loss. 'Gala-Rose, huh? Unusual – but then, so are you. OK, let's get started Gala.'

'You mean right now?' She stared at him, astonished.

'Sure now. When else?' With the cigarette dangling from the corner of his mouth he began moving strobes into place.

'But what about my make-up . . . and I didn't bring my things, the right clothes . . .'

'Forget it Gala-Rose – you'll do fine just as you are. Go and sit over there, behind the frame and just relax while I set up.'

Seated behind a white styrofoam cut-out that framed her head and shoulders, Gala blinked into the strong lights, feeling more like a patient on an operating table than a potential number-one fashion model. Frowning through the glare she watched Cam, who was still busy re-arranging lights, wishing she had thought to bring some make-up along. Here she was about to get her precious photos at last and all that she had learned at model school was going to waste. Rummaging through her bag she came up with a black mascara and a pink lipgloss. She smoothed the gloss over her eyelids then across the tip of her cheekbones, where the light would hit, and added a touch of mascara.

'OK, Gala-Rose, into the camera please.' Gala stared at him seriously as he took his shot. Flapping the polaroid print to dry it Cam inspected it critically. The girl looked just like a startled rabbit, all pink eyes and pale ears . . . 'Jesus! Tell you what Gala-Rose,' he said with a smile, trying to put her at her ease – 'let's try again, and this time try to relax your mouth. Think of something that makes you happy . . . a puppy, a new boyfriend, a dish of cold chocolate ice cream . . .'

Gala laughed, thinking of the ice cream and Cam snatched his shot quickly. This time the print was better, at least her face was animated instead of a paralysed blob. 'Here we go again,' he said, 'just remember that ice cream, how cold it felt in your mouth.' Adjusting the light to throw more shadows on her face, he picked up the Rollei and began shooting.

Shoulders down, head erect, Gala stared anxiously into his

lens, trying hard to think of ice cream and puppies, but the rapid clicking of the camera only made her worry more about the way she looked and a slight frown split her brows.

Ten minutes and two rolls of black and white film later Cam knew it was no good. The girl was as tense as a coiled spring – but damn it, he couldn't just waste the night and the studio. Gala-Rose was the biggest challenge he'd had yet and she had a definite quality, if only he could get her to relax. 'Great, Gala,' he called beaming at her, 'just great. You're a natural for the camera. Come on down a minute and have a rest while I think of what we'll do next.'

Pink with pleasure at his compliment, she emerged from behind the frame, sinking into the sofa as Cam pulled the cork from a bottle of white wine and filled two glasses. 'Here sweetheart,' he said gently, 'you've earned a drink. Nothing's ever easy the first time, is it?'

Gala accepted the glass cautiously. She had never drunk wine or spirits, but the pale-coloured liquid looked cool and innocuous as lemonade and besides, she didn't want to seem inexperienced.

'What's your story Gala?' asked Cam, perching on a stool in front of her, sipping his wine and thinking what an odd little thing she was. But yet when she turned her head like that, her neck was full of grace and the curve of her cheek was quite beautiful . . .

'I'm from Garthwaite – a mining town near Leeds. I worked at an exercise studio there.'

'That's what gave you such a good figure I suppose,' he commented encouragingly.

Gala smiled at him as she took a sip of her wine. In no time she was telling him about her Mam and the new husband, about her childhood dreams of Jessie-Ann Parker and how they had fired her ambition to be a model.

'If you do half as well as Jessie-Ann, you'll be OK,' commented Cam, picking up his camera and focusing on her eyes . . . they were the clearest grey and so large they dominated her face throwing it off balance, 'especially now she's married to one of America's richest men.'

An image of beautiful Jessie-Ann wrapped in sables and dripping with diamonds, all heads turning in her direction as she swept into some grand restaurant on the arm of her handsome new husband flashed through Gala's head as Cam clicked busily on his camera. Lucky, lucky Jessie-Ann. Lucky never to have felt shy or nervous, lucky to be bursting with beauty and self-confidence, lucky to be such a success – and now luckier than ever to have found love with a rich handsome husband – for Gala had no doubt that Jessie-Ann's husband would be *very* handsome. She took another gulp of her wine, still thinking about Jessie-Ann.

Putting down his camera Cam topped up their glasses and lit a cigarette. She was a mystery, this little Yorkshire lass, one moment he thought she was beautiful and the next she looked like an overgrown, underweight child. If only he could capture those elusive moments when she wasn't thinking about herself, when her guard and her inhibitions were down – *then* he'd have something.

'What do you do with yourself in London Gala?' he asked, taking a seat next to her on the sofa and sliding his arm comfortably across her shoulders. 'Do you have friends?'

'Not yet,' she admitted, 'but once I begin working I suppose I'll meet lots of people.'

Her loneliness showed in her eyes as she glanced at him over the top of her glass, and Cam squeezed her shoulder encouragingly. 'A beautiful girl like you is soon gonna make friends, I mean look – you're here aren't you, and we're friends already.'

Was it true, she wondered, was he her friend? He must be. Just look how he was helping her, taking her pictures, telling her she was beautiful . . . no one had ever told her that before. Could Cam, with his artist's eye and his camera see more in her face than she saw herself in the mirror . . . ?

'Look Gala, I know lots of people, there are parties all the time, I'll give you a buzz next time I'm throwing a little soirée for a few friends. You'll enjoy it, a little wine, some food, good music, dancing . . . I'll bet you're a great dancer, you're built like one.'

She smiled at Cam again, pleased. He really was attractive in a hard, masculine sort of way . . . 'Macho' she supposed the word was. He had thick dark brows and brown eyes and there was a faint dark stubble on his cheek where he needed to shave . . .

Cam leaned forward and kissed her lightly on the cheek, 'Well what d'ya say? Shall we try again?'

This time it felt easier and she gazed into the camera, in between little sips of wine, shifting her pose as he directed, and smiling at him. She remembered to hold her chin up though and keep her spine straight and glance over her shoulder the way they'd taught her at model school . . .

Jesus, it was no good, thought Cam, he still wasn't getting it. But he *knew* she had it, he just knew. If only she weren't so stiff, so *posed*; if only she'd drop that phoney smile . . . What he wanted from Gala-Rose was the essence of her innocence expressed in her wide clear eyes . . .

'Come on down, Gala,' he called, 'let's have another break and then we'll do some more.'

Gala clambered down from her high stool, blinking her eyes to clear them of the glare and stretching stiffly. Her back ached from sitting upright for so long, and her knees were a bit wobbly. Her head was beginning to swim too, and she felt quite dizzy.

Cam turned off the big strobes, leaving just the lamp over the table. Pouring some wine he carried the glass across to her and settled beside her on the velvet sofa. 'Here, sweetheart,' he handed her the glass. 'How did it feel this time?'

'Oh much better, much, *much* better thank you. Was I all right?'

'Terrific.' His arm rested nonchalantly along her shoulders and Gala relaxed against him, sighing with relief. She suddenly felt a thousand per cent better, relaxed, confident. Cam must be some kind of genius . . . She glanced up at him in surprise as he removed the wineglass gently from her hand and set it down on the table in front of them. And then his mouth was on hers, and he was kissing her and it felt wonderful, just marvellous, so warm and friendly as though it were the most natural thing in the world.

Her mouth opened under his and she tasted his winey kisses as his hand caressed the shorn nape of her neck. And then his lips travelled from her mouth and down her throat and Gala gasped with shock as his kisses drifted lazily across her nipples, projecting her into a whole new set of emotions. She waited, trembling for what he would do next, longing for him to touch her yet afraid he might . . . her body craved the strong male touch of his hand under her shirt, the silken flicker of his tongue on hers. Her head whirled with wine and erotic emotions as Cam drew away from her. Running a finger along her trembling lips he whispered, 'All right Gala, let's take those pictures of my beautiful girl, lovely, lovely Gala-Rose.'

Pictures? She'd forgotten all about them, lost in her dreamy pleasure . . .

Gala watched numbly as Cam slowly unbuttoned her blue cotton shirt. Her limbs felt heavy and languorous, as though she were under water, there was no way she could have stopped him, even if she wanted to . . . 'Here,' he whispered, sliding the shirt from her shoulders, 'this is what we need from you Gala – this is the true you. And you are very, very beautiful.'

Cam gazed at her naked breasts admiringly and, as if watching a scene played in slow motion, Gala saw his head bend towards her and then felt a jolt of exquisite pleasure as his lips closed on her small pink nipples and his large firm hands caressed her . . . Regretfully, Cam lifted his head. 'Beautiful Gala, you're so lovely. Now – let's get to work!'

Putting his arm around her he helped her back to her stool facing the camera.

'Here, wrap your shirt around you,' he said, tucking it across her breasts and under her arms . . . 'I want your shoulders and neck to be free. That's it Gala, great.'

Gala sat watching him quietly, her long neck drooping, her mouth slightly open, her eyes lazy with longing. *That* was the expression he wanted. That – and the fragile-boned slender shoulders, the shorn head and the long vulnerable neck . . . Gala looked like a child-bride eager for knowledge . . . Eve before the first bite of the apple . . .

The shrill of the telephone shattered the link between her eyes and his camera and cursing, Cam strode across the studio to answer it. 'Hi Cam? It's me, Lindy. I'm free sooner than I thought. I'll grab a cab and be over in fifteen minutes.'

Regretfully Cam replaced the receiver. Still, he supposed he had enough. But he'd better get the girl home before Lindy arrived . . . it wouldn't take Lindy more than a second to realise what he'd been up to. 'Sorry Gala,' he called, hurrying across the studio towards her, 'I've got to go . . . an urgent call from . . . from my Mum. I'm . . . er I'm needed at home.'

Avoiding her startled gaze, he whisked the blue shirt around her shoulders, pushing her thin arms into the sleeves as though he were dressing a child. 'Great sweetheart,' he said, 'you were fantastic.' Thrusting her coat at her, he hurried her towards the door. 'I'll get you a taxi,' he called, rushing ahead of her, down the alley towards the busy street.

'A taxi . . . but what about . . . I mean . . . when shall I see you again?' asked Gala following him, clutching her coat across her suddenly chilly breasts.

'Give me a buzz sweetheart, and we'll see what we can do about that party.' A taxi hailed down by his urgent arm screeched to a halt and opening the door, he thrust her inside.

'But my pictures . . . ?' cried Gala, as he slammed the door, 'what about my pictures . . . ?'

'Call me,' he yelled as the cab pulled away, 'in a day or two . . .'

Gala gazed after him bewildered as he disappeared back down the alley.

'Where to, Miss?' asked the cabdriver.

Where to? Where was she going? She couldn't even think straight . . . her head was swimming from all that wine and she was trembling with emotion and shock . . . She was going home, she supposed . . . but home was only the single room in Earl's Court. A lonely, lonely room. Sadly, she gave the driver her address, retreating into her thoughts, remembering Cam's kisses, the touch of his hands on her breasts, the way she'd felt about him as he took her photograph. Looking into the lens had been like looking into his eyes, intimate and sensual . . . Shivering, she wrapped her coat closer around her, smiling at her new secret. In a few days she would see him again. And, in a few days she would – at last – have her pictures. Feeling already like an experienced model, Gala rested limply against the shabby leather cushions of the black London taxi, heading for home and dreaming of Cam.

*

Dino Marley watched the little scene at his reception desk, as the odd-looking girl in the Sunday-best dress and jacket and the cropped hair spoke with his receptionist. His own model was taking for ever in make-up and he was getting impatient. Dragging nervously on his cigarette, he eavesdropped on their conversation, wondering idly what the girl wanted. There was something familiar about her . . .

'Cam left these for you.' Thalia, the receptionist handed the girl a large brown envelope. 'He said to tell you to leave your number and he'll be in touch.'

Of course, thought Dino, she was Cam's stray – the one who'd blown in off the streets. Cam had shown him the prints and he'd thought that she had fine eyes, and especially in the ones where she'd been looking lazily into the lens, her long slender neck seeming barely strong enough to support her full, childish face. There had been more than a hint of sensuality in the curve of her mouth, an allure in those wide innocent eyes . . . perhaps he should do something about her, try her for that new lingerie catalogue? 'Ready Dino,' called his model.

'Right,' he turned back to the studio. Thalia was taking the girl's number. He'd get in touch with her later.

The receptionist wrote down Gala's telephone number carefully. 'Right then Miss Rose, I've got it. I'll tell Cam you called in. He'll be real sorry to have missed you, but he's really busy all this week.'

'It's not "Miss" Rose,' explained Gala automatically, 'it's just Gala-Rose . . . like Jessie-Ann.'

Thalia stared at her, hiding a smile. Cam had surely got himself a weird one here, no wonder he wanted to avoid her.

Picking up the brown envelope, Gala walked to the door, her shoulders drooping. She had tried telephoning Cam for a week now, and each time he was busy on a shoot or he was out . . . she might almost have thought he were avoiding her, but then she remembered the warm intimacy of those hours together, how he'd told her she was beautiful, the feel of his kisses and the touch of his hands and she felt certain then that he wasn't. She had called him again first thing this morning and the receptionist had told her again that Cam was busy all day but if she wanted to come by, her pictures were ready. Gala had hoped she might see Cam there, she'd hoped he would kiss her, she'd hoped he'd invite her to one of those fun parties he'd mentioned. It would feel so different going to a party on Cam Mace's arm, as Cam Mace's girl . . .

Smiling wryly at her naïveté as she watched her leave, Thalia crumpled the piece of paper with Gala's number into a little ball and tossed it into the basket – along with the rest of the day's rubbish.

Back in the privacy of her room, Gala inspected the photographs carefully, gazing for a long time at each one before placing it face down on top of the others in a neat pile. When she had finished, she got up and stared at herself in the mirror. *This* was who she was, wasn't it? *This* was the Gala she'd seen reflected back at her every day of her life. The face in the photographs wasn't the cool, elegant model-face she'd expected to see, it wasn't the fantasy Gala-Rose. *That* girl, with her heavy-lidded eyes and drooping neck, her moist mouth and breathless gaze was an unnerving stranger. She was different, provocative, *alien*.

These weren't model pictures! There was no way she could show them to an agent. They were shameful, blatant . . . *That* girl looked as though she wanted to be kissed – to be made love to . . . It was worse than if she'd shown herself naked. Those pictures revealed her loss of innocence as surely as if she'd committed the final act.

Blushing with shame, Gala picked up the prints and tore them across deliberately, and then again, ripping them into tiny shreds so that no trace of that Gala-Rose would ever be seen again.

Fox and Martin's 'Bouncy Leisurewear' showroom occupied the ground floor and basement of a dilapidated Victorian building on Ganton Street, whose peeling paintwork and dusty, weather-stained windows only confirmed the shoddiness of the new season's hot pink and lime green polyester jumpsuits on display. Mr Martin and Mr Fox had been left behind after Carnaby Street's tide of success in the sixties had ebbed, and with it any glow of creativity. Their product now was the cheapest and the brashiest, aimed at the young market wanting a brief fling with glamour for very little money. Lurex and glitter had featured strongly in their less-than-successful winter season, and now, with spring already well-advanced, the new 'holiday' line was giving them trouble.

Wearing a green halter top and brief pink shorts Gala paraded for the three men sitting on cracked plastic chairs at the end of the room. All had kept on their overcoats and hats in the near-freezing temperature of the damp basement showroom and as she spun around showing them her back, Gala wondered if they could count the goosebumps on her pale, chilled legs. Like a Christmas turkey, she thought bitterly, only not nearly as plump and appetising.

'Hold it Gala,' called Mr Martin, 'Mr Fineberg wants to take a closer look at the material.'

Staring into the space above their heads, Gala waited while Mr Martin and the buyers inspected her bra and shorts and Mr Martin explained that the fabric was 70% nylon and 30% polyamide. Grabbing a fold of her shorts intimately between his finger and thumb Mr Martin shifted his fat cigar from one side of his mouth to the other, grinning at his customers. 'Nice bit of stuff, eh?' he winked, 'soft and springy, no wrinkles on this model!'

Amid hearty laughter the three men sat back in their chairs and Gala walked indifferently back to her changing room. Pulling across the dusty curtain she unhooked the little halter top and removed her shorts, reaching for the next garment – a yellow, full-skirted sundress and the only thing out of Fox and Martin's entire line in which she felt she looked half-way decent.

'Gala!' The curtain was yanked back and Mr Martin's pale eyes absorbed her greedily as she grabbed the dress and held it in front of her naked breasts. Blushing angrily, Gala glared at him. 'I've told you before Mr Martin, knock if you want me,' she said through gritted teeth.

'Yes, well, you're a model love and I've seen it all before,' he replied, still staring. 'And let *me* give you a little bit of advice Gala – don't *tell* me anything! Got that? And another thing – try to smile every now and again will ya – the buyers would appreciate it.'

'There's nothing to smile about,' retorted Gala, turning her back on him and climbing into the dress.

'Yeah? Try laughing at my jokes love – you never know where a little laugh might get you.'

Gala dreaded to think. Instead she zipped up the dress and silently re-applied a tangerine lipstick that didn't suit her but was the only one not killed by the clamouring colours of the clothes she had to wear. She'd had this job for five months now and each week that went by, she asked herself how much longer she could stand it. How much longer could she bear the squalid surroundings; the peeling walls with their rusty overlay of a half a century of nicotine, the grimy little washroom with the cracked, stained toilet and the broken wash basin where she was supposed to rinse their coffee mugs (all part of the job, Mr Fox had told her when she'd applied for the position of 'showroom model'). Brushing back the blonde hair that was a shade too yellow because she could no longer afford to patronise a good salon and had to make do with a cheap and cheerful place in Soho, Gala breathed a sigh of relief that at last her hair seemed to be growing. For months it had seemed to be in a state of suspended animation, stunned like she was, by its sudden cropping. Besides, it had been a bitterly cold winter and without a mantle of hair to mask her chilled ears she had felt like a shorn lamb. A woollen cap had been her only answer, making her look like a skier in search of a far-off slope or a refugee from an Iron Curtain country. Somehow it hadn't mattered, just getting through this winter had been all she'd cared about.

Waking each morning to the four walls of her bare one room flat, Gala's first thought was of her rapidly dwindling bank account. She had tried every way she could to economise, walking everywhere instead of taking the tube or a bus but then her shoes – the cheap copies of the beautiful Rossetti brogues she'd coveted in their Bond Street window – had worn thin and the repair man said they were plastic and unrepairable. So her economy had cost her another pair of shoes and after that she started taking the bus again. But there were no more McDonald's burgers, no cups of coffee in a cheap café to while away an empty hour, no movies and, worst of all, no television. Even her treasured magazines had to be passed up, and her reading was now limited to the *Evening Standard* because of its job listings.

She had made no friends in London. There were people she passed in the hallway or coming out of the shared bathroom, to whom she said good morning or good evening, but somehow they never met her eager eyes and shy smile, but hurried off, busy with their own affairs. Debbie Blacker had written once or twice, asking a trifle anxiously how she was faring, and Gala had written back – quick, excited little notes that sounded as though her life were too busy and full to sit down and write a really long letter.

When she'd finally landed the job at Fox and Martin's her first feeling had been one of relief – not so much at the prospect of a salary cheque every week, but at finally being able to call herself a model. And it was surely better than handing out leaflets in the Earl's Court Road for the same hairdresser who'd shorn her head, or waitressing in the dingy café for little pay and fivepenny tips.

Mr Fox, who had interviewed her, was a sweet little man whose large family was his entire life. He was sixty-three years old and for him Fox and Martin's ups and downs in the world of cheap fashion had long since lost their priority. Mr Martin, the younger partner, had been a problem from the beginning. He was forty-seven, short, stocky and balding with a sweaty skin and pale watery eyes. Whenever she turned her back on him Gala could feel his eyes on her, watching her as though he had her naked. But when she would spin round and confront him, he would just stand there, a cigar permanently locked into the corner of his mouth, ash drifting across his polyester shirt front, leering at her.

In Gala's opinion Mr Martin was just as cheap as the clothes he manufactured and she pitied Mrs Martin, who she had never met but knew existed from his frequent apologetic telephone calls to his home in the suburbs explaining that he'd been held up in town on business. Gala knew better. She'd seen Mr Martin emerging from one of Soho's sex-palaces on Rupert Street, a pink-painted 'theatre' where tired-looking 'models' writhed naked on sleazy nylon-sheeted beds, displaying 'all they'd got' for a couple of pounds, before flinging on a coat and trudging round to the next 'sex-theatre' to repeat their performance, and so on through Soho's endless neon night.

It would have been all right if Mr Martin had restricted his watery-eyed, itchy-handed favours to the sex shops, but right from the start his hands had been all over her. Pulling a sleeve into place he would manage to slide his hand down the side of her breast; feeling the material he would flip her skirt high; examining the fit of her shorts he would run his moist hands across her buttocks. And he never knocked when she was in the changing room, waiting until he knew she would have had time to take off her clothes to catch her in her bra and pants.

Her cheeks scarlet with anger at his latest affront, Gala marched down the showroom in the yellow dress, twirled swiftly in front of them and then headed back for the changing room.

'Hey! Wait a minute Gala!' Mr Martin's nasal East-end accent made her sinuses ache just thinking about it, and her stride unbroken, she continued on towards the changing room.

'Gala. I said wait! Come back here. Mr Fineberg and Mr James haven't had a chance to see the skirt properly.'

Gala hesitated a moment and then turned reluctantly back again. In the white high-heeled shoes Mr Martin favoured for his model ('makes the legs look longer love – your crotch'll be under your armpits wearing these') she waited, one foot neatly placed in front of the other, toe pointing out model-school style.

'Mmmmn,' commented Mr Fineberg, 'nice, very nice . . .'

'Turn round Gala, show the man the back detail,' commanded Mr Martin.

Gala spun obediently.

'Feel the fabric Morrie,' Mr Martin said, 'forty-five per cent cotton this one. This is class – a rip-off of a dress on sale in Harrods right now for ninety-five quid.' Grabbing a fold of her skirt he flipped it up quickly, holding it aloft so that her pants showed, laughing as Gala struggled to pull herself away. 'How d'ya like that detail Morrie, eh? Pretty good, isn't it? I'll bet it could be yours too, for a few quid!'

Mr Fineberg looked away uncomfortably as Gala finally ripped her skirt from Mr Martin's clutch. Hands on her hips she loomed over him as a tirade of rage spilled from out of her. Losing all Miss Forster's elegant vowels and reverting to her native York-shire dialect, Gala finally let him have it. Her insulted body trembled with rage and her cool grey eyes were narrow and dark as she spat her opinion of Mr Martin to his face. 'You disgusting little creep,' she yelled, 'you're paying me to model – not to run your slimy hands all over me, or grab free peeks when I'm changing. Go home and lift Mrs Martin's skirt – it'll make a change from those painted doxies in Sexarama . . . oh yes, I've seen you coming out of there . . . . it's easier for you there isn't it, they're not wearing skirts or knickers and you can look all you like for your money, you dirty little man!'

Mr Fineberg and Mr James edged towards the door as Gala grabbed Mr Martin by his necktie and pulled him from his seat. 'You know what you are? You're a pervert,' she screamed, 'only you try to hide it under a jolly old slap and tickle routine. Well not with me *Mr* Martin – oh no. You've got the wrong girl here . . . you've gone too far this time *Mr Martin*.' She let go of his necktie and he dropped back into his chair, stunned into silence by her outburst.

As she stalked back to the changing room and flung on her clothes, gathering her possessions into a bag and buttoning her coat with a strange calm, Gala thought she heard him shout that she was fired, but she preferred to think she'd simply walked out.

The only trouble was there were no more jobs. Youth had flooded the market and even work as a waitress was hard to come by.

After a couple of months of no work and no income and increasing bad dreams, she left her familiar Earl's Court digs and took a tiny room in a back street near Paddington Station, and from there her life seemed to go steadily downhill. She tried all the employment agencies and showrooms. She re-visited the Model Agencies but no one wanted her, not with her brassy hair with its roots showing darker and her unstylish look. Even to herself Gala had to admit that she had lost the fresh, youthful innocence that had at least been hers a year ago when she had left Yorkshire. Now she looked tired and thin with a permanent frown of worry between her brows and the taint of failure about her.

And each morning as she awoke the pictures of Jessie-Ann adorning her damp-stained wall, mocked her with their clean, successful All-American blonde image. Jessie-Ann had never been reduced to this. Jessie-Ann had always been a star.

Gala had considered her family in Garthwaite to be really poor – but now she knew better. She'd never heard from her mother and, after the first few months, she'd given up writing, ashamed of her failure and too hurt by the fact that her mother had finally abandoned her in favour of her new husband and new life. As far as her mother was concerned, Gala was no longer her responsibility. The twenty pounds pressed into her hand as she was leaving had said it all! Looking around at the shabby, worn room, scene of a hundred different temporary lives, Gala knew that this was the bottom line. It was serious. And all her fantasies couldn't help. She was Hilda Mirfield and she was lonely and afraid. And desperate.

She saw the ad in the *Evening Standard* a few nights later. With a mug of coffee clutched in her cold, mittened hand, she ran her eye down the list of job vacancies. And there it was. 'Wanted, young, attractive girl, fit, athletic and in good shape, to work as a receptionist/hostess at La Reserve.' Gala knew La Reserve was Covent Garden's latest and most luxurious Health and Beauty club. Sipping her coffee thoughtfully, she remembered how happy she'd been at the 'Figure It Out' salon in Leeds, and how good Debbie had said she was with the clients. This job could be the answer to her prayers – but of course, she would need to look good – better than the clients so they could see what the club could do for *them*.

Carrying her little mirror to the window she examined her face, fluffing up her limp yellowing hair despairingly. Maybe one of those do-it-yourself highlight rinses would help, and she still had her leotards from her 'Figure It Out' days. Her jeans were decent and she would press her yellow sweater and polish her shoes . . . she might be a failure as a model, but she *knew* she'd be good at this job. Surely they'd jump at someone with her experience. All she wanted was a chance to prove herself.

It didn't work out quite like that. The manager at La Reserve was haughty and she'd already interviewed at least two dozen other girls for the job by the time Gala got there. 'Sorry,' she said, without even bothering to soften it with a smile, 'but you're the wrong type.'

Glancing down at her too-white, too-slender figure in the shiny

114

blue leotard and then at the curvaceous, rosily-glowing, sun-tanned girls pacing through La Reserve's lushly-carpeted corri-dors, Gala understood only too well what she meant.

Crossing Floral Street, she walked aimlessly through the bust-ling area of Covent Garden Market wondering what to do next. She'd spent almost all her money and she simply had to get a job.

A wave of giddiness swept over her suddenly and she clutched the railings by the stair leading to the lower level of the arcade. She hadn't eaten that morning because she'd been too nervous, and her stomach rumbled angrily. To hell with it, thought Gala wearily, she'd buy herself a cup of coffee and think about every-thing later.

Tears threatened as she sank into a chair and she bit her lip sternly, studying the well-thumbed menu. 'Just a cup of coffee please, and a piece of apple pie,' she told the waitress.

Thalia Weston studied her from across two tables. 'I know that girl,' she said finally to her friend, 'but I just can't place her.'

'Mmm,' said her friend, studying Gala, 'whoever she is, she looks anorexic to me.'

'Got it!' cried Thalia. 'Cam did some pictures of her once. He told me to get rid of her when she came in looking for him. He said she was a bit of a "stray" and he didn't want her chasing after him.' She sighed exaggeratedly. 'A receptionist's life is a tough one y'know. But I'll tell you what, Cam took these really weird pictures and nobody thought anything of them until Dino saw them – said he might be able to use her in a photo-journalism shoot he was doing. Can you beat that? Well, of course I had to tell him I'd thrown away the girl's address and he was really pissed off. Of course that was ages ago and he's forgotten all about her. Still,' she stared at Gala thoughtfully, 'I think I'm gonna get myself that girl's address again – just in case.'

'I shouldn't bother,' commented her friend dismissively, 'the girl's a wimp.'

'There's no accounting for taste,' grinned Thalia, making her way through the tight-packed tables towards Gala.

'Hi,' she greeted her cheerfully, 'remember me?' Gala stared at her puzzled. 'Thalia, the receptionist at Marley's.'

'Oh. Yes, of course.'

'Listen, we seem to have lost your address, but I've still got Cam's pictures of you on file. Dino thought he might use you once, and Cam tried every which way to find you but seems nobody knew where you were.' She laughed, 'Or even *who* you were. I guess Cam got the exclusive eh?' She winked knowingly at Gala, jangling her armful of gilt bracelets as she fished in her purse for pen and paper. 'How about giving me that number and address again, just in case?'

Gala stared at her, dumbstruck . . . Cam had those dreadful photos . . . Dino might have used her . . .

'Well,' said Thalia impatiently, 'I've got to get back to work you know.'

Quickly Gala gave her the address. 'There's no telephone,' she said apologetically.

'That's OK, I'm just taking it on the off-chance. But it's unlikely to happen again. Still, good luck then, Gala-Rose.'

In a whirl of pleats and jangling metal she whisked back to her friend and Gala watched as they climbed the stairs from the café and from her life. Of course Dino Marley would never want her for anything, the whole idea was ludicrous. Why, she couldn't even get a job like the one she'd had in Leeds, with Debbie.

She wandered from Covent Garden to Soho and in one of its maze of seedy back streets she spotted a burgundy-painted store-front with the words, 'Lindy's Wine Bar' painted in already-faded gilt on the windows. And a little sign propped in the corner, 'Bar-Person/Waitress Wanted.' Gala closed her eyes, not wanting to see it. Then she remembered her rent was due again on Friday – and every Friday after that, and she remembered too, the icy-blue eyes and unsmiling face of the rent-collector. And she was hungry. Gritting her teeth, she pushed open the door and went in.

In those first dreary months working at Lindy's Wine Bar, she wept every night when she got home; buckets of tears, releasing the resentment she felt serving in the seedy, strip-lit bar. Lindy's customers consisted of Soho's transient drifters and minor-hoodlums and left-over football-supporters anxious to keep on drinking until they fell on their faces, or started a fight and were thrown out on the street by the bouncer, Jake.

If it weren't for Jake, Gala would have quit after a week, too terrified of the clientele and too contemptuous of the mean-faced proprietor to stay, but with Jake there she felt safe. He was six-three with the burly shoulders of an ex-rugby forward and the biggest hands Gala had ever seen . . . Jake could crunch a man's face with one swift, slicing jab of those hands – Gala knew because she'd seen him do it. And yet he had the kindest eyes . . . sometimes she thought they were like the eyes of an innocent little boy. Jake was the only person Gala knew who was worse off than she was. Not because he *had* less, but because he'd lost more.

Jake's family had a large country house in Wiltshire that had been theirs for generations as well as an expensive flat in Eaton Square, and they also owned a beautiful villa in the hills above Nice in the South of France. He had earned the dubious distinction of being thrown out of one of England's top public schools for running a betting ring – he'd actually done quite well out of it, he told her. Then he'd been expelled from the expensive, tough Scottish school where character was formed by five mile cross-country runs at dawn in all weathers – and the weather could be pretty grim in Scotland in winter. Jake had refused to run; he'd refused to climb icy mountains; he'd refused to set sail on rough seas in a small ketch with the others – telling them that nobody in their right minds would do such a ridiculous thing. If it weren't that he was a star rugger player they would have chucked him out right away. But, for the sake of the school-team and his distracted parents, they kept Jake on – until he was caught drinking in the local pub and accused of fornicating with the local lasses. Then he was out – and the hallowed portals of the best of British education saw him no more.

Jake went on to raise hell and to play rugger for Cardiff and then internationally for Wales, boozing and carousing in between to the delight of the tabloid press and the despair of his coach, until one bright, sunny, crisp day in Paris at the Wales–France International, just as he emerged from a scrum, a veil of darkness misted his eyes. Lurching down the pitch after the others he'd stared for a few minutes at the yelling crowd and then he'd fallen, like a stone, to the ground.

A stroke, they said, at twenty-two! His parents never visited him in hospital; they'd washed their hands of him years before. He'd brought their well-known and reticently-guarded family name into the cheap press, besmirching it in the worst way, and as far as they were concerned, he no longer existed. A small sum from a family trust fund paid monthly into an account at a bank in the Haymarket ensured that he would have a roof over his head and would never starve. But, as far as society was concerned, Jake Maybrook didn't exist.

'I was lucky the stroke only left me with this paralysis on one side of my face, but the rest of me functions "A-number-one",' he told Gala over a cup of coffee in Valerie's Pâtisserie on Old Compton Street, a couple of weeks after she'd started working at Lindy's Bar. 'After that I sort of gravitated to my natural habitat. But what about you Gala? You don't belong at Lindy's, you're too gentle. Lindy's needs girls like Rita (the other waitress) brash and tough, and not averse to a quick one with a customer for a tenner. You're not like that at all.' Smiling his peculiar, lop-sided grin, because only half his facial muscles now functioned, he reached out and ran his hand along the lean slope of her cheek. His giant fingers were as gentle as a kitten's paw with sheathed claws. 'You're just a kid,' he added, 'you should be home with your mother, going to parties and looking for a nice young husband.'

'Never! I'll *never* do that,' Gala retorted fiercely. Biting into her almond croissant, she chewed morosely while Jake watched her, sipping his espresso and smiling. Swallowing the last delicious morsel – it was the best thing she'd tasted in months – she washed it down with scalding hot coffee. Then gazing into Jake's kind brown eyes she confessed her sorry tale – everything, from her childhood fantasies and her mother's shaming saunter through the taverns and the men of Garthwaite, to her foolish ambitions to be a famous fashion model like Jessie-Ann Parker. She even told Jake her real name.

'Mmmmn, Hilda Mirfield,' he said, three cups and four pastries later, 'no, that's definitely not you. And just because it was the name bestowed on you by unimaginative parents is no reason you have to live with it. To me,' he added, in his cultured upper-class accent that was so at odds with his rough appearance, 'to me you are Gala-Rose . . . well maybe you're still a Gala Rose*bud* – but you'll get there one day. Don't give up, Gala.'

'But look at me,' she wailed, oblivious to the interested stares of the odd mixture of actors, media persons and Soho's shopkeepers, dawdling over their coffee at Valerie's formica tables amidst a haze of cigarette smoke, 'I'm too thin, my hair's a mess, I'm scruffy and out of fashion. I'm a *wreck*, Jake, I can't afford to keep up the standards needed to be a model. That's why I'm working at Lindy's, they don't mind the way I look as long as I can serve fast enough and clear off tables and give the right change. And I'm going to save every penny I can so maybe one day – next year perhaps – I'll be able to start again. After all, I'm only just eighteen.'

'Of course you will,' he replied, squeezing her hand encouragingly, 'you just stick with it Gala-Rose. You know,' he added, cocking his head on one side and regarding her critically, 'I'm a bit of a connoisseur about women and you've got what it takes . . . there are good bones under that pale flesh, and long, long legs under those jeans. All you need is a touch of the glossy life . . .'

'All I need is a magic wand!' she replied bitterly. But from then on she considered Jake Maybrook her best friend. Her *only* friend.

She stuck it out at Lindy's through the long winter months, eating the one free meal a day she was allowed from the greasy microwaved offerings on Lindy's menu, until her stomach rebelled and more sensibly, she went back to eating salad sandwiches cut from a wholewheat loaf that lasted her the entire week. Occasionally, when the need became too great, she succumbed to the luxury of a McDonald's burger or to a small portion of chicken from a take-out place. And sometimes she and Jake would sit over coffee in Valerie's, or else after work, when all else seemed closed, Jake would take her to a small café-club he knew, a hazy, smoky, after-hours drinks place where he'd feed her an enormous steak that with her shrunken stomach, she could

119

never finish and she ended up taking home most of it wrapped in napkins and a plastic bag to be eaten as sandwiches the next day.

Except for the times when he lost his car gambling, Jake made a point of driving her home every night in his battered little Metro, squashing his oversized frame behind the wheel until it seemed his knees were under his chin. He crouched like a rear-gunner in the turret of a bomber in a wartime movie as they cruised the quiet night-time Oxford Street en route to her shabby rooming house on a grimy, littered street, behind Paddington Station.

Gala never asked Jake in for a cup of coffee because she was ashamed of the soullessness of her room. There was nothing there that expressed who she was, or what she felt – the colours she liked, the flowers, the scents, the music . . . it was as anonymous as the day she'd moved in. Not a single penny had been spent in futile attempts to make it feel like home, because in her heart she knew that it never could. And if she kept it this way – transient, impersonal – then it kept alive the myth that one day, she'd move on from here into a home of her own; to some small apartment with a bedroom and a sitting room, with her own compact little kitchen and sparkling clean bathroom, and she would fill it with colour and flowers . . .

Then Jake asked Gala to his apartment on her day off. 'One of my many talents is that I'm a great cook,' he said. 'Besides, I get my money today and I can really splurge – nothing but the best for us tonight Gala.'

He served her thin green asparagus, the first she'd ever tasted. It was out of season and came from Fortnum & Mason's and her eyes grew round with delight as she savoured its delicate flavour. Remembering the disaster with Cam she took only one or two sips of the champagne he'd poured, but as Jake bustled around happily in the minute kitchen of his Chelsea flat, grilling fresh salmon and concocting a dill and cucumber sauce to accompany it, Gala relaxed. This wasn't like with Cam, Jake was a true friend, he'd never, *never* do anything like that. She blushed, staring into her softly bubbling champagne glass, remembering Cam's kisses, Cam's hands . . .

There were strawberries for dessert and Jake had bought delicious dark chocolates with exotic-tasting centres, 'to put a bit of weight on your bones,' he teased.

They sat, side by side, on Jake's slippery leather chesterfield sofa, holding hands, and Gala giggled because somehow she kept sliding off. Jake laughed at her – and then he kissed her lightly on the tip of her nose. 'If I were a good guy,' he told her solemnly, 'which I'm not, I'd ask you to marry me Gala-Rose.' He turned away, his twisted young-old face suddenly bitter. 'For the first time in my life I'm regretting what I am,' he murmured.

Gala stared at him for a few moments, stunned, and then she said, 'But you can't marry *me*, I'm not *anybody* . . . I mean you're a *Maybrook*, you don't mix with girls like me.'

'*Don't say that* Gala-Rose!' he retorted angrily. 'You are *you!* I see your gentleness and your innocence, and your own particular brand of beauty. And someday, someone else will see it too . . . it's too precious for the likes of me. I'm no good my little Gala, I've always done what I want to do when I wanted, just like a spoiled brat . . . only spoiled brats become men, and then where are we?' Sighing, he took her hand in his, kissing each finger in turn. His un-paralysed profile was silhouetted against the light and for a moment Gala had a glimpse of the rugged masculine good looks that had once been his, before his mouth covered hers in a tender, lingering kiss.

'There,' said Jake briskly, 'that's out of the way, once and for all. Now, having fed and watered you, *and* kissed you, I think it's time I took you home. I've got an appointment at a casino and I feel lucky tonight . . .'

Gala knew that he'd probably gamble every penny of his monthly allowance – and more – at the casino and in all probability afterwards he'd get drunk and, like before, he'd be caught peeing up against a tree in Mayfair or fighting in Berkeley Square because they wouldn't let him into a nightclub, and he'd end up at Beak Street Police Station on drunk and disorderly charges. 'Don't do it Jake, please,' she whispered urgently. 'Don't gamble all your money away, don't get drunk . . . *please*. For me.'

Jake gave her his usual cheerful, crooked grin as he shrugged on his jacket. 'Sorry sweetheart,' he replied, 'but I can't promise that, not even for you.'

As he dropped her off at her rooming-house Gala watched the tail lights of his Metro disappear down the street, wishing that she could love him like a woman and not like a sister. Maybe then she would have been strong enough to change him.

Jake's drinking seemed to get worse from that point; she noticed him many a night arriving for his work as Lindy's bouncer already smelling strongly of whisky, and although he never drank at Lindy's because Leonard Linsen, the manager, wouldn't allow it, he disappeared at frequent intervals to the neighbouring pubs and bars, returning red-faced and aggressive. Gala met him several mornings for coffee at Valerie's and tried to talk to him about it but mostly Jake would be so hung over and morose, he'd just sip his espresso and stare down at the old formica-topped table until she gave up in despair and just held onto his hand instead.

'It's no good you know,' he said to her one morning, facing her on the grimy sidewalk of Old Compton Street, 'just look at this Gala-Rose.' He held out his trembling hands to show her and she stared at them, horrified. 'I can't stop it,' Jake said, 'God knows I've tried . . . oh, I'm not all bad though you know, good Scotch soothes the pain in my head but it also puts a tremor in my hands. It's a vicious circle Gala, and not one I'm prepared to break.' She took in his unshaven face and haunted expression and then he turned on his heel and strode off, weaving his way rapidly through the crowds with the old expertise of the rugger-forward of yesteryear.

Upset and on edge, Gala showed up for work that evening, hurrying through her tasks with mechanical ease and a numb heart, worrying about Jake who sat slumped over the bar, a single pint of beer in front of him. The beer had been there since ten o'clock when he'd started work and it was still untouched at 11.30. He looked particularly rough, with three days' stubble showing on his chin and a rumpled dark blue pinstripe suit. He looked, thought Gala with a sinking heart, the very travesty of the young-Englishman-about-town.

'Here's your wages Gala,' said Leonard, the boss, handing her a sealed envelope, as he always did on Friday nights. Gala stuffed it in her pocket and hurried to serve the two men leaning on the bar. They wore striped rugby club supporters' scarves wound around their necks, and were demanding a 'drop of the hard stuff'. 'And two jacket potatoes love, with cheese,' they called, lurching to a table with their drinks. Dashing into the kitchen, Gala shoved the potatoes into the microwave, her mind on Jake. The Metro had disappeared again so Jake must have lost it gambling – and he wasn't drinking tonight. That could only mean one thing, he was broke and his credit was so bad he couldn't gamble any more – or even get a drink. Fishing in her pocket Gala stared at her own brown wages envelope. It would contain exactly sixty-five pounds – the amount due to her after tax and NHS deductions. After she'd paid her weekly rent of thirty-five pounds plus the minimum money she needed for fares and to feed the gas meter and a pound a day for food, there would be around twenty pounds left. She'd been scrimping and saving like a miser these last few months, aiming towards her goal of returning to modelling next year and she had two hundred and forty pounds in the bank. But if Jake needed money she would give it to him – he would have helped her, willingly, she knew it. Besides, she loved him.

Whisking the baked potatoes from the oven she hurried through the bar and put them on the table in front of the already raucous rugby supporters. There were an awful lot of them tonight, there must have been a big game at Twickenham . . . Welsh they were too, and looking for trouble but not quite drunk enough yet to seek it. Jake had better be ready for it though, tonight . . .

Walking to the end of the bar, she leaned her elbows on the counter. 'Are you all right?' she enquired, smiling at Jake anxiously.

'I'm all right Gala-Rose. I'm just not drunk, that's all.'

'Because you're broke, is that it?'

'Partly. But not entirely. There are other reasons. Wales was playing England today at Twickenham. I went there to watch my old team win – and they did. Without the help of yours truly, Jake Maybrook!' His eyes were bitter as he stared into his flat beer. 'Rugby was the one good thing in my life,' he murmured . . . 'until you came along of course,' he added with a flash of his old gallant humour. 'But damn me, if it didn't nearly kill me.'

Fumbling in her pocket Gala brought out the brown envelope. 'Take it Jake,' she urged, 'put it in your pocket and go home – drink champagne tonight not Scotch. If you must get drunk do it in style – and get drunk *at home*. You'll feel better about this in the morning.'

Jake looked at her bemused. 'But what is this love? A love letter – to me?' His big laugh boomed around the bar, and heads turned to see who was being so funny. Slitting open the envelope, he pulled out the contents. 'You're offering me money?' he whispered. '*Your hard-earned wages?* Oh Gala-Rose, my little love, I don't deserve such devotion. You want to pay for me to get drunk in style so that I can drown my sorrows about rugby. Well, thank you darling, but no. I can't accept.' He pressed the notes back into her hand, 'Keep it love, believe me, you need it more than I do.'

The notes fluttered onto the counter, sopping up the spilled beer as she tried to give them back to him. 'There's fifty-five pounds here,' he said sternly. 'That's too much to be flashing around in a dive like this. You'll be mugged before you know it!'

'Fifty-five?' Gala stared at him puzzled.

Jake counted it rapidly. 'Right. Fifty-five.'

'But there should be sixty-five – that's what I always get.'

Jake stared at her, and then he said, 'Tell me, do you usually open your wage packet here?'

'Oh no, I always wait until I get home. Then I take it to the bank the next morning.'

'OK. I'll tell you what to do. Go right now to our friendly boss, show him your fifty-five pounds and let's see what he says.'

Gala stared at him dubiously, 'Why? Do you think he's cheating me deliberately?'

Jake nodded. 'I'm willing to bet on it. It's an old trick – just an extra tenner in his own pocket . . . go on Gala, ask him.'

Gala walked slowly to the opposite end of the bar where Leonard was sipping coffee and reading the day's racing results. 'Yeah?' he asked, looking up grudgingly, when she spoke.

'Mr Linsen, I'm ten pounds short in my wages,' she told him, 'there's only fifty-five pounds here.'

'Bullshit,' said Linsen indifferently. 'You got the same wages you always do; if you've lost some that's your problem.'

'But Mr Linsen, I just opened it here – now . . . I couldn't possibly have lost ten pounds,' replied Gala reasonably.

'No? And how do you prove that? How do I know you haven't already slipped it in your bag, or your pocket. It happens all the time with bar-staff. Well, I'm sorry, but it won't wash on me . . .'

'Mr Linsen,' protested Gala, trying hard to stay reasonable, 'you must have made a mistake this time. I can't afford to be short – I need all the money I earn.'

'Yeah? Well try working a bit harder, then maybe you'll earn some tips . . . You should be like Rita . . . work "after hours".'

Her face scarlet with anger, Gala stalked back to Jake. 'I knew it,' said Jake. 'I've seen the little shit pull this with other staff too. Wait here Gala, I'll take care of him . . .' Sliding from the stool he made his way across the bar.

'Here,' called a thin little man in a striped scarf and a Welsh accent, 'if it isn't bloody old Maybrook.'

Half a dozen heads swivelled as Jake paused near them, 'So what?' asked Jake calmly.

'Nothin', nothin',' he muttered, assessing Jake's size.

'Right then,' said Jake continuing on his way towards Linsen.

'Three bloody Welsh caps, the star of Wales rugger and look at him,' marvelled the little man. 'Poncing around in a bar like a bloody poofter.'

Gala stared apprehensively at the drunken rugby supporters as Jake, ignoring them, reached Linsen. The crowded bar had fallen suddenly silent and all eyes were on Jake.

'Give Gala the tenner, Linsen,' he said quietly.

'What d'ya mean, give her the tenner? She got her wages, same as usual. You don't see Rita grumbling do ya – hey Rita, you've got your wages don't ya?'

'Sure do.' Rita fished out a sheaf of notes from the bosom of her low-cut blouse, 'and I'm willing to earn some more!' she added, winking boldly at the guffawing customers.

'If Gala's stashed it away and expects to get another tenner out of me, she's got another think coming.'

'No she didn't stash it away Linsen. *I* opened that wage packet, and I counted the money. Come on now. Give her the ten pounds and let's not have any more fuss, shall we?'

Jake's clear upper-class voice reached every corner of the silent bar as he loomed over Linsen.

'Looks like a fight,' commented one of the rugby supporters, knocking back his pint and flexing his muscular shoulders in anticipation.

'Nah,' commented the little man, 'that poofter's too scared to fight. He's had all the stuffing knocked out of him by the Frogs . . .'

Jake grabbed Linsen by the neck, 'A tenner Linsen, and *now*!' he said through gritted teeth.

'Fuck you, you're fired,' snarled Linsen.

Jake hit him squarely on the nose and amid the sound of crunching bone and a splatter of blood Linsen slid to the ground, a faint gurgling sound emerging from his throat. Reaching into Linsen's pocket, Jake removed a ten pound note from his wallet. He carried it carefully across to Gala and laid it in the palm of her hand. 'Now go into the back love, and get your coat. I'm taking you home. It's time you got yourself a new job.'

Gala stared at him, horrified. Jake's blue shirt was spattered with blood and the knuckles of his hand were puffed and bruised. 'Jake, I didn't mean you to do that . . . I only wanted to help you . . .'

'Never mind Gala-Rose. Just get your coat, and then we'll go home,' he said patiently, rubbing his eyes with his bruised hand.

'Are you all right Jake?' she asked worriedly.

'Just the usual headache that's all. Somehow it's been worse today . . . I suppose it's because of the game,' he said wistfully, 'if you could have seen it Gala . . .' his speech slurred suddenly as he murmured . . . 'it was just like old times . . .'

'You've broken his nose, you creep,' yelled Rita, crouched over Linsen at the far end of the bar, 'you're supposed to beat up the drunken customers, not the boss! Call an ambulance Gala!'

'Beat up the customers?' cried the heavily muscled rugby fan, strutting forward, 'we'd like to see this old has-been try, eh lads? Look at him . . . smart in his blue suit and his posh English voice. How did they ever let you play for Wales lad? Eh, tell me that now?' Arms folded he waited challengingly in the centre of the room.

'I'll be right back love,' Jake said calmly to Gala, 'I've just got one more thing to take care of here.'

126

The rugby fans rose *en-masse* as he approached them, glasses and bottles clutched in their hands, ready for a fight.

They stared in amazement as Jake stumbled and then clutched the counter for support.

'Drunk then is he?' laughed one. 'Well poofters never were good drinkers were they . . .'

Straightening his shoulders, Jake took two more steps towards them, facing them silently, swaying on his feet. 'Jake, Jake!' screamed Gala as he lurched forward. And then he fell with a solid fifteen-stone thunk onto the floor of Lindy's Bar amid the spilled beer and discarded cigarette butts.

Jake and Leonard Linsen shared the same ambulance to hospital and the police very kindly took Gala with them. But it was no good. Jake had been dead before he hit the floor.

There was a little paragraph in Nigel Dempster's gossip column in the *Daily Mail* and a brief report of the findings of the autopsy – a massive cerebral haemorrhage. Then Jake's family had him shipped back to Wiltshire. Gala supposed that now Jake was dead he was finally respectable enough to be received at home again. She tried to telephone his father, explaining that she was a friend of Jake's and would like to attend the funeral, but his secretary told her coldly that it was to be private, for the family only.

On the day of the funeral Gala crouched, terrified, in her lonely bedsit, sobbing for Jake and lost love. Jake was the protective brother she'd never had. With her, he had always been the perfect English gentleman, even though his family considered him worthless and a loser. In other circumstances she would most certainly have fallen in love with him – but, she thought sadly, had the circumstances been different then Jake wouldn't have loved her. He would never have met her; he'd have been caught up in his own life, going to all the smart parties and dinners and meeting those lovely girls she only read about in the newspapers. Poor, dear Jake. Drawing her flimsy curtains against the cold dark night, she sobbed for the empty world without Jake, and for herself.

5

Jonathan Morris Royle was seven pounds and two ounces of sheer delight. Jessie-Ann lay back against the white pillows of her hospital bed, her sweat-streaked hair combed back neatly from her pale face by a sweet young nurse and the baby in a wicker bassinet at her side. Harrison's joy showed in his face when he held his new son in his arms, exclaiming at his dark hair when he'd expected blond, and marvelling at the blueness of the baby's eyes – though Jessie-Ann warned him that they could change colour – but in fact, Jon's never did. Even grandmother Rachel Royle unbent beneath the power of her new grandson's smile – as wide as his mother's, though toothless. And Marcus came rushing down from Princeton, his arms full of yellow roses for Jessie-Ann and a six-foot-high teddybear for his new brother.

'He's real small,' he said touching the baby's hand tentatively.

'Don't worry, he won't bite,' she grinned, 'not yet anyhow.'

When Harrison came to visit her that evening, he was carrying a flat, buff-coloured suède box. 'I know you never want anything, and you're the most difficult girl to buy presents for,' he said opening the box, 'but blue is the colour of your eyes – and your son's.'

She gasped in amazement as he clasped a necklace of sapphires and diamonds around her throat, showing her the exquisite matching earrings. Stung by Rachel Royle's appraisal of her, and only too aware of the fact that most of the world figured she must have married Harrison for his money, Jessie-Ann had steadfastly refused to let him buy her anything. 'I've worn things like this when I modelled, but I never dreamed of *owning* them,' she exclaimed, turning her head to and fro so that the large pear-shaped sapphires surrounded by brilliant diamonds, sparkled in the light. 'But Harrison, I really can't keep them.'

'Of course you can,' he said firmly, 'they are to commemorate our son's birth. And naturally you'll need a new dress to go with them. I thought in a few weeks, when you feel up to it, we could fly over to Paris and get you some things.'

The months of pregnancy had not been easy ones for Jessie-Ann, though nothing had been really physically wrong with either her or the baby. It was just that she'd felt nauseated most of the time and therefore she hadn't eaten properly, and one thing had led to another. She could tell that Harrison worried about her – possibly more than he might have normally, because of Michelle – but now the worry was over. She was back to her old self, hungry and happy, and ready for anything.

In the end though, they didn't go to Paris because she couldn't bear to leave the baby. But she did go home at last, to show off Harrison and Jon to her family and friends.

Scott and Mary Parker had visited them once in New York, when Jessie-Ann first knew she was pregnant, and, upset by morning-sickness, she had never been more glad to see anyone in her life.

Jessie-Ann had always been close to her Dad – closer even than with her Mom, because taking care of three growing boys had been a full time job for Mary Parker. And somehow she and her Dad had always been in tune; they looked alike – he was a big blond giant with blue eyes – and they thought alike; sometimes she even knew what he was thinking before he said it. 'My little girl' he'd always called her affectionately, as he swung her onto his broad, safe shoulders when she was still small; and 'my big girl' when, as a teenager, she just grew and grew. When Jessie-Ann had called them on the phone from Eleuthera to tell them she was married, it wasn't her mother who had regretted losing the big white wedding for her only daughter – she had been too pleased that she had 'found someone to look after her at last', and that she was happy. But her father had said, 'Somehow I always pictured taking you down the aisle myself Jessie-Ann,' and, catching the tremor of emotion in his voice, her eyes had filled with tears.

Her parents' visit to New York hadn't been the happy event she'd expected, though it was a relief to let her mother take care of her – only her Mom knew just how to make her feel more comfortable, and when she needed a warm drink, or a cool cloth on her aching head. Jessie-Ann had been unable to face a restaurant or even take them around the city – and this was only the second visit of their lives. Harrison had laid on a limousine and a driver and theatre tickets and dinner reservations, looking after them like a good son-in-law, and she hoped they'd enjoyed it, but she still suspected that the grand apartment and its priceless furnishings and works of art had intimidated them . . . And Rachel Royle hadn't helped to make them feel any more comfortable.

Her father had battled on gamely through a lengthy dinner, discussing wines with Harrison, telling him of his favourite Christmas bottles over the years, and she knew that later Harrison had sent him a case of each one. But her poor mother had been subjected to Rachel's scrutiny as she picked out the family history with a few astute questions.

Scott Parker was a smalltown man. The son of a printer, he'd made it into Michigan State, graduating cum laude in English. He'd gone into journalism, covering the state for the local rags and finally achieving his modest ambition to run *Spring Falls Gazette*. It had been love at first sight between him and Mary Allison, and she'd married him fresh out of high school. Mary was a cultured, well-read woman who enjoyed her life and her small horizons, but she was no match for Rachel, chic and dagger-sharp in her black Chanel suit and burgundy satin blouse.

Jessie-Ann had grasped her mother's hand under the table as Mary Parker glanced at her worriedly in yet another awkward pause in the conversation. 'You look great tonight Mom,' she'd said encouragingly. 'I love that pink dress.'

'Your father said it was too young for me, but I thought it was pretty anyway,' she'd replied, pleased.

'Pink is such a difficult colour, don't you think?' commented Rachel. 'Especially when one is over the age of thirty.'

Jessie-Ann had glared at her mother-in-law, 'Bright pink was one of Schiaparelli's favourite colours,' she retorted, 'as well as Chanel's. And Lagerfeld uses it all the time . . . it's very fashionable.'

'I wouldn't know about fashionable.' Rachel spread a wafer of toast with a minuscule amount of butter and they watched her precise movements, fascinated, 'I found a style that suited me when I was twenty-five and I've worn it ever since – regardless of so-called "fashion".'

She had kept her parents away from Rachel after that, guarding them from her mother-in-law's barbs as protectively as if they were her children. 'She seems a very nice woman,' her mother had commented a touch doubtfully, 'and so smart. But then, with all that money I suppose she can't help but be smart.'

'You mustn't let all this go to your head,' counselled her father, when they were leaving, 'and remember Jessie-Ann, you can always come home.'

But could she? The thought nagged in her brain as their private jet, with Harrison at the controls winged westward at more than five hundred miles an hour, towards Spring Falls, Montana.

The split-level, ranch-style home on the big corner lot on leafy Billings Avenue looked exactly the way it always had. It was timber-framed and painted white, with a post and rail fence protecting the backyard and a green lawn sweeping down to the sidewalk. Kids in sweatshirts still rode bikes along the sidewalks and practised basketball into nets above garage doors. Windows stood open in the warm spring evening and snatches of rock from the teenagers' everlasting MTV station mingled with birdcalls and the barking of dogs.

'Your typical smalltown scene,' grinned Jessie-Ann, stepping from the hired Mercedes station wagon with Jon clutched in her arms. She had given the nurse a week off, wanting to be alone with the baby and Harrison and her family, and besides she knew that with his grandmother around, there would be no need for any extra help. The visit was to be kept simple – she had no intention of descending on her hometown like a celebrity jet-setter, surrounded by the trappings of wealth. All she wanted was for everything to be the way it had always been.

Her Mom's beaming face and outstretched arms welcomed her and Jessie-Ann handed over her precious bundle, folding back the blanket so that they could see Jon's sleeping face.

'He's a darling boy,' her mother exclaimed happily, 'so handsome – and so like Harrison!'

'You certainly know the way to a man's heart, Mary Parker,' said Harrison, grinning as he put down all the impedimenta a new baby needs to travel with.

'Welcome Harrison!' Scott Parker shunted the two pale grey Weimaraner dogs to one side. 'Get down Seth, Jared!' He pushed them through the door, closing it behind them. 'Jessie-Ann?' Then her Dad's arms were around her and she knew she was home at last.

'Here's your grandson,' she said proudly. The baby opened his blue eyes, smiling doubtfully at the new faces.

'That's your smile all right,' observed Scott, pleased, 'I remember it from when you were his age. I just wish your brothers were here – they'd remember it too.'

Jessie-Ann's elder brother, who took after her father, was a professor of English at Berkeley and her middle brother was doing his internship at Chicago's Cooke County Hospital. Her younger brother, who had always loved the outdoors life and the wilderness, was a Forest Ranger at Yellowstone National Park.

'Next time,' she murmured, wishing that they were home too, 'we'll plan it better.'

The living room windows stood open onto the screened wooden porch and Jessie-Ann stared in surprise at the plump, dark-haired girl standing there. It was someone she knew, someone from the past, but yet she couldn't quite place her . . .

'Hi,' the girl said, smiling shyly, 'I guess you don't remember me. I'm Laurinda Mendosa . . . we were in the same class at Spring Falls High . . .'

'Sure I remember,' cried Jessie-Ann, smiling, 'you were the one who was always so good at math . . . you used to leave us all standing! Didn't you go on to the University of Oklahoma? I expect you're a whiz in computer sciences or something by now?'

Laurinda looked embarrassed, 'I . . . I sort of dropped out . . . my Mom was ill and I was needed at home. I work as a book-keeper now – at the *Gazette*.' She smiled shyly at Jessie-Ann, 'Your Pa surely keeps me busy.'

'Worth her weight in gold,' boomed Scott Parker, 'Laurinda keeps us solvent – I guess the old *Gazette* would just go bankrupt without her.'

'Sounds great,' said Jessie-Ann, wondering what Laurinda was doing here. 'Laurinda, this is my husband, Harrison Royle.'

'Nice to meet you Mr Royle,' said Laurinda offering a plump-fingered hand to Harrison. He noticed that the nails were bitten down to the quick, and they looked red and raw.

'We moved from Ninth Street to Billings Avenue five years ago,' Laurinda told Jessie-Ann, 'and Mrs Parker has been just great. She found someone to look after my Mom during the day and she keeps an eye on things for me when I'm working.'

Jessie-Ann vaguely remembered an ailing mother but really it was hard to place Laurinda at all – except for her spectacular ability at math.

'Now Laurinda, you know I'm only too glad to be of help,' called Mrs Parker, heading for the kitchen. 'I've got coffee brewing, why don't you stay and have a cup with us?'

'Thanks Mrs Parker, but I'd better be off. Mom's alone and she gets anxious if I'm away for long. Nice to meet you Mr Royle,' she added, looking nervous, 'and nice to see you again Jessie-Ann. It sure seems like a long time since Spring Falls High . . .'

'It certainly does.'

'That's a real cute baby you've got there,' said Laurinda suddenly, 'I'd be glad to baby-sit any night, if you folks want to go out to dinner?'

'That's a great idea,' exclaimed Jessie-Ann, 'I'd like to take Mom and Dad to the Old Mill for supper . . . you'd love it Harrison,' she reassured him, 'it's good down-home food – just the way you like it. Apple pie almost as good as Mom's.'

'Not my Mom's,' he commented with a grin.

'Thanks Laurinda,' Jessie-Ann said walking with her to the door, 'I'll take you up on that offer.'

'Any time Jessie-Ann,' she replied shyly, 'as I said, your Mom's been real kind to me. I'd be glad to be able to do something in return.'

'Well!' exclaimed Jessie-Ann, returning to the den, and throwing her arms wide. 'This is it Harrison. Home . . . roots . . . it's where I'm from. And where I'm at!'

Harrison settled himself comfortably on the big, old plaid sofa and a ginger cat emerged from underneath, jumping on his knee and purring. 'Well, it seems the family accepts me,' he commented, smiling.

With a sigh of relief, Jessie-Ann sank down next to him, kicking off her sneakers and unbuttoning the top button of her jeans . . . 'Look what you did to me,' she complained to her sleeping son in his carrycot beside them, 'that's an inch on my waist at least!'

'You're still too thin to my way of thinking,' said Scott Parker, carrying an ice bucket with a bottle of champagne. 'Thought we'd have this rather than coffee – after all, it's a celebration, isn't it. Now, where are those glasses?'

'What's for supper Mom?' called Jessie-Ann, heading for the kitchen in search of the glasses.

'Your favourite of course, pot roast and vegetables, green salad and strawberry shortcake.'

'I never, ever eat pot roast except when I come home,' cried Jessie-Ann, hugging her Mom, 'because no one makes it quite like you.' It didn't matter that the evening was too warm for pot roast, it was exactly what she felt like.

Although she kept an anxious eye on Harrison through supper, Jessie-Ann needn't have worried. In jeans and a blue oxford shirt with the sleeves rolled up, he looked as relaxed as she had ever seen him, enjoying the pot roast and her father's stories of the traumas of running a local paper. Jessie-Ann felt proud that he was so handsome and so easy with her family; after all, it was very much a far cry from his usual world. While the two men took a stroll round the block with the dogs, and her Mom gave the baby his bottle, Jessie-Ann cleared and stacked the dishwasher.

'He's a real nice man, Jessie-Ann, you're lucky to have found such a good husband,' commented Mary Parker.

'Yes,' her eyes were starry as she thought of him, 'I know.'

Later she dragged out her old High School Year Book and she and Harrison pored over it together while she pointed out her special friends. 'That's Joannie Lawrence,' she told him, 'my *very* best friend. I think we practically lived together for five years – she was either here at my house or I was at hers. Isn't she beautiful – all that lovely dark curly hair? She's married to a dentist – we'll

134

see them tomorrow. And this is Kip Jackson – all the girls had a crush on him. And there's Ace!' she squeezed Harrison's hand as he peered closely at his rival.

'Ace is doing real well,' interjected Scott, 'he's with the Green Bay Packers – that boy plays real good football!'

'And here's Imogen Raikes,' said Jessie-Ann, 'and Marly Jerzinski . . . and oh look, there's Laurinda!' Peering closer, she examined the girl's pudgy, unsmiling face. 'Now I remember,' she cried, 'Laurinda's Mom was married to a Mexican! He was dark and swarthy with wavy black hair all shined up with haircream. He was a real creep – always eyeing the girls up and down when he came to get Laurinda from school . . . he never used to let her walk home with the other kids. In fact, now I think of it, Laurinda was always alone.'

'Poor girl,' said Mrs Parker, 'her father ran off with a waitress at a diner in Billings – left his wife and child without even so much as a goodbye. They've never heard from him since. If you ask me, Mrs Mendosa's better off without him, but there's no accounting for taste. Of course she's always been a sickly woman – but since he left, she's sort of . . . well – leaned on it – if you see what I mean. No one's ever quite sure what's wrong with her, but she's an invalid all right. And poor Laurinda had to give up college to look after her. Let's face it,' she added pouring more coffee, 'Laurinda's not the prettiest of girls, and with Mrs Mendosa clinging to her, she's not likely to find a husband. It's a pity she had to sacrifice a potential career – a great pity. If you ask me, the best thing for her would be to get right away from here, away from her mother. Laurinda's very good at her job and she could earn more than your father pays her on the *Gazette*.'

'That's for sure,' agreed Scott, stretching out in his favourite chair by the window, 'Laurinda's more than just a book-keeper, she's damned near a genius with figures. Yes, it's a pity about Mrs Mendosa – but those are the breaks, though in my opinion there's nothing really wrong with her – except maybe a fondness for the bottle . . .'

'Now Scott, you don't know if that's true . . .'

Jessie-Ann remembered that she and Joannie and Kim Bassett,

135

who all lived on Billings Avenue, had to pass by Laurinda's house on Ninth Street on their way home from school . . . they'd dawdled deliberately so as not to keep up with Mr Mendosa as he walked his daughter home, reluctant to catch his too-intimate glance. A shiver ran down her spine as she thought of that silent, shuttered house where the shades were always drawn to keep out the sun and the doors and windows firmly closed against their neighbours. She thought how lonely poor Laurinda must have been – not that she had felt much sympathy then. Laurinda was one of those girls outside her magic circle and Jessie-Ann had been far too involved in her own full, happy life to even think about the Laurindas of this world. Besides, she'd hated the way Mr Mendosa looked at her. Even with her back turned she could feel his eyes boring into her. But now she was feeling guilty for having been so selfish. Poor Laurinda, thought Jessie-Ann, she even had to sacrifice her one talent – maths – to her mother . . . It was so unfair . . .

The next day she took Harrison to see her old school, and wondered why it all looked so much smaller and less exciting than she remembered. They ordered sodas in the drugstore, sitting in the same red plastic booths of her youth, watching as the kids burst in, fresh from class, claiming tables as the boys pushed and shoved for places next to the prettiest girls. Those who knew her called, 'Hi'. Others lingered by their table to stare at Jessie-Ann the celebrity, and when she smiled, they asked for her autograph. 'Who's the old guy,' a pert twelve-year-old with straight blonde hair and wide eyes, asked her, 'is he famous too?'

'She could be you – fifteen years ago,' said Harrison, laughing at Jessie-Ann's indignation, as the kid walked away.

That evening she took Harrison and her baby round to Joannie's for a barbecue supper. Afterwards Harrison and Joannie's husband Pete Stevens watched the football game on TV while she and Joannie put the Stevens' two exuberant kids to bed. Later Kim came by with her husband, Tad Kramer, who was doing really well in fast-food franchises. Tad joined the men in the den while the three women sat in Joannie's immaculate bedroom with its matching Nettlecreek daisy-pattern bedspread and curtains.

'What's it like Jessie-Ann?' they demanded, 'tell us how it *feels* to be married to a millionaire?'

Looking at her childhood friends waiting on the big bed, their eyes wide with anticipation, Jessie-Ann wondered what to tell them. 'It's just like being married to any other guy,' she shrugged at last, 'except of course that Harrison's special.'

'Sure, he's special, he's as handsome as Matt Dillon and he's got more money than Rockefeller,' laughed Joannie. 'But tell us what your *life* is like. Do you get to buy whatever you want in Royle's stores?'

'That never occurred to me . . . but Harrison did offer to take me to Paris to do some shopping,' admitted Jessie-Ann, laughing.

'Paris!' they shrieked, 'Shopping! God, we're lucky if we get as far as Billings! Tell us more . . .'

Jessie-Ann told them about the wonderful apartment with its twenty-eight rooms. She described the art treasures and the Persian silk carpets, 'his and hers' onyx bathroom suites, the swimming pool and the gymnasium. She told them about the houseman and the cook and the maids, she told them she never need lift a finger . . . in fact she never had an *opportunity* to lift a finger, because Jon had a nurse to look after him too.

'So?' asked Kim, her round eyes sparkling. 'What do you do all day?'

Jessie-Ann stared at her friends sadly, 'But that's just it you see – for the first time in my life, I don't *do* anything!'

'Sounds like heaven to me,' yawned Kim, 'it seems like I've been getting up at five in the morning with yelling kids for years . . .'

'But it's not *heaven* Kim. I married *Harrison*, not *his money*! Running Royle's is a bit like having a demanding mistress. Harrison hates parties and fuss. He works hard and he likes to stay home nights with me and Jon. In fact, if it weren't for Jon coming along when he did, I think I might have gone crazy. I wanted to open a model agency and get back to work, but I don't think Harrison really understood why.' She sighed, thinking about it. 'So you see, it's not all roses being married to a rich man.' Catching their sceptical glance, she said defensively, 'I suppose I sound like a spoiled brat, and I don't mean to . . . I'd rather be

137

married to Harrison than be the most successful woman in the world . . . But still, it would be sort of nice to combine the two,' she added wistfully.

Lying awake that night, Jessie-Ann glanced around her old room. She looked at her dressing table with its girlish ruffles and the white four-poster draped with broderie-anglaise frills. She took in the family photographs on the walls, the old books and the stuffed animals spilling from the shelves which had been built by her Dad, and which she had painted bright red one summer weekend; this was her past, and this was what Harrison loved about her. But in order to continue to be the person that Harrison had loved and married, she needed a new challenge, the excitement of meeting new people, of chat and gossip and constantly ringing telephones. She needed to have her own stories to tell Harrison when he came home at night. She needed to be her own person. In fact, what she needed was *work*.

She stared at Harrison's sleeping face, at the firm mouth that kissed her so passionately, at the hollow curve of his eyesockets, the broad brow, unfurrowed and relaxed in sleep; she ran a tentative finger over the blueblack stubble on his chin and touched his dark hair, letting her hand slide along his neck and along his hard, muscular chest . . .

Harrison's eyes opened, meeting hers in the moonlight. 'Still awake?' he murmured, wrapping his arms around her, 'come here darling . . .'

Jessie-Ann yawned contentedly; now that she had worked out her problems, she could sleep. She would broach the subject of *Images* again, when they returned to New York.

6

Laurinda Mendosa sat on the old plaid sofa in the Parkers' cosy den, staring at the singer on television. He was dark and swarthy with black, very glossy hair, and he was singing in Spanish. He reminded her of her father and Laurinda flicked the remote control to change the channel quickly. She hadn't meant to think of her father tonight . . . she didn't *want* to think of him! She was here at the Parkers to baby-sit; not that she cared about helping Jessie-Ann, but because she wanted to please Mrs Parker. Mary Parker was a good woman, and she always kept her house bright and shiny clean. It was a welcoming sort of house, shabby but nice. There were always lots of people at the Parkers too, friends and neighbours just dropping in casually, without even telephoning first. And if it were supper time there'd be something good on the stove, or else there'd be coffee and a freshly baked chocolate cake – Mrs Parker made the *best*. And she was a *wonderful mother*. The sort of mother Laurinda should have had, but that was just another example of the way life was so unfair; *she* got that drunken old sot for a mother – and Mrs Parker got that cunt Jessie-Ann for a daughter!

Laurinda closed her eyes, the filthy word trembling redly in her mind, as though it were written in her brain in fire . . . that's why she always typed the letters in red.

'Jessie-Ann you whore . . . Jessie-Ann you evil temptress . . . Jessie-Ann you cunt . . . flaunting your body in front of the world . . . teasing . . . tempting . . . luring men into things they never should do . . .'

'Hi Laurinda.' Jessie-Ann whirled into the room and began rummaging amonst the cushions on the sofa. 'Have you seen Jon's musical duck? He just won't go to sleep without that tune playing over and over and we can't find it anywhere . . .'

'Here it is,' replied Laurinda shakily, holding up a fluffy yellow duck with a bright orange beak, 'I found it on the floor.'

'Ah well,' said Jessie-Ann dusting it off quickly, 'I guess a few of the Parker household germs won't hurt him, after all they never hurt me!'

Laurinda noticed Jessie-Ann was wearing a tight blue silk skirt and a simple matching top and she'd wrapped a long blue and coral and yellow silk scarf around her waist. The skirt stopped short of her knees and she wore high-heeled blue sandals and dark stockings with seams that made her legs look as though they went on for ever . . . Laurinda stared at the seams fascinated . . . they were like arrows leading her eyes up, and up . . . that's why Jessie-Ann wore them of course, something new to lead men on . . . she wasn't satisfied to have married a rich man . . .

'They're back in fashion again,' said Jessie-Ann noticing her stare, 'don't you remember, when we were about fifteen, they were all the rage? Golly, that seems a long time ago. I'll be right back Laurinda, I'll just give Jon his "night music" . . .'

Laurinda had always hated the way her Pa had looked at the girls at school – especially Jessie-Ann. He'd wait outside the school, just hanging around, watching, a little smile on his coarse-skinned face, and always with a wooden toothpick sticking out of the corner of his mouth, and his hands in his pockets . . . she knew he was touching himself, watching the girls . . . and her cheeks had burned with humiliation and fear . . . She'd always try to be first out of class, running down the hallway to beat the others, but he'd say to her, 'Hey kid, what's your hurry . . . let's slow it down a little huh?' and he'd lean against the wall, picking his teeth, and waiting . . .

Even at twelve Kim Bassett had had breasts; Laurinda had heard the other girls giggling about it in the locker room – she'd even seen them herself when Kim was getting out of the shower, big and round, and under her pink wool sweater they jiggled a lot. Not that that was Kim's fault, a girl couldn't help the sort of body she had . . . but her Pa couldn't take his eyes off them. And Joannie, too, was sort of round and very pretty; but it was Jessie-Ann that her Pa really lusted after.

Jessie-Ann was always skinny but she had a curving bottom and

140

high budding little breasts, that stood out under her thin cotton T-shirt. Her father would wait until the three of them appeared on the steps, and then he'd saunter lazily down the road, never looking at Laurinda, walking slower and slower until the girls caught up to them and passed them. Giggling amongst themselves, they barely noticed her of course. *She* didn't count. *She* was fat, and her skin was coarse, like her father's, and *she* had too much body hair, she'd been shaving her legs since she was eleven.

At school Laurinda felt as if she were enveloped in a cocoon of shame and silence. Her only solace was the cool passion of higher mathematics whose complexities appeared to her as simple and fascinating as a jigsaw puzzle. But *she* wasn't one of the 'chosen' group; *she* wasn't invited to the parties, the picnics, the dances, *she* didn't go skating with them, nor up to the mountains skiing; *she* didn't get asked to sleep over and share their secrets . . . she never even knew what they were giggling about – unless it was about her . . . and her weird father, and her drunken mother . . .

Then her father would walk more quickly to keep up with the girls. His eyes would be fixed on Jessie-Ann's tightly-jeaned bottom, watching her every stride as though he were seeing her naked. When the girls had turned the corner, he'd hurry Laurinda into the house, pushing her ahead of him down the hall and into her bedroom. And then he'd do things to her – things she didn't even want to think about – while her Momma rattled pots and pans in the kitchen, pretending to be busy, acting like she was unaware of what was going on, and deadening her senses with another bottle of Southern Comfort.

Laurinda had been so frightened, she hadn't known what to do. Her father was a violent man, she'd seen him aim casual blows at her mother, cuffing her out of the way as though she were a dog, and even when Laurinda was still so small she barely reached his knee, he'd beaten her for being 'wicked'. Never just 'naughty', like the other kids . . . she was always '*wicked*'! She couldn't remember when she'd first realised that her Pa enjoyed it . . . she just recalled standing there, trembling, staring in horrified fascination as he slid his wide brown leather belt out of the belt-loops of his grey corduroy pants, knowing what was to

141

come. 'You've been wicked again Laurinda,' he'd say, putting her across his knee and pulling down her pants, 'you're a wicked little girl . . . you are a sinner Laurinda . . .'

There had been no escape and no one who could save her. Who would believe her shameful story? Her own mother would deny it, she was certain of that. Her father was a respectable man – he worked as a gardener at the big houses up on Royal Mount and the ladies there were all very pleased with his work. He kept his roving, lecherous eye for Laurinda's contemporaries, not those 'smart old dames', as he called them.

Laurinda escaped to school each day, dreading the moment when she had to return, dreading walking behind Jessie-Ann, hating the girl's knowing backward glance – as though she under-stood what was going on, hating her confident walk and her innocent blue eyes, hating Jessie-Ann's pert, cute little rump in its tight, tight jeans . . . hating Jessie-Ann for what she was doing to her . . .

And she envied Jessie-Ann too, envied her warm, happy home, her strong, blond father and her warm, comforting mother . . . she'd envied her three protective older brothers who looked after their little sister like medieval knights protecting their fair lady . . .

Each afternoon, when Laurinda entered her shuttered silent house that was clean as a new pin, because when her mother wasn't drunk she cleaned house with the zeal of a fetishist, covering the sofa with plastic wrappers and commanding them to remove their muddy shoes, each afternoon Laurinda's heart would feel as though it were swelling, threatening to choke her, as she walked ahead of her father into her bedroom . . .

She had tried to tell her mother, sobbing and burning with shame, her body bruised and painful, but her mother had shut her up brusquely, telling her she had too much imagination, that her father was simply helping her with her homework. And her hand had reached under the kitchen counter . . . as Laurinda glanced back on her way from the room, her mother was standing there, head back, the bottle of Southern Comfort uptilted, just pouring it down her throat . . .

After a while though, the girls had gotten wise to her father's predatory stares; they'd lingered behind, defying him to walk even slower than they, giggling and whispering, and her Pa had grabbed her hand, hauling her off down the street angrily, muttering to himself in Spanish. But the worst had come later, when they were older.

Jessie-Ann was fifteen when she won the model contest. There had been a photograph of her flaunting her body in a revealing white swimsuit that was cut so high up her crotch and so low in the back you could practically see everything. Her father had been sitting, reading the evening paper, and he'd stared at Jessie-Ann's picture for a long time. Then, unbuckling his belt, he'd gotten up and jerked his head in the direction of her room, stepping closer, menacingly when she remained, riveted to her seat by fear. This time it had been different, this time it wasn't just the touching . . . this time, with Jessie-Ann's picture placed next to Laurinda's head, he'd straddled her, crushing her with his weight as he thrust into her, wounding her with his big horrible thing . . . scorching her with shame, branding her for ever . . . It was then that she had written the first letter . . . pouring out her hatred . . . she'd told Jessie-Ann just what she thought of her, repeating the words she'd heard her father use as he stabbed at her over and over until she'd bled. After she'd written it and put it in the mailbox near the school, she'd felt such a relief, as though the whole burden had somehow been lifted from her. She could now expunge the memory of her Pa and his searching hands and panting body from her mind.

Laurinda had quite enjoyed the fuss that followed. She hadn't expected such an outcry – it was exciting, watching what went on and knowing that *she* was the cause of it all. She – *and* her Pa. The police had waited outside school, checking everyone. In the days that followed her Pa had suddenly become busy with extra work in those fancy gardens up on Royal Mount, avoiding the school. But after a while it had all died down and things went back to normal . . .

A year later, when her Pa had run off with the sixteen-year-old waitress from Billings, Laurinda had felt pity for the girl. But her own ordeal was over . . . maybe now she could lose herself in the purity and beauty of mathematics.

Mrs Parker hurried into the den, patting her short, neatly-set grey hair and smiling. 'That baby is out for the count,' she told Laurinda, 'I guess you're not gonna have too many problems with him tonight. He surely is the best-behaved child I've ever known – and he certainly doesn't take after his mother in that respect. My, was she a naughty one, I always said she was thoroughly spoiled by her father and her older brothers.'

"A *naughty* child," thought Laurinda . . . "not a *wicked* one . . . like me . . ."

'You look real pretty tonight Mrs Parker,' she offered, 'I like that pink dress.'

'Why, thank you Laurinda. I bought this when I went to New York to visit Jessie-Ann and Harrison,' she glanced down at it worriedly, 'somehow it seems to suit Spring Falls better though!'

'Are we all ready? Our reservations are for 7.30.' Scott Parker hated to be even a minute late for an appointment and he jingled his car keys impatiently until Harrison and Jessie-Ann appeared.

Fumbling in her purse, Jessie-Ann brought out her precious sapphire earrings and flicking back her hair she slotted them neatly into her pierced ears, shaking her head to make sure they were secure. 'What do you think Laurinda?' she asked, 'aren't they wonderful? They're so fantastic everybody is sure to think that they are fakes! In fact, Harrison,' she added teasing, 'I swear I saw some exactly like these in Bloomingdales the other day.'

They were real sapphires and real diamonds! thought Laurinda, stunned . . . "and Jessie-Ann hadn't so much as glanced in the mirror when she put them on. She'd just simply tossed her head, showing off her trophies, telling her husband they looked like fakes . . ."

Fishing in her purse again, Jessie-Ann brought out the suede box and clicked it open, showing the matching necklace to her mother and father, 'Harrison gave them to me when Jon was born,' she told them proudly, 'but I think the necklace needs a grander dress and a grander occasion than dinner at the Old Mill!' Mr and Mrs Parker exclaimed over their beauty, watching as Jessie-Ann placed the necklace back in its box and stuffed it casually into her purse.

'Hurry up girls,' called Scott, making for the door, 'it's time to leave . . .'

'Jon's bottle is in the kitchen Laurinda, and his juice is in the refrigerator,' Jessie-Ann told her, 'and you have the number at the Old Mill House if you need me . . . but I guess everything's gonna be all right.'

'Help yourself to coffee,' called Mrs Parker, 'and there's a fresh marble cake – baked today. We'll be back around eleven I guess.'

Laurinda watched them drive off in Scott Parker's white Buick and then she closed the door firmly and locked it. Leaning back against it, she stared around the Parkers' house, noticing that the oatmeal carpet in the hall was wearing thin, and the floral curtains were faded from the sun. She sniffed the mingled fragrances of freshly-brewed coffee and newly-baked cake, and the pot-pourri that Mrs Parker kept in little china bowls scattered throughout the house. "*This* is a true home," she thought.

She walked to the kitchen, her face relaxing into a smile as she poured herself a mug of coffee and cut a large slice of cake, taking it into the den and settling in front of the television again. Thank God, the Mexican singer had gone and there was a situation comedy about one of those proper American families where the father is always wise and understanding and tolerant, even though his typical teenage kids drive him crazy – and his wife is capable and beautiful . . . and everybody makes jokes and is funny and at the end of the programme they always made a point of letting you know that they all loved each other a lot. Munching the cake morosely, Laurinda thought it was only the same old American dream. It was just a myth. She went into the kitchen to cut another slice of cake – it would be disastrous for her latest diet – which had lasted all of two days, and she'd probably break out in a dozen spots tomorrow, but Mrs Parker surely knew how to bake.

On her way back to the den, she thought she heard a wail from the direction of Jessie-Ann's room. Glancing up the stairs, she hesitated . . . there it was again. So much for Jon's being a good baby, she guessed this was his night to be different! Maybe the kid knew *she* was looking after him? Laurinda shrugged her shoulders indifferently. Let him wait, a good cry would probably do him good, spoiled little rich brat! Damn, now she'd spilled coffee on Mrs Parker's carpet! Putting her fresh cup of coffee and her cake on the table in the den, she rushed back into the kitchen to find a cloth, scrubbing at the small stain anxiously. There, it had just about gone. Relieved she rubbed at it again. Yes, it was OK and Mrs Parker would never know how careless she had been. God, that kid surely made a racket. Closing the door of the den, she settled herself comfortably on the sofa, propping her feet on the coffee table and turning up the sound on the television. She'd just be in time to catch the news, she always enjoyed seeing what was happening around the world. Somehow it took her out of Spring Falls . . .

When she carried her cup back to the kitchen half-an-hour later, the baby was still crying, only now it was a loud frightened wail. God, the neighbours would be around if she didn't shut him up! With a sigh, Laurinda walked slowly up the stairs to Jessie-Ann's room. Leaning over the ruffled white crib she peered at the baby. Suddenly silent, he stared back at her with Jessie-Ann's direct blue eyes. His face was red and blotched from crying and his breath came in huge, sighing sobs. Laurinda hadn't expected him to look so sort of sweet and helpless and she felt quite sorry now that she'd left him to cry, but kids had to learn that they couldn't just interrupt grownups, they had to know their place.

Picking him up, she realised that he was wet and she laid him on the changing table and removed his diaper. Averting her eyes from his masculinity, she pinned a fresh diaper around him hurriedly, wrapped him in his blanket and then carried him downstairs.

Laurinda held Jon uneasily on her lap as he glugged happily on his bottle, thinking that Jessie-Ann didn't deserve a baby like this – or *any* baby. Jon couldn't help having Jessie-Ann for a mother though, could he? Just the way she couldn't help having *her* mother – *and* her father. Wiping the baby's milky chin she smiled at him, and, as he stared back at her she wondered what he was thinking, wishing he didn't look quite so much like Jessie-Ann. The baby heaved a contented sigh, and his eyelids drifted slowly downwards and soon he was breathing evenly, fast asleep in her arms.

Laurinda stared in wonder at his innocent face. This was the first time in her life she had ever held a baby; it was the first time that she had ever held *anyone* in her arms – and it was certain that nobody had ever cradled *her* like this as a kid. And of course *never* now that she was a woman. Leaning her head back against the cushions Laurinda closed her eyes, suffused with a new kind of happiness, holding the baby against her breast.

'Well now, look at that. Isn't that just darling?' cried Mrs Parker, 'both of them asleep like that.'

Laurinda awoke with a start. 'Oh I'm so sorry Mrs Parker, I didn't mean to fall asleep . . . it was just that Jon was crying so much and then we both got so comfortable here on the sofa, and when he finally went to sleep again, I didn't want to disturb him.'

'You're spoiling him Laurinda,' said Jessie-Ann, picking up the baby and hugging him. 'Come on you little rascal, have you been giving Laurinda a hard time then?'

They seemed so much a family, thought Laurinda enviously, as she slipped on her jacket, you could tell they'd had a good time together.

'Thanks Laurinda,' said Harrison, tucking a fifty dollar bill into her pocket.

'Mr Royle, I can't take that,' she protested, handing him back the note, 'really I didn't do it for the money – and anyway this is far too much.'

'I always believe in paying what a job is worth,' replied Harrison firmly, 'and your services were valuable tonight.'

Laurinda smiled at him guardedly, 'Well thank you then Mr Royle.' As he held open the door for her, she hesitated, 'Would it be OK if I came tomorrow, just to see the baby again?' she asked suddenly.

'Why of course, we'll be glad to see you.'

He watched as Laurinda hurried down the path, dodging the sprinklers, then walked more slowly to the very end of Billings Avenue and the shabby, two-bedroom frame house she called home.

The next afternoon Laurinda sat on the floor of Jessie-Ann's bedroom, watching little Jon kicking his legs in the air as Jessie-Ann packed. She dangled the yellow duck over the baby's crib, laughing delightedly when he reached for it.

Jessie-Ann glanced up at her, amazed. She'd never heard the girl laugh before. Poor thing, it really was a pity about her family – but there was still something about Laurinda that made her uncomfortable . . .

Laurinda sighed exaggeratedly. 'I'll sure be sorry to see you folks go,' she offered, quietly.

'We'll be back before too long,' said Jessie-Ann, rolling up the blue silk outfit and thrusting it into the big Louis Vuitton leather sack. 'A model's trick,' she explained catching Laurinda's startled glance. 'If you roll the clothes, they don't crease and you can get lots more in.'

Laurinda remembered the only time she had gone away – those weeks in college before she'd been forced to come home – packing her few outfits carefully between layers of fresh white tissue, ironing and folding . . . 'If only I could get away from here,' she said in a low voice, 'I can't tell you what it's like Jessie-Ann. Oh I know Mrs Parker thinks my Mom's an invalid, but the plain truth is that she drinks. Southern Comfort is what keeps me chained to Spring Falls.' She laughed bitterly, 'If it weren't for your Dad giving me a job and not minding when I have to take time off – although of course I always make up the time later, I'm very conscientious about that – well, I think I would just go crazy.' Dropping her eyes, she added softly, 'I just don't know what I would have done to myself.'

Jessie-Ann dropped the bundle of clothes she was about to cram into the bag and stared at her, aghast. 'Laurinda!' she cried, shocked, 'things can't be that bad!'

'Oh yes they can.' Laurinda's voice trembled and a tear slid down her puffy cheek as she went on, 'I've never really talked to anyone about it before . . . not even Mrs Parker. My Mom doesn't even care *where* she is – or even if I'm here – as long as she has someone to take care of her and keep her supplied with booze!' Catching Jessie-Ann's shocked glance she added quietly, 'Believe me, it's better to buy it for her than have her be without – then she's like a madwoman. She'd kill to get hold of drink! Sometimes I dream of getting away – to New York even – and getting myself a decent job. Maybe I could go to school at night and study accounting; I could learn all about tax law and corporate law . . . I dream that maybe it's not too late . . . that maybe some day, I could be *somebody* . . .' Her voice trailed off in tears, and she sniffed miserably, adding, 'If only I could get a job in New York.'

Thrusting the dress she was holding into her bag, Jessie-Ann sat down on the bed and stared worriedly at Laurinda. God, the girl had gotten such bad breaks . . . if only she'd known, maybe she'd have taken more interest in her at school, tried to help her a little, instead of always sniggering with the others about her awful father . . . but Laurinda had always seemed so remote and a little strange . . . even now she found it hard actually to *like* her . . . Standing up, Jessie-Ann walked over to her son, taking his small hand in hers. Jon gurgled happily, clutching the little yellow duck in his small tight fist and waving it around. She had everything, thought Jessie-Ann guiltily, everything any woman could want . . . 'Thank you for telling me Laurinda,' she said gently. 'I'm truly sorry you are so unhappy. If you like I'll ask Harrison to see if there's an opening in the Accounting Department of his office in New York. I don't know how much they pay, but I expect it'll be enough for you to get a small apartment, and you'll surely be able to go to college at night.'

Laurinda's small, lustreless eyes held a new gleam as she looked at Jessie-Ann. 'Would you really do that? *For me? Really, Jessie-Ann?*' Her face clouded again, 'But I can't leave my mother – she's helpless, and I can't afford to keep her *and* live in New York.' Bursting into tears, she sobbed, 'Oh dear, it just won't work.'

For the life of her, Jessie-Ann couldn't bring herself to put a comforting arm around the plain, ordinary looking girl. 'Now don't you worry about that,' she said. 'We'll speak to my Mom and Dad and work out how we can get Mrs Mendosa hospitalised, there must be some place where she could undergo a cure . . .'

'A cure!' Laurinda's bitter laugh mingled with her tears. 'There's *no cure* for my mother. Oh no, Jessie-Ann. She'll have to be institutionalised. *My mother needs locking up!*'

Jessie-Ann gasped, horror-struck by Laurinda's vindictiveness.

'You don't know her,' Laurinda muttered quickly, catching her shocked glance, 'you don't know the half of it. She's likely to set fire to the place one night, with her smoking and being drunk, and she'll kill herself – *and* me!'

'Don't worry Laurinda,' Jessie-Ann said finally. 'I'll get my Dad to help. He'll see what needs to be done.'

'And Harrison? You won't forget to ask him too?' Laurinda's voice was painfully eager.

'I promise,' agreed Jessie-Ann. 'You'll be in New York – and your new life, before you know it,' she added, managing a smile.

Laurinda pushed herself up from the floor smoothing her crumpled cotton skirt. 'Thank you Jessie-Ann. And thank Harrison for me too. I don't know what I'd have done without your family. I can't believe that soon it will be all over – and I'll be out of this nightmare. Well . . . goodbye then.'

Laurinda held out her hand awkwardly, and as she took it Jessie-Ann thought how cold and clammy it felt, despite the fact that the room was warm. 'Goodbye Laurinda,' she said, 'and good luck.'

7

Thrusting his hands in his pockets, Harrison gazed moodily out of the window of his fiftieth-floor office-eyrie. A pile of glossy real estate brochures lay on his desk, gift-wrapped in pretty gold paper and tied with a scarlet bow.

Tomorrow was Jessie-Ann's birthday and he'd planned to surprise her by buying her that ranch in bluegrass country she had told him she had dreamed of owning since she was a little girl. His property consultants had searched for two months and their half-dozen choices – from which Jessie-Ann would make the final decision – had all been thoroughly vetted for their investment value as well as for their charm. She would be able to keep the Arabian horses he planned to buy her in some of the most up-to-date stables in the US. She could school them in an all-weather manège, and train them over jumps in an indoor equestrian centre; without make-up and wearing blue jeans, she could ride all day over her own land, enjoying her horses and the freedom of the open spaces she longed for. Perhaps, thought Harrison, when little Jon was older, she would teach him to ride – he'd have his own pony and maybe a couple of dogs too. And in the evenings, when Jon was asleep in bed, he and Jess would settle down lazily in front of a roaring log fire, she with a glass of the California Chardonnay she preferred, and he with a tumbler of his favourite old Malt Whisky from Scotland; there'd be something like Brahms' Double Concerto on the record-player and she'd curl her long legs under her and rest her head against him, and the dogs would be sprawled on the rug at their feet . . .

The trouble with his birthday surprise, Harrison realised, was that he had somehow converted Jessie-Ann's dream to suit his own. What she had wanted was *to earn* that ranch. In Jessie-Ann's dream, along with the ranch there was also her model agency. *Images* was to be her proof to the world and to herself that she was more than just her model girl image. But the trouble with that plan was that he wasn't at all sure that she could. Jessie-Ann was no businesswoman. She would be a pushover for every sob-story, she wouldn't be able to turn anybody away. Yet she was confident that she would succeed, sure that she knew exactly what she was doing. All she needed was a home for *Images* – and Harrison to say yes.

As Harrison paced the cream and rose-coloured Bokhara rug he realised he was changing Jessie-Ann from the girl he'd married. She was quieter, and she smiled less, and she had no stories and gossip with which to entertain him when he came home in the evening; and young Jon only filled a part of the day.

Let's face it, he thought gloomily, I want to buy her the ranch so that I can have what *I* want – my beautiful down-home girl by my own fireside, wanting no one and nothing but me, and Jon . . . but the reality wasn't like that. He couldn't buy Jessie-Ann her dream – all he could do was try to help her achieve it. And maybe that way, he'd get what he wanted too.

Buzzing his secretary, he asked her to get his Manhattan real estate broker on the phone – he had a job for him – and he'd have exactly eighteen hours in which to achieve it.

Rachel Royle stalked out of the elevator on the fiftieth floor of the Royle building on East Sixty-first and Madison, bestowing regal smiles left and right as she walked through the big open secretarial area, pausing now and then to enquire after some long-term employee's health or to greet a vice-president en route to a meeting. It gave her endless satisfaction to see that, as always, the offices were a hive of activity, and that no one lingered by the coffee machine gossiping. Royle employees were well looked after – their working conditions were climate-controlled, comfortable and well-lit; everything – from the typewriters, copiers and word processors to the vast computer complex – was the most up-to-date; a subsidised canteen operated for the staff of twelve hundred serving excellent health-oriented meals; and the medical insurance policy, the pension plan, the holiday allowance and profit-sharing bonus scheme all contributed to a contented work-force, happy in their jobs.

Her husband, Morris Royle had created all this and, for Rachel, it was a living monument to his memory. The fact that Harrison had successfully expanded Royle's until it was a giant corporation was double cause for satisfaction, for didn't it just go to prove that she and Morris had taught him the proper values? When his father had died, she had been able to lean on Harrison for the strength she'd needed to get through those first terrible months, and he had been a loving and supportive son – Rachel didn't know what she would have done without him. Of course Morris had left *her* in control of the company with 36⅓ per cent share holding, while Harrison had 30⅓ – the remaining 33⅓ shares were publicly owned. And while Harrison was very much in charge of the company, Rachel would never relinquish that final controlling vote because she owed it to Morris to keep his trust in her. That's why she still took an interest in what was going on, regularly attending the Board meetings and the Annual General Meeting, where she always appeared on the platform, ready to answer any questions without fear that she wouldn't know the answers – because Rachel knew *exactly* what was going on at Royle's. Just the way she knew what was going on in her son's life.

She stopped at Jeannie Martin's desk in the big outer office to say hello. Jeannie was Harrison's personal secretary – with a secretary of her own plus two assistants. Hers was a responsible and important job and she had been with Harrison for more than twelve years now. Jeannie knew as much about Royle's business as Rachel did, and almost as much about her family.

'Morning Jeannie,' Rachel called, nodding hello to the assistants and to the dowdily dressed dark-haired girl who seemed out of place in the executive suite . . . Rachel thought she must check on that, the girl didn't look the right calibre for their fiftieth-floor offices!

Laurinda nervously shuffled the sheaf of papers containing the previous month's figures from the eastern stores, peeking at Mrs Royle from the corner of her eye, wondering who she was. My she was smart though, in that navy blue suit with the yellow silk blouse, and those pretty shoes . . . it was exactly the way she would have liked to have dressed, if only she could afford it . . .

'Good morning Mrs Royle,' said Jeannie pleasantly, 'how are you today?'

'Mrs Royle!' thought Laurinda, 'this must be Harrison's mother!' Waiting for the assistant secretary to finish her phone call, she stared furtively at Jeannie and Mrs Royle, eavesdropping on their conversation eagerly. She had volunteered to bring the statements up here when the boy whose job it was had failed to turn up – because Laurinda had deliberately omitted to summon him – hoping that she might see Harrison. In fact she often went out of her way to try to see Harrison, finding excuses for coming up here from the lowly tenth-floor accounting-offices, hoping she might bump into him in a corridor or the elevator. Once she had, and Harrison had nodded politely and asked how she was getting on; but she'd only had time to say 'fine thanks Mr Royle' before he'd got out.

Laurinda hadn't realised until she'd started work here, in the bookkeeping department, just how *important* a man Harrison was. He'd had the power to get her a job in his massive company and change her entire life. And he was so handsome, and so kind, and so . . . sort of – God-like. How that evil Jessie-Ann had captured him she didn't know . . . or rather she did! All Jessie-Ann had to do was twitch her tail like a bitch in heat and the men came running – and poor Harrison was no exception. It wasn't his fault, he couldn't help it . . . no one was safe from her!

'Is it your birthday then, Jeannie?' asked Mrs Royle, pointing to the gold-wrapped parcel on her desk.

'Oh no Mrs Royle, that's Jessie-Ann's birthday present from Mr Royle – or at least it was. I think he's just changed his mind.'

'Changed his mind?' Rachel frowned, staring at the parcel. 'What was it then, books?'

'More than that. Real Estate brochures – Mr Royle wanted to buy her a ranch – out in bluegrass-country, and Jessie-Ann was to make her choice from half a dozen he'd found. Now he says he knows something she wants more – or rather, *first*.'

'I wonder what that is?' queried Rachel, drumming her fingers impatiently.

'I understand it's the new premises for her Model Agency,'

replied Jeannie, adding with a laugh, 'it doesn't seem like such a good swap to me . . . I'd take the dude ranch anytime!'

'I think you're right, Jeannie,' called Rachel, her pale cheeks flushed with sudden anger as she headed towards Harrison's door. It was the first she'd heard about a model business and she intended to find out what was going on right now!

Laurinda gazed after Mrs Royle, stunned. She'd thought that now Jessie-Ann was married – and to a man like Harrison, that she would have mended her evil ways, that she would stay home and look after Jon and her husband – but obviously one man would never be enough for Jessie-Ann. She wanted to be back where she came from, out there in front of the cameras and on the catwalk, parading around so that men could stare at her again, lusting after her . . . Laurinda clenched her fists angrily, crumpling the sheets of paper.

'Yes, what is it?' asked the assistant secretary abruptly, the girl seemed to be in a daze . . .

'Oh, oh . . . here are the figures Mr Royle wanted.' Laurinda thrust the sheaf of papers towards her, noticing suddenly how crumpled they were. 'Oh dear, I'll go back and get you fresh copies . . .' she muttered, embarrassed.

'No need. And you could have just left them on my desk anyway – there was no reason to waste time waiting around.'

'Sorry, sorry,' muttered Laurinda, scuttling towards the door.

The girl glanced after her curiously, 'Who is that nut?' she asked of no one in particular, as she turned away and began to study the figures.

'Good morning Mother,' said Harrison, kissing her on her smooth, well-powdered cheek. She smelled of Chanel No. 5 – as she had for as long as he could remember.

'Harrison, I came to tell you that I'm planning a little party for Jessie-Ann's birthday tomorrow. I've invited some of my friends – and some of yours. And Marcus is coming down from Princeton . . .'

'That's very kind of you Mother,' he replied, wondering why she hadn't asked Jessie-Ann's friends since it was *her* birthday, 'but I'd already planned to take her out to dinner – alone.'

'You're too much alone,' commented Rachel coldly, 'and it's

time that Jessie-Ann met some people, *real* people I mean – not just the sort of person she met when she was a model. I have several good causes in mind that she could lend her name to. After all she is quite famous and there are children's charities that would benefit a great deal from her association with them. As you know the work can be quite demanding,' she glanced up at him through her lashes, 'but of course it wouldn't interfere in any way with her home life, with you and Jon.'

Harrison stared at her amused. He knew his mother well enough to spot one of her little plots. 'Sorry Mother,' he replied evenly, 'but I think Jessie-Ann's going to be pretty busy for a few months – she's planning on opening her own Model Agency.'

'And you are buying her the premises?'

Their dark eyes locked as he replied, 'That's right, yes.'

Rachel sprang from her chair. 'Don't you think that your wife's place is at home? After all Harrison, she's not married to some sales clerk or to an accountant! *She's Mrs Harrison Royle!* And what about your son? Isn't he entitled to have his mother home when he needs her . . . the child is only four months old and already she's planning on leaving him . . . what sort of mother is that?'

'Jon has a very capable nurse and Jessie-Ann would never leave him alone,' replied Harrison evenly, 'and you know as well as I do Mother, that she adores Jon . . . it's out of the question that she would ever "neglect" him.'

Rachel smoothed back her wings of silver hair into their chignon, 'And you know as well as I do Harrison, that apart from anything else, Jessie-Ann is no business woman. She'll have you doing all the work, sorting out all her problems; she'll be bothering you with trivia when you have this corporation to run . . . doesn't the girl realise what is involved?'

'She sees me when I come home at night, tired, wanting nothing more than a drink and a quiet meal together . . .'

'I warn you now, that if you allow her to pursue this, those peaceful evenings will become a thing of the past! Think again, Harrison, for your own sake.'

'I've already thought of my own position – and I think it's time that I – all of us – considered Jessie-Ann's. You are right, she may not be a great business woman, but she's entitled to try,' Harrison shrugged, 'if she fails, then we can always sell off the property.' He didn't add that what he really wanted to say was not *if* she fails . . . but *when* she fails . . . for he knew that what his mother said was true. If she were a success his peaceful days alone with Jessie-Ann were numbered.

'Don't say I didn't warn you,' Rachel replied coldly, stalking to the door, 'and I'll expect you both tomorrow – at eight?'

'We'll be there,' he promised, smiling ruefully.

At the age of twenty, Marcus Royle was a younger version of his father, tall and athletic, with a muscular, wiry body – but with a shock of fair hair where his father's was dark. Marcus played a great game of tennis and was an excellent swimmer, as well as being a more than competent sailor. He was now in his junior year at Princeton and enjoying life very much.

He'd brought Jenny, a girl from college to Rachel's party for Jessie-Ann, warning her up front that she would get the double-edged scrutiny from his grandmother when he introduced her; and Gran had run true to form, eliciting Jenny's background in three or four oblique and carefully casual questions, so that she had her pegged accurately on the ratings. Of course the 'ratings' were Rachel's own, and Marcus didn't give a damn! It just so happened that Jenny's family was as well-off as the Royles – and their money was older – railroad money from way back – not just two generations.

Taking Jenny by the hand he pulled her through the crowd to meet his father and Jessie-Ann. As usual his 'step-mother' looked fantastic – in white silk, that made her golden skin look soft and warm, and her hair look like the colour of late summer wheat-fields. He sure hoped Dad knew how lucky he was – because not only was Jessie-Ann stunning, she was also a sweet-heart. You could see her love for his father shining from her eyes.

'Happy Birthday Jessie-Ann,' he called, kissing her on the cheek.

'Marcus! How lovely to see you. I hope you're not cutting too many classes to be here? Never mind, I'm glad you came anyway. A birthday wouldn't be a birthday without you.'

157

'This is Jenny Carter-Putnam,' he said.

Jessie-Ann smiled at the pretty, dark-haired girl. 'I'm glad you could come Jenny,' she said, 'we need someone to keep Marcus in line.'

'For that,' he said severely, 'I might not give you your birthday present.'

'Then I take it all back!' she laughed, 'I didn't mean it, I promise you.'

'You can damage a guy's reputation, making statements like that,' Marcus said, grinning as he handed over a small box.

Tearing off the silver ribbon Jessie-Ann stared at its contents in delight. 'Oh Marcus, how clever of you, how wonderful . . . look Harrison.'

It was a miniature portrait of herself, painted with infinite fineness and patience by some artist with a delicate touch, on a smooth oval of ivory, framed by a narrow band of gold.

'Why that's wonderful Marcus,' said Harrison, pleased that his son had chosen such a sensitive gift – and one which had obviously taken him a lot of trouble to have made.

'I had it copied from my favourite picture of you,' Marcus told her, 'it's the way I always think of you.'

'I'm so pleased Marcus,' she said gratefully, 'more than that – I'm touched.'

'It's no more than you deserve,' he said lightly. 'Now, what has Dad bought you – probably Paris or something equally as staggering.'

Harrison laughed. 'My gift is much more modest.'

'Your father has bought me a building – it's for *Images*. I'm going to open my agency at last Marcus.'

He knew all about Jessie-Ann's dreams, and he knew his father too. A quick glance at Harrison's face reassured him that for the moment anyhow, Harrison seemed happy to let his wife do her own thing. The conflict between them had been only too obvious to him.

Circling the room with Jenny by his side, Marcus greeted the crowd of family friends and acquaintances, noticing that there was no one present who Jessie-Ann might have invited.

'It was a surprise party Marcus,' his grandmother said reprovingly, when he questioned her about it, 'how could I ask Jessie-Ann for her friends' telephone numbers – that would have given the game away.' He stared at her in amazement as she glided off to talk to her guests, marvelling at her ability to arrange matters so that they always came out her way.

Taking Jenny's hand he guided her through the crowd towards the hallway and the elevator. 'Too many old folks in there for us,' he explained, grinning, 'let's get ourselves a bite of dinner and then head over to the Palladium.'

Harrison glanced at his watch and then at Jessie-Ann. He had a dinner reservation for nine thirty at a little Italian place she knew. 'Shall we?' he asked, sliding his hand across her warm, silken shoulders, longing to be alone with her.

'No one will miss us now,' she agreed, easing through the crowd with Harrison following. In the silent grey-suède elevator he smiled at her guiltily. 'Mother'll never forgive me for that,' he said.

'But I will,' she laughed, kissing him.

The tiny Italian restaurant was a place Jessie-Ann had frequented before she was married, and was just around the corner from her old Central Park West apartment. She'd thought it would be fun to return there with Harrison, away from their usual smart haunts, but the restaurant had changed hands and she stared at him in dismay over the plate of overcooked pasta smothered in a thin, bright red sauce. 'It's still better than Rachel's party,' said Harrison comfortingly, and they both laughed; and they ate the pasta and drank too much rough red wine and Jessie-Ann told him that she'd never had a better birthday present in her life, and she'd never been happier.

Their chauffeur-driven Rolls-Royce was waiting to take them home and in the elevator Harrison pulled her long blonde hair back from her face, and stared at her with that dark, intense gaze that had attracted her from the first. 'I love you Jessie-Ann Royle,' he whispered as the elevator doors opened into the apartment.

Arms around each other, they walked through the vast silk panelled corridors to their room and, barely waiting to pull off their clothes, they made passionate love in their newly decorated apple-green and white bedroom, that reminded her a little of her old room in Montana.

'I love you Harrison,' she murmured afterwards, 'you are my happiness – you and Jon.'

'Why do you need *Images*?' Harrison asked her bewildered, 'when you have so much?'

It was a question that Jessie-Ann was unable to answer.

8

Caroline awoke with a start, staring in puzzlement at the ceiling painted with a midnight cloudscape of moons and stars, slowly remembering that she had moved only yesterday into this converted loft in New York's lower East Side, belonging to an artist friend. She had agreed to apartment-sit while Timmo Sanshi spent six months in Italy finding new inspiration for his next Manhattan exhibition in May. Lucky Timmo! She could use a bit of inspiration in life herself! She had been so sure New York would be her key to a whole new life, but so far nothing seemed to be going quite right.

Broadway was proving even harder to crack than Shaftesbury Avenue and, despite her newly acquired speed-typing course, no producer seemed to be in need of an assistant. Instead Caroline had taken a job as a sales assistant in a smart Park Avenue boutique, but after Maudie's, she'd found it dull. Its rich customers wanted to be made over into exact copies of the latest fashion photographs in *Vogue* even though they were usually much shorter than the models – and often weighed twenty pounds more! Bored with their striving to turn couture into a uniform, Caroline had found a job as a receptionist at a small gallery on the East Side – and that's where she'd met Timmo.

He was small and fragile-looking and half-Japanese, with a shock of silky black hair cut like a shaggy Beatle, and pebble-dark, nearsighted eyes behind thick glasses, that saw the world slightly differently from most people. Timmo's lop-sided, multi-perspective acrylics mixed shapes and space and non-colour in a uniquely attractive way and he was already making a name for himself internationally. But though she had made friends with Timmo and some of the other artists displaying at the gallery, Caroline was restless. On the promise of a position in the Fine Art department at Sotheby's in Manhattan she'd left the gallery but when the Sotheby's job had fallen through at the last minute she'd been very glad to accept Timmo's offer of his apartment – rent-free – in return for her custodial care. It was a tremendous stroke of luck, coming at a time when her financial situation was at a new low. Without the need to pay rent, at least she was sure of a roof over her head and could afford to eat until something else came along.

Caroline gazed at Timmo's painted stars hoping that fate was pushing her in the right direction and that the job at the McConnell Gallery would be the break she needed. She had been a firm believer in fate all her life and, with the exception of one or two disasters – like when Pericles Jago came into her life – it had rarely let her down. She knew that 'luck' was only a question of being in the right place at the right time.

Clutching Pericles' paisley silk pyjama jacket around her small-boned frame, she shivered as she switched on the lamps, staring approvingly at the line of brass uplighters ranged along the inner wall, and thinking worriedly about the future. She still had this foolish dream of working in the theatre – she was willing to start right at the bottom – she'd make tea, run out for sandwiches, sweep floors even – anything to get a foot through the door. If only she could find a door to get through!

Wandering through the loft she examined Timmo's work. The massive anthracite grey and white acrylic surfaces somehow emphasised her loneliness, bringing memories of Pericles. Chilled by the bleak canvases and her thoughts, she looked out of the windows at the snow falling steadily from a sky that matched Timmo's paintings onto a view of New York's shabbier rooftops and buildings, and the sullen, grey-brown Hudson River. Only last night the same windows had seemed to frame a magical kingdom, festooned with the illuminated tinsel-loops of Manhattan's bridges, promising glamour and excitement.

It's no good moping, Caroline told herself sternly, New York was out there, just waiting for someone like her! Tuning the radio to WNEW, she hummed along with Sinatra's 'My Way', belting out the last chorus and forcing herself into a more optimistic mood as she fixed herself some coffee. Running her hands through her short curly brown bob, she did a little jig to get her circulation going, and then she cushioned her head in the triangle formed by her arms and did a Yoga headstand. She grinned at herself reflected in the dark glass of the cabinet doors as she carolled loudly, 'I did it *my* way,' feeling a hundred per cent better. Fate was smiling on her already, she felt sure of it, and somewhere out there, in wonderful glittering Manhattan would be the job of her dreams – if not the man of her desires.

Harrison stared out of the windows of his fiftieth-floor office, watching the snow spiral slowly downwards and wondering what to do about Jessie-Ann. Since she had opened *Images* a couple of months ago, she'd gone from a laughing, animated, carefree girl, to a subdued young woman with an abstracted air. Whenever he asked her about *Images* – careful not to say 'What's wrong?' – just 'how's it going?', she always flashed him a brilliant smile and replied, 'Great, it's OK. I'm doing fine . . . ' leaving him with a sneaking feeling that for once in her life Jessie-Ann wasn't speaking the truth.

He turned to look at her photograph, silver-framed on his big rosewood desk, assessing the changes that *Images* had made. The worried frown and the fact that she never discussed things with him could only mean one thing – she wasn't finding the instant acceptance that she had anticipated. Poor Jessie-Ann, his heart went out to her, the jungle world of big business was showing her its indifferent claws and she wasn't used to rejection.

Harrison paced the floor worriedly. Even though he hadn't really wanted her to open *Images*, he couldn't bear to see her hurting. His hand on the telephone, he contemplated calling her and saying, 'let's have lunch – meet me at 21', just the way they used to; but somehow he felt sure she would say she was too busy, faking him out that all was going well.

'Oh Jessie-Ann, Jessie-Ann,' he groaned, resuming his pacing, 'all I want is for you to be there when I come home at night – you and Jon . . . you don't need to prove yourself to *me*!'

He admitted he was jealous of her independence and new life, but how could he allow his jealousy to stop him from helping her? He had never suggested it – because he knew she was determined to make it as Jessie-Ann Parker, not as Mrs Harrison

Royle – but it would be easy for him to send some business her way. All he had to do was make a call.

Harrison contemplated the bank of telephones on his desk silently. If he made that call it would put *Images* on the road to success – and there was a chance he would lose Jessie-Ann in the process. But if he didn't try to help her, he wouldn't be able to live with himself, knowing she was unhappy. *Goddamnit, all he really wanted was the old Jessie-Ann back, the sunny Montana girl greeting him with that big 'Hi' and a great smile, straight from the heart, when he got home at night.* It was Jessie-Ann's spirit that had captured him even more than her beauty, and if he could give her back her spirit then that's what he must do. Sighing, he buzzed his secretary and placed his call.

Images was located way down on Third Avenue, tucked between a couple of seedy buildings – nothing fancy, just another empty store-front walk-up – but it had high ceilings and space and the area was on the upswing. And its glossy bright blue door with the curving blue neon sign – *Images* – above, opened onto Jessie-Ann's new life.

Her white-brick-walled office was hung with scarlet bulletin boards awaiting the exotic faces of her new *Images* models – those she had yet to find. There was a futuristic blue-steel and leather sofa and a couple of comfortable white-tweed chairs, and her bright blue lucite desk held a battery of scarlet telephones from which she planned to make all those international calls, placing her models in the most important *Vogue* shots and advertising campaigns.

Sitting at her shiny blue desk, she stared at the pile of square white envelopes with her name and *Images* address typed neatly in red on the front. There were now sixteen altogether and after the first two she'd had no need to open them to know exactly what they would say. The theme was crude and monotonous – and very frightening.

And whoever it was had known all about *Images* – almost before they were open for business. The very first day there had been one waiting for her as she'd walked through *Images* door. She'd thought it was a letter from Harrison, maybe wishing her luck . . . but it was the same filth, typed in red . . . and now there was something else . . . he was not only threatening her – this time he mentioned Jon!

YOU ARE NOT GOOD ENOUGH TO BE A MOTHER. YOU MUST DIE SO YOUR CHILD CAN BE BROUGHT UP IN INNOCENCE . . . AND I'M COMING CLOSER . . . YOU NEVER KNOW WHEN I MIGHT APPEAR . . . IT'S TIME FOR REVENGE AND THE KNIFE IS IN MY HAND . . .

She had glanced fearfully at the curtained windows, suddenly aware that she was completely alone. In a panic she'd picked up the phone and dialled Harrison's number. Then before it had time to ring she slammed the receiver down quickly. It was her first day in business and the very first thing she was doing was asking for Harrison's help. She could just imagine Rachel's triumphant 'I told you so – just one day on her own and she's already in trouble . . . if Jessie-Ann were home with her child where she belongs, these things wouldn't happen!'

'Damn Rachel,' she'd thought, fighting back the tears, she'd lived with these stupid letters for years now – she would deal with them by herself. Picking up the receiver again, she'd dialled the number of the ManCo Detective Agency.

'We're dealing with a pathologically obsessive mind here,' Jack Halloran of the ManCo Detective Agency had told her. 'But the fact that disturbs us now is the change in tone from the letters you got before. It's not just the usual porn, there's this new threat of violence here that makes us really unhappy. Mrs Royle, I'd like you to re-think your decision not to inform your husband.'

'No,' she'd replied fiercely, 'I'm not going to bother Harrison with this. After all, I was getting the letters way before I met him. This is *my* problem and I don't want him worrying about me.'

Halloran had sighed, fingering the letter and reading aloud snatches that caught his eye – 'you should be pierced with sharp knives as you have caused others to be pierced', he'd quoted ominously; 'you are not good enough to be a mother so you must die so that your child can be brought up in innocence'; 'It's time for revenge and the knife is in my hand . . .'

His voice had trailed off and she'd stared at him, wide-eyed with alarm. 'I'm not saying there's anything to these threats Mrs

Royle, but you are married to a prominent businessman and that fact may account for the turn the letters have taken. Before, the author seemed content with name-calling – filthy though it was. Won't you please reconsider telling Mr Royle?'

'I want Harrison kept out of this,' she'd replied stubbornly. 'It's something I have to deal with alone.'

'OK,' he'd said with an exasperated sigh, 'but let's not take any chances shall we?'

The very next day a burly young man in jeans and a heavy plaid lumber jacket, looking as innocuous as any workman, had arrived to keep vigilance over her. Sometimes he patrolled the icy street in front and sometimes he sat in the back office, his feet propped on the table drinking endless cups of coffee and rustling the newspapers annoyingly as he sifted through the day's racing form. But he hadn't stopped the letters from coming.

Halloran had finally told her that they were at a dead-end unless the anonymous madman made a move, and Jessie-Ann simply decided to ignore the whole thing – except for keeping Ed Zamurski in the back room. With Ed around she felt safe, but even so, she never opened the letters because she knew their contents would only frighten her more.

Her smart office seemed oppressively silent and pushing aside the envelopes, Jessie-Ann stared gloomily at the telephone, willing it to ring.

Her first week in business she'd sat confidently at her desk dialling every contact she knew on her scarlet telephone; she'd called every account-executive she knew at every ad agency; she'd called all the top-flight photographers as well as some of the lesser ones; she'd spoken to fashion editors at every magazine, catalogue and journal, plus all the models she knew. 'Hi, it's Jessie-Ann,' she'd called happily, 'I just wanted to tell you about *Images*.'

Of course everyone had been *thrilled* to hear from her, they'd been *delighted* with her news and eager for her gossip . . . but no one had called her back. No models haunted her doorstep begging to be taken onto her books, no photographers or fashion editors rang demanding her – or her models' services, though she had assured them she'd be able to get exactly the types they wanted; and no magazines or ad agencies called seeking the new looks and fresh faces that she'd assured them she could deliver. Of course that wasn't quite true. She was caught in the old chicken or the egg syndrome . . . she couldn't go ahead and search out 'new faces' unless the fashion editors and advertising agencies guaranteed her the work.

Sighing, she flipped a tape onto the machine and closed her eyes. The Mozart Requiem cut out the rustle of Zamurski's paper and his irritating smoker's cough, and it matched her mood perfectly as she contemplated *Images'* bleak future. Should she call everyone a third or even fourth time? And become someone whose calls were always answered by a secretary with an impersonal 'sorry, he's away today, I'll leave him your message'? Jessie-Ann knew that route . . . hadn't *she* been guilty of avoiding people like that a couple of times in the past?

The unfamiliar high-pitched bleep of the telephone penetrated her consciousness, disturbing Mozart's beautiful solemnity, and she leapt with surprise, flipping off the tape with one hand and reaching for the receiver with the other.

'*Images* here. Good afternoon,' she said breathlessly.

'Afternoon Jessie-Ann. Stu Stansfield here.'

'Stu! Hi, how are you?' Nicholls Marshall was one of New York's biggest international advertising agencies with offices in London and Paris as well as Manhattan, and Stansfield was the account executive she'd met on her Royle Girl interview. A call from him could only mean business.

'We'd heard you'd opened a new model agency, and as you know, we're always on the lookout for good new faces.'

'Sure,' she replied, wondering frantically where she was going to find the good new faces.

'Of course it would be impossible to use new faces for our *major* advertising campaigns,' Stu went on, 'but we do have catalogue work to offer, and you know that's always a good lead-in for new models. If you can supply the right girls Jessie-Ann, we'd sure like to put the business your way.'

She had a sudden suspicion she knew just which catalogue he had in mind and her heart sank. 'Do you mean the Royle catalogue?' she asked in a small voice.

'Certainly do, Jessie-Ann. Seems a good opportunity to keep

it in the family,' replied Stu jovially, 'and I can't think of anyone better to coordinate it all. With your flair and know-how, all of us here at Nicholls Marshall are convinced we'll have a really great catalogue this time around. And I'm sure I don't need to tell you how much it's worth business-wise, in hard cash . . . we're talking four, five hundred pages here.'

'I know Stu. I remember the catalogues,' she answered quietly.

'It's just a question of the right person for the right job, and we are all convinced that person is you.'

'Thanks Stu. I appreciate that,' she replied politely, making notes on the clean pad in front of her as Stu gave her preliminary details of the job. 'Thanks again,' she said quietly when he'd finished. 'I'll get back to you later this week and let you know what I can do.'

So that was it! Harrison had realised that she couldn't pull *Images* together by herself and had come to her rescue. Jessie-Ann's cheeks burned with embarrassment. *She had been so sure she could make it on her own, and the way she had always planned. Damn it she didn't want to be stifled by the Royle aura!*

Tears of anger and defeat trickled down her face as she thought over Stu Stansfield's call. He was talking large amounts of money, but even so, she couldn't accept the job. She didn't want a lift up the ladder of success from Harrison. And anyway, she realised defeatedly, she had no new models to offer, and no idea how to go about putting together an entire catalogue.

It seemed as if Rachel Royle had been right after all, she thought, stifling a sob. Rachel had been so smug and smiling on her visits to Jon the last few days, and you could bet it was because she had sensed defeat. What could she do, Jessie-Ann wondered, dabbing at her tears with a fresh wad of Kleenex? Should she take on just the fashion section and do it all herself? Mrs Royle modelling Royle's catalogue – that should go down big with Rachel!

'Sorry Miss,' called the New York cabbie, jolting Caroline from her dreams of Broadway success, 'we got traffic backed-up all the way down Third – you'd get there quicker walking . . .'

Wrapping her big yellow duffel coat around her, Caroline

braved the icy wind ripping through New York's canyons, as she hurried down Third Avenue in search of the McConnell Gallery. The girl who'd given her the directions on the phone had said to look for a small street – almost an alley – snaking off between a Vietnamese restaurant and an Italian grocery store; but with the wind blowing the snow in her eyes, it was impossible to find it. She walked the same block three times before she spotted what she thought must surely be it.

Turning thankfully into the side-street out of the wind, she glanced from side to side looking for McConnell's, but could see nothing that resembled an art gallery. The street was drab and littered, and the only place that looked the least bit interesting was the whitewashed building with the brightly painted blue door and a blue neon sign above. *Images* was all it said, with no explanation as to its business and Caroline stared at it doubtfully. For all she knew it might be a high-class brothel. Still, even if it were, someone there would be able to tell her where the McConnell Gallery was. Tapping smartly on the door, she walked in, and stared in astonishment at Jessie-Ann's familiar face.

'Goodness,' Caroline exclaimed, shocked, 'I didn't expect to find *you* here!'

'Do we know each other?' asked Jessie-Ann, mopping her swollen eyes on a soggy Kleenex.

'No, we don't,' said Caroline with a sympathetic smile. 'Actually I was looking for the McConnell Gallery but I seem to have ended up in the wrong place – as usual! I'm awfully sorry,' she added, embarrassed, 'I'll push off and leave you to your misery.'

Despite her tears Jessie-Ann laughed. 'Please don't go,' she begged, realising that it was probably the first time she'd laughed in a week, 'I can't stand being alone with my misery any longer.'

'That bad, eh?' asked Caroline, sympathetically.

She nodded. 'That bad.'

'Tell you what,' Caroline suggested impulsively, 'it looks awfully lonely in here. If you can show me where the McConnell Gallery is, I'll guarantee you a drink – it'll only be white wine or designer water though – the New York conscience and diet drinks!'

Jessie-Ann laughed again, emerging from behind her lucite

desk and offering Caroline her hand. 'I'm Jessie-Ann Parker,' she said.

'The whole world must be aware of that!' exclaimed Caroline. 'I'll tell you something, when I was at school it was *your* pictures *my* boyfriends pinned on their walls – and now I see why. Even with your red eyes you're beautiful. Not that I *mind* you being beautiful,' she added with a grin, 'but I think I should warn you I've always hated tall girls!'

Ed Zamurski's bulk filled the doorway between the offices and Caroline stared at him in surprise. He was as out of place in the sharp, chic, city office as a cowboy at a vicarage garden party. 'You all right Jessie-Ann?' he enquired shrugging his big shoulders into a faded red-check Pendleton jacket.

'Just fine Ed. I'm on my way to the McConnell Gallery with . . .?'

'Caroline,' she told them beaming. 'Caroline Courtney.'

Ed Zamurski paced a few yards behind them as they hurried along the icy street in the direction of the Gallery. Glancing nervously over her shoulder, Caroline decided that he must be Jessie-Ann's 'minder' . . . but why on earth should she need one? Was Harrison Royle afraid his wife might be kidnapped, or what?

Jessie-Ann just knew she was going to like Caroline – she was the most refreshing person she'd talked to in months. She followed her into the McConnell Gallery smiling as Caroline's dismissive glance swept the dark, abstract oil-paintings lining the walls. Then she told the owner firmly that she didn't think his job was suitable for her. With that she swept Jessie-Ann off to the Oak Room at the Plaza for drinks.

'Try treating New York as if you were a tourist,' she advised Jessie-Ann blithely, 'that way it's much more fun. Now tell me, would you have come to the Oak Room usually? Of course not. But my dear, just look at all those men!'

Her eyes rounded with pleasure at the sight of so many apparently unattached men, drinking bourbon on the rocks and discussing terribly important business deals, making Jessie-Ann laugh. In no time at all she found herself on her third champagne cocktail and confessing all her problems to Caroline. 'You see, I just can't seem to get started,' she admitted finally. 'I expected the phones to be ringing all day with offers of jobs, and I thought models would be lining up at my door asking to sign up with me – I mean, *I worked* with all these people Caroline – *for years!*'

Caroline stared around the Oak Room, her face impassive, sipping her champagne cocktail, and Jessie-Ann glanced at her uncomfortably. She'd done it again, opened up her big mouth . . . of course this stranger wasn't interested in her tales of woe. 'Sorry,' she muttered, pushing back her chair to leave, 'I shouldn't have bothered you with all my problems . . .'

'Sit down!' commanded Caroline. 'Can't you see I'm thinking!' She frowned, nibbling on a handful of peanuts, as Jessie-Ann sat, surprised.

'It seems to me,' she said at last, 'that you are not thinking in broad enough terms. *Images* itself is a good idea, but it's only the core of a much wider concept. What I mean Jessie-Ann, is why represent only the models? Tell me, who earns the most money per day – the top model – or the photographer? And the answer to this next question is something you know from experience – *who lasts longer?* Isn't the person behind the camera *the true star*? And that person will still be around twenty years from now – only getting better. Think of it as *theatre* Jessie-Ann! Think of all the people involved in creating "a star" – the make-up artists, the hairdressers, the fashion stylists, the models and the photographers. *Of course you should represent them all*! And why not take it a step further and have your own studios? Then you could supply everything a client needs all under your own roof. Sell them a *package* Jessie-Ann!' she concluded triumphantly, her face alight with enthusiasm.

Jessie-Ann stared at her, wondering if she could be right? Of course there was no way *Images* would be able to persuade already established photographers and top models to come in on such a scene, but hadn't her idea originally been to start with fresh new faces? Today's photographers-apprentices and today's small-town beauties were tomorrow's stars . . .

'Any photographer who signs with you should get the use of your studio at very special rates,' Caroline decided, 'and let *Images* buy cameras to rent out to the photographers, because when they are just starting out they can't afford to buy the best;

then they'll be able to choose from your models and book your make-up people and stylists. Of course,' she added, a trace of doubt creeping into her voice for the first time, 'you'll need to find a studio and that might cost quite a lot. In fact, to get it all off the ground economically, I'm afraid you're going to need quite a lot of capital – or, at least a couple of really big jobs.'

'You're not going to believe this,' exclaimed Jessie-Ann excitedly, 'but the reason I was crying this morning was because someone offered me exactly that – *a really big job*.'

'*You were crying over that?*'

'It's for Royle's,' admitted Jessie-Ann, 'I know Harrison must have asked his advertising agency to let me do the catalogue. *Images* was my own idea and I guess I just don't want to feel like Royle's are giving me a helping hand.'

Caroline shook her curly head at Jessie-Ann's foolishness. 'Take it,' she advised, 'how else do you think other people get where they're aiming if not by using every contact they've ever made? The Royle catalogue will set you on the road to success.'

Jessie-Ann suddenly felt the return of her natural joie-de-vivre. 'Tell you what,' she exclaimed, 'the old warehouse in back of my office is for sale. It would make a great studio, and I've got enough money saved to be able to buy it without asking Harrison . . .'

'And you know what else?' asked Caroline, 'I know young models in London who'd *die* for a shot at the bigtime in New York! We'd need to search here and in Europe, for exciting young photographers; we'll check whose assistants are up and coming. We'll place ads in *Women's Wear Daily*, and call back all your establishment contacts in the ad agencies and tell them what you're up to. And we'll need a great PR – someone who'd make *Images* sound the most exciting and intriguing event in the fashion world for years . . .'

'Caroline, you're a *miracle*!' exclaimed Jessie-Ann happily. 'Just as I'm about to quit, you fall through my door from out of nowhere, and give me all the answers I'm looking for!'

'Good,' replied Caroline, 'because I was looking for a few answers myself. I need a job.'

Jessie-Ann's uninhibited laugh rolled through the murmur and clink of the cocktail hour in the Oak Room. 'I was just about to say – I can't do without you. Images *needs you, Caroline Courtney!'*

9

Danae's brand-new and ruinously-expensive Rollei lay unused in a corner of her tiny apartment along with the second-hand Hasselblad, the Nikon and the Polaroid, the special lenses and the tripod. Every now and again she ventured out on the streets of Manhattan or into the countryside, taking pictures of soaring glass buildings or wind-tossed trees, developing them afterwards in the make-shift darkroom that was also her tiny bathroom. She'd arranged the results along her apartment walls until they finally covered the entire cramped space and it was costing her a fortune in film and lab expenses, for the special grained papers she needed – money she could no longer afford. Most of her father's legacy had been spent on equipment, and what was left had been used to pay the rent on her apartment until the jobs came along. But so far her ads in the trade journals had not resulted in a single commission and she realised, reluctantly, that the transition from 'Brachman's Assistant' into 'Danae Lawrence – Great Photographer' involved far more than just letting it be known that you were available.

After six months, she'd finally faced the fact that she would have to look for another job, but positions for assistants were scarce, and trekking around the photographic agencies she'd discovered their books were already overloaded with would-be Avedons, Baileys or Terry O'Neils, all just as convinced of their own talent as she was.

Danae had pinned all her hopes on this morning's interview with a photographer's agent and she stared at him, baffled, when he said bluntly that she'd better be prepared to start at the bottom.

'But I did! *I mean I was Brachman's assistant for two years!*' she cried, spilling her sample colour slides onto his black and white tiled floor in her agitation. He flicked the ash from his filter cigarette, watching impatiently as she scrabbled on the slippery tiles, recapturing her photographs. 'It's the chicken or the egg,' he said. 'The Alieri pics were OK – but you never followed up on them. If you wanted to specialise in candid shots like those – then that's what you should have been doing all this time. Maybe you should go back to Brachman – see if he'll help you, maybe he'll let you do some of the shots, get a few credits . . . now *that* would mean something. But these . . .' he waved his cigarette disdainfully at her portfolio, 'these are all meaningless. Of course I'm not saying they're not *good*,' he added hastily, as he met Danae's stricken gaze, 'but you have no credits and no name. And therefore,' he said with a dismissive shrug, '*no impact*!'

Danae thought bitterly of her London pictures and Brachman's stolen credit, as well as her Tomaso Alieri photos that apparently were worthless too, credit-wise, 'Damn it,' she thought, fighting back the tears, 'oh damn, she never cried . . . *never* . . . not even when she was little and her mother forgot to come to pick her up at school . . .'

'Look, I'll tell you what,' the agent said, writing her name on the pad in front of him, 'I'll keep you in mind if anything comes through.'

'Thanks.' She dabbed at her eyes, knowing that of course he didn't mean it.

'Jesus!' he exclaimed, eyeing her tears angrily as he stalked towards the door, holding it open and hurrying her through. 'I'm an *agent* y'know, not *God*! I can't *create* work for unknowns. Remember I've got to earn a living too – and fifteen percent of Danae Lawrence surely ain't gonna pay my overhead!'

She could hear him still muttering angrily about 'girls who wanted to start at the top' as he slammed his office door and hurried back to answer his constantly-ringing telephone.

Her own phone was ringing as she unlocked the door to her apartment later that evening. Dropping her leather jacket and her portfolio on a chair, she rushed to answer it.

'Hi, Danae,' said a familiar voice, 'this is Rick Valmont.'

'Valmont!' she exclaimed, wondering what on earth he could want. She hadn't spoken to him since Brachman had fired her. 'Well . . . hi . . . I mean, how are you?'

'Listen, Danae, I've left Brachman and I'm setting up on my own. I've got quite a few jobs lined up and I'm gonna need an assistant. I remembered you were pretty good when you were with Brachman, and now I hear you need the work?'

Valmont was offering *her* a job? But she *hated* Valmont – and he despised her . . . or at least he had when she was in competition for his position with Brachman. But Valmont also knew that she was a hard worker, and no doubt he planned to use her the way Brachman had – fetching and carrying, constantly at his beck and call. *Oh it was so unfair! She* should have been employing *him. She* was a far better photographer than he was . . . she'd always thought Valmont's lighting crude and she'd noticed how often Brachman had had to correct him . . . and the shots that he'd set up had turned out stiff and ungraceful, and without any meaning. Yet here he was, in business, while she couldn't even get arrested!

'Well, Danae,' Valmont called, sounding impatient, 'what do you say, yes or no? I'll pay you what Brachman paid and you can start right away.'

'Right away?' Cradling the phone against her chest, she considered. It would mean that she'd be earning money for the first time in six months – but he was offering her only the same salary Brachman had, and the bastard knew that Brachman had underpaid her simply because he was Brachman and could get away with it! Valmont was trying to get her cheap . . . damn it oh damn it, it was a man's world all right. 'Let me think about it, Valmont,' she said, managing to keep her voice steady, 'I'll give you a call tomorrow and let you know.'

'Make it in the morning – early,' he commanded, 'or I'll have to get someone else.'

He hung up without saying goodbye and Danae slammed down the phone angrily. Slumped in a chair she contemplated her snow-stained suede boots that were already beginning to look a little shabby. The copy of *Women's Wear Daily* that she'd picked up at the news-stand lay on the floor next to her portfolio, and picking it up she flicked through its pages, examining each photograph and its credit jealously. The PR blurb about *Images* jumped out at her from its pages – a new agency with its own studio included in a package deal . . . they were offering work for 'the right' young photographers . . .

She was waiting on *Images* doorstep early the next morning, scuffing impatiently up and down the snowy alley off Third Avenue, staring at the brightly lacquered door with the legend *Images* in glinting blue neon above. It was, she prayed, the door to her future.

A short while later Danae perched on the edge of Jessie-Ann's blue desk, watching their faces anxiously for a reaction. She breathed a small sigh of relief as Caroline sifted slowly through her New York pictures and smiled. If she were smiling, it must mean that she liked them . . . she was over hurdle number one! Fingers tightly crossed, she forced herself not to stare at Jessie-Ann who was poring over her London negatives displayed on the lightbox, trying hard to appear more nonchalant and at ease, afraid that if her anxiety showed she might put them off. She hadn't realised that *Images* would be Jessie-Ann, but that was a bonus because they spoke the same language . . . if only they liked her photographs . . . if only they liked *her* . . . if only . . . oh please, *please* say 'Yes', she prayed, glancing over her shoulder again, trying to catch the expressions on their faces . . .

The girl was a genius, thought Caroline excitedly, her photographs were worthy of an exhibition! Danae had framed the windy, grey sky in the piercing glass tips of Manhattan's sky-scrapers, giving them an unreal, other planet look, as though they were lost towers trembling in a futuristic time-warp. Caroline's trained, artistic eye noted the imaginative composition, the contrasts of grainy texture against smooth, the dramatic play of shadow and light . . . 'These are wonderful,' she said, holding one at a distance and studying it admiringly, 'look, Jessie-Ann, they're fantastic!'

'And so are these,' agreed Jessie-Ann glancing up at Danae, 'but I'm afraid I've seen them before – in *Vogue* – under Brachman's name.'

Danae blushed furiously as they stared at her. 'Of course you have,' she retorted, 'but that's because Brachman stole my credit! He was taken ill in Paris when we were photographing the collections last fall and he sent *me* to London instead. That's *my* work you see there – I chose the models, the locations, the clothes . . . *everything*. Of course you don't have to believe me,' she

177

added defiantly, 'and I know it sounds crazy, but it's true. Brachman stole my work. The man's a megalomaniac. I should know, I worked for him for two *long* years!'

Jessie-Ann wondered if it were only Danae's credit Brachman had stolen . . . she knew the photographer – and his reputation with women. 'Of course I believe you,' she replied, 'Brachman is capable of anything; life holds no rules for that self-proclaimed genius. How *dare* he steal your pictures! Caroline's right, your work *is* wonderful. Oh I'm so thrilled,' she cried, crossing the room in two long strides and throwing her arms around her. 'Will you consider joining us, Danae? You'll be our very first photographer. In fact, you'll be our first *anything*! But I warn you, you'll have to take your chances, we've only just started!'

'I'm all yours,' she replied, not knowing whether to cry or laugh with relief, 'just tell me what you want and I'll do it.'

'Danae,' said Caroline with a grin, 'you can take your pick from the entire Royle catalogue. Where do you want to start?'

Her eyes widened with amazement. 'You mean Royle's *whole* catalogue?'

'Right! It's our first job. And it's all yours – or as much of it as you want,' cried Jessie-Ann. 'Oh I know it's just catalogue work, and not a ten-page spread in *Vogue*, but we'll get that one day, I *know* we will. So, are you with us?'

Danae ran her hands excitedly through her rumpled copper mane, 'Of course I'm with you! It's like the Three Musketeers – "one for all and all for one", as d'Artagnan would have said . . . and I promise you this, Jessie-Ann, Caroline,' she beamed at them each in turn, 'you'll get the best catalogue Royle's has had in fifty years!'

There was a knock and they looked round at the young couple standing by the door. The boy was maybe nineteen, stylish with a slick, thirties-looking haircut and an ancient black overcoat from the same era. The girl was a foot taller than he, slender as a reed, with elongated features and a wide scarlet mouth. Her thick black hair was cut in a perfect asymmetric slant and hung smooth and straight to her fragile shoulders. Wound about in layers of scarlet, grey and black knits, she looked superb.

'Hi,' he said confidently, 'my name's Hector, I'm a hairstylist.

178

And this is Anabelle – she's my model. I brought her along so you could see her hair. I've got photographs as well, but I thought there was nothing better than real life – so here she is.'

'But she's *fantastic*!' cried Jessie-Ann, in delight. 'And so is her hair.' Her sparkling blue eyes transmitted the message to Caroline, it was beginning to happen at last. *Images* was on its way!

After that, it seemed as though the place was perpetually crowded with would-be stylists, models, and photographers, and Jessie-Ann was forced to retreat into the back office along with Ed Zamurski, to interview all the hopeful young applicants, while Caroline manned the front desk and fielded the telephone calls. Sometimes she thought the phone would never stop ringing, but it was at six o'clock, when they finally locked the door, that the *real* work began.

The warehouse in back of the office had been converted into a simple whitewashed studio with a gallery at one end, and Danae moved her equipment in immediately. The Royle catalogue clothes were already hanging on rails ready for photography and she and Jessie-Ann sifted through them expertly, discussing what sort of models to use, and style and format. They talked long hours into the night, while Caroline took notes of what they needed, and interviewed a succession of young and talented stylists until Danae found a girl who suited her and understood what she wanted.

At the end of six weeks, *Images* had a dozen models on its books, and one other photographer, as well as half a dozen stylists, hairdressers and make-up artists. Danae was already cutting a swathe through the Royle catalogue work, giving their simple traditional fashions a glossy new look in luxurious settings of panelled, firelit rooms and spacious flower-filled terraces. She created the ambience of Wimbledon in the *Images* studio for Royle's new line of tennis wear, and a smart young poolside party for their swim-wear, keeping her colours bright and primary so they seemed filled with sunshine. But Merry McCall and the 'Royle Girl' line were being photographed on the West Coast by Dino Marley, flown in specially from London. It upset her, but

179

Danae knew now that she'd make it to the top. She had her foot through the door at last, and she would work as hard and as long as it took to gain recognition. The first seeds of the power that would make her strong against the Brachmans of this world were in her hands – and it was a power that would make her stronger than any of her rivals – *and* any of her models or sitters.

10

On the tenth floor Laurinda waited for the elevator to descend,
hoping she'd timed it right. If the conversation she'd overheard
at the coffee machine this morning was correct, then Harrison
was flying to San Francisco and would leave the building no later
than 11.30. She pressed the buttons again, examining her watch
anxiously, hoping she hadn't missed him, but it was still only
11.25 and she'd been here for ten minutes, checking every elevator
as it descended. She'd been absent from the accounts department
for ages because she'd gone to the ladies' room first to brush her
hair, applying her new cerise lipstick to her dry lips and spraying
herself lavishly with the perfume she'd bought to use on special
occasions. And what could be more special than seeing Harrison?

With the exception of Scott Parker, Laurinda had never found
anything to admire in any man. She despised them all. But
Harrison Royle was different. His politeness towards her – treating her as though she were his equal – his gentleness, and especially his pushing the power-buttons and getting her to New
York and this job – as well as getting her Mom out of her life –
had given him a god-like status in her eyes.

With a bit of luck the elevator would be empty and it would
be just the two of them . . .

Laurinda had expected Jessie-Ann to be a bit more friendly
once she came to New York, thinking she would be able to
infiltrate her life, but the months had gone by and she hadn't
once been asked over to the Royles' luxurious apartment for a
bite of supper or to babysit for little Jon – let alone to one of the
fancy parties she supposed Jessie-Ann was always giving. And of
course, she rarely managed to see Harrison alone in the office –
even though she'd made a thousand excuses to go up to the fiftieth
floor, until the secretary had told her, sharply, to stop wasting
her time and send the messenger instead. But it was Harrison
who had made sure someone found Laurinda a little studio

apartment, and the Parkers who had seen that her mother was looked after in the State facility. And good riddance too, her mother could stay there for ever for all Laurinda cared – she was surely never gonna go back and visit her! If only it was as easy to get rid of her father – oh not physically, he was long gone in that sense – but his image stuck in Laurinda's mind, and even when she forced herself to forget him he resurfaced, subliminally, like in those clever television commercials.

She could still recall, as if in a big-screen close-up, his coarse, pocked skin; she could feel its grainy, sweaty texture as he loomed over her; and she could smell his odours of stale sweat and ammonia . . . Laurinda could remember her father's arrogant strutting walk and the way his lank black hair fell across his brow, shining with grease, and in her dreams she felt the bulk of his body stabbing her . . . The only thing she couldn't remember about her father was his voice . . . though she could recall every word he'd ever said when they were alone together in her room. They were the same words she used in the letters to Jessie-Ann – because it was *Jessie-Ann* who deserved them . . .

With a ping the elevator doors slid open jolting Laurinda back to the present and her startled eyes met Harrison Royle's.

'Going down Laurinda?' he asked pleasantly.

'Yes . . . Yes please, Mr Royle.' She stepped inside quickly. Harrison was alone and she had a few seconds when he was all hers!

'How are things?' asked Harrison with a tired smile, his mind a million miles away – or at least a couple of miles – just as far as Third Avenue and *Images*. He'd asked Jessie-Ann to come with him today to the preliminary meetings for the new 'Royle Girl Show' in San Francisco but even though he'd said he could use her advice, she'd been too busy. Ever since she'd met that little dynamo, Caroline Courtney, things were really happening for *Images*. Of course the Royle catalogue job had given them the financial input they needed and now they were busy putting the finishing touches on their studio and searching for new talent. All it meant to Harrison was that now Jessie-Ann was too busy to spend a week in San Francisco with him. Oh she was apologetic and sweet, but he had to admit it hurt . . .

'You look awful tired, Mr Royle,' offered Laurinda with a concerned smile.

'What? Oh, do I, Laurinda? Well, it goes along with the job I guess. Royle's keeps me on the move,' he replied, wondering whatever possessed the girl to wear that unbecoming shade of lipstick – and that overwhelming musky perfume; it was so strong it took his breath away. 'How's the work going?' he asked, edging further into his corner of the elevator and managing a smile. 'Keeping you busy are they?'

Laurinda sighed. 'That's just it, Mr Royle, they don't keep me busy enough. Oh it's not their fault,' she added hastily, 'it's just that I'm real quick and – well the fact of the matter is, Mr Royle, the position is really too junior for someone with my capabilities. I know I'm still fairly new here, but really I'm a lot better than some of the others in the office.'

'I'm sorry to hear that,' replied Harrison, as the elevator door opened, 'but I'm afraid there's not much I can do about it. Seniority counts in offices like this you know. Of course you mustn't think you owe Royle's any loyalty, Laurinda, just because of the way it happened. We're not a company to hold a person back from new opportunities.'

'Oh, Mr Royle,' she gasped shocked, 'I wouldn't dream of leaving you! Unless . . . well – I just sort of wondered . . . oh well, no it doesn't matter . . . you're in a hurry and anyway I can't ask you any more favours . . .'

Carson, his chauffeur, already with the door of the Rolls open, was waiting, but the girl looked so distressed, he couldn't just walk away . . . after all she was Jessie-Ann's protégée . . .

'What is it, Laurinda?' he asked, stepping to one side to let the other passengers leave the elevator. 'Are you worried about your mother? You know Jessie-Ann and I will do what we can to help.'

'That's just it, Mr Royle. I wonder if Jessie-Ann *could* help me. I haven't liked to ask because I know she's so busy . . . but well you see, I'm a small town girl, Mr Royle, and I feel lost in this big company. I thought if Jessie-Ann needed someone to help with *Images* – well it would suit me down to the ground. I really feel I'd be valuable there – I'm very good at my job . . . I'd surely see that *Images'* books were kept in tip-top shape. It

183

would be more like family you see, and I could help in other ways, like I did for her father.'

Laurinda's dark eyes glinted with a hint of tears and Harrison glanced at her nervously. 'I understand,' he said quietly. 'You feel like a small cog in a big piece of machinery here at Royle's. I guess for someone from your background, it's all a bit anonymous. I'll speak to Jessie-Ann and see what she can do.'

Laurinda watched as he hurried through the glass doors and into the waiting car. As the chauffeur pulled out into the busy mid-morning traffic she noticed Harrison pick up the car phone and dial a number. Perhaps he was already calling Jessie-Ann about her. Her plan was working. Soon she'd be able to be near Jessie-Ann all the time – and then she'd see that she kept to the path of righteousness. She would save Jessie-Ann from her own evil – and God forgive her if she didn't repent!

11

Stu Stansfield liked what he saw. Danae's photographs for the Royle catalogue were clean, crisp and contemporary; she'd managed to make the clothes come first and the models second, yet they had personality. They were young but not aggressively so, and those used for the matronly and larger sizes managed to look mature and approachable. Even the little kids were regular kids, not the sort of brats you wanted to heave a kick at! And although all the photography had been done in *Images* studios, she'd managed to infuse the sets with warmth and sunshine, so that no one would ever guess it was just a set – or else she'd gone the other way and lined up her swimsuit models in front of a frankly-fake backdrop, whooping and leaping and hollering, with rubber-ducks, water-wings and toy sailboats clutched in their hands. And her sumptuous oak-panelled library made Royle's inexpensive line of fake-furs look regal enough for a Queen.

Stu leaned back in his leather chair, hands clasped behind his head, smiling happily. Royle's catalogue this year would steal a little of the Laura Ashley romanticism, plus a hefty dash of the glossy travel-brochure . . . landscapes, transatlantic liners, lavish country houses. No more page after page of flat photographs . . . Danae Lawrence and Jessie-Ann had revolutionised Nicholls Marshall's entire approach.

It was a good thing Rachel Royle was away on a cruise because she was certainly not going to approve; in fact that was probably the understatement of the century! It was Rachel who had always insisted that the catalogue stick close to her late husband's original concept, with only minor changes over the years. And Stu couldn't say she'd been wrong because Royle's mail-order sales had never faltered; but neither had they increased. He could feel the beginnings of an almighty family row brewing here, once Rachel got a look at it. But it was Harrison himself who had instructed them to give Jessie-Ann and *Images* a free rein, and it was up to him to handle his mother. Please God he could cope! A fight with the indomitable Mrs Royle was not something Stu looked forward to.

The red light on his phone blinked insistently and he picked it up, still concentrating on the batch of photographs spread across his desk. '*Images* for you, Mr Stansfield,' his secretary informed him.

He waited for the click to connect him and then said, 'Hi, Jessie-Ann, how're y'doing?'

'Mr Stansfield, this isn't Jessie-Ann. It's Laurinda Mendosa, *Images'* bookkeeper. Sorry to bother you, but I thought I'd better talk to you first and then maybe you can speak to your accounts department.' Laurinda paused for a moment, but he said nothing so she continued. 'You know of course that *Images* is a very new company, and it would surely help our cash-flow situation here, Mr Stansfield, if your accounts department could be a little more prompt with their payments on the Royle catalogue work. They have been a month or six weeks late on every payment so far, and you know how difficult it is for small businesses to take that kind of cash-flow pressure?'

'I wasn't aware of that situation,' commented Stu, surprised.

'People in your position rarely are, Mr Stansfield, but it is a common accounting ploy. I'd just be grateful, in this case, if you could see it doesn't happen again. After all, we wouldn't want Harrison to get too upset would we?'

He stared at the receiver, stunned. This girl was *threatening* him! And how come *Images'* bookkeeper called Harrison Royle, *Harrison*? 'I'll get my chief accountant on to it, Miss Mendosa,' he said, replacing the receiver abruptly.

Laurinda sat back in her chair, a satisfied little smile playing around her lips. When Caroline returned she'd be able to tell her that from now on Nicholls Marshall would pay on time! She knew Caroline had been worried about it.

Now she had her foothold at *Images*, she planned to consolidate it; she would make herself indispensable . . . good old trustworthy Laurinda who could be relied upon to do her work efficiently – as well as any other odd jobs that nobody else could find time for. Oh yes, in a very short while they'd wonder how they ever managed without her! She'd already put that slimy bastard Stansfield in his place. He'd *know* who she was from now on, she'd made sure of that by dropping Harrison's name.

Last time Stansfield had been here, he'd been all over Jessie-Ann, hugging and kissing her, smarming around her because she was Harrison's wife. He'd praised Danae to the skies too, and chatted with Caroline about London and about art, but he'd never noticed Laurinda, waiting in the background. She was just an office employee to him; but that's where he was *wrong*. He didn't know that she was Harrison's friend, that Harrison looked after her, helped her . . . and he didn't know that she counted herself as Harrison's guardian angel, and that soon it would be *she* who was looking after *him*. Harrison needed her, and so did young Jon, and one day they would be grateful that she was there, in Jessie-Ann's place.

Opening the top left hand drawer of her workmanlike metal desk, she took out a box of Kleenex, feeling in the soft layers of tissues for the blunt-handled pruning knife she'd hidden there. The blade was worn thin from years of use and the tip was broken where her father, in a towering rage, had once hurled it at their kitchen door. He'd used the knife for pruning roses and lilacs, and had spent hours stropping it against an old hard-leather belt, until the edge was honed to a gleaming fineness that could slice through a tough-skinned watermelon in one swift, easy blow. Laurinda remembered the two halves, gleaming coral-red with their seeds scattered and their juices dripping from the plastic-topped kitchen table, staining her mother's immaculate linoleum-tiled floor.

But it wasn't time for that yet, she told herself briskly. There was a lot to be done first. Her main problem was how to get closer to Harrison. She had still never been invited to his home, but then Jessie-Ann spent so much more time here at *Images* it wasn't surprising. The only way she could see to get to Harrison was through young Jon. He was over a year old now and toddling all over the place. Jessie-Ann had the Nanny bring him to *Images* most afternoons because she was too busy to get home to see him, and all those stupid models and hairdressers treated him as though he were a little pet dog, taking it in turns to cuddle him,

187

bringing him toys and giving him lipsticky kisses. Already they were corrupting his innocence! And already his mother's tainted life was being imposed on him.

Laurinda replaced the knife carefully in the box of Kleenex and closed the drawer. Time was of the essence; for little Jon's sake she would have to make a move soon. But she must make her plans carefully. And they must be foolproof. Then she would free Harrison and Jon from Jessie-Ann's corruption, and, when it was all over, naturally she would take her place. *She* would protect Harrison from evil and of course baby Jonathan would be like her own son.

Caroline emerged from her meeting with *Images*' newly appointed PR company, well pleased with what she had accomplished. Now that *Images* was solidly into business, she meant to see that its name became a household word, and the sooner the better. Already it was being picked up in the trade magazines, and talked of on Seventh Avenue, as well as the Madison Avenue gossip. With the clinching of the Avlon Cosmetics deal the time was exactly right for the big PR push.

It was Jessie-Ann who'd initiated the Avlon deal, but it was Caroline who had brought it to final triumphant completion. And Danae's work had been examined – practically under a microscope – by Avlon's advertising agency execs. The new photographs she'd taken of Jessie-Ann – casting her in a different, softer, more mature and gentle role, sort of a cross between Grace Kelly and Catherine Deneuve instead of the young, healthy-animal Jessie-Ann – had flipped their minds. Danae had the Avlon Cosmetics job in *her* pocket and *Images* had one of advertising's most lucrative contracts of the year in *theirs*.

All they had to do now was find the right model. Jessie-Ann had refused to do any more modelling, so that was out – even though she could have earned a fortune. And although money was the least of her personal problems it was still *Images* main one because they were eager to expand. Caroline flipped mentally through the short list of their accounts; there was Royle's of course, and the nationwide travel company wanting a new season's brochures, and then there was the rock group who needed an album cover and PR shots plus several smaller, but prestigious accounts. And now Avlon.

Stepping briskly, she cut across Madison and headed cross-town down Fifty-First, towards Third Avenue. The sun was shining suddenly on what had been a grey October day, and just last week she'd moved into her own proud little apartment on Central Park West, close by the Lincoln Centre. Absolutely everything was right with her life . . . or *almost* everything. She'd never heard another word from Pericles Jago, though she had dutifully done her tour of the Galleries for him.

It wasn't that she'd actually *minded* that much when Pericles married Evita, thought Caroline, dodging traffic like a true New Yorker, but she minded being taken for a fool. And she had been foolish about Pericles. *Very* foolish. 'Never again,' she thought, turning the corner into *Images*' narrow street, from now on she'd be footloose and fancy free, and she'd commit her heart to no one. Anyway, work left her no time for love, and her life was all the better for that. Face it, Caroline she told herself, grinning, as she pushed open *Images*' door, in the six months *Images* has been in business, you've never been happier in your entire life!

Images was growing faster than any of them had ever imagined; Danae was cutting a mini-swathe through the photographic and advertising world with her innovative, fresh look, and with her grainy, black and white shots – often in outlandish locations – and her throwaway approach to grand clothes and casual wear alike. *Images* had already grown from a single studio to two and they were wondering how to juggle their finances so that they could expand further and purchase the building next door, which would give them enough space for two *more* studios.

Caroline liked to think that *Images* was Broadway in capsule form, each studio putting on its own show, sometimes two or three, or even four a day. A morning, a matinee and an evening performance – and each had its own cast of characters, scenery and script. It was exactly Caroline's métier and she'd immersed herself in it totally, as had Danae and Jessie-Ann. And therein lay a problem. It was all right for Caroline to play the lady executive – full-time – but Jessie-Ann had a husband and a child and a home life that demanded *equal* time. And the simple fact was that Jessie-Ann wasn't doing that. Caroline sighed as she shrugged off her coat and turned to examine the pile of mail on her desk. It was the one cloud on *Images*' horizon, and it surely loomed like a big one!

'Caroline, can I talk to you for a minute?' asked Laurinda.

Caroline noted Laurinda's white silk blouse, buttoned to the neck, and the black dirndl skirt that made her look even lumpier than usual. Her coarse, frizzled dark hair was pulled back from her low brow and secured with steel grips, large enough to skewer a turkey and Caroline sighed in despair. Even though the girl was wearing lipstick, it was the wrong colour, the cerise had already turned bluish on her sallow, olive skin. Stepping back a pace to avoid Laurinda's musky perfume, she wished she liked the girl more, but somehow Laurinda seemed unaware of the small polite-nesses that lubricated the wheels of any relationship. There were no smiles, no preliminary greetings, no small-talk or gossip, and none of the generous charm that abounded in *Images*' hand-picked models and clients. Caroline would never have chosen Laurinda to work for *Images*, the girl simply didn't fit in at all, but she'd had no choice. Laurinda had been thrust upon her, so to speak. Even Jessie-Ann, who was the kindest person and who had helped Laurinda originally, had balked when Harrison had suggested she work for *Images*. Anyway, here she was, and to give the girl her due, she was good at her job.

'Laurinda,' said Caroline kindly, 'have you ever thought of letting Hector have a go at your hair? He's really a genius you know – just look what he did to my unruly mop!' She shook her brief crop of curls vigorously, laughing as her hair arranged itself charmingly back into place.

'Thank you,' replied Laurinda stiffly, 'but I'm happy with my hair the way it is. I don't feel the need for fancy styles the way . . .'

She broke off abruptly, but Caroline knew she'd been about to say 'the way you and Jessie-Ann do'. She shrugged, that was Laurinda's problem. 'OK, Laurinda, what did you want?' she asked, businesslike once more.

'I just wanted to tell you that I called Stu Stansfield and arranged for the Royle catalogue account to be paid on time in future.'

Her face lit up in a half-smile of triumph as Caroline stared at her curiously, wondering how this mouse had had the balls to call Stansfield. Calling the head of one of Manhattan's top agencies and getting him on the phone was a feat akin to calling God – collect!

'I thought it was time someone put them in their place,' continued Laurinda, 'and I explained to Mr Stansfield that, as a new business, we needed to maintain our cash flow.'

'And what did Mr Stansfield say?'

Laurinda patted her hair, and smiled again. 'Oh he quite understood, especially when I explained that Harrison might not like it.'

Caroline pursed her lips in a low, emphatic whistle. 'Jesus! You said that?'

'I sure did. And it worked. Well, anyway, that's that. I'm getting all the accounts onto our new computer system, Caroline, and soon we'll be able to check exactly where they stand at a moment's notice. And then I'll make sure to chase them up.'

'Thank you, Laurinda.' Caroline watched the girl's heavy, slightly waddling exit, still stunned by the fact that Laurinda had used a touch of blackmail on Stansfield. Jessie-Ann would not like that – she would not like it one little bit. In fact, Caroline decided prudently, it would be better if Jessie-Ann knew nothing of Laurinda's little episode. She'd be ripping-mad to know that Harrison's name had been used on *Images*' behalf – even when it came to being paid by his company. It was fortunate that she was away, on location with Danae, because this was one item Caroline was certainly keeping under her hat!

By three o'clock Caroline had taken care of most of the accumulated mail on her desk, and was contemplating a cup of coffee – though somehow a cup of coffee alone hardly seemed worthwhile, sharing was half the fun. But the studios were empty this afternoon, the first session wasn't booked until six o'clock. Even Ed Zamurski was gone – permanently – Jessie-Ann had shown her some of the frightening letters and Caroline had recoiled in horror at such degenerate filth . . . it was worse than mere porn; these were the bottom of the barrel ravings of a sexual lunatic! But Jessie-Ann had thought she no longer needed Ed Zamurski and,

191

oddly enough, she hadn't received that sort of letter in months now.

'Hi there. Are you *Images*?'

Caroline's heart did a familiar little two-step and her mouth felt dry as she stared at the vision before her – a vision she knew well. Calvin Jensen had thick, slightly-waving dark blond hair slicked back from a broad forehead into a shoulder-length mane. He had narrow greenish eyes, strong tense bones, a wide firm jaw, and the year-round golden tan of a globetrotting top male-model.

'I'm Calvin Jensen,' he said in a slow, western drawl, 'this is *Images*, isn't it? I am in the right place?'

'Certainly you are,' gasped Caroline. 'Won't you take a seat please, Mr Jensen?'

Calvin laughed, giving her a display of strong, square, perfect white teeth, un-enhanced by crowns or bonding. Calvin was, quite naturally, physically perfect. And even though his broad shoulders were draped in the softest black leather jacket (by Armani), his tapering hips and strong legs covered in fine tweed (by Versace) and his tanned chest clothed in a plain white shirt (Ferre), Caroline was only too aware of what was beneath. Calvin had the immediate impact of a beautiful sexual animal, and who was she to fight it?

'You're English,' he said, lowering his large-framed body gracefully into a white-tweed chair. 'I was just in London on a job. Nice city – nice people. But I didn't meet one who spoke like you. You know, you sound sort of like "Brideshead Revisited".'

Caroline laughed, 'Do I really sound like that? I'm sorry.'

'Don't be sorry. I like it.' Leaning his elbows on her desk, Calvin stared into her eyes. 'I've got good instincts you know,' he murmured. 'I can feel when to trust a person, and I know I can trust you. What's your name?'

'It's Caroline . . . Caroline Courtney.'

'Perfect, sweetheart, that is just *perfect*. Yeah, I really like that . . . Caroline Courtney, huh? A high-class name for a high-class girl. What are you doing here at *Images*?'

'I work here,' she admitted, blushing. 'In fact I'm Jessie-Ann's partner. I run the business side, getting new jobs and organising the schedules for the studios, while she takes care of the models and the creative end. With Danae, of course. Danae is *Images'* photographer, and she's about to become our third partner.'

'I've heard of her,' drawled Calvin, his eyes holding Caroline's, until she glanced away, embarrassed. 'In fact, you might say that's why I'm here. I've had a pretty good row with Hilary Gough at Modelmania – my ex-agent.'

Caroline held her breath . . . his *ex*-agent? . . . Could it be that Calvin was looking for a new agency? God, anyone in New York – anyone in the *world* – would take him on in a minute. Calvin worked all the time, he was a virtual money-machine . . .

'I also had a bit of a run-in with Brachman,' continued Calvin, settling back in his chair and propping his feet on Caroline's desk as she stared in fascination at his six-hundred dollar Italian cowboy boots, fashioned from the softest, supplest leather she'd ever seen.

'Tell me what y'think of these?' he demanded, pulling a sheaf of polaroids from the slouchy Vuitton tan-leather satchel he carried over his shoulder. 'Come on now, Caroline, your honest opinion please?'

Wiping her suddenly moist palm on her yellow linen skirt, Caroline took the pictures from him, carefully, avoiding touching his hand. In them Calvin, suntanned and truly beautiful, wore nothing but a pair of brief underpants. She shuffled through them, frowning. In some he wore boxer shorts, in others a plain vest and pants . . . but somehow all the sexiness had been diluted by the conventional pose of a million innocuous underwear ads throughout the years. 'They're blah!' she exclaimed contemptuously, 'how could *Brachman* do this to you!'

Calvin leaned closer across the desk. 'I can't figure it out. D'ya think maybe he's jealous? I mean the guy's getting old and all that . . . Either that or he thinks I'm a faggot . . . or maybe he's a faggot?'

Caroline laughed. 'You'll have to speak to Danae about that, she's our resident expert on Brachman. Danae worked with him for two years.'

'Yeah? Is that so . . . well, I'll tell you, Caroline, I wasn't about to have my career ruined by these God-awful pictures and I told Brachman exactly that.' He grinned at her. 'You can imagine what happened – the guy went berserk, said quite a few nasty things about my character . . . "No need to get personal," I told him, "all I'm saying is that these pictures are the pits!" Now I ask you, what's wrong with that?' His narrow green eyes twinkled at her from beneath blond brows, as he continued, 'Anyway, Brachman calls Hilary Gough and she comes tearing around and rips into me . . . *Me!* "Lady," I said to her, "aren't you forgetting somethin'? *I'm* your client – not this old has-been photographer. You wanna represent him, go right ahead. Me – I'm walkin'." And that's exactly what I did – except I showed Brodie Flyte these polaroids before they had time to get back to him.'

Caroline licked her lips nervously, absorbed in his story. Brodie Flyte, née Broderick Fienstein, was a rough, tough guy from the Bronx, who'd graduated into fashion directly from the streets. He was now one of America's top designers, and his turnover – with his ready-to-wear lines as well as the couture – was already quoted at almost a billion dollars a year. She'd read somewhere that he was looking to his new, unisex, mass-market underwear line to tip the sales over the billion mark. 'And what did Brodie Flyte say?' she demanded eagerly.

'Brodie's an old buddy of mine, I knew him when he first started and I've always done his shows. He took one look – just like you did – and said, "These are crap. What's the asshole playing at?"' Calvin grinned at Caroline's shocked expression. 'Brodie talks like that,' he explained, 'it's only his clothes that look refined.'

She burst out laughing. 'So now what?'

'I told him I'd left Hilary and Modelmania and he said, "Good riddance – how about trying something new? I hear nothing but good things about *Images* . . . Jessie-Ann Parker surely knows her stuff, and they've got a new girl photographer who's really hot." So,' Calvin leaned back, smiling contentedly, 'here I am. And if this new girl photographer is as good as she's made out to be, Brodie and I would like her to do the Bodyline ads.'

Caroline was too stunned even to reply . . . Brodie Flyte's new underwear could make *Images* – or break it . . . it would be *Images*' responsibility to come up with the right look, to get the message across that simple boxer shorts and Y-fronts and cotton vests could be sexy as hell on girls as well as boys . . .

'The ad agency is Monahan, Karnelian, Marks,' Calvin told her, 'they'll fill you in on details of the campaign. Me, I just show up for the pictures.' Smiling his dazzling white smile, he stood up and slung his leather satchel across his shoulders. 'Gotta go,' he told Caroline, staring intently into her eyes, 'I'm on my way to the gym – an hour's squash, twenty laps of the pool, a half hour on the Nautilus . . . and then, what are you doing for dinner tonight?'

'I hadn't thought about it yet,' she murmured shyly, marvelling at his stamina. If she'd been doing all that, she'd have simply crawled home to bed.

'Great. Why don't I come to dinner at your place then? Eight o'clock OK? You got the address?'

Caroline scribbled her address on the back of an *Images* card. 'Great,' said Calvin tucking it into his shirt pocket. Leaning across the desk again, he put his hand under her chin. Tilting her face up to his, he stared at her for a long moment, and she waited breathlessly, aware of the smoothness of his tanned skin, the darker golden glint of his sun-bleached hair and his firm, passionate mouth – so close to hers.

'You are one very beautiful lady, Miss Caroline Carstairs,' he said at last, turning away and making for the door.

'Courtney,' she called after him. 'It's not Carstairs, it's Courtney.'

'See you at eight, Courtney.' With a wave, he strode through the door and was gone.

Caroline slumped back in her chair, her pulse racing and her mouth dry with excitement. She'd forgotten all about *Images* and Brodie Flyte . . . Calvin Jensen was coming to dinner!

12

The Brodie Flyte underwear campaign had become a priority job, and Danae scarcely had time to gloat over the gossip-columns' stories of Brachman's tantrum and his deadly-dull pictures that had lost him the year's most lucrative job. *And* lost it to the girl who was once his assistant! She had always thought that when the moment came, she would savour it slowly, glorying in Brachman's downfall, but she was so absorbed in the challenge of Flyte's 'Bodylines', that it took her entire attention.

After endless discussions with the people at the advertising agency, Monahan, Karnelian, Marks, the brief she had been given was a fairly loose one, leaving her plenty of leeway creatively. Of course they'd balked a bit at first, when she'd said she wanted to use a girl as well as Calvin. Her idea was to use them together as lovers in a rumpled bed; but she'd promised them she would find exactly the right innocent-looking young model. She swore that if they just left it all to her, she'd give them something tasteful and different – and a real eyecatcher. 'A touch controversial,' she'd stated with a cocky grin, 'after all, if you wanted the conventional, you should have stuck with Brachman.'

'Just don't go over the top, Danae,' warned Konrad Karnelian, 'we aim to sell this underwear to *everybody* in the country – and that includes the dudes out in redneck-land, and in bluegrass country and the Rocky Mountains, as well as sharp New Yorkers.'

'Right,' Danae replied briskly, 'I'll give you exactly what you want – all I ask is the freedom to do it my way.'

'You're on,' agreed Brodie Flyte, liking the girl's confidence, 'but get the fucking thing right this time or I'll chop your balls off.'

'*Mr Brodie!*' exclaimed Danae, 'that's no way for an underwear-tycoon to talk!'

Brodie sighed, 'You're right, lady, I spend so much time with those cut-throats on Seventh Avenue, I guess I've forgotten how to talk to a nice person.' He grinned at her and Danae grinned back. Brodie Flyte was OK; small, dark and volatile . . . but even though she knew that he was 'interested' that was as far as it went – or as far as she would *allow* it to go. She was concentrating on her career as the one-woman dynamo, the whiz-kid of the camera world . . .

The first problem came when she told Calvin he was to share his ads with a girl. 'Jesus Christ,' he said looking plaintively at Caroline, 'that's death for a male model. All I'll be is background to some sexy chick.'

'No way,' promised Danae, 'this chick will be so innocent the public's gonna be afraid for her honour! Come on, Calvin, it's a chance to step out of the Versace mould, you'll look great in Brodie's silk drawers and a T-shirt – with a girl . . .'

'What do you think, Courtney?' asked Calvin, taking her hand.

He looked so uncertain, Caroline felt that he wanted her to make the decision for him. 'I'd trust Danae,' she replied quietly, 'she's a genius. You'll have the best photographs you've ever done – I'd be willing to bet they'll be considered works of art.'

'OK then, the lady says yes.' Calvin turned his brilliant smile on Danae, shaking her hand warmly. 'You've got a deal. Just let me know when.'

'Leave a number where we can reach you,' she said.

'Aw I guess you can get me at Courtney's most nights,' replied Calvin, nonchalantly.

Danae raised her eyebrows and Caroline blushed. 'It's not quite the way it sounds,' she murmured. 'It's just that Calvin came to dinner last week, and he seems rather to have made himself at home.'

Danae shrugged and said with a grin, 'I can think of worse things to happen. Just make sure he doesn't disappear. I'll see you in a couple of weeks, Calvin. Meanwhile, I've got to get on a plane to London tonight. No, it'll have to be tomorrow. *Tonight* I'm shooting an album cover for Phil Edgar & 'Hurricane'. And *today* I've got some shopping to do.'

'Oh yeah?' asked Calvin interested, 'where?'

'Saint-Laurent,' replied Danae airily, 'where else?'

'But why?' asked Caroline.

'Because I always promised myself that when I made it I'd wear Saint-Laurent – and now's the moment. Because Calvin and Brodie and my new model are going to make my fortune.'

'No . . . I meant why are you going to London – tomorrow . . . and anyway, what new model?'

'The one I'm off to London tomorrow to find of course. We need a totally new face, a new look – innocence and sex. And where better to find that combination than Europe? I've got good contacts in London, and if necessary I'll comb the city streets until I find *exactly* what I'm looking for. So you'd better all wish me luck – because the success of Brodie Flyte's knickers nationwide depends entirely on my little expedition!'

It was true that Calvin seemed at home in Caroline's small apartment. He'd shown up for dinner that first night, with his hair still wet from the shower, clutching a bunch of pale creamy-yellow roses in his large square hands. He'd worn a smile that Caroline might almost have considered shy, if he weren't one of the world's most photographed men. 'They reminded me of England and you,' he'd said, handing them over to her, and planting a gentle kiss on her warm cheek.

She'd arranged them in the wide crystal bowl that she'd discovered in an antique shop on Second Avenue, and then she'd offered him a drink. 'Do you have any Badoit?' he'd asked, just as she was about to reach for the gin and tonic.

'Sorry, just Perrier.'

'OK then, with a twist . . . but I'll send you a case or two of Badoit. I always drink it – naturally carbonated water y'know, it's better for you.'

Slumped into one of her small Victorian velvet chairs, he sipped his drink, while Caroline nervously poured a gin and tonic for herself. There was something about Calvin – not just his looks, though honestly, she'd never seen anything more elegantly graceful and – let's admit it – sexy, than the man opposite her. Calvin even made sipping a glass of water a state-of-the-art gesture! She wondered if it was his absolute openness and simplicity that threw her off balance. There was none of Pericles' subtle manoeuvring here. She just knew that Calvin Jensen would say exactly what he meant every time – take it or leave it. Just like he had with Brachman.

'What's for supper?' he enquired, engagingly. 'It sure smells good.'

Caroline had rushed from the office to Grace Balducci's on Lexington, gathering goodies in a rapid sortie of their departments; fragrant ogen melons from Israel; fresh strawberries from California; lobster tails from Maine; baguettes baked that morning in Paris; Normandie butter; freshly-made spinach tagliatelle; hot-house tomatoes that she'd pounded with red peppers to make a sauce, brewing it with sprigs of fresh basil. Calvin was a slender giant, but she felt sure he would eat and eat . . . and she had overbought just to be sure she'd bought *enough*.

'It's a surprise,' she smiled at him, 'would you like to open the wine?'

He removed the cork without inspecting the label, sniffing it critically. 'Good,' he said approvingly, 'yes, that's good.' He filled the lavishly oversized glasses and took a seat at the table opposite her.

'Pasta first,' said Caroline wondering why she felt so foolishly nervous as his green eyes locked into hers, 'and then lobster tails with a light salad, and fruit for dessert.'

'And good fresh bread from France,' he added pleased. 'A guy could get used to this Courtney, y'know that?'

'Tell me about yourself,' suggested Caroline, sipping the Puligny Montrachet, and toying with her pasta.

'Me? Oh I'm just a guy from California – San Diego way, close to the Mexican border. My Pop's in aerospace and my Mom ran off with some other guy when I was around sixteen – she said it was because my Pop was never home – he was always working. I did a year at USC Santa Barbara but then I was picked up by a magazine doing a feature on college kids. From that I got a job modelling tennis gear, and then some sailing shots . . . it just sort of took off from there. I'm twenty-four years old, unmarried and clean-living. How's that for a bio?'

Caroline laughed. 'I wish mine were as uncomplicated.'

Calvin's narrowed green eyes met hers. 'Well then, Courtney,' he said gently, 'you'll have to tell me what's complicating your life, won't you?'

And later, after dinner, and half-way through a second bottle of wine, she did. Sitting on the sofa with her head resting on Calvin's chest, his arm draped gently across her shoulder, she'd told him all about Pericles and Evita – the whole miserable story. Only somehow it seemed even tackier, told out loud.

'Forget him sweetheart, the guy's a creep,' was Calvin's only comment. Then he'd yawned and said, 'Jesus, I've got a job in the morning, I'd better get some zzz's . . .' and he'd headed for the door. 'Wait a minute,' he said, turning suddenly and striding back across the room towards her. 'Thank you very much, Ma'am, for a delightful evening. And great food. Can I come again tomorrow night?'

Caroline laughed. In anyone else it would have seemed brash, but Calvin in this mood was as innocent and appealing as a beautiful puppy.

'You may,' she'd agreed, 'but I can't guarantee this sort of banquet every night. I'm a working woman.'

'Sure you can,' he'd retorted, 'you're *super-woman*, aren't you?' And then he'd put his arms around her and kissed her, on the mouth this time, lingeringly, and so very, very nicely . . .

That was seven nights ago and Calvin had been to her place for supper every single one of them. Caroline suspected that, despite all her good intentions, her heart was taking over from her mind again. But she was trying awfully hard not to let it – even though his kisses were delicious, and even though he hadn't yet made any attempt to seduce her. And that was a question she worried over, in bed at night – alone – after Calvin had gone. *Why* hadn't he? What was wrong with her? Because there was certainly nothing wrong with Calvin Jensen.

13

Dino Marley refilled Danae's champagne glass, inspecting her critically. She looked pale and tired despite the make-up and the smart black designer suit that he recognised as Saint-Laurent. And it wasn't just the fatigue of jet-lag. 'You look a bit different from the last time we met,' he commented, 'as though life – or maybe success – has caught up with you.'

'You mean I've lost my girlish joie-de-vivre,' sighed Danae, sipping the wine.

'Just a touch,' he agreed with a grin, 'but I guess life is tough at the top?'

'Don't put yourself down, Dino Marley,' she retorted, 'you've been at the top for more years than you probably care to remember. I'm hoping it's only the first few that are tough. But I'm here for the same reason I was last time – I'd like your help. I'm searching for a new girl for the Brodie Flyte Bodylines campaign. I want someone who's totally unknown – or at least who hasn't been hawked around by the agencies. London is the best place in the world to find that sort of new talent – and I've got about a week to do it. Do you have any ideas?'

'Not one,' replied Dino cheerfully, 'but I know who will. My ex-assistant Cameron Mace . . . he must have met – and seduced – at least fifty per cent of the new young hopefuls haunting this town. And he's probably photographed most of them too. Cam's the man to help you on this quest.'

'Cam – of course!' She remembered now how helpful he'd been on the Brachman shoot.

'He's set up on his own now. I'll have him back here tomorrow around four,' Dino promised her, 'with his pictures.'

Cam had certainly been busy, thought Danae, sifting slowly through the pile of photographs the next afternoon. Some of the photographs were good and some of the faces interesting, but they didn't have what she was searching for. After an hour, she pushed the pile to one side dispiritedly. There were one or two possibilities, but they didn't 'grab' her the way she'd hoped . . . she was still seeking that special elusive quality and it simply wasn't there in these girls' eyes.

Thalia Weston, the beautiful receptionist, fluttered importantly into the room. 'Sorry to disturb you, Miss Lawrence,' she said with a smile, 'but Dino found these pictures in the old files. He thought you might like to see them.'

The photographs were all of the same girl. She was very young, obviously inexperienced and child-like, with a wide jaw and large apprehensive eyes. Yet her neck was incredibly long and graceful and her shoulders heartbreakingly slender and in some of the pictures there was a hint of allure, even though she looked more than a little scared. Danae imagined teaming that childlike, innocent face with sophisticated dresses that breathed sex and decadence . . . or with Brodie Flyte's unisex 'Bodylines'; she could see now exactly how to shoot this campaign . . . *This face* was the inspiration she had needed!

'Where's Cam?' she asked Thalia.

'He had to go out on a job, Miss Lawrence, he won't be back tonight.'

'I must find this girl,' exclaimed Danae, 'I *must* know who she is. I've *got* to find her . . . right away.' Now that she'd decided, she couldn't wait to meet her, to see if what she saw in Cam's photographs was really there . . . She simply couldn't wait until tomorrow . . .

Thalia glanced at the photograph. 'That's easy,' she said with a smile, 'I have her address on file. That's Gala-Rose.'

'Gala-Rose,' breathed Danae . . . 'Oh, Gala-Rose, I'm gonna make you famous . . . soon *everyone* will know your name!'

The doorbell made a fluttering attempt to ring and then sank back into silence, as though unable to raise itself out of long disuse. Gala stared at the scarred brown wooden door in astonishment; no one ever rang *her* bell – except when the rent-collector called. He made the rounds of all the rooms every Friday evening: and those who couldn't pay always managed to be 'out'. It made no difference though, the man was always there when they came back.

The doorbell made another rough coughing sound. Then there was a sharp rapping. Gala felt a chill of fear. Today *was* Thursday, wasn't it? She hadn't made a mistake . . . no she couldn't have. Could the rent collector, whose foreign name she'd never quite caught, have made an error?

She wouldn't answer it, Gala decided. In this area a girl didn't just open her door because someone rang the bell!

'Gala-Rose?' cried a sharp, feminine American voice. 'Are you there?' Whoever it was was *banging* on the door now. 'Look, Gala-Rose,' the voice said cajolingly, 'if you *are* there, please open up. I'm a friend.'

Gala stared at the door, her grey eyes were wide with shock. 'But I have no friends,' she murmured, 'not since Jake . . .'

'Please,' pleaded Danae, '*please*, Gala-Rose, don't be afraid, let me in.'

Gala waited in silence, a trembling hand at her throat.

'Damn it,' yelled Danae, beating on the door, 'I've come all the way from New York to find you. Get this goddamn door open – and now!'

Gala shot across to the door and pulled back the bolt, peering at the irate red-haired girl facing her.

'Jesus!' breathed Danae, pushing her way in.

The two girls eyed each other in silence for a moment and then Danae held out her hand. 'Danae Lawrence, photographer,' she announced. 'I got your address from Marley's.' She smiled at Gala, trying hard not to let her dismay show in her eyes. Gala-Rose, the model she was planning on making into a star via national magazines, billboards, posters, and even videos, was just a painfully thin child with defeated eyes and raggedly cut mouse-blonde hair – she was a waif clad in nondescript grey clothing. Her only touches of colour were the cool, clear, positive grey of her eyes and a brave flash of day-glo pink socks.

Danae talked rapidly about her job as a photographer and how she'd come to London seeking new faces and had seen her pictures at Dino Marley's while Gala just stood there, seeming too stunned to do anything but listen. As she moved around the room Gala's eyes followed her like a snake hypnotised by a mongoose.

203

'Come here,' called Danae, 'over by the window. Let me look at your face.'

'I'm sorry, Miss,' Gala said quietly, 'but you've made a mistake. I'm not a model. I've never worked as one. Those pictures I did with Cam were the only photographs I've ever had taken – and then I wished I hadn't.'

Their eyes met and a flicker of emotion passed between them. 'I know exactly what you mean, Gala-Rose,' Danae replied gently. '*I understand*. But you know, those were fine pictures. And looking at you – even now like this, I can see there is something special about you.' With her head on one side, she held Gala's chin in her hand, turning her face to the light from the window so she could see each profile. 'Amazing,' she said finally, 'do you realise, Gala-Rose, that you have a virtually symmetrical face? Almost nobody has two matching profiles, but you do! All the measurements of your face are even . . . They're not classically perfect, but you have a special sort of beauty. It's the sort that needs a little work,' she added cheerfully, 'but it's there all right. Under the grime.'

Gala glared angrily at the chic red-headed vision in the expensive black and white suit. 'Just because I'm poor doesn't mean that I'm unwashed,' she retorted.

'Bravo, Gala-Rose,' laughed Danae, 'and you're right, of course. Do something for me, Gala, will you, just walk across the floor, yes right across the room and back again . . . I know this may sound crazy but I'm serious . . . that's right, turn when you get to the door; now stop, right there, just let your bones arrange themselves . . . mmmmnnn, yes . . . OK . . .'

'But why?' asked Gala breathlessly, 'what's this all about?'

'Work,' replied Danae, 'work as a model. It's about a very important advertising campaign – coast-to-coast, USA . . . it's about *money*, Gala-Rose, about *fame and fortune* . . . although we'll have to *un*teach you a few things first. I'm talking top-level, instant-exposure-time here, Gala-Rose, and *you* are the girl for me!' Danae eyed Gala impatiently as the girl simply stared at her open mouthed. 'Wait a minute,' she commanded, 'take off those bag-lady sweaters and let's have a look at your shoulders – and the rest of your body . . . bodies are important in this game . . .'

Blushing, Gala removed layers of jerseys, emerging in her too-often-washed greyish underwear.

'You're not anorexic, are you?' Danae demanded suspiciously, eyeing the long elegant bones protruding too prominently through Gala's translucent flesh. 'Anorexics are too much trouble.'

'I am certainly *not* anorexic!' retorted Gala, close to nervous tears. 'It's just that I just can't afford to eat properly.'

She glared at Danae, and Danae recalled herself, in the not-too-distant past, when Brachman had posed her in front of his camera in Paris and accused her of putting on weight . . . 'It's just that I can afford to eat regularly now,' she remembered replying . . .

'The hell with all this,' cried Danae. 'Let's you and I go out and get ourselves some dinner, Gala-Rose.'

Sweeping Gala into a taxi she commanded the cabbie to take them to a restaurant nearby, nothing fancy but with good food.

'Indian,' decided the cabbie, heading for Queensway. 'Best food – and best value – in Britain.'

Ordering a lavish Indian banquet that would have fed six comfortably, Danae watched with fascination as Gala munched her way through chicken tikka and tandoori lamb masala washing it down with icy glasses of lager. There was something so innately graceful about the girl's every movement it took her breath away. Gala-Rose was something so special she felt privileged to be the one who would develop her. Gala-Rose was näive, untried, brand-spanking new . . . and she, Danae Lawrence, could *create* this face, *create this person*! It would be almost like giving birth, she thought, meeting Gala's limpid, satisfied gaze as she wiped her mouth with her napkin and heaved a small sigh of utter satisfaction. Danae smiled at her, feeling like Professor Higgins with Eliza Doolittle in the first act of *Pygmalion*.

'So you'll come with me then, to New York?' she asked.

'When?' breathed Gala.

'How about tomorrow?'

'Tomorrow!'

'Well, at the latest, next week. We've got a lot of work to do on you, Gala-Rose, before you become the "face of the year".'

'The face of the year,' murmured Gala, thinking suddenly of Jake. Oh dear, darling Jake, hadn't he'd always said that one day, someone would come along and see exactly what he saw in her? Whether it was beauty or not she wasn't sure . . . but this girl wanted her to work. She would be a model, at last. And dear Jake, sweet dead Jake, had been right.

14

Jessie-Ann's English Nanny pursed her lips, shaking her head as Jonathan, one leg tucked under him, crawled rapidly across the studio floor in a sideways sliding movement, gaining momentum on the slippery boards. When he reached his goal – the area of bright lights and people – he sat back on his haunches, blue eyes sparkling with interest, enjoying the heat from the halogen lamps and taking in the action, suddenly deciding he'd like to be part of it too.

'Jonathan!' exclaimed Nanny, striding purposefully towards him, arms outstretched ready to whisk him away.

'Aw leave him, Nanny,' called Phil Edgar, guitarist and lead-singer, as well as composer of most of 'Hurricane's' hit singles – many of them extracted from the half-dozen platinum albums that the group had cut over the past five years. 'The kid's OK, he's enjoying himself,' he drawled, 'ain't ya, Jonathan? Well? What d'ya say, kid, besides "ooh" and "ah" and "Mommy"?' Folding his six foot three frame down to Jon's level, Phil gazed solemnly into Jon's wide blue eyes and the child gazed solemnly back.

'Really,' tut-tutted Nanny, 'those lights are far too bright for him, they'll harm his eyes . . .'

Standing in the doorway, Laurinda watched, unsmiling. Just look at that great depraved hoodlum of a rockstar! Hadn't he once been arrested, accused of sex with an underage girl? It had all died down later, but he must be guilty as hell. He'd probably paid off the girl's parents to withdraw their charges . . . she knew how these things got hushed up . . . family secrets . . . And he was touching baby Jon, *picking him up*, grinning that stupid grin and tossing him up in the air, while the other guys in the group laughed at them. Laurinda itched to reach out and slap Phil Edgar's face, she'd like to rake her nails across his eyes . . .

Phil wandered across the set with Jon tucked casually beneath his arm and his guitar slung across his shoulder. He took a seat on the central, throne-like chair and put young Jon on his knee, then smilingly offered the child ten-thousand dollars' worth of guitar to play with. The baby's face lit up as he gazed up at Phil and then back down at the fascinating new object in front of him. Tentatively his fingers explored the strings, making tiny plucking noises as he tugged them. 'That's music, kid,' grinned Phil . . . 'you've got the makings of a true rock star there.'

'Well *really*!' muttered Nanny, heading towards the door. 'Where is Mrs Royle?' she demanded, brushing past Laurinda, her face a thundercloud.

'In her office,' Laurinda told her, tagging along behind, eager to hear what was going to be said.

Nanny thumped once on the door and walked in. 'Mrs Royle,' she cried, ignoring the man sitting opposite Jessie-Ann, her face crimson with annoyance, 'I really must speak to you. At once!'

Jessie-Ann frowned. It was wrong of Nanny to interrupt her meeting with Carlo Menaghi, Vice-President of Avlon Cosmetics . . . unless something had happened to Jon . . .? 'What is it, Nanny?' she asked anxiously, 'where's Jon?'

'That's exactly it, Mrs Royle, young Jon is out there in Studio Two – under all those hot lights – with those dreadful rock and roll people. He's actually *sitting* on the man's knee!'

'That man?' asked Jessie-Ann, puzzled. 'You mean Phil Edgar?'

'*Exactly*, Madam!'

Nanny's face was thunderous and beyond her, Jessie-Ann caught a glimpse of Laurinda by the doorway; the girl's deepset eyes were fixed on her with a cold glint in them that suddenly chilled her heart.

'Wait a minute,' exclaimed Carlo Menaghi, 'you mean *Phil Edgar*'s in that studio with *a kid* sitting on his knee! *This* I'd like to see! The only thing Phil usually has on his knee is a great-looking girl . . . Jessie-Ann, this is a first!'

'Come on,' she cried, laughing, 'let's go and see.'

Hurrying past the furious Nanny, they found the studio a scene of peace and tranquillity. Danae was roaming the set, rearranging props and murmuring commands to her assistant. Her copper hair was already messy despite the yellow headband and the sleeves of her white satin shirt were rolled to the elbows. She wandered barefoot between the five rangy guys who comprised the group 'Hurricane', arranging them according to some inner vision of what she needed.

'Hector,' she called, 'I want their hair combed, neatly, please.'

'Aw come on, Danae,' they grumbled good-naturedly, 'what's with the hair-combing bit?'

'Monica?' she summoned the stylist, ignoring their complaint, 'I want five white shirts, with stiff collars, neatly ironed.' Monica gulped and headed for the phone.

'Jesus,' exclaimed Phil, 'you wanna make me look like my Pa?'

'Right,' beamed Danae. 'Or almost right. Isn't the title of this new album, "Sunday Session"? OK, we'll leave your unshaven chins, and your long hair, as well as your degenerate young faces – *youngish* faces,' she amended, amidst laughter, 'because you guys are all now over twenty-five, but we're gonna put you in your "Sunday best". White shirts buttoned to the neck, hair neatly combed – perhaps with a touch of water to slick it down. This is gonna be a straight-on family photo – like you'd find in an Edwardian family album. And Phil, you'll sit right there in the middle, with Jon on your knee. It's perfect,' she cried excitedly, 'just great . . .'

Jessie-Ann and Carlo filed quietly from the studio, smiling. Danae had it all under control, her creative juices were flowing, the guys in the group were happy, and young Jon was having a ball playing with the guitar and being the centre of attention.

'Everything's OK, Nanny,' Jessie-Ann called soothingly. 'Danae's using Jon in these photographs so you may be here for some time. Just check to make sure he's dry, and then keep an eye on him. OK?' Her dazzling smile failed to placate Nanny, who stumped off towards the studio, her white-overalled back expressing her displeasure.

Sighing, she flopped in her chair, pressing the button for her secretary and ordering coffee. It was getting tougher and tougher to juggle her home life and her work, and Nanny certainly wasn't making it any easier! And now she seemed to see less and less of

Harrison – somehow it always worked out that he was away when she could have made it home early; and just when she was frantically busy Harrison would be in New York. And somehow he seemed to be away more often now.

Of course, it was all her fault, but she'd explained to him that these months were critical for *Images*, and that soon it was all going to work out and be great. But right now it was just sheer, hard, time-consuming work! She hated feeling guilty about enjoying what she was doing, because she really loved Harrison and when they were together life was wonderful . . . yet although Harrison always said he understood, sometimes she wondered if he did, truly? The only way she really got to be around Jon was by bringing him here, but Nanny was so difficult. She was a prim and proper blue-blood-type Nanny who'd worked for a friend of Rachel's and she wasn't at all the type of person Jessie-Ann would have chosen herself. What she had wanted was a young girl, someone who could play the same silly sort of games she would have played with Jon herself, as well as change his diapers and see that he ate all the right things and take him to the paediatrician for his check-ups. What she'd needed was a girl who was flexible enough to fit in with her changeable lifestyle.

'It's a tough life,' commented Carlo, reading her troubled expressions. It wasn't difficult for him to fathom the conflict. 'I've got to hand it to you women though, you get out there and do a good day's work and as well you have to juggle all the rest.'

Jessie-Ann smiled ruefully. 'That's exactly what it is, Carlo, a juggling act. But that's my problem. Now, about the skin-care promotion in October . . .'

Harrison roamed the empty halls of his apartment, pausing now and again to study a painting; a Cézanne in the small study that he particularly liked; the immense Rubens that dominated the drawing room; a mystical English garden painted by David Oxtoby in the library. He picked up a smooth piece of rock crystal, exquisitely etched by the Austrian, Gernot Schluifer, and examined it minutely, running his fingers lovingly over the delicate

210

tracery. Replacing it, he prowled on, picking up an *objet* here, a leather-bound book there, admiring and replacing, and all the time wondering when Jessie-Ann was going to get home.

He checked the simple Blancpain moonphase watch that she'd given him on his last birthday. It was eight thirty and she'd promised to be home an hour ago. He could call her, he supposed, but obviously she was still busy . . . 'I wonder,' he thought, 'if Merry is busy too, in Washington?'

Washington DC was where the 'Royle Road Show' was currently appearing, using half a dozen models to present the new line.

Meredith McCall, the 'Royle Girl', was the typical long-limbed all-American model – a Jessie-Ann, thought Harrison, with glossy chestnut hair and laughing eyes – and such a great smile. The Royle line under her name was selling as fast as it hit the racks and the 'Merry McCall look' was where it was at on campuses nationwide. Merry had made the line an enormous success with her extrovert beauty and vitality. And it was Merry who set the pace, flying from city to city to appear personally at each store, touring endless campuses with the fashion show, appearing coast-to-coast on breakfast TV and late-night chat-shows, looking like the girl next door every guy wished had lived next door to them!

Harrison had intended to appear at only the first of the 'Road Shows' in San Francisco, but to his surprise he'd enjoyed himself. Since then he'd made a point of catching up with the show at a dozen different locations, flying himself in his Gulf Stream jet and literally dropping in on them, out of the blue. He admitted to himself that it was Merry he went to see – she was always cheerful and she always looked great. And she always had time for him. In fact all he had to do now was to pick up the phone and say, 'I'll be out there in a couple of hours, Merry, how about dinner after the show?' and he was certain she'd be pleased to see him. What's more, thought Harrison dangerously, *he knew he would be pleased to see her*.

Somehow Merry McCall made him feel that he counted in her life in a way he didn't in Jessie-Ann's. Maybe it was just because when he and Merry met they were both on neutral ground away from her home-life and away from his – yet together in the same game – the Royle Road Show?

He wandered into the nursery, picking up Jon's building blocks, and absently stroking the mane of his big wooden rocking horse, but it seemed even lonelier in there, without the sound of Jon's eager babble of greeting, or the soft sigh of his breath when he slept.

Walking quickly back to his study, Harrison poured himself a shot of bourbon. He'd already told Warren, the houseman, that he would not be needed any more that night, and but for the ticking of the clocks, the huge apartment was totally silent. He thought wistfully of the animals he had always wanted as a kid: just small, city ones would have been fine – he'd fancied a little sheltie dog and maybe a frisky blue-point Siamese – but his mother had never allowed household pets, claiming she was prone to allergic attacks of asthma, though Harrison had never witnessed one. 'Very well then,' she'd finally agreed, 'get a dog and see me have an attack if that's what you want' . . . so of course, he never had. Perhaps he should think about getting one now, pondered Harrison, at least it would be company. He stared at the telephone hoping it would ring, but he knew Jessie-Ann was lost in her own busy world.

He wondered if it was his fault. Right from the beginning, he'd put her on a pedestal as the ideal American girl; the one who would look great whether she were walking the dogs, or at a school prize-giving, or an opening night at the Opera. The girl who would not only be the perfect image of a wife, but who even if she didn't *cook* him the applepie, would at least see that he was served it occasionally. *And* in his own home, not in some restaurant. *And* preferably in front of a nice fire, on a quiet, dusky autumn evening, with maybe the end of a good football game on television, or perhaps the soft strains of Vivaldi on tape . . . and maybe a baby or two playing sweetly on the rug at their feet. But now she was Jessie-Ann of *Images*.

Harrison drank his bourbon at a gulp. He'd married her to escape from his eighteen years of loneliness, only to find himself lonely! And suddenly he found the possibility of Merry McCall's welcoming arms distinctly inviting.

Checking his watch again, he reached for the telephone and called Mat Gabler, his pilot, arranging to meet him at La Guardia airport in half an hour. Then he placed a call to the Watergate Hotel in Washington DC, and Merry McCall.

15

Calvin lay full length on Caroline's navy-blue flannel sofa, his long, denim-clad legs hooked over one arm, and his favourite old white loafers dangling from the tips of his bare brown toes. He wore a soft blue cashmere sweater and, with his arms folded beneath his head, he was as comfortable as a drowsing cat.

Caroline sat opposite him in the velvet Victorian chair, immersed in a thick sheaf of papers filled with columns of figures – the month's accounts thrust upon her by Laurinda just as she had been leaving the office that evening. Occasionally she would glance up and meet Calvin's half-closed eyes, or if he were lost in a dream – as he often seemed to be – then she would simply look at him, absorbing his fluid, graceful beauty as she might a painting in an exclusive gallery.

She had known Calvin for three weeks now and, except on the occasions when he had flown off on location for a modelling job, he had shown up at her apartment every evening. Sometimes, when she had been working even later than usual at *Images*, she had arrived home to find him lounging against her door, arms folded, just waiting for her, and the sight of him as he unfurled himself and strode smiling, along the corridor to meet her, had gladdened her heart in a way that Pericles never had. But still Calvin had never done more than simply kiss her hello, or goodbye . . . sweet, tender, lingering kisses. Were they, wondered Caroline, the kisses of a brother for a sister? No . . . definitely not . . . there was sensuality in those warm lips. But for some reason Calvin never went any further.

Thrusting the papers aside, Caroline glanced at her watch. It was almost ten o'clock and apart from sharing the bottle of champagne Calvin had brought and a few little slivers of Gruyère cheese, they hadn't yet eaten. As far as she could remember, the refrigerator was depleted, and anyway, New York was glittering outside her windows and she felt like being part of it – even if it were some simple restaurant where they could be together . . . perhaps they might even go to a disco or a club afterwards . . . Calvin knew all the most 'in' places.

Kneeling by his side, she leaned across him and gazed into his eyes. 'Hi,' she said.

Calvin smiled at her, a smile of such sweetness she wanted to kiss him there and then. But she didn't.

'Hi,' said Calvin. 'You finished?'

'Yes, and I'm starving. How about you?'

He ran a finger along the curve of her cheek. 'Sure, I could eat something.'

'Let's go out, Calvin,' cried Caroline, her hazel eyes sparkling. 'I want to eat sumptuous food and dance until dawn.'

Calvin ran his hands through her short, silken curls. 'Whatever you say, Ma'am,' he agreed, uncurling himself from the comfort of the sofa.

Caroline ran into her bedroom, changing hurriedly from beige linen pants and sweatshirt into a soft silk-jersey Jean Muir outfit, bought what now seemed like a decade ago at Maudie's, but still one of her favourites. Its short black skirt stopped just above her knees, and the fuchsia low-necked jacket – buttoned with a row of tiny loops down the front – clung as only that soft, sexy fabric could. With lacy black stockings and high-heeled black suede shoes; a glittering fake-fantasie necklace of jet and diamonds and huge matching earrings; a touch of powder, blusher, shadow and lipstick and a huge splash of Ysatis and she was ready.

Calvin had a two-day growth of beard because he wasn't working and he'd simply thrust his feet into his ancient white loafers and shrugged on a rumpled black linen jacket. Caroline thought that any other man would have looked merely scruffy, but Calvin managed to look chic.

'Well?' she demanded eagerly, 'where are we going?'

He gazed at her with those lazy green eyes. 'I thought you had somewhere in mind?'

'But don't you have some favourite place you'd like to take me?' she asked, puzzled.

'Sure, well I guess so – but why don't you choose, Courtney? I'm happy to go along with whatever you say.' Calvin smiled his easy smile and Caroline decided it didn't matter who made the decision on where to go. 'There's that lovely new Italian place on East Fifty-eighth,' she suggested, taking his arm and urging him through the door, 'why don't we try that?'

Even though it was late, the restaurant was still full. Caroline waited for Calvin to slip the customary folded dollar bills into the maître d's hand, but he was glancing around the place, oblivious to such mercenary transactions. They'd have to wait ages unless something were done, she thought, fumbling in her purse for a ten dollar bill. The maître d' palmed it discreetly, permitting her a smile. 'In five minutes, Madam, if that's all right? May I suggest a drink at the bar? Come this way, please.'

'What're you drinking, Courtney?' asked Calvin, hooking himself onto a tall stool next to her. Caroline decided on a Kir Royale. Tonight was going to be fun, somehow she felt more 'together', more *intimate* here with Calvin in this crowded restaurant, than when the two of them had been alone in her apartment. Maybe this would be the night that Calvin kissed her properly, the way she knew she wanted to be kissed by him . . .

He waved across the restaurant to someone he knew and she peeked over his shoulder curiously.

'That's Brodie Flyte,' he told her, 'with Marisa Kell, a model.'

Caroline had not yet met Brodie and she checked him out with interest. Then Marisa turned and waved too, blowing a kiss at Calvin. Caroline stared into the pink bubbles of her Kir Royale, consumed with a sudden jealousy.

'Marisa's very beautiful,' she murmured, pretending to sip her drink.

'Yeah. I've worked with her often,' said Calvin, 'we're old friends.'

'And we are only new friends,' commented Caroline, unable to hide the edge in her voice.

'New friends?' He toasted her with his drink. 'More than that, Courtney, *you* are my *best* friend.'

She gulped down her Kir. 'Best friend' was not exactly what she'd had in mind . . .

The maître d' signalled that their table was ready. En route Calvin paused to say hello to Brodie and Marisa, dropping a kiss on the model's pale, smooth cheek. Her lingering return kiss left the soft scarlet imprint of her lips on his face and Caroline longed to wipe it away, but instead she smiled politely as she was introduced.

'You've got lipstick on your face,' she said haughtily, when they were ensconced at their cosy corner table.

Calvin rubbed at his cheek ineffectively. Impulsively she leaned over and scrubbed his skin with her handkerchief.

'Thanks, Courtney,' Calvin said, studying his menu intently. After a few moments he closed it and said, 'What shall we eat?'

She stared at him in surprise, 'Well, what do you fancy? This is a very good menu, there's plenty of choice.'

'That's the trouble, there's too much. You choose for me, sweetheart.' Sitting back in his chair, he smiled at her easily, waiting for her to make the decision.

Summoning the waiter, Caroline ordered for both of them – angelhair pasta with a basil and tomato sauce, and after that carpaccio, thin slivers of beef with a garlic and mustard dressing.

'Wine, sir?' The waiter looked expectantly at Calvin, who simply shrugged and glanced at Caroline.

'Red or white?' she queried.

'Red,' he said positively.

'Well done!' retorted Caroline, laughing, 'at last you've made a decision!'

'It's just that I'm not good at that sort of thing,' Calvin explained, looking plaintive, 'and I know whatever you choose will be right.'

It was in the middle of a mouthful of pasta that Caroline realised why Calvin hadn't made love to her yet. Calvin was simply incapable of making *any* decision; he was like a little lost boy, he needed to be looked after, he needed his meals planned, his work arranged, his sleep peaceful. *And he needed her to make the first move.*

'Calvin,' she said, picking up her glass of Barolo Riserva, 'we're going to drink a toast.'

'What are we toasting, Courtney?' he demanded, taking up his glass.

'You'll find out later,' she murmured, as he took her hand

across the table and squeezed it, 'but meanwhile, let's toast to friendship.'

Back at her apartment, he lingered by the door, waiting for her to ask him in. 'But you know you can always come in, Calvin,' she told him.

'Courtney, my folks brought me up never to take liberties with a lady – and you are the "ladyest" girl I've ever met.'

'Is that the reason you don't make love to me?' she demanded, still standing in the open doorway. 'You think I'm too much of a lady?'

'Look at it this way,' he replied gently, fixing her with his narrow gaze, 'sex is easy . . . it's not something I've ever had to look for, and most times that's all it is. It's a high, it's warm, it's kinda companionable, but when it's over it's over.' Calvin shrugged, propping his lean frame against her door. 'It's just that I get this feeling with you, Courtney, that it's a whole other ballgame.'

As their eyes linked with longing, Caroline took his hand and drew him into the apartment. Kicking off her shoes she pushed the door closed with her foot. 'Tell you what, Calvin Jensen,' she whispered, sliding into the circle of his arms, 'why don't we just find out?'

Calvin's kiss was different this time, teasing open her willing mouth, tasting her, holding her close to his hard, slender body. Caroline could feel a tremor run through him as he lifted his mouth from hers and stared at her so intently, she felt he must surely have a blueprint of her features in his brain. And then suddenly he picked her up, hefting her easily in his arms, and carried her towards the bedroom.

'Let me undress you,' he said, throwing his jacket to the floor. Caroline looked down with dismay at her jacket with the long row of tiny round buttons hooked with their minuscule fabric loops, like the stays of some Edwardian lady. But Calvin's hands were nimble and the buttons were open in a minute and he was sliding the soft little jacket from her shoulders . . . as well as the wisp of peach lace bra . . . Calvin held her while she stood on the bed to wriggle out of her tight skirt and stockings, and then as she crumpled down onto the bed again, he lay across her,

218

kissing her gently, first her mouth, then her closed eyes, then her brow, her earlobes, the tiny fluttering pulse at the base of her throat . . . Pushing him away, Caroline fumbled with the buttons of his shirt. 'Wait,' she said. 'Now I want to undress you.' She removed his shirt, running the palms of her hands over the smooth skin of his back. Then she unbuckled the braided tan leather belt, waiting while he slid out of his French jeans.

Calvin knelt at her feet, his hands on her hips, kissing her tender, fleshy inner thighs; he kissed the soft hollows behind her knees, he cradled her foot in his hands and kissed her warm, scarlet-nailed toes; and then, when she felt she could bear it no longer, he hooked his fingers through her brief silk underpants, removing them gently, burying his face in that warm, scented place, kissing her and coaxing her until trembling, she begged him to stop . . . she needed him . . .

'Sweetheart, oh sweetheart,' groaned Calvin as he entered her, and 'Ah, Courtney, my love,' as she wrapped her legs around him. 'You're made of silk and satin,' he breathed in her ear, and she moaned in pleasure under his expert caresses. Shaking with passion he screamed, 'Jesus, Courtney,' as the long orgasm shook him.

Lying quietly in his arms, her body feeling as though it had just returned from another planet, Caroline knew there was nothing of the little lost boy about Calvin in bed.

He moved into her apartment gradually, sauntering by at first with his precious Vuitton satchel that contained all that was most important in his life – his latest pictures; his old snapshot of his dog, 'Bugsie'; clean underwear and socks; Eau Sauvage after-shave; a pair of well-worn jeans and a couple of cashmere sweaters from W. Bill of Bond Street, London.

Prowling her apartment one Sunday, he announced, 'What this place needs is a cat!' The following evening he appeared clutching a slender, silver grey, cross-bred Siamese that slid fluidly from his arms like a sliver of mercury. The cat fixed them both with a clear yellow-eyed stare, and proceeded to inspect the place from corner to corner. Finally, satisfied, it curled up on the sofa, making itself comfortable.

'He's yours, Courtney,' said Calvin, 'he's gonna look after you when I'm away, working. I picked him up at the pound. He's called Cosmo Steel – because he's that steely grey colour. I named him myself,' he added proudly.

Little by little, more of Calvin's stuff appeared, scattered among Caroline's less exotic possessions . . . his squash racquets dropped behind her front door after a game; magazines from Italy, France, Australia; his mail picked up from his own apartment and left lying around, mostly unopened, and covered with stamps from a half dozen different countries. Burning with curiosity, Caroline examined the handwriting on the envelopes, trying to decipher whether these were feminine correspondents, but she managed to resist the urge to open them and find out. Then came his clothes, beautiful garments from top designers, as well as his rumpled collection of old jackets; there were two dozen identical pairs of Gucci loafers and at least three dozen shirts from Paris, Rome and London. There was his work-out gear and his power-walking gear, and his tapes, and books . . .

After a month, Caroline made the decision that they should take a bigger apartment together, with enough room for her things as well as his. It was she who found the place, dashing out between urgent sessions at the office. It was Caroline who organised the move and found time to make the new place gracious with pleasant furnishings, curtains, lamps, rugs . . . it was a little English enclave on the twenty-fifth floor of a Manhattan skyscraper, with a view from their king-sized bed of the Chrysler building's pinnacle, lit up green like a Christmas tree.

Calvin had never been happier in his life. Being with Caroline was as comfortable as being with an old friend, and yet more exciting than any sexual relationship he'd ever experienced. A new dimension of sensuality had emerged between them, and on long, quiet Sundays – Caroline's only free day and usually the only day that he too could be sure of being in town – they lingered late in their spacious bed, with the curtains half-drawn and Cosmo Steel curled at their feet, just lazing and loving. They paused now and then to fix a bowl of muesli for Calvin and toast and tea for Caroline, scattering sections of the *New York Sunday Times* across the floor as they finished them. As evening approached, they'd rise lazily. Later, showered and refreshed and dressed casually in sweaters and jeans, they'd stroll around the block to the little neighbourhood French restaurant for supper.

These Sundays were the best days in Calvin's entire experience, and for the first time in his life he was absolutely certain of something. *He adored Caroline Courtney*. She had made sense from his muddled, hurried life. He felt better when he was with her, more secure . . . he no longer had to be thinking constantly about his next moves because Caroline took care of him, business-wise as well as at home.

When he was with Caroline, Calvin was as content as Cosmo Steel, the cat. It was only when he had to travel, which he did frequently, that he became restless and insecure and then his only consolation was the little unit he worked and travelled with. Proximity and the feeling of being separated from the rest of the world bred affairs like shipboard romances . . . there were always eager young models, and there was lonely Calvin, sorry for himself at being separated from Caroline . . . and they *were* so very pretty, and he *did* enjoy sex, for what it was . . .

16

On Danae's instructions Hector had bleached Gala's hair a deliberate Monroe-blonde, cropping it short up the back so that her neck looked even longer and more delicate. He'd left it longer on top, shaping it into a jagged uneven fringe so that in the sunlight it looked like a fluffy, silvery halo. As an alternative 'look', he'd given Gala a ruler-straight side-parting, slicking back her hair with gel until she appeared to be a very young, very blonde, nineteen-twenties dandy. 'Put her in a tuxedo and it'd be tough to know if she's a boy or a girl!' he told Danae triumphantly.

'Brilliant, Hector!' exclaimed Danae, inspecting her approvingly, 'it's *exactly* what I wanted.'

Gala glanced at her anxiously from beneath the new fringe, glad that Danae seemed pleased. She would have shaved her head, had Danae said it was necessary, because she wanted so badly to please her, to do well for her . . . she would do anything in the world to make this a success for Danae . . .

'OK, Gala, now I'm gonna show you what you get to wear for this job,' announced Danae. 'Come over here.'

The packets of Brodie Flyte underwear were spread across the worktable in the studio and Danae unwrapped some for Gala to see. 'OK,' she said, 'let's see you in these.' She held out a pair of knickers, cut exactly like a boy's Y-front underpants – only these were in lilac silk. A brief matching vest, like a racing swim suit with wide armholes that left the shoulderblades free, came with them, and Gala clutched them doubtfully. Danae held up a masculine version of the same outfit, in white sea-island cotton – as soft and fine as silk but, in Brodie Flyte's view, more butch. 'These are Calvin's,' she said.

'Who is Calvin?' asked Gala, bewildered.

'Calvin's the guy you'll be sharing this job with,' she replied, burrowing amongst the pile of underwear.

'Calvin Jensen is a top model Gala, you're lucky to get to work with him first time out,' interrupted Hector. 'Besides, he's a great guy.'

Gala glanced apprehensively at the underwear and then at Danae. 'I hadn't realised I'd be working with a man,' she said, blushing.

'You'll be working with another *model*!' snapped Danae, 'and if he can take his clothes off for the camera, then so can you.'

'Yes, yes, of course . . . I'll go and put these on,' Gala murmured, hurrying into the dressing room.

'She's a bit shy, your new chick,' observed Hector, polishing his nails.

'She'll get over it,' replied Danae, calmly, 'or at least, *I hope* she'll get over it. Come to think of it, Hector, she'd *better* get over it – for my sake as well as hers.'

They were laughing together as Gala emerged from the dressing room wearing the lilac knickers and vest, and despite her resolve to forget her silly inhibitions, she shrank from their gaze.

Danae prowled around, inspecting her like a trainer with a thoroughbred filly before the big race. In the month that she had been in New York, Gala had been to exercise class every day; she'd worked out on Nautilus machines, she'd taken dance class, and she'd lifted weights under the supervision of a top instructor. She had swum twenty laps and done a half hour of yoga exercise morning and evening, as well as meditation at night before she went to sleep, to bring her down from all the day's hyper-activity. Danae hadn't let up on her; she'd nagged her, bullied her, encouraged her . . . she'd even swum with her and accompanied her to class. Danae was creating a star and Gala was going to be in perfect shape before she faced her camera.

On her special high energy, low-calorie diet, Gala was no longer emaciated; her face had bloomed again into little-girl softness and there was a hint of roundness in her cheeks – but this time there were *bones* there too . . . her cheeks had delicious hollows, and her eyesockets looked as if carved from ivory. Gala had perfect long legs with just enough muscle to pass for a young athlete in the lens of the clever camera. Her hips were as tapered as a boy's, with a tight round rump, long waist and small, high breasts. 'Gala,' said Danae happily, 'you could start a whole new fashion in bodies – you look terrific.'

Gala relaxed. Danae thought she looked all right and somehow, even being photographed in underwear didn't seem to matter as much, after all it was only like wearing a bathing suit, just a tiny bit more revealing . . .

'Try on the other things,' commanded Danae, 'and after that Isobel wants to experiment with some make-up.'

Danae had scarely let Gala out of her sight since she'd brought her to New York; the girl was staying in her new studio apartment on the border of Greenwich Village and when she went out to her classes, or to *Images*, it was under supervision. The only parts of Manhattan Gala had seen were those stretches she'd glimpsed from taxis between the Village and West Fifty-seventh where the exercise studios were, or en route to Third Avenue and *Images*. She spent her evenings alone if Danae worked late – which she often did – eating chicken salad with low-fat yoghurt dressing, and watching television, switching from channel to channel eager to devour all the glamour America had to offer. She had not yet visited Central Park or the Empire State Building; she had not tasted a hot dog or a pizza; and she'd never been to a single one of New York's remarkable restaurants. But she had been to Bloomingdale's.

Jessie-Ann had taken her to the famous store and outfitted her with a simple basic wardrobe. Danae had left instructions that Jessie-Ann was to scrap everything that Gala owned and start from the bottom up, so they'd swept through department after department, choosing underwear and pyjamas, bathrobes and slippers, basic jeans and shirts and Reebok sneakers. They'd bought an oversized jacket with wide padded shoulders, some linen pants, a couple of skirts, a few big sweaters, plus belts, shoes, and a huge soft squashy handbag that Gala regarded with a mixture of pleasure and dismay, because she had nothing to carry in such a beautiful bag.

'Gala honey,' said Jessie-Ann affectionately, 'you are the most basic person I've ever met. You have absolutely *no greed*. I can think of a dozen models I might have brought in here who would have demanded the *most*! And the most *expensive*.'

'I think I'd rather earn the money first,' Gala had replied, 'it gets me nervous buying on HP – hire-purchase . . . that's what credit is called in Yorkshire,' she'd explained with a smile, seeing Jessie-Ann's puzzled expression.

But nevertheless, the new clothes had brought her more pleasure than she'd known in months and, simple though they were, they had been put together with Jessie-Ann's flair. Now Gala felt prepared for America. There was no longer any need to be ashamed of her appearance; she was part of 'the scene'.

Over a cup of coffee, she'd told Jessie-Ann, in confidence, about her childhood, and how she'd always kept her pictures pinned on the wall, as her image of perfection, glamour and success, wishing she could be like her. Jessie-Ann had laughed, looking exactly the way that Gala knew so well from photographs, and told Gala that she was probably going to be a far better model than she had ever been. It wasn't true of course, but still Gala thought it was nice of Jessie-Ann to say so.

'Right, guys,' called Danae, 'tomorrow Calvin will be here and we can get our two models together. I need a few rehearsals for this one. OK, Gala?'

'OK,' beamed Gala. Everything was just fine. Danae knew exactly what she was doing.

17

Marcus occupied one of the coveted 'fireplace' rooms in Blair Hall, the same one that his father had lived in when he was at Princeton. It's appearance and general state of student untidiness had probably changed very little since Harrison's days. Between them, Marcus and his room-mate had arrived at the simple conclusion that if you left your clothes and your sports gear, your books and papers and the general debris of life, exactly where you dropped them, then the stuff simply accumulated in daily layers. If you wanted anything, you just sifted down through the layers like an archaeological dig, until you came to the appropriate day – and there it was. Their system was foolproof, but their gothic-windowed room was a scene to break any mother's heart!

It was while he was searching for his favourite grey sweatshirt and already down to layer six, that Marcus came across a two-week-old copy of *People* magazine open at a picture of his father and Merry McCall. Even though he was late for crew practice and should have been at the Boathouse on Carnegie Lake – like *now* – he was compelled to stop and look at it more carefully. They were caught in the light of a flashbulb as they were leaving a San Francisco restaurant called the Fog City Diner. Merry was gazing up at Harrison with an adoring smile, and his father had his arm around her pretty shoulders and was gazing back at her with a look of tender indulgence. 'Regular twosome Merry McCall and Harrison Royle dining together – again . . . while the lovely Jessie-Ann stays home and looks after her two babies – *Images* and son Jon . . .'

Regular twosome? His father – and Merry McCall? Marcus re-read the blurb uneasily. Harrison had told him just a couple of weeks ago that the Road Show was the main reason for the astronomical sales of the Royle Girl line, and he was aware that his father often flew out to the Show's latest location to check on his pet project. Or maybe he was just checking on Merry McCall?

Placing the magazine on his desk – the only neat sector in his half of the room – Marcus stared at the photograph for a long moment before turning and heading for the door. Grabbing his cycle from the rack, he peddled furiously through the campus and down Elm Drive, turning left along Faculty Road towards Carnegie Lake and the Boathouse.

At six-two and weighing 175 pounds, Marcus had the lean, hard body and broad muscular shoulders of a champion rower and was a member of the Princeton crew. Ever since he'd been a kid, he'd had two passions – boats and buildings. It was during family holidays with his father on Martha's Vineyard and Eleuthera that he'd learned the craft of sailing. Later but when he was still very small, on long treks with Harrison through Europe he'd discovered his love for architecture. It was always Marcus who'd begged to stop so that they could explore a ruined Abbey in France or a great Byzantine Mosque in Istanbul, or a Quattrocento Venetian Palazzo. Princeton's graduate school of Architecture loomed in his ambitions, like a trophy to be won. Only there would he be able to achieve his life-long ambition to learn how to design the sort of buildings he considered to be 'living sculptures'. He was working steadily towards his architectural goal, and at the same time enjoying the physical high being a member of crew gave him. And, in between, he managed to commit himself to a pretty hectic social life.

Marcus was as attractive as his father, with more than his fair share of his late mother's charm, plus a touch of tenderness that was uniquely his own. He was a young man certain of his place in the world and of his value in it. He was sensitive and he was fun to be with; he enjoyed reading Shakespeare's sonnets and Donne's love poems; he liked the music of Satie and Mozart, as well as Dire Straits and Bruce Springsteen. He had girlfriends, with whom he often shared his dreams and occasionally his bed, and guys he liked to hang out with. His life was crammed to the hilt with work and fun.

But as he wheeled his bike into the yard and slung it into the rack, Marcus's mind wasn't on the immediate practice session on Carnegie Lake. Nor, as he viewed the two-thousand yard straightaway rowing course, assessing the wind before walking to the Boathouse, was his mind on tonight's party being given by Janie Ardley, with whom he had quite a nice thing going. Marcus was thinking about Jessie-Ann.

Even as he hefted the shell with the other members of the crew, flipping it over as they came to the water's edge and lowering it into the lake, he was wondering whether she had seen the magazine, and if there had been other items in the gossip mags or in the tabloids? It was the phrase 'regular twosome' that worried him . . . implying that Merry and his father were often seen around together. Of course Merry *was* the Royle Girl and it might all be perfectly legit, after all his father was deeply committed to Royle's new project. Marcus pulled harder on his oar in rhythm with the cox's count, wondering if his father was also committing himself to Merry McCall? A few months ago he would have dismissed the idea as crazy but, the last couple of times he'd been home it seemed to him that Jessie-Ann had been going in one direction and Harrison in another. Could his father really be infatuated enough with Merry to jeopardise all he had going with Jessie-Ann? Or was he just angry with her for neglecting him? There was no doubt that Jessie-Ann was deeply involved in *Images* and that she no longer had the time for Harrison that he wanted.

The cox signalled them to rest and he leaned on his oar, sweat matting his thick light hair and his muscles screaming for release. If there were something going on it was both their faults. How could they be such fools he wondered angrily, when they stood to lose so much. Because he was certain his father loved Jessie-Ann, just as he was certain that she loved Harrison.

He was damned if he was going to stand by and let them make a mess of things. He'd drive to New York this very afternoon; he'd find Jessie-Ann at *Images* and without her knowing, check to see if she had heard the rumours. Then he would get his father alone and find out what the scene really was. And if the rumours were true, he was going to do his damnedest to convince his father that he was being a fool, and that he risked losing Jessie-Ann and his young son Jon, and all they stood for in his life.

Images was in a state of hushed excitement. Danae had meant to start shooting Brodie Flyte's 'Bodylines' campaign at two thirty that afternoon but she'd been delayed by a terrific fight with Calvin who had refused to let her cut his hair to match Gala's. She was only just getting the show on the road, at four o'clock.

Caroline had come to her rescue of course. She'd taken Calvin aside trying to reason with him, stroking back his hair soothingly, the way she might an unhappy child. 'Remember when we first met?' she'd asked him gently, 'didn't I tell you then, just to leave it all to Danae and you'd have the best pictures you ever had in your life? *Trust her Calvin*, she knows what she's doing.'

'I've got other jobs booked,' replied Calvin, anguished by indecision, 'they're used to me looking like this.'

'Then maybe it's time for a change,' retorted Caroline. 'You'll still be *Calvin* – just a new aspect of you.'

Caroline had finally almost convinced him when he'd seen Gala-Rose.

Calvin stared at her suspiciously as he shook her hand. Gala wore a long, white terry bathrobe and no make-up. With her platinum hair side-parted and slicked back with gel until it fitted her beautifully-shaped head like a gleaming little cap, she looked shy and gawky.

'Jesus,' he muttered to Caroline, as he turned away, 'the kid looks like a ventriloquist's dummy. Is this Danae's idea of a joke?'

'*Trust her*, Calvin,' insisted Caroline.

He shook his head doubtfully. 'This is my career you're messin' with, Courtney,' he replied, sitting resignedly in front of the mirror as Hector brandished his scissors. 'I hope you all know what you're doing.'

Isobel worked on Gala, using the formula she and Danae had arrived at the night before. On her right profile she used a foundation of porcelain paleness, a flush of lavender-pink defining the hollows in her cheeks, a flicker of amethyst accentuating Gala's deep eyesocket and a careful smudge of grey swept around her eye. She applied dark grey mascara, and filled out her eyebrows with the faintest, feathery strokes of lavender pencil, painting her soft mouth into violet petulance. On Gala's left profile Isobel used a golden colour foundation, flushing her cheek a healthy coral and adding sunshine to her bronzed face with yellow eyeshadows and a glitter of golden dust to match the gold shimmered coral mouth. The right side of her body was powdered into immaculate paleness while her left was anointed with golden body make-up. Gala swivelled from side to side, staring at two reflections in the mirror and finding two totally different personalities. In one she was a wild little wood nymph, a Puck who'd never emerged from the forest's dark-greenness into the clear light of the fields; and in the other, a golden racing-limbed young athlete from ancient Greece, ready for the very first Olympics . . .

'Fantastic!' declared Danae, looking her over critically. 'OK, Isobel, now on to Calvin. And, Gala, I need you for some practice shots.'

Gala followed her obediently, avoiding Calvin's stunned gaze as she passed by . . . God, he was *so* good-looking, and so . . . so *New York*! He'd done jobs like this a thousand times and knew exactly what to expect, but she supposed he was used to working with experienced models. He travelled the world and like Jessie-Ann, he did the top European fashion shows. *Calvin was a star!* Her heart sinking, Gala sat on the edge of a narrow, silk-sheeted bed while Danae gazed into light meters and shouted commands to her assistant, Frostie White, who was hefting the halogens around uncomplainingly.

Jessie-Ann hovered on the sidelines, smiling encouragingly as Gala's frightened eyes met hers. 'It's OK, honey,' she called, dashing over to give her a quick hug, 'we're all here rooting for you – it's gonna work out just great. Do you have any idea how *fantastic* you look? I honestly don't know which half of you is more beautiful . . . you're just a knockout, Gala-Rose, and you'd better believe that, because it's *true*!'

Calvin strolled nonchalantly into the studio clad only in Brodie's brief pants. His tanned body gleamed from Isobel's expert attention and his shorn blond hair was parted low at the side and slicked back to match Gala's.

Caroline's heart skipped a beat as she watched him step into the circle of lights and even Jessie-Ann, used to beauty as she was, gasped. 'Caroline,' she whispered, 'our Danae certainly knows what she's doing. Just look at the pair of them!'

As they sat on the bed, Gala's left profile was towards the camera. Her lithe body leaned into his as Calvin put his strong arms around her.

'Closer,' commanded Danae. 'And, Frostie, mess up that sheet in the background a little will you . . . I want it to look as though they'd just stepped out of that bed. Gala, you're looking a touch stiff there – how about a glass of wine to loosen you up a little?'

'No!' she cried, the awful memory of Cam and that night at Marley's studio returning suddenly . . . It's OK, she told herself nervously, this isn't like with Cam, this is *professional*. I'm a real model now, and I'm working with the best.

'It'll be OK you know,' Calvin murmured in Gala's ear, 'it's only a job hon', just lean close to me, get real comfortable. Danae'll let us know what she wants us to do. Did anyone ever tell you you have fantastic eyes? You do, you know, grey as English skies, I'll bet. Where are you from, sweetheart?'

'I'm from Yorkshire,' whispered Gala, allowing herself to sink a little closer towards him – but somehow Calvin was so . . . so *naked*. And so was *she*, just these little silk underthings . . .

'I was there once,' said Calvin, surprising her, 'the dales and all those sheep and low dry-stone walls . . . beautiful it was. Stayed at a quaint old inn somewhere up on the moors at Grassington.'

'*You've* been to *Grassington*?' squeaked Gala, amazed.

'Sure have, sweetheart, drove all around there – and loved it . . . Doesn't that make me almost family?' he added with a grin.

'Almost,' she admitted, smiling.

Calvin tightened his arms around her as Frostie finished fixing the sheet.

'Right,' called Danae, 'we're rolling.'

It was seven thirty and Gala waited in the dressing-room, wrapped in her voluminous bathrobe and trembling with exhaustion. She'd thought it was all over, but apparently they were just taking an hour's break and then they would start up again, using a whole different approach. Her face had been wiped clean of the exotic make-up and her hair had been washed one more time and finger dried by Hector, this time into an angel's fluff. Watching her reflection in the long mirror with its border of light bulbs, she thought she resembled a well-scrubbed, half-plucked chicken! With a sigh she heaved her aching legs onto the counter and took a desultory bite of the chicken sandwich. A glass of champagne waited, untouched, on the counter near her feet, and as she chewed she watched its bubbles rise steadily to the top and disappear. She put down the sandwich again, she just couldn't eat. She was still too on edge. Leaning back in the chair, she closed her eyes, re-living the past few hours . . . Calvin's warm body next to hers, the rumpled silk sheet and her half exposed breasts; the hot blush that had coloured her cheeks and made him smile, the feel of . . . of his *maleness* next to her. But still Calvin hadn't made her feel the way she'd felt with Cam that night, or even the way she'd felt about Jake . . . maybe what she'd felt for Cam was *sex*, and she knew that she had *loved* Jake. She was grateful to Calvin for helping her, easing her into feeling just really *comfortable* with him. 'It's all pretend, kid,' he'd told her, 'I'm pretending I'm crazy about you and you're pretending that *maybe* you're crazy about me . . . and the way it's gonna look in the pictures is all up to Danae. You and I'll just do our own thing here on this bed – the rest is up to her.'

Danae had warned them that after the break they were to lose the romantic, sexy mood; she wanted them to be vital and vivacious, glad to be alive. They'd be leaping through the air, she'd told them, and doing handstands and vaulting . . . and then next week there would be some summery, beach shots . . . it seemed this Brodie Flyte job would go on forever . . .

Marcus waited a full minute before he spoke, just standing in the doorway taking in the wondrous blonde waif with the angel's haircut and the sweetest, softest mouth. Her eyes were closed and he stared at her face, at the delicate curves of her alabaster eyelids and the firm straight nose, and the sweet curve of her cheek. Who could she be?

'I hate to disturb you,' he murmured, apologetically, as Gala's eyes shot open in surprise, 'but there's no one else about.'

'They've all gone round the corner to Blakey's,' she replied hurriedly, 'it's the break you see, and they were hungry.'

'And you're not?' Marcus asked, observing the uneaten sandwich.

Gala eyed him warily, she was all alone in the studio and she'd never seen him before – yet there was something familiar about him. 'They'll be back in a minute,' she told him, wrapping her robe closer, 'in fact they should be here right now.'

'That's OK, I'll wait. It's Jessie-Ann I've come to see really.'

Then he must be here on business, thought Gala, relieved. Whoever he was he had a nice face, a *reliable* face. And he was *very* attractive. She liked his brown eyes and his mop of dark blond hair – it hung shaggy and straight, falling into his eyes. '*Who* was he?' she wondered, as they stared at each other in silence. 'Do you know Jessie-Ann?' she asked at last.

Marcus grinned at her. 'Sure I know her, she's my step-mother.'

Gala sat up with a little gasp. 'Your *step-mother*!'

'Crazy isn't it? But Jessie-Ann's married to my Dad. I'm Marcus Royle.' He offered a firm handshake, and Gala bit her lip in embarrassment, she'd been almost rude to Mr Royle's son . . . how stupid of her . . .

'I beg your pardon . . .' she stammered, 'I just didn't know who you were.'

'Of course not.' Marcus slumped into the chair by her side and their eyes met in the mirror. 'And?' he asked.

She gazed back at him, puzzled.

'*Who* are *you*? No, don't tell me . . . You are Titania, you are Wendy without Peter; you're Tinker Bell or Puck . . . *What* are you? I'm lost . . . I can't put a name to such a rare face? Are you a famous model? *Should* I know you?'

Gala laughed and Marcus thought he'd never heard such a joyous sound in his entire life. 'I'm just Gala-Rose,' she answered, snuggling deeper into her robe and smiling at him in the mirror, 'and I'm not famous. But Danae and Jessie-Ann tell me that I will be when the Brodie Flyte Bodylines campaign is launched on the unsuspecting world.'

'Tell me, Gala-Rose,' he said leaning closer, 'what does a mere mortal guy like me have to do to get a soon-to-be-famous model to have dinner with him?'

Gala laughed, all her fears and worries, all her nerves and

inhibitions had suddenly disappeared. Marcus Royle was warm and real – and he was *fun*. And fun was not something she could remember experiencing very often. 'To have dinner with you?' she repeated, an impish smile curving her lips. 'Well, first you'll have to ask Danae.'

'*Danae!*' Marcus's expression of mixed surprise and horror made her laugh.

'Danae brought me here from London. She sort of manages my life – and so far I've not been allowed out – for dinner – or anything else.'

'We'll change *that* situation right away,' Marcus said firmly, taking her hand in his, 'you're having dinner with *me* tonight. Please?'

Gala traced the line of calluses across the palm of his hand with her finger.

'Rowing,' he explained, as she glanced at him questioningly, 'but you haven't answered me.'

She smiled, her grey eyes as clear and translucent as a forest pool. 'I'd like that,' she answered shyly. In fact, she could think of nothing in the entire, whole wide world she'd like more than to have dinner with Marcus Royle.

The bed had been replaced by a backdrop of brilliant blue skies and scudding clouds and hot lights lit the scene with the power of a noonday sun. Calvin, already changed into bright primary-blue boxers and racing vest, waited calmly for his instructions. Beneath her robe Gala wore the identical outfit in poster-paint red. 'I don't think I can do it,' she whispered to Marcus suddenly nervous again . . .

'Sure you can – when I'm not around. Anyhow, I have to talk to Jessie-Ann,' he said, heading tactfully for the door and almost falling over the girl standing at the back in the shadows.

'I'm sorry,' he cried grabbing her arm, 'I hope I didn't hurt you, stepping on your foot like that.'

'That's OK,' muttered Laurinda.

'You're sure now?' Marcus hesitated. He'd really stepped hard on her foot, it must have hurt like hell, but he hadn't spotted her there, in the dark . . .

'Sure,' replied Laurinda, shaking off his hand and moving away. 'I'm OK.'

'Well then . . . sorry again.'

She watched him disappear through the door, a glimmer of interest in her sullen eyes. Surely that must be Harrison's son? What was *he* doing here? What was Jessie-Ann up to now? You'd think things had gone far enough for one day without Marcus Royle getting into the act. After that *shameful* session this afternoon when they'd made that poor young girl Gala strip almost naked and roll around in bed with Calvin . . . it didn't take an expert to know what Calvin was feeling with that great bulge concealed in his pants . . . God, it made her shiver just to think of it . . . she hadn't wanted to watch, it brought back all the ugly memories, as if she were lying in that bed, but she'd been unable to tear her eyes away from the scene. Danae had made Calvin lie on top of Gala; he'd just sort of rested on his arms, pushing his body away from her . . . and Laurinda had seen the expression in his eyes, the hot, searing look that had passed between the two of them. Jessie-Ann would have Gala's lost innocence to add to her evil record this week, because it was for sure the girl was corrupted now. And just look at the way she'd been staring at Marcus Royle . . . all warm and glowing. It was enough to make Laurinda vomit, that sort of look . . . it brought back all those ugly memories of the way her father used to watch Jessie-Ann, lusting after her . . .

'Right, you guys,' called Danae, 'hold hands and when I count to three, start *jumping*!'

Lurking in the shadows, by the door, away from the bright, hot lights and the charmed circle of beautiful people, Laurinda watched in silence.

Jessie-Ann put down the phone and kissed Marcus, hugging him tightly. 'Am I glad to see *you*!' she exclaimed, 'at least one member of the family is home! Are you staying the night? Harrison's away and I thought maybe you and I could have dinner?'

'Dad's away?' asked Marcus, casually.

Jessie-Ann sighed, 'We're not organising our lives very well right now. I'm always free when Harrison is away – and when

235

I'm busy, then of course that's the time he's home!' Her blue eyes were wistful as she thought of Harrison, and Marcus knew she was unaware of the gossip. He'd be willing to bet though, that if there *were* something going on, half of New York would be talking about it by now. What was it they said, the wife is always the last to know? Oh shit, he thought gloomily, this was really trouble . . . he'd have to get a hold of his father and try to talk some sense into him before it went too far. 'Sorry I missed Dad,' he said casually, 'when will he be back?'

'Oh, Monday or Tuesday. He has meetings in town all next week.'

'About dinner,' said Marcus grinning, 'you should have caught me earlier, I've got a date.'

'Jane?'

He shook his head. 'Gala-Rose,' he replied with a nonchalant grin.

'*Gala-Rose?*'

'Why so surprised? She's only the most beautiful girl I've *ever* seen – step-mothers excluded of course!'

'OK,' she laughed, 'but you'll have to get past *Danae* first! But knowing you, you'll even charm our very own dragon-lady slave driver. Have fun, Marcus. And take care of her – she's breakable.'

'I will,' he promised. And he meant it.

18

Laurinda sat on the floor of her apartment with a small sharp pair of scissors in her hand, surrounded by dismembered magazines and newspapers. She wore a pair of thin surgical gloves just as she did when she typed the letters because she was too smart to be caught by such a naïve thing like fingerprints. On her left side lay the neat pile of clippings she'd gleaned over the last two months, all of them featuring a photograph of Harrison and Merry. There weren't that many but there was no doubt in Laurinda's mind that Jessie-Ann had driven Harrison into the arms of another woman – and it was the *wrong one!* That woman was meant to be her, Laurinda . . . *she* was destined to take Jessie-Ann's place so that she might look after Harrison and his son. And after the *shameless* behaviour at *Images* the last few weeks she knew that it was time to make her move. First she would save young Jon and then she would take care of Jessie-Ann.

Laurinda stared around her tiny, studio apartment. No one ever came here; she was as isolated as if she were living on a farm in Montana, but it was a singles apartment-block, inhabited by young people struggling to make it in Manhattan, living on credit and the optimism of youth. A child would be as conspicuous here as an elephant. She must find another apartment, further out in the suburbs, where she could merge into the normal background of women with children.

It wouldn't be easy. She would have to make her plans carefully. The question was would Jessie-Ann alert the police or would she wait for a ransom note from the 'kidnapper'? And would she realise that it was Laurinda? There was always that risk of course, but she'd bet that Jessie-Ann would be afraid to contact the police in case the 'kidnapper' harmed the child. Laurinda could see in her mind's eye the 'ransom' note, written in red letters like the others so that Jessie-Ann would *know* it was aimed at *her*. Only what she wanted as 'ransom' was not money, but Jessie-Ann. The time she wasted by not going to the police would give Laurinda just enough time to carry out the rest of her plan.

Picking up the little pile of clippings, she carried them to the table and stuffed them inside an envelope. Then she took the old typewriter from its hiding place in the kitchen cupboard and began composing her letters, so that she would have them all ready for the big day. And this very afternoon, she intended to take the subway out to Queens where she'd look for a new apartment. She wanted something suitable for a woman and a child, on a busy street where they wouldn't be too noticeable. She would make sure to tell the landlord that she was a single parent, and that at present her boy was staying with his grandparents in Montana, but that he'd be back with her real soon. And then when she'd finally got Jessie-Ann alone, that's when she'd really tell her what she thought of her, the truth . . . the whole truth . . . nothing but the truth . . .

She watched the letters appearing on her sheet of paper, dreamily composing obscenities with a smile of satisfaction, like a child at playschool pleased with its first attempts at making words.

Harrison glanced up in surprise, a pleased smile touching the corners of his mouth as Marcus strode through the door. It wasn't often that his son came to see him at the office. Even though Marcus was over twenty years old, he could still see the little blond boy who'd haunted his elbow seventeen years back, waiting to be counted in as his Dad's friend and companion.

'Good to see you, son,' he exclaimed. 'But what brings you here mid-week? No trouble at college, I hope?' He laughed as he said it, because Marcus had always been one of the steadiest boys he knew – he worked hard, got good grades, and he rowed crew. What more could a father ask?

'I'm here for two reasons.' Sitting opposite his father, Marcus leaned earnestly on the polished, uncluttered surface of the desk. 'It's kinda hard to say this but . . . well, Dad, I've been reading a few things in the gossip columns recently – about you and Merry McCall. I guess it's all being blown out of proportion by the press, but I'm worried about Jessie-Ann. I surely wouldn't like to see her hurt.'

Harrison leaned back in his swivel chair, fingertips pressed together avoiding Marcus's eyes. The boy had put it as delicately as he knew how; he hadn't *asked* him if there was anything going on between him and Merry, he'd merely presented him with the question that Harrison asked himself most often – what about Jessie-Ann? He certainly didn't want to cause her any pain . . . he loved her and he still wanted her, desperately. But Merry was filling a void in his life that he hadn't expected to find there. 'You're right, Marcus,' he replied finally, 'the press is playing things up. Merry and I are often together when I visit the Royle Road Show, but it's nothing that you – or Jessie-Ann – need worry about.'

Marcus recognised he was being put off, but he'd made his point. Whatever was going on between Merry and his father was their business, but he sure as hell wasn't going to let his father jeopardise Jessie-Ann's life – and love, without a fight. 'I know Jessie-Ann hasn't heard anything about it,' he said. 'I guess she's too busy with *Images* to have time to read the popular press. It would break her heart, Dad, if there were any . . . any *trouble*. And I think maybe it would break yours too?'

'You've made your point,' replied Harrison coolly, 'and I appreciate what you're saying. I can assure you I've no intention of hurting Jessie-Ann. Now,' he added briskly, gathering up some papers and thrusting them into his black leather briefcase, 'there's a meeting downtown I'm already late for. Maybe we could have dinner tonight?'

'Sorry, I've got a date. It's kind of an important date,' he added, looking at his father seriously. 'I've only known her a few weeks, but I'm in love with this girl, Dad.'

Harrison's eyebrows rose. 'Love, eh? Well, it gets to us all in time, son.'

'It's serious, Dad – at least it is if I can persuade Gala that I mean it.'

Harrison glanced at his watch, he was already five minutes late. 'Sorry, Marcus, but I really must leave. Why don't you stop by and see Jessie-Ann. And don't worry about "love". At your age it comes and goes.'

'Not this time,' replied Marcus quietly.

'Can I give you a lift somewhere?' Harrison asked in the elevator. 'I have the car waiting downstairs.'

'Thanks, I'll walk.'

'Goodbye, son. Give me a call – maybe we can all have dinner later in the week? Bring this new girl you're so crazy about. Wait a minute though, I have to be in Chicago this weekend . . .'

'That's OK, Dad, we'll catch up.'

'Fine. Good to see you, son.'

It was too bad, thought Marcus sadly, as the big car pulled from the kerb, that both Harrison and Jessie-Ann were too busy to see what was happening to them, and too busy to listen to him when he had something important to say.

19

The envelope with her name and address typewritten in red was
lying on Jessie-Ann's desk, tucked in with the morning mail, and
as soon as she saw it the old fear set her pulses racing and her
heart pounding. What was it they called the atavistic reaction to
fear or threat? Fight or flee . . . that was it. And she wanted to
flee from *this*! Picking up the envelope by a corner she tossed it
into the waste basket, but then she glanced back at it uneasily.
There was something different about the envelope this time, it was
bulky and heavy. She forced her gaze away from the wastepaper
basket, whatever it was, she didn't want to know.

The envelope lay there, amongst the rest of the day's trash,
until late afternoon. The studios quiet and the secretaries gone
for the day and unable to resist her curiosity, she fished it out
trying to decide whether to open it.

Laurinda paused in the doorway, a triumphant little gleam in
her eye as she watched the changing expressions flitting across
Jessie-Ann's face . . . uncertainty . . . anger . . . and fear. Laurinda felt the savage pleasure of possessing power over another
person; Jessie-Ann was *hers* – hers to manipulate any way she
wished. It was *she* who called the tune now – and she was gonna
make sure that Jessie-Ann *danced* to it . . . she'd dance and dance
and dance . . .

Her face flushed with excitement, she strode into the room.
'Here are the Avlon figures, Jessie-Ann; I thought you should
know that they're pulling the old trick of not paying on time; I've
given them the usual reminder.'

Jessie-Ann glanced at Laurinda without really seeing her. She
was still thinking about the envelope, wondering what it contained
that was different . . .

'And we'll have to keep our eye on any "non-*Images*" photographers who rent the studios and hire our models,' continued
Laurinda. 'I've been after Dickson Cross for a couple of months

now, but he always claimed he hadn't been paid yet by *his* client, Blissful Fashions.'

'Oh?' she queried, barely listening.

'Yes. But I nailed that down too, I got on the line to Blissful and asked when they intended to pay Cross, because he owed us and wasn't paying until *they* did. They told me they'd paid Cross six weeks ago.'

'Really?'

'Naturally, I got on the phone right away and told *Mr* Dickson Cross that unless he paid like *yesterday* – he'd be on *Images'* black books and would not be able to use these studios again. His cheque came this morning.' She waved it in front of Jessie-Ann's eyes.

'Great,' she replied wearily.

'You OK, Jessie-Ann?' Laurinda enquired, enjoying herself. 'You look tired – or maybe you're *upset* about something?'

'You're right. I am tired. I'm going home. I'm sure I'll feel better in the morning.' With one swift movement she swept the bulky envelope back into the waste basket. Picking up her purse she headed for the door. ''Night, Laurinda,' she called over her shoulder, 'thanks for all the information. See you tomorrow.'

Laurinda glared angrily after her and then she grabbed the waste basket and retrieved her letter. Jessie-Ann wasn't getting away this easy. She'd find that letter on her desk again tomorrow morning – and every morning after that, until she was *compelled* to open it!

Kissing Jon goodnight before he went to bed, Jessie-Ann closed her eyes, clutching the boy to her as though afraid to let him go. Jon was tall for his twenty months, with a thin, elastic little body and knobbly knees appliquéd with an assortment of scratches and bruises, a tribute to his adventurous nature. With his shock of dark hair and big, dark blue eyes, young Jon Royle had a waif-like charm that was a true heart-stealer. He hugged his mother back tightly and then wriggled free, heading for his rocking horse for 'one last ride', before bed.

'Push, Mommy, push me,' he commanded, sensing Jessie-Ann's

lenient mood and taking advantage of the extra minutes while he could.

Jessie-Ann pushed, smiling at his delight as the little horse bucked faster. 'Hold on, Jon,' she warned, 'we don't want you falling off again.' He really looked so cute in his yellow sleepers and those little cowboy boots – from which he refused to be parted. Nanny had to place them at the foot of his bed where he could see them and they were the first thing he asked about in the morning. Little red cowboy boots, she thought with a surge of love, that's all it took to make him happy. She wished Harrison were here to kiss him goodnight, but Harrison was away more nights than he was home these days.

With a helpless sinking feeling in the pit of her stomach, she wondered where had they gone wrong? They seemed to see each other less and less, and when they *were* together, did they really talk to each other? She loved him . . . she was sure of it, and he was kind and loving towards her, in an absent-minded sort of way. But where was the passion that had bonded them right from the beginning? And what had happened to make them lose sight of the priorities in their lives? She knew a good deal of the problem was because of the time she'd spent away, working, but was it *entirely* her fault? Harrison was away so often too, now . . .

'More, Mommy, more,' chortled Jon, his face crumpled with glee.

'No more, young man,' she said firmly, 'it's way past your bedtime. Off with those boots now, and into bed.'

'Where's Daddy?' he asked, lying back against his Garfield pillow.

'Daddy's working,' she murmured, bending to kiss him. 'He'll be home tomorrow.'

'Home,' Jon muttered drowsily, his eyelids already drooping.

''Night, my little love,' whispered Jessie-Ann, bestowing a final kiss on his warm forehead. Jon yawned, his eyes shut tight. He'd be asleep before she left the room.

In the small sitting room a table was set for one. Salad, cold chicken, a half-bottle of chilled champagne – her favourite drink and usually a great pick-me-up at the end of a long day. The

243

houseman hurried to open the bottle and pour her a glass, and then he departed, closing the door softly.

The sound of surging traffic penetrated faintly into the apartment, and its wide windows framed a blue-black sky, lit from below by the glare of the street lamps and traffic and a million twinkling windows. Suddenly she felt very small and very alone. 'Why, oh why,' she implored the Manhattan night, 'why is it all going wrong now, when everything else is going so right?'

Images had really hit the headlines with Danae's outrageously erotic photographs for Brodie Flyte's 'Bodylines'. Calvin, clad only in Brodie Flyte's indiscreet underwear, displayed on giant billboards from LA's Sunset Boulevard to New York's Times Square, had set the country's female population atremble with vicarious pleasure. And the androgynous, split-personality, Gala-Rose was the talk of New York, one moment a night-time boy/girl nymph, her long silken legs entwined with Calvin's, and her soft, pale childish mouth hovering breathlessly over his, their matching short sleek blond heads lending a titillating question to their embrace; and the next moment, she was a streamlined golden hoyden, breasts half exposed in a twist of silken sheets as she lay in Calvin's arms. And then, in contrast there were the ads with the two of them leaping with childlike abandon, hand in hand into the sunshine of a blue day, all colour and grace and joyous lustful life.

Danae had stepped to stardom on Calvin's body, thought Jessie-Ann moodily, and Caroline had fallen in love with him. Well, she couldn't blame her, what woman could resist the urge to look after Calvin? And now – New York, always eager to snatch the new and different and discard the old, had latched onto Gala as England's personal gift to the fashion and hype industry. Danae had done a ten-page spread on her for *Vogue* that had sent ripples through the entire media . . . Gala in blue jeans and sweater all graceful long limbs, and naïve charm; Gala in false curls and haute couture, short black velvet and long, long legs, her round, childish face made over so she looked like a wicked little harlot out on the town; Gala in ten-thousand-dollar organza ballgowns looking, with her short hair, like a fallen angel; and Gala, casual in her own clothes, a big check jacket and baggy pants, gripped at the waist with a five-inch-wide braided leather belt, sitting on *Images'* floor with her legs crossed, violet shadows of exhaustion under her eyes, at the end of a long day.

There were pictures of Gala everywhere you looked, in every magazine on every news-stand, and already she featured daily in the gossip columns, appearing at parties – always carefully chaperoned by Danae, to promote Brodie Flyte's Bodylines, and also to promote *Images*.

And of course, Danae was going from strength to strength. She had more work than she could handle – her schedule at *Images* was booked solidly for the next ten months. And right now she was off on a shoot on some island with Gala. Danae was now a full partner along with Jessie-Ann and Caroline, and *Images* had more business than it could handle. Jessie-Ann supposed that *Images* could have floated on the work from Royle's alone, but with Avlon and Brodie, and *Vogue* using them regularly, and the other young photographers bringing in good business, they were really poised to take off.

Then why, Jessie-Ann wondered, having achieved what she had *wanted*, all she had *worked* for, did it all suddenly seem meaningless? She knew the answer to that one. It was because there was no Harrison waiting to listen to her achievements; no Harrison to congratulate her – no Harrison to *share* it all with, damn it!

She paced the room, thinking jealously of Merry McCall, telling herself that she was glad she didn't have to go through the effort of being the 'Royle Girl', and the strain of *always* looking her best, yet she admitted that in an odd sort of way she was jealous of Merry . . . it might have been *her* out there on the road with Harrison . . . *she* might have been all carefree fun and laughter instead of the harried businesswoman she'd become. Of course she was a *little* bit worried that Harrison was spending so much time on the road with the Royle promotion team – and Merry – flying off each week to catch up with them in Chicago or Houston or San Francisco, but she trusted him completely. Still, she wondered uneasily when it would end.

She slumped wearily into a chair, kicking off her Maud Frizon black suede and alligator pumps and burrowing into the cool silk cushions, seeking the softest spot to lay her tired, aching head. It wasn't *all* bad, she supposed bleakly; Danae was on top of the world; Gala was transformed; and Caroline was in love . . . three out of four wasn't bad for the *Images* team. Only *she* was utterly and desperately miserable.

20

Now that 'Success' with a capital 'S' was finally falling, *deservedly*, into her lap, Danae had determined to hold out for exactly what she wanted, right from the start. With the example of Brachman indelibly stamped on her memory, and the old adage 'Begin as you mean to go on' as her motto, she'd decided that only the best would be good enough for her. Not that she meant to be difficult – though if necessary she would be – *outrageously* difficult! But she knew instinctively that in order to stay at the top, you needed to surround yourself with only the best people. She used only the best models – and that didn't necessarily mean the well-known ones, but the ones *she* considered tops; and she had made a rule that all locations were to be chosen personally by her. Danae was rationing Gala-Rose's appearances like sugar in wartime, rejecting any but the top modelling situations for her protégée, and even then, using her sparingly, because she knew only too well how New York could gobble up a fresh face and spit it out six months later – unwanted because it had been over-exposed. And of course, only *she* photographed Gala-Rose.

The little Caribbean Islands' plane carrying Danae and her entourage of four models plus a make-up guy and Isobel, who always did Gala's make-up; Hector, the hairdresser; a stylist; a fashion editor from *Vogue*, and Danae's assistant, plus a cargo of clothes, hats, accessories, shoes and jewellery and her photographic equipment – prepared to land on the tiny Harbour Island, a place that Danae had considered sufficiently off-the-beaten track to suit her style, and to liven up *Vogue*'s January issue with a flash of sunshine and beach-chic. Through the suddenly-tilted window she spied a breathtaking curve of palm-fringed white beach, lapped by a sea in ten shades of blue. Beyond lay an aquamarine lagoon, its crystal clarity and sweeping curves rivalling those of the black-tiled swimming pool belonging to the island's single hotel, the Harbour House. The luxurious pink hacienda and its bungalows sprawled enticingly between the sea and the lagoon, offering every creature comfort within its cool terracotta-tiled halls.

The small plane banked again, bringing whoops of mock-horror and laughter from the group. Danae's window suddenly framed only a flawless sky, brilliant as blue enamel in the afternoon sun. Success had happened so fast, she thought, staring into the blueness, that sometimes she felt if she paused to think about it, the whole delicate structure might collapse. Her life was a whirlwind of action – but it was *creative* action! Brodie Flyte had given her a shot at the big-time and it was *her* concept and *her* photographs that had attracted nationwide attention. It hadn't all been good, of course, there had been criticism from some worthy locals across the country who'd objected to her 'erotic pictures' decorating their highways and city streets on billboards ten feet high. But the bad publicity had triggered even stronger interest in the series of ads and Brodie Flyte's Bodylines had sold in undreamed of quantities.

Brodie himself had taken her out to dinner – at Le Cirque (nothing but the best for Danae Lawrence – ace photographer, he'd said). He'd held her hand throughout the meal even though she'd complained it made it very difficult to eat, but they'd drunk lots of champagne and laughed a lot and she'd enjoyed being with him more than anyone she could remember – except Brachman. But still she hadn't wanted it to go any further than just friendly hand-holding and a goodnight kiss.

'It's because I'm just a rough, punk guy from the Bronx,' Brodie muttered moodily, when she'd shown him to the door of her apartment and said 'goodnight', *very* firmly. 'I don't know how to treat a girl like you, that's the trouble isn't it?'

'Brodie,' she sighed, 'forget the "guy from the Bronx" bit. You know as well as I do that you're an attractive, creative, sensitive man who's on the best of terms with most of the top ladies in this land. If they have no complaints, then why should I? You are *a charmer*, Brodie Flyte, *and you know it*!'

'Then if I'm so goddamn charming why don't you let me stay?'

The look of aggrieved innocence on his rugged face had made her laugh, but she'd been determined to stick to her plans – even though Brodie *was* charming, *and* he *was* interesting, *and* he *was* attractive. But she had vowed to put all her energy into her work. And besides, she just knew Brodie Flyte would be trouble – he would demand too much. Too much time, too much passion, too much energy. At any other moment in her life, Danae might have said yes . . . but not now.

'Home, Brodie,' she'd said, urging him through the open door. 'I've got work to do tomorrow.'

'So have I,' he complained.

'Then we both need our sleep, don't we? Thanks for a wonderful evening, dinner was delicious and I enjoyed being with you.'

'Career women!' complained Brodie thrusting his hands in his pockets and slouching down the corridor. 'Call me, Danae, when the pressure of "business" eases up,' he'd yelled, over his shoulder.

And that had been that. Sometimes, alone in her apartment after a long day when she was still brim-full of its surging energy and excitement, Danae had considered calling him, but Brodie wasn't the kind of guy to be happy with an occasional night . . . so in the end, she'd never called, and instead she'd spent those evenings with Gala.

Gala had her own apartment now, in the same building as Danae so she could still keep an eye on her, and Gala had said it made her feel more secure, knowing she was there, just two floors up. Poor insecure little Gala, she'd been so reluctant to leave the haven of Danae's studio, afraid the loneliness she'd felt in her Paddington bedsit would return, but once Marcus had appeared on the scene, her views had changed.

Danae hadn't counted on 'love' entering Gala-Rose's life so soon; somehow she had always thought of Gala as being *hers*. *She* was the one who told Gala how she should look, what she should wear, how she should act with the press and what publicity parties she should go to. Danae had chosen her apartment and controlled her diet. Gala-Rose had been *her property* – until Marcus Royle came along.

It was amazing, she thought, as the plane skimmed the dusty white runway, the way Marcus had changed Gala. She'd even gone out with Marcus a couple of weeks ago without so much as *asking* her if it would be all right, even though they'd had that important first *Vogue* shoot the following day. And after Danae had spent a sleepless night prowling the apartment, Gala had returned at 6 a.m. looking exhausted, with huge shadows like lavender bruises under her grey eyes. They'd had dinner at '21', she'd told Danae excitedly, and then they danced at these fantastic clubs Marcus knew, three different ones, and then they'd gone for breakfast at some little all-night diner in the village – 'and we just talked and talked . . .'

Danae had glowered at her silently, her eyebrows a straight line of disapproval, and then she informed Gala that not for Marcus Royle or anyone else – she didn't care if it were a Prince of England, there was *no way* Gala ever went out the night before a job. *Any* job – never mind the one that was probably going to change her entire life. 'It's only the most important day of your life,' she'd declared scathingly, as Gala wilted before her eyes, 'and you mess it up by staying out all night. Just look at you!' She'd hauled Gala in front of the mirror forcing her to look at her tired reflection, recounting the damage she'd done until the tears came. 'For God's sake *don't cry!*' Danae had wailed, throwing her arms around her, 'your eyes will swell and you'll look even worse . . .'

'What can we do?' Gala had whispered, trying her best to quell her remorseful tears.

'We'll go right now to the Club,' Danae had declared, leading her towards the door. 'You're going to do twenty laps of the pool, and then you're going to have a sauna, and then another plunge in the pool to cool you off. And then you're going to have the best massage you ever had, plus a facial. You're gonna drink some juice and nibble on a salad – and you'll feel as though you've been away on a week's vacation.'

It had all worked out OK and in one photograph she'd even used the shadows beneath Gala's eyes to emphasise her shot. Gala wore a short, glittery, sexy little dress and flimsy high-heeled gold sandals, and Danae made her trail the sable cape on the floor, drooping her head, like a tired little rich girl on her way home from the party, a streamer and a balloon still clutched in her hand. And ever since then, Gala had been obedient to her commands, although Marcus still loomed on Danae's horizon, as a threat.

'Will we be back by the fourteenth?' Gala had asked, just last week.

'Why?' she had demanded, suspiciously, 'what's the hurry?'

'It's just that Marcus wants to take me to the Harvard/Princeton game,' she'd replied, blushing. 'I mean, it's OK if we're not. I don't mind a bit.'

'We'll be back,' Danae had answered abruptly, knowing that it mattered all too much. But she didn't like seeing her power over Gala slip, little by little, from her hands. She had *created* the girl; it was she who should reap the rewards of Gala's new image, not Marcus Royle! She didn't want Gala in love – she wanted her to work!

'Isn't it beautiful?' exclaimed Gala as they strode across the small gravel forecourt into the whitewashed shed that masqueraded as the airport terminal. 'I've never seen such brilliant colours in my whole life. After this, England is going to seem sort of - faded.'

'Don't you believe it,' retorted Danae, 'there are as many colours in a green landscape in England as there are in that blue sea out there. It's just a question of adjusting your sights – and your filters! OK now, let's get started! Come on,' she cried, marshalling her troops and issuing orders to her assistant, 'let's get moving. Check on the limos, where's the rep from the hotel, we'll need maps of the island, and cars . . .'

'Danae,' sighed Maralyn, the weary *Vogue* fashion editor, 'relax. What with the stop in Miami and then the delay in Barbados, it's been twelve hours since we left New York. Let's just get to the hotel, have a bath and, please God, a drink and room service. And then it's into bed for me. We'll think about locations tomorrow.'

'*You* will think about locations tomorrow,' snapped Danae, 'but I'm gonna think about them tonight.'

Her little group surveyed her gloomily. 'Hey, Danae,' complained Hector, 'since when did you become a slave-driver?'

She flushed angrily, sitting silently in the limo on the way to the Harbour House. She didn't consider herself a slave-driver;

she was here to do a job and she was determined that it would be the *best*, the *most perfect* photographic work ever. She would drive herself to get better and better each time, searching for ways to make each shot different, more dramatic – more *daring*. She was determined that no one would ever be able to say that Danae Lawrence's work had become 'samey'! And she was prepared to put *all* her energy and time into her work, even if the others weren't. Except of course, Gala-Rose, who would always do just what Danae asked.

The Verandah Bar of the Harbour House was a wide wooden terrace with a bamboo counter and high stools, open on three sides to the dark, warm, sapphire-blue night. There were low wicker tables with deeply-cushioned chairs, and a wide-bladed wooden fan stirring the soft tropical warmth into a facsimile of a breeze. For Vic Lombardi, showered, shaved and cool at last, in white cotton pants and a loose blue shirt, it was the closest point to heaven he'd seen in three months. The tall rum drink concocted by Julio, the smooth, smiling barman, was iced to perfection and the prospect of a dinner where he would sit at a *real* table with a *real* crisp linen cloth and matching napkin – and be served *real* food by white-gloved waiters, was something to be savoured slowly, like the drink. It beat crouching in some swampy jungle, munching two-day-old rations of cold rice mixed with whatever else he could scrounge from the guerrillas, which is what Vic had grown accustomed to over the past months. In fact the prospect definitely called for another drink. Besides, thought Vic, that would give him a chance to observe the antics of that exotic-looking bunch who'd spilled into the bar a half-hour ago, looking as exhausted as he felt.

He watched, disappointed as they soon drifted off, one by one, until only the red-haired girl and the waif-like young blonde were left.

'Oh for God's sake, Gala-Rose,' exclaimed Danae as the girl yawned again, 'you might as well go too! Call room-service and ask them to send you a chicken sandwich – no mayo – and then get some sleep or you'll be a wreck tomorrow.'

'But I thought we weren't shooting tomorrow? Don't we have to find the right locations first?'

'Of course we do,' she retorted, nettled, 'but it would be great if you didn't have shadows under your eyes again. And remember to keep out of the sun. I don't want strapmarks all over the place, and anyhow Isobel will provide you with the necessary sun tan from a bottle.'

'But it's so lovely,' wailed Gala, 'I want to swim and lie in the sun . . . oh all right,' she added hastily, catching Danae's irate expression. 'I know, I'm here to work.' Dropping a kiss on Danae's cheek, she trailed tiredly along the verandah, through the scented tropical gardens back to her bungalow.

Picking up her Nikon, Danae focused it on the departing girl, adjusting the shutter until she had the right amount of light, catching a quick shot of the pale, blonde Gala in a white dress against the background of dark tropical greenery, a long gauzy scarf trailing behind her in the slight breeze . . . a ghost-girl in the jungle . . .

She slid onto a bamboo stool at the bar gazing mournfully, straight ahead. 'What'll it be, Miss?' asked Julio, polishing a glass.

'Oh I don't know,' she murmured, 'whatever's long and fresh and very cold.'

'Try this,' Vic pointed to his tall glass packed with ice and fruit and sprigs of mint, 'it's the Harbour House's version of a Planter's Punch.'

Danae's greenish eyes were cool as she glanced at him. She wasn't ready for a chat with the 'tourists' tonight, all she really wanted was a drink. Still, this one looked a bit different from the usual suntanned holidaymaker, here for the booze and the broads. He was in his thirties, she guessed, and he was too short and definitely too thin. He had light brown eyes and dark hair with a slight wave and he looked the way she felt, cool and wary.

'Thanks,' she replied, 'maybe I will.'

Vic watched as she took a fresh film from her purse and re-loaded her camera. She had great hair, he thought, the colour of a tropical sunset, and pretty eyes, even if they were a touch chilly.

'That your hobby?' he enquired, as Julio placed the drink in front of her.

Danae glanced at him icily. 'Of course not.'

253

'Sorry,' he shrugged, grinning, 'and on second thoughts instead of that drink maybe you should have a hot cup of coffee – it might help thaw the icicles.'

Danae swivelled her stool away from him, towards the bar. 'It's just that I don't particularly feel like company.'

'Fair enough.' Finishing his drink in one long swallow, Vic nodded goodnight to Julio and ambled lazily in the direction of the Patio Dining Room. If the lady didn't want company, then that was OK with him. Besides, all he really wanted was that dinner. He'd surely dreamed of it often enough.

The dining room was exactly the way he'd pictured it, in those long, bug-infested nights in the wilds of El Salvador, foot-sore and exhausted, his ears still shattered from the daily shelling, keeping his eyes alert for trouble but dreaming of a bottle of good champagne, chilling beautifully in a silver bucket, icy drops of water frosting its sides. Dreaming of the bars he knew or delicious dinners in civilised restaurants was a ruse Vic often used on his treks around the world as a roving reporter for NBC television. He found it kept him sane in the worst moments of stress. And those moments weren't the ones when all the action was happening, because then he didn't have time to think; he just tried to keep his head down and do his job – and that was to get the *real* news back to the people, to give them the sights and sounds and smells of war, instead of just words and charts and plastic models. Vic Lombardi had been roving the hot spots of the world with his 'crew' – a cameraman and a sound man – for six years now, and he could imagine no more interesting way of life. But boy, he sure enjoyed the good things of life when he had a few days' break.

The Pol Roger Sir Winston Churchill Vintage 1979, which he'd chosen from the wine list both in honour of the great warrior after whom it was named – and because it was a great champagne, waited in the ice bucket by his table, looking just the way he'd imagined it all these weeks. A few couples dined quietly at the pink-linen draped tables, and a large man, an islander, immaculate in white dinner jacket, was playing the piano, delicate melodies of Satie and Ravel and Debussy as well as Jerome Kern and Rogers and Hart, just the way he had the last time Vic was here.

Satisfied that nothing ever changed except for the better at the Harbour House, he turned his attention to the menu.

'Excuse me?' The red-haired girl stood by his table, running her hand through her already rumpled hair and smiling at him apologetically.

'I'm sorry,' said Danae, 'I didn't mean to be rude. I thought you were just another tourist, on the make . . .'

Vic threw back his head, laughing. 'So what's made you change your mind about me?' he asked, pulling out a chair for her.

'Well then of course, I recognised you. I feel such a fool for not knowing immediately.'

'No reason why you should. Besides, I don't usually look this clean on television,' he replied as she took a seat.

'I really *admire* your work,' she exclaimed, leaning forward in her chair, 'but it must be terrifying, being out there with all the bullets flying.'

Vic shrugged, unsmiling. 'Sure it's frightening, but that's my job. I'm a reporter and that's the only way to get the news to the folks back home.'

Danae clutched her Nikon eagerly. 'I wonder . . . I mean would you mind? Well, the fact is, you have a very *interesting* face, Mr Lombardi. I wonder if you'd mind if I took some pictures of you?'

She gazed at him so intently that Vic thought her entire happiness must depend on simply taking a snap of him. He shrugged. 'If it's that important to you Miss . . . ?'

'It's Danae. Danae Lawrence., And it *is* important. I'm a *professional* photographer. Maybe you've seen some of my work?' He looked puzzled and she hurried on, 'The Brodie Flyte Body-lines ads? And the Gala-Rose ten-page spread in September *Vogue*? Avlon Cosmetics . . . ? No?'

Her face fell as he shook his head, and Vic smiled at her sympathetically. 'Sorry, Danae, but I've been out of the country so long, I guess I'm behind the times. So, that's what you're doing here, shooting a fashion layout?'

'We just arrived this evening but the others are all so tired they've gone off to bed.'

'But not you?' Vic signalled the waiter to pour the champagne.

'*Never* me . . . I just wish it were daylight so I could go off and scout locations. I can't *wait* to get started! They call me a "slave-driver",' she admitted, shamefaced, 'but it's just that I love what I do and I expect them to feel the same way. Especially Gala-Rose.'

'The willowy-wisp blonde?'

'That's her. I suppose I just expect too much from people. I expect them to have *my* energy, *my* dedication . . .'

'And I suppose *they* are only taking fashion pictures?'

Danae glanced at him sharply. Was there an edge of sarcasm in his words?

'Look, Danae Lawrence, I'll make a deal with you,' said Vic, 'have dinner with me, and then you can take all the pictures you like.'

Danae gazed into his light brown eyes, remembering the last time a man had said those words to her – Tomaso Alieri in Rome – and remembering too how that evening had *almost* ended. 'It's a deal,' she agreed, laughing.

'What's so funny?' he demanded.

'Oh nothing . . . nothing, really,' she replied, still smiling.

'Then you should try laughing more often,' he said softly, 'it suits you, Miss Lawrence.'

'Tell me about yourself,' she demanded, over a light-as-a-feather mousse made from fish caught off the Island that morning. Sipping more of the wonderful champagne and listening to him talk, she decided she really liked his looks; she liked his faintly olive skin and his strong, lean, stocky body. And she liked his firm-jawed sensitive face with the little lines radiating around his young-old eyes . . . eyes that she wanted to capture on film. And she wanted to photograph the champagne flute clasped in his large hand, like a fragile crystal flower.

Leaning on her elbows, Danae watched fascinated as Vic ate his way through several superb courses. She had not seen anyone enjoy food so much since Gala-Rose had eaten at the Indian restaurant that first night.

'I'm New York born and bred,' he told her, 'though as you've probably guessed, my family's Italian . . . immigrant lower-east side, then the Bronx and then the suburban comforts of Long Island – in three generations. Not the smart section of Long Island though,' he confessed, with a grin, 'my Pop drives a cab. He made enough to get my brother and me through college with not too much left over, but he and my Mom are happy together in their comfortable tract house. I guess he's pleased when he sees me on television, though my Mom never watches the news any more because of me. She said the only time she saw me it scared the hell out of her. She can't understand why I want to spend my life dodging mortar shells in Beirut or explaining yet another mound of slaughtered bodies in India or El Salvador. Mom says prayers for me every night,' he told Danae, as they sipped their champagne, 'and I like to think it helps. It's sort of like wearing a good-luck charm.'

'But *why do you do it*?' she asked. '*Why* risk your life for a TV news report?'

Vic grinned, that same lopsided grin she'd caught on those same news reports. 'Somebody's got to do it, how the hell else do we all know what's really going on? You can't go through life in blinkers. At least showing the world the *facts* of war, the senselessness of it all, the slaughter of the innocent . . . maybe it makes us all more aware, and maybe, just *maybe* something will be done about it.'

'It's not just for the adventure then?' she persisted.

Vic drained his champagne glass, and ordered another bottle. 'Maybe, a little of that too,' he admitted. 'Meanwhile I'm on "R & R" – rest and recreation – for a few days until the next bout of Latin American trouble, and I'd sure like to enjoy it with you, Danae Lawrence.'

His nice brown eyes held a question that Danae avoided, putting her camera to her eye and framing him in her lens.

'The question hasn't changed,' Vic commented leaning back easily in the comfortable chair.

'I'm here to work,' she replied, her voice muffled.

'What about all that spare energy? You and I are two of a kind, Danae Lawrence. You're an adventurer, just like I am, but in a different world and I'll bet that the New York fashion magazine scene is even tougher than jungle warfare! But even adventurers should know that all work makes a dull person!'

Despite herself Danae laughed, snapping away with her Nikon.

'Just turn your head to the left a little,' she commanded, 'that's right . . . no, just a touch more this way. Right! Got it! Now look away into the distance . . . God, you're wonderful to photograph, you have such a great face, all angles and craggy planes . . .'

'Is this how you talk to all your models?' he demanded, putting out his hand and pushing away her camera.

'They're not nearly as interesting as you,' she replied, 'except Gala-Rose, of course.'

'Of course.' His eyes narrowed as he caught her glance. 'You want to come dancing with me, Danae?'

'I'd love to,' she agreed, all her good intentions suddenly swept aside.

He held out his hand and as she took it in his, a little electric current seemed to run between them . . . a magical link, matched by the look in their eyes.

Vic's arms were around her and her head was resting against his shoulder, as they danced to the soft, sensual Latin rhythms of the five-piece group who played nightly in the Captain's Club at the hotel. She hadn't meant to be doing this, thought Danae dreamily, she was supposed to be in her room, planning out tomorrow's action, giving the job her total concentration. Instead, here she was, clasped in this stranger's arms and so aware of his heartbeat next to hers that she could think of nothing else. She was aware of the scent of his skin and the faint citrusy sweetness of his cologne; her finger traced the line of muscle across his shoulder where her hand lay, and as she lifted her eyes to his, she felt she was drowning in a new, sensual emotion.

With a happy sigh, she drew her gaze away, burying her head in his shoulder; there had been other men in her life, boyfriends and lovers – and Brachman – but never before had she known this immediate physical impact. She felt helpless to stop what was going to happen . . . and what's more she didn't want to stop it. In fact, she knew if anyone had asked her right now, what she wanted most in the world, it would be to make love with Vic Lombardi.

The music stopped and they paused, arms still around each other. 'The moon's up,' murmured Vic, sliding his hand down her bare arm and sending small tingles of expectancy through her body. 'Would you like to take a walk along the beach?'

The tropical night air wrapped itself around them as, hand in hand, they strolled at the water's edge. Tiny white-frilled waves whispered onto the sand, the soft sound mingling with the dry rustle of palm fronds and the constant whirring of cicadas. They paused, absorbing the beauty of the scene, a beauty Danae knew that at any other time would have had her reaching for her camera and planning how to use it in her lay-out. Yet right now, nothing mattered but this man whose light-hearted veneer concealed an intensity of purpose. She turned within the circle of his arms . . . and then Vic Lombardi was kissing her, and she never wanted him to stop . . .

The Harbour House's bungalows were scattered through thirty acres of grounds, spaced well away from each other and screened by luxuriant trellises of climbing bougainvillaea and flowering oleanders. The exotic fragrance of some night-blooming flower filled the air as, arms around each other, they walked up the low steps into his bungalow, clutching their shoes and scattering sand from their feet over the cool, terracotta tiles. 'A shower,' murmured Danae, in between kisses, 'I'm too sandy . . .'

Vic kissed her as he unbuttoned her sleeveless white satin shirt, sliding it from her shoulders and revealing her high, pointed breasts. He pulled off his own shirt and held her close, and the feel of his flesh on hers was almost more than Danae could stand. 'Beautiful, lovely Danae,' he murmured, bending his head and taking her small coral nipple in his mouth . . . She moaned, gripping his thick dark hair, pulling him closer, she wanted to absorb him into her body, to touch him, to taste him . . . she needed him, desperately . . .

In the luxurious bathroom Vic turned on the shower and then they removed the rest of their clothes. He stood naked in front of her, the symbol of his desire drawing her eyes, her hands, her mouth. She couldn't resist him, kneeling in front of him, she tasted his passion until he pushed her away roughly, his body trembling. 'Wait, wait . . .' he begged, pulling her into the shower and then it was his turn to kneel in front of her. With infinite gentleness Vic sponged her feet, washing off the sand. He soaped her smooth body and Danae flung back her head, moaning in pleasure as he explored her softness.

'Please,' begged Danae, 'please, Vic . . . oh please . . .' Her body convulsed in a great, aching outpouring of pleasure as he lifted her onto his erection, clasping her close, closer, even closer, filling her with his passion . . . until, still shaking, they clung together, the cool water mingling with their sweat, running in rivulets from their hair and down their backs.

'Danae, oh Danae,' he whispered, dropping tender kisses on her face and smoothing back her wet hair, darkened to a denser colour by the water. 'Like ancient Etruscan copper,' he murmured, leaning back to study her. 'How beautiful you are, a wild, wet mermaid . . . Venus rising from the sea . . . or in this case the shower.'

They laughed, breaking the erotic spell. Vic folded her into a huge white terry robe and wrapped her red hair in a towel, turban-style. With her knees still trembling, Danae followed him out onto the terrace overlooking the whispering, moonlit sea.

As they watched the moon's path across the peaceful swell of the sea, she turned her head to study the man who had just summoned a passion in her that she hadn't known she possessed. Vic's profile was silhouetted against the blue-black sky and without the direct light he looked younger and more vulnerable. His dark hair was curling slightly as it dried, falling across his brow, and he lifted an impatient hand and pushed it away, turning to meet her eyes. For the first time in her life Danae knew she was in danger of falling in love.

'Well, lover?' he asked, fixing her with that intense gaze.

He'd only to look at her like that to send tremors through her entire being, thought Danae. 'Well?' she queried.

'I was just wondering what it is about you. This is no ordinary encounter, Danae Lawrence, you realise that?'

She nodded, tracing the lines on his face with a smooth finger.

'I don't feel this way about every girl I meet – even after three months in the wilds! It's more than a mere bodily response to a lovely girl; there's a deeper passion, something I can't explain – all I know is I don't want to let go of you.'

She knew he was right, what they had was true *passion*, the sort poets wrote about and tragic lovers killed themselves over. But she also knew she must keep her head, she must remember she was a career girl . . . Danae Lawrence – ace photographer. It's only *passion*, she reassured herself, just passion that's all – not love. But, 'Don't let go of me,' she said to Vic, sliding her arms around him and pressing herself closer, 'oh please don't let go of me tonight.' And then his mouth was on her eagerly open one, and his hands were caressing her, and the magic was starting all over again . . . under that warm night blue sky, with the sound of the sea and the palms and the cicadas in her ears and the glory of his body on hers.

21

Gala had been really worried about Danae when she hadn't shown up for the seven o'clock breakfast meeting. Of course she wasn't the only one who'd failed to show – the other models had simply turned over, hiding their heads under the sheets when Gala had gone to their rooms to try to wake them; and Maralyn, the fashion editor had left a 'Do Not Disturb' sign on her door in four languages – with 'And This Means You, Danae Lawrence!' scribbled underneath! It was the same story with the others, no one seemed prepared to emerge and enjoy this wondrous sparkling morning. Not even Danae, although Gala had knocked and knocked on her door. Finally, because no one ever locked doors on Harbour Island she'd gone into her room calling Danae's name, but her bed hadn't even been slept in.

It was all right, Gala told herself, returning to the bungalow she shared with Jane, the dark-haired model. Danae had probably been up since five and was out even now, scouting locations. She must have realised that the rest of them wouldn't get up, and typically, she was doing it all herself. The maid had already made up her room.

Sipping a glass of orange juice on the terrace and gazing at the vista of an almost-still blue sea, trying to analyse the exact point where it merged with the sky, Gala imagined it must have been exactly like this in the Garden of Eden. Luxuriant blossoms tumbled from every wall and arbour and the lush foliage had a special shining greenness. The brilliant clarity of the sunlight made the landscape almost dance with colour in a way it never did in England's misty, grey rainwashed countryside. But if it were really the true Garden of Eden then Marcus would be here with her.

She hadn't thought it possible to miss someone she'd known only a few weeks as much as this, but she felt she'd known Marcus for ever. Of course she wouldn't tell Danae, but Marcus had telephoned her last night . . . just to say 'Hi' and 'I'm missing you' and . . . 'I love you' . . .

Sometimes, thought Gala, sipping her juice, she felt dizzy from love. It was a softly spiralling emotion that whirled you round and round, slowly at first, then so breathtakingly fast that your heart was in your mouth and your head swam just from sheer *joy*. And joy was a completely new emotion for her. Thinking back to her childhood, she couldn't remember one single moment when she'd felt the sheer exultant pleasure she got from just being with Marcus Royle. There had been times when she'd been *happy*, like when she worked for Debbie Blacker, and when she'd made friends with Jake, but never *joy*. It was a feeling that placed a smile on her face and made her bubble with easy laughter, it swelled her heart with wonderful new emotions as she held Marcus's hand and walked with him through Central Park or sat next to him in a red leatherette booth, eating pizza and drinking rough red wine from Italy; or when she danced with him, body to body, in some dark and glitzy Manhattan disco . . . *whatever* she did with Marcus was sheer pleasure. But she hadn't yet made love with him.

She stared at the big yellow bee who'd tumbled into her glass. Picking up a spoon she fished him out, setting him on the table where he fluffed out his wings and stretched his tiny legs, drying out in the sun. It wasn't that she didn't want to make love to Marcus, it was just that they never went that far. They held each other close, exchanging passionate kisses until she felt delirious with pleasure, but then Marcus never went any further. He'd stroke her short sleek hair, caress her face, smooth the long curve of her back with his strong hands and she would just lie there, waiting for the moment when he might touch her breast . . . but he hadn't. And of course, she couldn't possibly touch him first, I mean *she just couldn't do that* . . . much as she longed to.

Perhaps it took time, worried Gala, searching the depths of her inexperience for a clue, maybe these things didn't happen right away . . . passion must take time to build.

If only Danae weren't so down on her friendship with Marcus, she would have asked her advice. But sometimes she felt as though she were walking a tightrope between the two of them, with Danae accusing her of allowing Marcus to monopolise her time when she should be concentrating on her career instead of running off to Princeton all the time; and Marcus telling her that she was dominated by Danae and that she should have a mind of her own. He simply didn't understand that Danae had *saved* her. *Without Danae she was nothing.* Worse – she was Hilda Mirfield – and she'd probably have been back in Garthwaite, working in the local pub or something. It was because of Danae that she had finally become Gala-Rose. And because of that she would love Danae for ever. There was nothing she wouldn't do for Danae. The only problem was, there was nothing she wouldn't do for Marcus either!

Sighing, Gala decided she'd go for a swim from that beautiful beach and then, remembering Danae's instructions, she thought she'd better just cover herself with lotion and a shirt and a wide-brimmed straw hat and lie in the shade and wait for Danae to return.

The group sitting at the tables under the thatched beach restaurant had enjoyed a delicious lunch supplemented by several tall crystal jugs of the Harbour House's special wine-cooler. Brimming with fruit and ice the drink looked – and tasted – innocuous, disguising the lethal wallop of wine and rum. They were in a very merry mood as Danae, in a white swimsuit and hiding behind black Raybans, sauntered alongside the pool towards them.

'Hi, Danae!' they yelled grinning. 'We've been here since seven! We've been waiting for you! Where's the Nikon, Danae? Been scouting locations, Danae?' and, 'So OK, Danae, when are we off? We're all here, present and correct and ready to march. Just say the word.' They dissolved into helpless giggles as, ignoring them all, she plumped into a cushioned wicker chair and ordered 'a very tall, very cold glass of juice' from the waiter. Removing her glasses she met their knowing smiles defiantly.

'Love those shadows under your eyes,' murmured Maralyn, 'and the black and blue marks on your arms . . . mmmmn, in fact you look great, Danae – a big improvement. Just like a woman fulfilled!' Vic appeared at the other end of the pool and with a cheery wave at Danae, dived in and began to plough smooth laps across the pool. 'Well now, I wonder?' Maralyn added, 'could *this* be the source of that happy little smile on your face?'

Gala noticed the new tenderness in Danae's glance as she watched the man in the pool and the easy, relaxed way she sprawled in her chair. This wasn't the Danae of yesterday; the tense, coiled Danae waiting to unleash her energy on her work, driving them onwards to new and greater things. Danae looked the way Gala felt when she was with Marcus!

Removing her eyes from Vic's bronzed wiry body, Danae smiled defiantly. 'So we all need a little relaxation,' she said, placing the iced glass against her burning cheek and enjoying its coldness, 'tonight we'll work.'

'Yeah, hooray,' they cheered, signalling the waiter to bring another jug of the Harbour House cooler, 'we'll drink to that.'

'Wait a minute, did you say *tonight*?' asked Maralyn.

'Sure did,' replied Danae, thinking of that beach by moonlight and the phosphorescent little waves, the graphic tufts of the palm trees silhouetted against the blue-black sky, and of Gala-Rose in a white dress disappearing into the shimmering green twilight . . . She felt the old surge of creative energy zooming back, only this time it was tempered with a little extra something – a certain special knowledge that she hadn't had before and that would now be reflected in her work. There was *nothing* – no experience or emotion – that couldn't be translated and used. What had happened with Vic last night would only add to the images she created in her work.

There was no doubt, thought Danae, that Vic interrupted her schedule – and her equilibrium. Long sensuous nights spent making love made her a later starter than usual – to the delight of the models. Except Gala-Rose who, annoyingly, was up and waiting in the terrace, sipping her juice like a good girl, at seven a.m. *promptly*!

It made Danae feel guilty when fresh from Vic's arms and a cool shower, she finally wandered up for breakfast at half past eight. Of course they had done that all-night shoot, catching first the sunset and then twilight, and then the deep-blue, starry night, waiting around a little beach campfire built by the hotel staff and stoked by willing hands, sipping champagne and waiting for the first hint of dawn to touch the horizon. And she'd caught that exact moment with Gala-Rose posed like a naiad in a fluttering dress of pearl-grey chiffon pressed against her slender figure by the dawn breeze, her upturned face painted peach and gold by the sun's very first rays, until *she* looked like the dawn of creation. After that session, Danae knew she had it in the bag, and that anything else she did at Harbour Island would be an anti-climax; but she took them around to deserted beaches and jungle waterfalls, shooting light-hearted stuff, full of sunshine and blossoms, that would make *Vogue*'s winter pages jump with colour and life and the promise of a better, sunshiny, glossy world.

Ignoring their knowing smiles and stares, she dined alone with Vic every night, eager to *understand* him better. It wasn't right not to really *know* the man she felt so passionately about – and she wanted all the dimensions that were Vic Lombardi, as well as the immediate one.

'Tell me more about yourself,' she demanded as they sipped their usual champagne before dinner.

He glanced at her lazily. 'What is there to tell?' he asked, thinking how very pretty she looked in that yellow silk dress with her coppery hair flowing free.

'What were you like as a little boy?' she persisted.

'As much a little creep as any other Italian kid on my block, I guess,' he replied with a grin.

'No . . . really. I mean what were your ambitions?'

'My ambition was to eat the biggest hero sandwich from Emilio's Deli – veal, sausages and peppers – as often as I could. And I wanna tell you, lady, that was *some* hero sandwich!'

'OK, OK,' cried Danae, laughing. 'I give up. No more questions.'

'Then it's my turn?'

'What do you want to know?' she asked, sitting up straighter and pretending to look serious.

'What are *your* ambitions?' Vic sipped his champagne, watching her through narrowed eyes. 'Come on,' he urged, as she hesitated, 'you never talk about yourself. Come clean.'

'I told you about my family, my life . . .' she retorted, defensively.

'And the ambition? You may as well tell me,' he said, taking her hand, 'because it shines from you like a beacon. You're a dedicated lady, Danae Lawrence. I just wonder . . .'

She waited breathlessly to hear *what* he wondered, but he simply sipped his champagne and said nothing.

'But I *am* dedicated,' she cried, leaning towards him earnestly, 'I'm *good* at what I do, Vic. I'm twenty-seven years old and I've made it to the top in a tough world. Do you have any *idea* of what it will take to *stay* there? OK, so I'm this year's success – don't you think I'll have to pull out every stop, try every trick in the book . . . come up with new ideas *constantly*, pull off a winner *every time* – in order to be next year's?'

'I understand,' he replied seriously, 'it's just that I wonder . . .'

'Well?'

'Is it worth it? Fashion pictures,' he shrugged, 'fun, yes. But they're frivolous, immediate, a passing show. After all, Danae, you're still only selling dresses to women who could just as easily go into a store and pick them off the rack. I mean – where's the *job* satisfaction? What do *you* get from it? Other than I guess, good money and your name in smallish letters on a page in *Vogue*?'

'They're *large* letters,' retorted Danae angrily, 'and I get paid a hell of a lot for my talent, Vic Lombardi!'

'I'm sure you do,' Vic sighed. Taking her hand he turned it palm-upwards and kissed it tenderly. 'I'm sure you do, darling Danae. And you deserve every cent of it. I'm not disputing your undoubted talent, nor your intelligence. Anyway, my magazine reading is limited to *Time* and *Newsweek*, with the *Economist* when I can get my hands on it, and every now and then *Jane's Defense Weekly* . . . and let me tell you Jane's pictures more often than not are blurry satellite photos of off-limits nuclear subs, or the latest secret planes caught by some spying camera. Not in your league.'

'Never? Never read *Town & Country*, *Harpers Bazaar*, *Tatler*, *Harpers & Queen* . . . ?'

Her expression of outraged amazement made him laugh and

Vic felt a little sorry that he'd put her on the line like that, but still she should know that there was more to the world than fashion pictures. 'How much does a little expedition like this one of yours cost?' he demanded, pouring more champagne.

'A lot. And all the champagne I can drink.'

'Touché,' he replied. 'I get to pay for my own.'

'You're in the wrong game, Vic Lombardi,' she retorted.

'Funny, I was just thinking the same thing about you.'

It hurt that he thought her work trivial and frivolous but Danae tried to rationalise it, telling herself he came from a serious world where 'pictures' were photographs of life and death. How could she expect him to understand, or to appreciate her success . . . because she *was* successful, back there in the *real* world of New York, where it counted. They sat in silence for a while and then Danae said, 'Could we just forget this whole conversation?'

'Sure,' he replied, 'and I apologise if I've been out of line.'

'How about dinner then?' she asked, striving to regain their old intimacy.

'It's a deal, as long as you promise not to talk about *Vogue* fashion and I promise not to talk about *Jane's Defense Weekly.*'

'I couldn't bear any more,' she cried, crossing her heart in mock-horror. But she really meant it. She wanted to keep things with Vic Lombardi exactly the way they were – a passionate island love affair, destined, like shipboard romance, to fade when they left to take up their real lives. Meanwhile, she wanted to savour every precious moment.

It was early Sunday morning, the seventh day and, as God intended, Danae had planned that they should rest. She wanted to spend an entire day and night alone with Vic, exploring the island in a rented jeep, staying at one of the small Island inns. It would be just the two of them without the others for ever looking over her shoulder making their everlasting wisecracks! They would all leave the island on Tuesday but Danae was putting the fact out of her mind, refusing to acknowledge it until it was upon her.

They were asleep, naked and warm, her leg wrapped across Vic, his arms around her, their bodies fitting together in perfect, easy harmony, when the phone rang.

'Jesus,' exclaimed Vic, emerging from several layers of sleep and grabbing the receiver. 'What is it?' he groaned.

Danae pushed the hair out of her eyes, leaning on her elbow watching him as he made rapid notes. 'Right,' he said. And 'OK, Bill. Yes, Gottcha.' And then, 'I'll be there. See you, fella.'

Dropping back onto the pillows he stared at the ceiling.

'What is it, darling?' asked Danae. But she already knew the truth.

'I'm catching the first flight back to Barbados,' Vic told her flatly, 'and from there to London and then on to Delhi. There's trouble in Amritsar again, they want me over there.'

'I see,' she replied, trying to hold together her emotions that were suddenly shredding at the edges. 'OK. Well then, you'll need to pack . . . I mean you don't have much time. I'd better help you.'

'That's all right,' he said gently, 'I'm used to doing it myself. I've gotten pretty good at it over the years.'

'Sure,' she muttered, sitting up with the sheet clutched around her, wishing she didn't want to cry . . . Jesus, this was ridiculous . . . he was just a guy she'd met on a holiday island, not really her kind of fella at all. If she'd met him in New York they probably wouldn't have had two words to say to each other . . . Vic was from *his* world and she was from *hers*. Hadn't he explained that pretty clearly to her the other night? '*Why* must you do it?' The words burst from her before she could stop them. '*Why* must you go . . . risking your *life*?'

'Sweetheart.' Vic held her to him carefully, as though she were the most precious porcelain and he were afraid she would break. 'I'm a journalist. This is my business. This is *my life*, Danae.'

'I see,' she flared, tears pricking her eyelids, 'you've got your life and our paths simply don't meet – except on neutral territory like this.'

'You've chosen your life too, sweetheart,' he said, holding her shoulders and gazing into her eyes.

'And you *despise* it!' she cried, letting anger disguise her despair at leaving him.

'Not despise,' he replied carefully, 'just . . . question.'

And then he hurried to pack his things and in less than half an hour she was standing on the terrace watching the Harbour Hotel's jauntily-awninged jeep drive him away – to the airport and points east. And out of her life.

22

Brodie Flyte was a nice guy, decided Danae. He was attractive in his own street-fighter way, he was charming and had a gift for non-stop amusing conversation that dissolved her into helpless laughter. He was also very successful and very rich. Then why, she wondered over dinner with him at The Four Seasons, was she still waiting for the thrill that was supposed to happen when a guy like Brodie told you he was crazy about you?

'I can't help it,' complained Brodie plaintively, 'all I needed was to fall in love with a photographer who's gonna take pictures that make other designers' clothes look better than mine every time we have a row! I fought it, Danae, and I lost . . . I'm willing to take the competition, photographically, that is. Will you be my girl, Danae Lawrence?'

'Ahh,' she sighed dramatically, 'for a moment there, I thought you were about to propose marriage?' He grinned at her disarmingly; his eyes were tired and his chin blue-black with a two-day growth of beard because he was working night and day on his next collection, but his pale blue shirt was immaculate and his suit a perfection of tailoring. He looked, thought Danae, the way a designer should look, elegant but casual, rugged and masculine . . . then damn it, why did she feel nothing?

'First things first,' he countered cheerfully. 'Y'want an engagement ring, is that it? We'll go tomorrow to Harry Winston's or Van Cleef's, Cartier? You choose. All I want is to give you a chance to find out first if you can live with a crazy guy like me. Actually, Danae, that's not true,' he added suddenly serious. 'I didn't ask you right out to marry me, because I was afraid you'd say no. I thought this way, I might just be able to ease you into it?'

'Brodie . . .' Danae ran her hand worriedly through her red hair, wondering what to reply. 'Look,' she said finally, 'can't we

271

just leave our relationship the way it is, for a while? I'm always happy when I'm with you, Brodie . . . I like you almost more than any guy I know . . .'

'*Like?*' he raised an eyebrow quizzically, '*almost?* Not good words, babe . . . I could live with "*like*" – for a while, at least until I could persuade you to reassess; but "*almost*" – now that leads me to think that there's some guy you "*like*" more than me? Right?'

Danae shook her head, staring down at the exquisite petal-led arrangement of fruits on the large white plate in front of her . . . but of course Brodie was right; she hadn't been able to rid herself of the image of Vic Lombardi ploughing powerful lengths up and down the inky pool at Harbour Island, or of his profile silhouetted against the royal-blue night sky, or his challenging eyes when he questioned the value of what she was doing with her talent, and the desire in them when he'd held her close, body to body in those sultry, tropical, passionate nights . . .

'It's OK, Danae,' said Brodie taking her hand across the table, 'just thought I'd give it the old college try, that's all. Are we still friends?'

'If you still want me as a friend?'

Her hazel-green eyes met his anxiously, and Brodie Flyte cursed himself for being a fool, but he really liked this girl; she'd gotten under his skin with that odd mixture of single-minded toughness and vulnerability . . . 'Sure I want you as a friend,' he replied, kissing her hand, 'and the offer still stands, Danae. Any time you say.'

But when his limousine drew up later at her apartment building, Brodie didn't suggest coming in for a nightcap, he just leaned across and kissed her lightly on the cheek. 'Call me next week, babe,' he told her, 'we'll have lunch. OK?'

Danae had decorated her spacious apartment lovingly in her signature colours of black and white, filling it with an eclectic mixture of high-tech and post-modernist pieces, adding flashes of colour in the dramatic abstract paintings that lined the walls; but tonight it felt impersonal and lonely . . . just a collection of objects and ideas. One wall was lined with gleaming steel bookshelves holding rows of black leather-bound albums, filled with every photograph she'd taken that she considered worthy of her talent. With memories of her previous cramped apartment and of her work pinned on every available surface, she'd decided never to display her work in her home, except for the one in her bedroom, a three-foot blow-up of the very first picture she'd ever taken of Gala, all wide innocent eyes and soft, sensuous mouth.

She pulled an album from the shelf and knelt on the glossy, black-lacquered floorboards and opened it. There was no need to turn its pages to find what she was looking for, the album fell open automatically at the close-up photograph of Vic Lombardi, taken at Harbour Island. She knew his face from memory, every tense line of it; his wide brow and dark hair, his fine eyes – narrowed and amused as he faced her camera, the determined set of his chin and the rugged nose . . . It was an uncompromising face, she decided, closing the album with a sigh, and she was a fool to let the memory of a footloose, dedicated newsman like Vic Lombardi change her life. She had received exactly one communication from him since they'd parted – a highly-coloured postcard of a temple in India, and her silly heart had done a double-flip as she read it . . . 'miss you, Danae Lawrence!' was all it had said . . . and he'd signed it simply 'Vic'. No 'love', no 'hugs', no 'kisses' – no passionate declaration that he couldn't live without her, when she was really afraid that maybe she wasn't going to be able to live without him.

But she might as well face it, she was going to have to. Vic had just flashed through her life like a comet – and she'd see him just about as often. Except on TV where he popped up regularly in some or other remote location where no *sensible* person would want to stay. After the first few weeks, she'd disciplined herself to stop searching the news reports for a glimpse of his face, and immersed herself more and more in her work and in her occasional dates with Brodie.

Picking up the phone she dialled her answering service. 'Hi, Danae,' the girl answered, 'Gala-Rose called – she said she'd call again later.'

'Later?' thought Danae. Gala should be in bed by now; they

had the Avlon 'Junior Skin' session tomorrow and she had to look her best for those close-ups. She took her other messages automatically, still thinking about Gala. Picking up the receiver again, she dialled Gala's number, but there was no reply and, turning away, she prowled moodily to the window, staring out at Manhattan's glitzy skyline, feeling even lonelier than before. So Gala was out – probably with Marcus Royle, who seemed to be monopolising her every free moment!

Wandering disconsolately into her bedroom, she shed her clothes and climbed into bed, shivering at the touch of sheets on her naked flesh. Curling herself into a ball she closed her eyes, hugging her arms around her, wondering just why she had been fool enough to turn down Brodie Flyte for the memory of a passing stranger like Vic Lombardi?

It was extraordinary how *luminous* Gala looked today, thought Danae, peering through the lens of the Hasselblad. Whatever she'd been doing last night had obviously had no bad effect on her – on the contrary, the girl positively *glowed*. Her eyes sparkled and her skin looked flawless . . . Gala looked like the kind of girl who might have just come back from a brisk five-mile hike across the hills, or who'd just sailed a yacht up the coast into Vineyard Haven – even though they'd been working all day! It was amazing how quickly Gala had developed the art of looking different on camera, she seemed to be able to change her personality effort-lessly now to whatever Danae – and the job – demanded. She was perfect for the ad-campaign aimed at the fifteen to twenty-four-year-olds because the whole concept was based on superb squeaky-clean skin and glowing health, and today Gala personi-fied both those ideals.

'Wonderful, Gala-Rose, you look *fantastic*!' called Danae, emerging from behind the camera. 'We'll take some polaroids just to check the light.' She watched as her assistant Frostie White took the shots, examining each one carefully as it dried. 'Can't fault you, Gala,' called Danae cheerfully, 'I don't even have to try on this – you're doing all the work for me!'

Gala gazed into the camera lens, imagining she was somewhere wonderful with Marcus, walking on a quiet beach perhaps, with the wind in their hair and the cool sand between their toes . . . he would take her hand and every now and then he'd turn to look at her, holding her eyes with his . . . and then maybe they'd kiss.

'Great, Gala . . . fantastic . . . just keep that dreamy look in your eyes for a few more minutes, then we'll try something different . . .'

Gala remembered Marcus, waiting for her in his room at Princeton. She had planned to take the five-thirty train and her gaze shifted anxiously to the clock on the studio wall. It was already four fifteen and Danae was still shooting. Even if she was finished in half an hour it would be a close thing, she'd have to try to get a cab and then battle across New York in rush hour – in full make-up too because she wouldn't have time to clean it off – and she hated Marcus seeing her in her 'modelly' look. She only wanted to be herself when she was with him.

'Jesus, Gala! What happened?' cried Danae. 'You lost it – just like that. All of a sudden you look like a harried suburban housewife on a bad day!'

Gala stared at her, hurt, as Danae called to the stylist. 'OK, Monica, get her into the English stuff from Joseph . . . maybe then she'll get her inspiration back.'

'Oh but I thought . . .' cried Gala, and then seeing Danae's ominous expression, she stopped.

'Yes, Gala? And what did you think? That we were finished for the day? Oh I caught your eyes on the clock. Just where do you think you are, Gala-Rose? In a factory where the buzzer goes off at four thirty and we all down tools and go home and the next shift takes over?' She glared furiously at Gala, at the same time thinking how great she looked. Gone was the pathetic waif from London – she looked like a slick, chic, strangely beautiful young girl from . . . where? Not New York, not California . . . no, Gala was *European*. And she'd gained such . . . vitality . . . look at her now, glaring back at her . . . she would never have done that a few months ago . . . And, goddamnit, she shouldn't be doing it now!

275

'I promised Marcus I'd catch the five-thirty train,' said Gala. 'I didn't realise we would be working this late . . . after all, we've been here since ten this morning . . .'

Danae felt the energy drain from her. She'd been coasting along, knowing that the session was going great, and now Gala had ruined it. 'It's always *Marcus* these days, isn't it,' she stormed, slamming the Hasselblad onto the table, 'that's all you ever think about. You mope around when he's not here, and when he is, all you want is to be with him! Never a thought for your work, or your responsibilities . . .'

'Danae, that's not true . . .' protested Gala, 'you know I'll work as late as you want, whenever you want . . . I've never put Marcus before our work . . .'

'And what about me?' yelled Danae. 'You don't care about *me* any more? *I'm* the one who brought you here, remember me? *I* rescued you from that hole you were living in in London . . . not Marcus Royle!'

'Of course you did, and I'll always be grateful,' murmured Gala, tears running down her cheeks, 'how can I prove it to you? I've already told you I'll work . . . I'll call Marcus right now and tell him I can't make it.'

'Don't bother!' retorted Danae, tears of self-pity running unchecked down her face and onto her white satin shirt. 'I *made* you, Gala-Rose, and now Marcus wants to steal you away. *Goddamn it, it's not fair!*'

'But I'll still be your model, Danae, I won't ever work for anyone else,' pleaded Gala, sobbing, 'I promise you I'll be available whenever you want me, just like now . . .'

'Oh yeah? I'd like to see that when Marcus says, "Hey, Gala, come on up to Princeton for the Yale game", and there's a shoot planned for the same afternoon? Or if I need you in Europe and all you do is moon around, looking dull on camera because you're pining for your lover? Love! Bah, *I hate love*!'

Turning on her heel she stormed from the dressing room, leaving Gala weeping helplessly. Brushing back her own tears on the sleeve of her satin shirt, Danae charged up the stairs and flung open the door to her office, slamming it behind her.

'Well, well,' said Vic Lombardi, smiling from her black leather

Eames chair by the window, 'what's all this? A war in the fashion world? A storm in the *Vogue* teacup?'

'You? Oh *you*!' yelled Danae tossing her copper hair out of her eyes and stamping her foot tempestuously. '*You shit*, Vic Lombardi! Why did you have to show up right now?'

23

Even lazing on her sofa, Vic looked more alive than most people would rushing down the street, thought Danae, as she reached for her camera, wondering if it were possible to capture that boundless coiled energy on film . . . not colour of course, a strong face like his needed definition and the shading and texture of black and white. But it was no good, the setting was all wrong. The eyes that looked into her lens had seen too much tragedy, they *knew* too much, and her stylised, indulgent apartment seemed strangely unreal faced with Vic's realities . . .

'I guess you're feeling better,' he commented, setting down his cup on the steel coffee table next to the remains of the take-out Chinese food, still in its cartons.

'What do you mean feeling better?' asked Danae suspiciously.

'You've got your camera in your hands again so I figured you must be feeling all right. Was it the Chinese food? Or was it something I said?'

Danae laughed, 'I'm sorry, Vic. I didn't mean to be rude. And so . . . unwelcoming.'

'Then you are glad to see me?'

'I wouldn't have asked you here this evening if I weren't,' she replied, busying herself unloading the camera and avoiding his eyes.

Vic leaned forward on his elbows, sipping his coffee and watching her. It didn't take a genius to see that Danae had been more upset today than she'd admitted, but so far, she hadn't mentioned it. 'Do you feel like telling me what that scene was all about this afternoon?' he asked.

She glanced at him cautiously and then went back to her camera, slotting in a fresh film. 'No.'

'Fair enough,' he shrugged, 'but whenever you do, I'm a good listener.'

'This would be too trivial for your intellectual ears,' retorted

Danae bitchily. Then putting down the camera, she looked at him, shamefacedly. 'Oh I'm sorry, Vic. I didn't mean that. It's just that – well my plans got a bit of a jolt this morning, and I suddenly felt disoriented, as though all I'd worked for over the past few years might suddenly disappear. Oh I know everyone thinks I'm tough and invincible. They don't know how *hard* it's been. No one starts out that way, Vic, do they? I mean I was just a regular little kid like all the others, going to a ballet school and playing softball – all that stuff. Career-women aren't *born* – they are made!'

'What you need, young Danae, is a change,' replied Vic with his old cheerful grin. 'And I'm just the guy to offer it to you. I'm off to Washington tomorrow. A new assignment – reporting the in-fighting in the nation's capital for a change. I'm hitting the diplomatic trail, Danae . . . parties, receptions, limousines and champagne. Why not come with me? Bring your cameras and grab a few pix of the power boys and girls at work – and play? I can guarantee it'll be full of surprises. And besides, I want you with me. What do you say?'

Why shouldn't she too snatch her happiness whilst she could? thought Danae, because it was for sure that with this man and his eventful, fast-action, ever-travelling life, it couldn't last. And in Washington she would have an insight into the seat of power . . . it would surely make a great photo-essay. The hell with it, she decided, shedding the responsibility of *Images* like a too-heavy cloak. 'I'll come with you, Vic,' she said, her eyes sparkling.

'What persuaded you?' he asked with a wry grin, 'Washington or me?'

'Both,' she replied simply.

Taking the camera from her hands he placed it carefully on the table.'I was hoping you'd say that,' he murmured, folding her in his arms, 'because that's the only reason I accepted this assignment. It was *Danae* and Washington, or no Washington.'

Resting her head against his shoulder Danae sighed contentedly . . . she *needed* Vic Lombardi tonight, she needed his calm assurance – his *strength*. Because under all her confidence, she was still uncertain and afraid sometimes. As she lifted her face and his mouth closed on hers she lost all her self-doubts and all her anger with Gala and all her worries about her career disappeared. She was just Danae, in love.

'This is it,' said Vic, marching her from the cab and up the steps into the Watergate Hotel on their way to their third party that night. 'This is where the deals are made – at embassy receptions and industry cocktails, and dinner parties put together by your society hostesses. Government decisions are finalised in hotel corridors and lucrative contracts are decided in the gentlemen's lavatory. We've probably met at least a half dozen spies so far, and you've never even recognised one!'

'I sure have!' she retorted, laughing, 'how about that fat guy smoking the big cigar at the Press Reception just now? I'll bet he's sold a few secrets in his time.'

'That, my dear ignorant Danae, was one of our nation's most respected Senators,' replied Vic, sweeping her ahead of him into the already-crowded room where a reception was being held to welcome a ballet company from an island that, not too many years ago, had almost caused a President's downfall. Grabbing a couple of glasses from a passing waiter, he manoeuvred them to a quieter place by the window, sighing as he handed her the champagne. 'God knows why I'm here,' he muttered.

'I thought you knew why?' she replied, her eyes meeting his in a deep, intimate glance.

'Touché,' he grinned, 'and you're right. God *certainly* knows why I'm here. It's because I love you.'

The champagne slopped from her glass onto his shirt and she looked at him, startled. 'Say it again, Vic Lombardi,' she demanded, 'just say that again . . . slowly and clearly . . .'

'I . . . love . . . you . . . Danae . . . Lawrence,' he repeated – so loudly and clearly that people turned to stare and smile. 'Even though you spill champagne all over me.'

'Sorry, sorry . . . oh, I mean . . . well, are you *sure*?'

'Of course I'm sure,' he replied, looking astonished, 'why do you even ask?'

'It's just that . . . Well, no one has ever been in love with me before,' she admitted.

Could she really mean it? he wondered, tenderly. Here she

was, Manhattan's tough little cookie sadly telling him that no one had ever loved her. Jesus, he wanted to wrap his arms around her, here and now, and tell her it was all right . . . 'Let's get out of here,' he said, grabbing her hand. 'I want to be alone with you . . . boy do I miss the island . . .'

'And our cottage, and the moonlit strolls along the beach,' she murmured, as he pulled her through the crowd, 'I've thought about you so much, missed you so much . . .'

'The Four Seasons Hotel,' said Vic to the cab driver, 'and we're in a hurry . . .'

Their suite was luxurious and filled with flowers and the bed was king size and waiting, and they wanted each other so badly . . . Danae was lost in his arms again, drowning in sensations and senses she hadn't known she possessed. Their lovemaking was urgent and desperate, as though they were afraid they might never again have the opportunity . . . but they would, she thought, surely they would. This was too strong to be just an affair, surely it couldn't end after these few stolen days together in Washington – time filched from responsibilities and reality . . . 'I love you too,' she whispered, entwining her body with his, 'don't leave me . . .'

Danae shifted her camera from one bare shoulder to the other because it was making a red mark on her skin. Her short Saint-Laurent evening dress with its tight, black silk-velvet strapless bodice and white puffball taffeta skirt was surely glamorous, but it left nowhere for a girl to hang a camera without it looking very much out of place. In fact after four days on the Washington social and political circuit, *she* felt out of place. She was out of sync here, out of her depth even . . . she was a lightweight in a serious world.

'I've no power here,' she'd complained rebelliously before they'd left for this Charity Ball in aid of the Save the Children Fund or was it the Friends of the Opera tonight? She'd lost track . . . 'On my home ground I'm king!'

'Queen,' he'd corrected, grinning.

'Sexist,' she'd retaliated. But she didn't mean it. She felt lost in Washington, as though her talent were unproven. She meant nothing in the corridors of *real* power. And for her, power had always been the real lure.

'There you are!' exclaimed Vic, 'I lost you in the crowd.'

'Just grabbing a few shots of the faces,' she muttered, lifting her camera.

'The same old glitterati faces,' he prodded, 'they're all the same, aren't they, Danae? And these are the women you knock yourself out to please.'

'It's not like that,' she said facing him furiously, 'the fashion industry is a major part of this nation's economy and I help perpetuate that. My photographs help sell millions of dollars' worth of goods.'

'Right . . . OK. If that's what makes you happy. You are surely good at it, Danae. I bet you sell more than anybody.'

'Damn it,' she cried through gritted teeth, 'why are you always needling me?'

Taking her hand, he drew her aside from the crowd. 'Because I think you are too talented for all this; you're too strong, too *real* to remain in this glossy world for ever. You need to expand, to grow, you need to prove to yourself that you offer more. And I know you can do it, Danae. *That's* why I needle you.'

'And exactly what do you suggest I do about it?' she demanded, flushing angrily. 'Do you expect me to give up all I've worked for – all I earn? And I'll tell you this much, Vic Lombardi – it's a dozen times more than you make! *You* couldn't keep me in Saint-Laurent, for Christ's sake!'

Vic stared at her coldly. 'You're right,' he said finally. 'I couldn't. And money's the true American milestone of success, isn't it? Well, excuse me, Danae, I've got work to do. After all, I must earn my bread.' Turning his back he disappeared into the elegant throng.

Jesus, thought Danae, her head aching, what does he expect me to do? Fly to Beirut? Risk my life like he does to take pictures of ruined apartment blocks and old ladies in black robes? I didn't put up with Brachman and run my ass off all those years to get shot at! I'm good at what I do, damn it, *everybody* says I'm the best. What the hell am I doing here anyway? Guiltily, she remembered her cancelled sessions . . . *she was risking her career for a man*! And wasn't that what she'd always sworn she would never allow to happen?

Fighting back tears, she headed for the ladies' powder room. Leaning over the basin, she dabbed cold water onto her face. It was no good, things would never work out between them. Even though she loved Vic, they were worlds apart in their thinking . . . Better she just disappeared, she thought, gathering up her purse and her camera; she'd just leave quietly and go back to New York where she *belonged*. Chances were, Vic would be so busy he'd scarcely even miss her . . .

24

The idyllic Princeton campus with its manicured green lawns and beautiful buildings – a mixture of white clapboard colonial, gothic stone and I. M. Pei modern seemed to Gala's dazzled eyes to be filled with pretty, casually confident girls. Even with Marcus holding her hand firmly, she felt out of place.

'Well, this is it,' announced Marcus, throwing open the door to his room.

Gala peered, stunned, at the chaos inside. Her own brand-new apartment was small, but she kept it neat as a new pin.

'Well, what do you think?' he asked proudly, 'my father had this very same room, more than twenty years ago.'

'Was it any tidier *then*?' she asked, awed.

He swept a chair clean, scattering an assortment of books and sweaters to the floor. 'You think this is a mess? You should just see some of the others! I'll have you know, Gala-Rose, this is one of the best rooms on campus. Let me show you where I sleep.' Taking her hand he led her into an L-shaped alcove where two narrow beds towered at ceiling height on long wooden stilts. The space beneath was a whirlpool of clothes and tottering towers of books, and despite her disapproval Gala laughed.

'But why do you sleep so high up?' she demanded.

'With the beds off the floor we get extra space and, as you may notice, we need it. OK. Now you've seen it all – you know where I spend my life – when I'm not with you, of course. Now I'm gonna take you to Conte's bar for pizza.'

Conte's, on Witherspoon, was packed and Marcus seemed to know everyone. Gala inspected the girls Marcus called 'hello' to, noting the way they did their hair – sleek and shining and long, sometimes held back with elastics in bunches or pony-tails. They wore sweatshirts and neat-collared blouses and bermuda shorts, showing off long suntanned legs. Some had sweaters tied casually around their hips or over their shoulders and all of them carried books or racquets and in Gala's eyes they all had an indefinable air of being the right people in the right place. Dazzled by their easy confidence, she stared at them, envying their access to a free, youthful world she had never dreamed existed even though they were the same age. She would have traded everything to be one of those carefree, clever girls who strolled so casually across Princeton's grassy campus, and who looked as though they *belonged*.

Marcus watched the different expressions crossing her face, wondering what she was thinking. Gala's delicate, enchanting beauty hid a multitude of uncertainties. Just how a girl who'd gone through what she had – and survived – could be so *un*-streetwise, was amazing. She was the most insecure girl he'd ever met, and the most vulnerable. Her life story had touched him deeply. He'd fallen in love with Gala-Rose immediately, but she had such a fragile sense of self-esteem he was afraid to disturb it by making any wrong moves. He wanted her to trust him, to believe implicitly that he would never hurt her, that he would love her for ever – because of course he would. She fascinated him, intrigued him, lured him with her simplicity and lack of conceit. Gala was famous, her face was known nationwide, and yet he knew she was totally unaware that every girl in the room was checking her out enviously, assessing her looks, her style, her sheer *presence*. Today because she wasn't working she wore no make-up, and her honey-coloured hair fell in a straight, simple fringe across her wide-spaced eyes. She was wearing a swirling denim skirt and a blue cambric cowboy shirt, clasped at the neck with an outsize silver and turquoise pin, and simple flat shoes. Gala looked like an immaculately-groomed young girl with her nails polished a surprising fuchsia, and her hair smelling deliciously of some grassy scent. Touching her cool hand, Marcus woke her from her reverie.

'A penny for them,' he murmured.,

'Ohh . . . I was just thinking . . . well, it's nothing really.'

'Let me tell you. You were thinking how pretty the girls looked. Sure they do. And *they* were thinking how great *you* looked. Didn't you catch them staring? They've probably never seen a famous model before – and certainly not such a beautiful one.'

'But these girls are *my* age, Marcus,' she said wistfully, 'and here they are in this marvellous school, without any cares and a wonderful future in front of them. I feel light years away from all this.'

'These kids had to work like hell to get in here,' replied Marcus sharply, 'and a lot of them have to hold down jobs in order to afford to *stay*. Maybe it seems to you as though it's one big jolly club and all we do is hang around and go to parties, but we're a pretty serious bunch. We're all putting in our time here as a stake in the future, building towards something. You've done it a different way that's all – admittedly, it was a tougher, lonelier way, but you are just at the beginning of a long and successful career. Don't you understand that these girls might *envy* you? That in their eyes, *you* are the lucky one, the one to be admired, to be copied?'

She stared at him, wondering why they would envy her – after all she wasn't anything really . . . she was only a body to hang clothes on, a face for Danae to print. Turning her hand palm-upwards, he kissed it softly. 'What am I going to do with you, Gala-Rose?' he groaned.

'Is that why you like being with me?' she asked suspiciously, 'you want to be seen around with a famous model?'

Marcus didn't know whether to laugh or be angry with her. 'I'm going to forget you said that, Gala,' he said quietly.

She eyed him repentantly. How could she have said such a stupid thing? Marcus Royle didn't need a 'model' on his arm for attention. He was attractive, rich, charming – and so *nice* . . . He could have had his pick of a dozen models if he'd wanted, he could have taken out any girl in this room. 'I'm sorry,' she whispered, 'don't let's fight.'

'OK,' he agreed, 'but it's time to talk about the spell Danae Lawrence keeps you under. Don't you realise she rules your life? If Danae tells you you look great, you believe her. You let Danae tell you what to eat – or rather what *not* to eat – and I bet you won't confess you had pizza this afternoon? Danae tells you what time you should be in bed, when you can get up – what time to show up and where . . . at the exercise class, the health club, the studio, the party . . . Damn it, I almost have to check with Danae before I ask you for a date!'

286

'But, Marcus,' she exclaimed, dismayed, 'you must understand that without Danae I would be nowhere – *nothing*! Danae picked me up from the gutter, she transformed me, *she made me into Gala-Rose* . . .'

'Danae didn't *create* you, Gala, she only *enhanced what you were*! She did the easy bit, glossing you up to suit what she needed. But what she really wanted was *you*. Gala – Hilda – the person you are, the person you've become. It's the person you are who is the famous model, not Danae Lawrence's puppet! And besides,' he added, leaning across the table and staring intently into her eyes, 'it's you – Gala-Hilda-Rose . . . that I love.'

Tears of happiness pricked at her eyelids . . . he loved her, she was sure of it now . . . he didn't just want the image on the billboards and magazines, he truly wanted that indefinable person that was *her*.

'I love you too,' she whispered, oblivious to the student-waiter in the red-striped T-shirt, waiting by the table, a huge sizzling pizza in his hand.

'OK, you guys,' he cried impatiently, 'break it up here. Let's get a bit of action now . . . half sausage, half mushroom, right?'

Their hands parted reluctantly as he slid the pizza onto the table between them. 'Two beers,' he called, 'comin' right up . . .'

'Will you marry me, Gala?' asked Marcus, across the pizza.

'Yes,' she whispered back happily. 'Oh yes, Marcus. I'll marry you.' Crossing her fingers under the table, Gala hoped he'd understand that she would have to speak with Danae first though . . . and make sure she understood . . .

25

A world cruise was something that Rachel Royle had planned often enough with her husband, but somehow, when it had come down to booking the luxurious suite she'd chosen on the Patio Deck of the liner, Morris had always found a dozen other activities that took priority. It was work of course; she'd always told him he worked too hard, just as often as she'd told him he must take a vacation. But Morris had been, by nature, a hard worker; work was what counted in his life – and very probably what killed him.

It was a pity, thought Rachel, that Morris hadn't taken the opportunity when he was alive, because, even though she'd finally had to do it alone, the world cruise on the liner *Queen Elizabeth II* had been very enjoyable.

Inspecting her appearance in the vanity mirror of the Rolls, she smoothed back an errant strand of white hair, admiring her lightly-tanned complexion. It was more a good, healthy colour than a tan, and naturally, she'd been most careful, using the Estée Lauder Sunbloc regularly and always wearing a widebrimmed hat. She settled back into the comfortable grey cushions as Warren drove the big car from Pier Seven through the push and shove of traffic on Wall Street, heading homewards.

The cruise had been a good experience. Of course there had been some people on board one wouldn't care to invite into one's home – the younger, flashier group – and then there had been plenty of those who thought that simply having sufficient money qualified them for admittance to the exclusive club to which she naturally belonged. Her little 'group', as she liked to think of it, had soon discovered each other through a natural process of mutual assessment and elimination, and they had managed very well, keeping to themselves, going to each other's cocktail and dinner parties, and playing bridge afterwards in the peace and quiet of the cardroom, without the need to go near that infernal disco. All in all, thought Rachel, she'd enjoyed herself thoroughly. There was already talk among her new friends, of booking the cruise for next year . . . and hadn't she heard that there were those who went every single year? Rachel could see why now, though if anyone had suggested it to her before she'd experienced the cruise for herself, she would have laughed at them for being utterly ridiculous.

Now that she was back home and on dry land, she was rather afraid she was going to miss ship life. In fact, her big apartment would seem quite empty this evening.

Still, thought Rachel, gazing out the window at Manhattan's traffic, there were compensations. She would get to see her eldest grandson tonight, because today was her birthday and he always came to supper on her birthday. And naturally, Harrison and Jessie-Ann would be there too. She'd catch up on news of her little grandson Jon, and how the business was doing, what was new and what was working and what wasn't. Including the Royle Girl promotion and the new catalogue. And she had a sheaf of delightful invitations in her purse to contemplate – requests for her presence at mansions in Dallas and Houston, and at a plantation in Virginia, as well as several quite stately homes in England and France . . . splendid people, all of them. Naturally, she'd be doing a little extra entertaining of her own now too, and it was very pleasant to be home and in charge again.

Gala was now one of New York's highest-paid models and it was Danae who'd advised her to buy an apartment. The idea of actually buying a home of her own would have seemed an impossible dream without Danae's encouragement and help, but now the tiny apartment was hers. There was still a chunk to be paid, but it was *hers* nevertheless. She'd decorated it all in white, banishing the loathsome memories of the sordid grey-brown rooms she'd been forced to live in in London.

Gala gloried in her all-white sofas and rugs, in her simple white silk curtains and her white-tiled bathroom; even the tiny kitchen had a white oven. Clothes were hung up as she took them off, shoes were stowed away in the spacious closets, and she walked barefoot so as not to mark the soft white carpet. She replenished the enormous bunches of white flowers frequently, cramming them onto the glass shelves, the coffee-table and the pretty, perspex desk – a smaller no-colour version of Jessie-Ann's blue one and a housewarming present from her. Marcus had given her a large, perfect curled white shell that he'd once discovered on the beach in Eleuthera and she kept it next to a serviceable white enamel alarm clock (because God-forbid she should ever be late for Danae's sessions) on her white-lacquered bed table.

Marcus was sprawled on her white sofa with his feet on the slab of glass that was her coffee-table, his hands behind his head, looking very comfortable. But there was a stubborn expression on his thin, attractive young face.

Gala sat on the edge of her chair, a worried frown between her eyes and her hands clasped tightly. She thought that in this mood Marcus looked exactly like the picture of Harrison on Jessie-Ann's desk; the same strong chin, the same positive arrogant nose and firm mouth . . . she had never met Harrison Royle but she'd be willing to bet that Marcus was a chip off the old block.

'Tell you what,' suggested Marcus, 'I'll take you out to dinner – how about that little French place we went to a couple of weeks ago, the one you really liked? Or there's always the Carnegie deli.' He grinned at her. 'I'll let you choose.'

'I mustn't eat that kind of food,' replied Gala automatically.

'The French place then, that's fine with me.'

'Marcus, *please*. You know you have to go to your grand-mother's tonight, you told me yourself you *always* go for her birthday.'

'OK then, I'll go. But you know my terms.' He re-crossed his legs on the coffee-table, inching further down into the sofa, looking as though he'd be happy to spend the next few hours exactly where he was.

Gala heaved a sigh of despair; he *knew* why she wouldn't come with him to his grandmother's. For one thing Rachel Royle hadn't invited her – in fact his grandmother didn't even know she existed! And Gala wasn't at all sure that Mrs Royle would be pleased about her relationship with Marcus. It certainly wasn't something she felt should be sprung on her tonight – without any preliminary discussion. Besides, from what she'd heard about Rachel Royle from both Jessie-Ann and Marcus, she was more than a little afraid of meeting her.

'Come on, Gala,' coaxed Marcus, smiling at her winningly, 'come with me – please? It'll be OK, I promise you. Jessie-Ann's gonna be there and you know she loves you, and my little brother Jon – and he *adores* you.'

'And your father – who doesn't know me . . . ?'

'My father's no problem, he'll fall under your spell right away. He's susceptible to beautiful women.'

'That leaves your grandmother,' said Gala, tightly. 'How is she going to feel when you bring some total stranger to a private family gathering?'

'But you *are* family, Gala. You're going to be my wife.' Uncurling himself from the sofa, he went to kneel beside her on the white rug. Producing a small blue Tiffany box from his pocket, he offered it to her. 'The first ring my father gave my mother, when they were only seventeen, was from a Christmas cracker,' he told her, 'and afterwards, when they got engaged, Dad had it copied for her at Tiffany's – in real diamonds and emeralds. She was buried wearing both her rings, but Tiffany still had the design on their files and I had it made for you. For us. I know my Mom would have been pleased to have you wear it.'

Tears of happiness brimmed in her eyes as he slipped the ring on her finger. 'Marcus . . . it's so beautiful . . .' She gazed enthralled at the ring that proclaimed to the world that Marcus Royle loved her. 'It's wonderful,' she whispered, as he clasped her in his arms, 'I love you so much.'

'Now that you obviously are a future Royle,' murmured Marcus, kissing her finger tenderly, 'will you come with me to my grandmother's birthday dinner?'

Still Gala hesitated. 'I'm just not sure it's the right time to tell them . . . couldn't we keep it our secret? Just for a while?' Even as she pleaded with him, she was wondering not only what Mrs Royle would say but how Danae would react . . . oh why did life have to be so complicated? she thought worriedly.

'No deal,' replied Marcus firmly. 'I want you to be my wife and I want the whole goddamn *world* to know it! And so should you.'

She knew he was right, she should be proud that Marcus loved her . . . they would be married and live happily ever after, just like the girls she'd envied in the Barbara Cartland novels she used to read behind the reception desk when things were slow at 'Figure It Out'. Suddenly the future seemed filled with optimism and happiness, with Marcus beside her she could take on the world . . . everything would work out perfectly, she just knew it . . .

Marcus was kissing her again, and she slid her arms around his neck, pressing closer, running her hands through his thick springy hair where it met the nape of his neck; she could even feel the firm pulse of his heart against her breast . . .

Removing his mouth from hers, he whispered, 'I love you so much, so very much, Gala . . .' She flung back her head, glorying in his touch as he placed slow kisses on her throat, and then his hands were on her breasts and she didn't even want him to stop touching her . . . she just wanted him to make love to her . . . never to let her go . . .

'Gala, we can't . . . I mustn't . . .' groaned Marcus, holding her away from him.

'It's all right,' she whispered, aware that his hands were trembling as he held her . . . 'I want you to . . .'

'And I want to – God, you must know that!' Gala's grey eyes were wide and filled with a longing that matched his, but she was the most innocent girl he had ever met in his life; her sweetness in the way she wanted to give herself to him right now, the very way she responded, made him hesitate. 'I don't want to rush you,' he whispered, holding her hands tightly in his, 'we'll be married soon, I can *wait* . . .'

Gala's eyes were dazzled with love for him, and an untapped fount of tenderness was welling inside her. It was a feeling of such true, *pure* love that she knew that there was no wrong in making love with Marcus . . . she wanted only to give her love to him . . . 'There's no need to wait, darling,' she murmured, resting her warm cheek next to his, 'we shall love each other for ever, so why must we wait . . . ?'

Marcus's hands were hard yet gentle on her body and she was drowning in his eyes, and then he was kissing her mouth, forcefully, not holding back his passion . . . and it was then Gala

**knew instinctively that making love wasn't only about giving . . .
it was about taking too, demanding things from your lover . . .
his kisses, his hands, his body . . . she too wanted to touch, to
taste, to take . . . Gala's eyes closed in ecstasy as Marcus claimed
her . . . ah, she hadn't known . . . that love was like this . . . that
it would all be so beautiful . . .**

26

Jessie-Ann sat at her dressing-table, brushing her hair and watching Harrison reflected in the silver mirror. He looked tired and abstracted, as though he had a lot on his mind. Was he worried about something at Royle's? Or maybe he wasn't feeling well? She knew he'd been working hard lately – *too hard* – he was always flying somewhere, LA, the Far East, Europe. Flinging down her brush, she padded across the bedroom towards him. 'Let me do that for you,' she said, taking the ends of his black silk bow tie and smiling up at him. Harrison was already dressed for dinner at Rachel's and as she tied an expert bow she thought how handsome her husband looked. She tilted her head on one side, assessing the new lines on his face. 'Hi,' she said softly.

'Hi there yourself,' murmured Harrison, with a faint smile.

'Did I ever tell you that I love you?'

'I believe I remember you telling me that.' His dark eyes met hers seriously.

'I never say things I don't mean,' she replied, a faint smile touching the corners of her mouth.

'Then I take it you still love me?'

It was said with such an air of wistfulness that Jessie-Ann's heart lurched. 'I haven't changed, Harrison,' she whispered. 'I may be guilty of being too busy with *Images*, but it doesn't mean I don't love you. It's just that . . . well, we seem to have a problem connecting these days, we don't talk much to each other lately . . .'

'You're a busy woman, Jessie-Ann,' he remarked, shrugging on his dinner jacket.

'And you're a pretty busy guy!' she flared suddenly . . . after all, it wasn't *all* her fault.

'That's true.'

'Damn it, Harrison, I'm sorry. It's just that . . . well, I guess my nerves are a bit ragged these days. Maybe you were right after all, maybe I should never have started *Images*. But now I'm committed and it's like having a child that you love a lot; you want to nurture it and look after it and see it grow, until it achieves its rightful place in the world. And there are always so many problems . . .' she added, thinking of the vile letter she had received only that morning . . .

'Anything I can help with?'

Harrison looked concerned and immediately she felt guilty. 'It's me who should be asking you that question, you're the one who looks as though you have inherited the world's cares! We haven't taken a holiday in over a year,' she said. 'Perhaps that's what we need, a couple of weeks in Eleuthera. We could even leave miserable old Nanny behind and have Jon all to ourselves.'

'Sounds like a great idea to me, when can we leave?'

Her face fell, as she remembered her commitments. 'Well, I'm kind of busy for the next couple of weeks, we're opening the two new studios and they're pretty well booked . . . and I really should be there for the next Avlon sessions because I can't trust Danae not to get carried away. She's getting a bit reckless these days . . .'

'Just let me know,' Harrison replied abruptly. He glanced at his watch. 'We're late for Rachel's birthday dinner. Better get dressed, Jessie-Ann.'

'I'm sorry, darling,' she muttered contritely – 'about the holiday I mean. I'll work it out, I promise you. I long to be alone with you – away from all this. I want us to . . . to *find* each other again . . .'

Harrison regarded her, unsmiling. 'Don't you think you'd better hurry? Remember that Rachel will have had a chance to look through the new Royle catalogue. It may be war tonight, Jessie-Ann.'

Jesus! She'd quite forgotten that Rachel hadn't yet seen the catalogue, but of course, she'd been away for three months on that cruise.

'Don't worry,' he added, 'the first sales figures are way up. *Images* is vindicated – though no doubt she'll still raise the roof about the changes.'

Jessie-Ann slipped into an expensively simple chiffon shift and waited for Harrison to fasten the little buttons at the back of her neck. He dropped a light kiss where his fingers had been. She swung round relieved. 'I thought you were mad at me?' she exclaimed, smiling again.

'How could I ever be mad at you when you look like that!' he replied gently. 'Now hurry.'

'I'm ready, I'm ready,' she cried, whizzing around the room, slipping on her silver sandals and collecting her bag. 'OK, Rachel, here we come!'

Rachel waited until she heard Parsons, her maid, ushering the first of her guests into the drawing room. Checking the exquisite gold and blue enamel clock on her desk under the big windows overlooking Park Avenue, she noted that they were ten minutes late. Typical of Jessie-Ann, she thought contemptuously, how that girl had ever held down a job where punctuality meant money, was beyond her. The Royle catalogue lay on her desk, its glossy cover depicting a smiling family group, the way it always had, ever since Morris Royle had taken over the business from his father. Only now it was different. *This* family was no longer the solid, salt-of-the-earth middle-American unit Royle's customers were used to seeing. *This* family did not give the appearance of people who spent long winter nights by the fire, mother knitting or busy fixing supper and father immersed in his newspaper, while Junior admired his new roller skates and his teenage sister displayed her new gingham dress. Of course it wasn't *exactly* like that, thought Rachel, impatiently, but somehow Royle covers had always given *that* sort of impression. You knew exactly what you'd find inside, good quality products, nothing too adventurous because you couldn't afford to get caught in quick fashion changes, solid furniture, brand-name household goods, everything you might need from kitchen to garden – all there in Royle's reliable pages. But each member of this modern-looking family held a glittering gold letter. Dad held up the 'R' – a younger father than Royle's normally used and too good-looking and athletic, as though he might get out there and actually play baseball instead of just watching the game on TV. Mom held the 'O', her pretty, discreetly made-up face and trim figure, smart in a silk blouse and linen skirt, proclaiming her a woman of today. Sister perched in a crook of the gold 'Y', wearing a brief leotard and tights and a big smile, while Junior gripped the 'L' crookedly, struggling to maintain his balance on his roller skates. A pair of toddlers in pink and yellow sleepers were propped against the 'E' while the apostrophe punctuating the name was held up by a large nail in a background of bright blue sky, and a cheeky little dog looking like an escapee from the pound, cocked its leg against the final golden 'S'.

The whole thing, fumed Rachel, was in extremely bad taste. The photography was a disaster. The house-settings looked overly-expensive, Royle's customers would be put off by them. And as for the bathing-suit pages – well! They were outrageously sexy – even she could see that! It was a disaster and Royle's figures for this quarter would surely prove it.

Harrison would have a lot to answer for tonight, she thought grimly. Just let him try to defend Jessie-Ann on this. Of course she'd known it was a mistake to let *Images* have the job and she saw now why they'd taken care not to show her the results before she left on her cruise. Never again, she vowed, she would *personally* see to that! With the catalogue under her arm, she marched into the drawing room pausing in surprise as she saw Marcus with a girl by his side.

'Grandmother Royle,' he cried, striding towards her throwing his arms around her. 'Happy Birthday – and welcome home! Gosh, Gran, what did they do – shrink you on that cruise! Didn't they give you anything to eat? There's nothing to you, you're as light as a feather.' Picking her up in his strong arms he whirled her around.

'Marcus! Please!' she cried, smiling despite herself. She'd always found her grandson irresistible, right from when he was a small boy. He was a true charmer and, now that Morris was gone, it was Marcus who held the key to her heart. 'I didn't know you were bringing a guest,' she said looking pointedly at Gala.

'This is a very *special* guest, Gran, my guest of honour,' replied Marcus. 'May I present my fiancée, Gala-Rose. Gala – this is my Grandmother Royle.'

'Did you say – fiancée?' asked Rachel, stunned.

'Sure did, Gran, I'm very proud to say that Gala has agreed to marry me.'

Rachel closed her eyes, still clutching the catalogue. It was too much – too *ridiculous* that he should even be thinking about getting married – or even engaged. He was far too young, and still in college . . . and who was this girl anyway? She was from no family that she knew personally – and she knew *everybody*. Opening her eyes again, she met Marcus's challenging gaze, but for once in her life Rachel was at a loss for words. 'I, well . . . does your father know about this?' she said at last.

'You're the first one, Gran. We only just found out ourselves, didn't we?' he smiled at Gala. 'Come on, Gran, aren't you going to congratulate us? At least come and meet Gala – that's why she's here, so you can get to know her.'

'I am certainly *not* about to congratulate you on what I can only think is a moment of youthful madness between you and,' she glanced at Gala, 'Miss Rose, wasn't it?'

'Gala-Rose – like Jessie-Ann,' murmured Gala, frozen into immobility under Rachel's icy stare. The older woman inspected her from top to toe and instinctively Gala drew herself taller, tilting her head arrogantly . . . I'm Gala-Rose, the famous model, she told herself silently. I'm successful, and earning more money than I've ever dreamed possible . . . and Marcus Royle loves *me*, I'm wearing his ring – and the imprint of his body. I'm proud of myself. And proud of Marcus too. I'll be *damned* if I'll knuckle under to this old woman's power . . .

'Gala-Rose?' continued Rachel smoothly. 'Well, dear, I can see that you are very young, but I must tell you now, that if you imagine a marriage to a member of the Royle family will ultimately net you a tidy fortune in the divorce courts – because obviously divorce would be inevitable – or maybe even *planned* on your part – let me inform you once and for all, Marcus will have no money of his own until he comes into his trust fund at the age of twenty-seven. If you are planning on getting married then you'd better be prepared to maintain him in the rather lavish style to which he is accustomed. As you know, Marcus,' she added, turning to her grandson, 'I had planned on leaving you the major portion of my assets, but if you proceed with this foolishness, then I shall remove your name from my will.'

'Just a minute, Gran,' exclaimed Marcus. 'I asked Gala to marry me. *Me, Marcus* – not the Royle fortune! My God, Grandma Royle, you've always thought the world revolved around the family business and its money – well, let me tell you, this time you've got it wrong!'

'It's quite all right, Marcus,' said Gala, her voice loud in the suddenly silent room, 'Mrs Royle, there's no need to threaten me or Marcus with your money. I'm making a great deal of money as a model and Marcus can have every penny of it if he wishes.'

'Hah! Another model!' snapped Rachel. 'As if whatever you made could compare!'

Harrison paused at the door, taking in the tense scene in the drawing room. His eyes met Jessie-Ann's for a moment, and then returned to Marcus and the beautiful blonde facing his mother in what was very obviously a battle.

'What the hell's going on?' he whispered to Jessie-Ann, 'and who is the girl?'

'If I read it correctly,' she murmured, pulling Harrison back into the hallway, 'I'd say that Marcus has just told Rachel he's in love with Gala-Rose. Maybe even that he wants to marry her.'

'In love? *Marry?* But who is she? How is it that I've never met her if Marcus cares about her this deeply? And anyway, he's too young to marry.'

'Gala-Rose is Danae's English model; she's a very charming, very sweet, gentle girl who also happens to be rapidly becoming a very successful one. You've never met her, Harrison, because you're not home often enough to meet *anyone* these days. And don't you remember how old you were when you first fell in love – *and* married? Like father – like son, isn't that what they say?'

'But damn it, Jessie-Ann, I knew Michelle all my life . . . this is different. I mean, how long can Marcus have known the girl . . . weeks? A couple of months . . . ?'

She gazed back at him a little sadly. 'It may not be the best example to quote,' she said quietly, 'but how long did we know each other before we married . . . a few weeks? *Less* than a couple of months. Why should you expect Marcus to behave any differently from his own father? And besides, I'm quite sure he loves Gala. Oh come on, Harrison, it's just the sweetest thing you ever saw, two beautiful young people desperately in love. It's Romeo and Juliet!'

Harrison's dark eyes met hers but she couldn't read his expression – there were too many thoughts, too many changes . . .

'Well then,' he replied thoughtfully, 'perhaps we'd better go in there and straighten out the situation – before my mother contrives to halt the course of true love.' Taking her hand in his, he kissed it lightly. 'I'm glad I married you, Jessie-Ann,' he murmured, 'even after knowing you only a couple of weeks. But . . .'

'But?' she asked, her blue eyes starry.

'But . . . we'd better go to the aid of those two young things.' Hand in hand and smiling they walked into the drawing room.

'Happy Birthday, Mother,' Harrison called, 'and welcome home. It seems cruising suits you, you're looking very well, if a bit . . . tense?' His dark eyes twinkled as he kissed her on either cheek and then held her at arm's length, examining her icy face. 'Yes, you definitely look well, Mother. What a pity you never managed to get Father to go with you.'

'It's a good thing your father isn't here tonight,' retorted Rachel, holding out the thick Royle catalogue, 'between this . . . disaster, and this . . .' she gestured towards Marcus and Gala standing hand in hand in the centre of the room, 'this *fiasco*! He must be turning in his grave!'

'It's not like you to be melodramatic, Rachel,' exclaimed Jessie-Ann, kissing her mother-in-law dutifully.

'Good to see you, Marcus,' said Harrison, embracing him. 'And this is Gala-Rose, of course. I've been hearing quite a lot about you from Jessie-Ann.' Taking Gala's hand in both his, he added, 'I must tell you that everything she said was extremely complimentary, and now I can see that she was right.'

Gala felt a little tremor of relief somewhere in the middle of her stomach, at least she wasn't going to have to take on the entire Royle family tonight . . .

'I may as well tell you right away, that Gala and I are engaged to be married,' said Marcus, watching warily for his father's reaction.

'Engaged? Is that so? Well, maybe it's a little sudden, but I guess you both know your own minds. As Jessie-Ann reminded me a few moments ago, I married young myself. So who am I to object? Congratulations to both of you. Does that mean I get to kiss my future daughter-in-law?'

Gala's face cleared in relief. 'Oh of course you do,' she cried, throwing her arms around Harrison impulsively, 'and thank you, Mr Royle . . .'

'There's just one thing,' he said, 'I must insist that Marcus finish college.'

'Nothing would stop me,' he replied grinning, 'it's gonna be a long haul, Father, but one day Royle's will have their own architect to design their new stores . . .'

'Bah,' exclaimed Rachel, glaring at them; it took an act of will to stop from actually stamping her foot – a thing she'd never done in her life! 'You know my views, Marcus – and I shall discuss them with your father later. Apparently, you're not only planning on going ahead with this foolishness, but now it seems you're also abandoning Royle's! *Architecture* indeed! And who, might I ask, will run the family business when your father retires? A stranger? However, the way things are going it's unlikely that there'll be any new Royle's stores!' Tossing the shiny catalogue onto an ebony lacquer table, she glared at Jessie-Ann. 'I must assume, this *travesty* is *your* doing?'

'Well, of course I can't take credit entirely,' replied Jessie-Ann, modestly, 'it's an *Images* production.'

'It's shameful!' cried Rachel, her pinched nostrils quivering with rage. 'How dare you change the Royle image and upset generations of devoted customers?'

'That's exactly it,' replied Jessie-Ann, suddenly enjoying herself. For once Rachel had her back against the wall; she was outflanked – and outnumbered. 'Royle's catalogue was out of date and out of style – it needed to catch up with the times. We merely used the sort of people you see walking down any suburban street. And I know because I was raised in one of those streets.'

'Rubbish,' snapped Rachel, tapping the cover with an immaculate rose-varnished finger nail, 'just look at this . . . this animal!'

'You know how it is with dogs,' replied Jessie-Ann easily, 'they can always be trusted to misbehave at the wrong moment. We thought it added a bit of reality.'

Rachel turned to her son . . . she was sure he must hate the catalogue as much as she did despite his loyalty to his wife, but let him try to deny the *facts*. 'Obviously the sales figures for the past two months must prove that this new "image" for Royle's is a disaster, Harrison. I suggest we cut our losses and simply re-issue our previous year's catalogue, adding inserts with those seasonal items and products we specially need to move. We should return to our old format immediately and organise a new catalogue as soon as possible. No doubt the photographers Royle have used for years – and who are loyal to us – will do a very satisfactory job, in the style established by your father.'

'It's not quite like that, Mother.' Harrison didn't want to upset her more but she had to hear the truth. 'The new catalogue has proven immensely successful. Sales figures are up a massive thirty-seven per cent over the same months last year. Not only that, Royle's catalogue is becoming something of a collector's item. It's the talk of Madison Avenue – and so is *Images*. Our catalogue is actually getting newspaper, magazine and TV coverage nationwide. In fact, Mother, I think Royle's should offer a vote of thanks to the three young women responsible – Jessie-Ann, Danae Lawrence and Caroline Courtney. Together they've taken Royle's out of the forties and into the eighties, and I think I speak for the rest of the management when I say we are all delighted with the results.'

Rachel clutched the edge of the black lacquer table wondering if she might faint. But no, she simply wasn't the sort to swoon, she'd always had the courage of her convictions and she wasn't about to change now, even though she might have to change her tactics a little. She didn't want to alienate Harrison by appearing unreasonable, and nor, for that matter, did she want to lose her grandson. 'I can't argue with those figures,' she said flatly, 'it seems I was wrong. I guess I'm just an older woman than I thought I was. I seem to be saying all the wrong things tonight.' She sank wearily onto the little gilt chair whose fine needlepoint cover she had worked herself, regarding the four of them through hooded eyes. 'I suppose you might as well open the champagne, Harrison, it seems we have more than just my birthday to celebrate.'

'We're leaving, Gran,' said Marcus, taking hold of Gala's hand, and heading for the door.

'No!'

Jessie-Ann stared at Rachel in surprise. Her voice had cracked a little – and could that be a glint of a tear in her eye?

'Bring Gala to meet your grandmother, Marcus,' Rachel said, managing a smile, 'it seems that I shall have to bow to your better judgement and just let you young people get on with things. We're going to drink to your engagement, *and* to Royle's successful catalogue. And then we'll all have dinner. Jessie-Ann, would you ring for Parsons and tell her that Gala-Rose will be staying for dinner? And then I want you to tell me how my other grandson is doing.'

Watching Rachel as she allowed Gala to place a kiss on her smooth, cool cheek, Jessie-Ann wondered what she was up to, because it sure as hell wasn't like Rachel to back down from any situation. One thing she was sure of, this wasn't her last word on Marcus's marriage, nor on the catalogue.

Later that night Jessie-Ann lay curled in Harrison's arms, still glowing from their passionate love-making, feeling happier than she had in months. She wondered if seeing Gala and Marcus so happy had somehow made them both understand what they were losing – their love-making had been almost an act of consolation, as if defying fate to take away what they had. Her priorities in life were suddenly clear – her man and her child. Maybe now that Caroline had *Images* firmly under control she could start easing herself away from the business little by little and begin to spend more time with Harrison. Because, now that she stopped to analyse it, life without *Images* was bearable; but life without Harrison was *unthinkable*.

27

It was ten o'clock on Monday morning and Caroline surveyed
her new office happily. *Images* had expanded rapidly and there
was now a total of four studios with a proper reception area and
a new efficient young receptionist at the desk. Each of the three
partners now had her own spacious office, and in a long, airy
room in the back, Laurinda supervised the book-keeping, hunting
out the late-payers like a hound on the scent of a fox, while two
young secretaries pounded endlessly on their typewriters.

Caroline had decorated her office herself using cool shades of
grey and white. There was a soft dove-grey carpet and a blue-grey
velvet sofa, a square, white-lacquer desk and lots of tall leafy
green plants. The effect was simple and restful. Placing an armful
of her favourite roses and yellow daisies on the desk, she hung up
her neat little Anne Klein jacket on the white coat-tree, pausing
by the window to inspect the new plants in their white containers.
The leaves were perking under the sunlight and Caroline smiled,
contentedly. Next to being home with Calvin, *Images* was the
only place she wanted to be in the entire world.

She'd really needed the extra space because somehow her office
had become a haven for the volatile bunch of people who were
Images' clients. It was always Caroline to whom the models ran
tearfully when they decided to throw a tantrum about the way
their hair or make-up looked; and, with a little charm and a hot
cup of tea, it was Caroline who made them feel that she really
cared about their careers and their problems with their boyfriends.
And in truth, she did. It was always to her office too, that errant
members of rock groups, in for album or publicity shots, wandered
in search of 'coke' . . . 'Cola is kept in the refrigerator,' she'd tell
them briskly. There had been times when she'd had no choice
but to close her eyes to certain things, but she was damned if she
was going to pander to any drug scene!

There was no doubt that she'd found her métier, she thought, busily opening the morning's mail. *Images* was like Broadway, but in capsule form, with each of the four studios putting on its own show – a morning, matinee and evening performance, with its own cast of characters and its own script. She ran *Images* efficiently, giving customers her personal attention. Her most recent coup had been to employ a chef so that clients no longer needed to rush around the corner to Blakeys or send out for food. *Images*' 'gourmet' touch with buffet meals was the talk of the fashion and advertising world, and it was just one of those little added incentives that were bringing in new clients almost faster than they could handle.

Efficiency, politeness, civility, were the watchwords that Caroline enforced at the studios. 'How kind of you to choose *Images*,' she'd say to new clients. 'I'm sure you won't regret your decision, and please don't forget to let us have details of any special requirements in food and wines. Our chef is splendid . . .' And, 'So sweet of you,' she'd reply, beaming when they thanked her at the end of a session. She always wrote follow-up letters not only to the account executives at the ad agencies and fashion editors at the magazines, but to the insecure members of the successful rock groups for whose publicity shots Danae was now much in demand. 'We do look forward to seeing you here again,' she'd write them, 'we so enjoyed the shoot. Thank you for using *Images* . . .' She saw that there was always a plentiful supply of chilled wine or iced champagne for visiting clients, and had taken special personal care of the crew from CBS who came to do a ten-minute spot about *Images* that had gone out nationwide, prime-time, right after the news, and had suddenly made their name a household word.

There was no longer any problem getting work, jobs were flowing in; the trouble was getting *paid* for it! And it was the big accounts that gave them the most trouble. Last night Laurinda had given her the breakdown of *Images*' monthly figures and their cash flow was really worrying. This expansion had been very expensive, despite the fact that Jessie-Ann had plunged in and bought the adjacent buildings with her own savings. It was the ever-spiralling cost of conversion plus the new equipment they needed that had drained *Images*' always shaky cash-flow and their overdraft was at a figure that made Caroline gulp! Of course, the payments would come in eventually, she thought, slitting open an envelope with her little pearl-handled knife and unfolding another bill, but if it weren't for the steady Royle business – and they were already well into next season's catalogue – *Images* might well have found itself in trouble.

Putting the bill in a pile with the others to give to Laurinda, she thought about Gala's engagement to Marcus Royle. She couldn't say that it was a total surprise, because they were so obviously besotted by each other, it was the only logical conclusion – to everyone except Danae! And what *Danae* would think of it was quite another matter. Thank God she was out of town for a few days, at least it kept the situation from coming to a head for a while longer, because there was surely going to be trouble when she found her protégée had defected!

Come to think of it, she didn't know exactly where Danae had gone. She'd simply called in and said, 'I'm taking a few days' break, be back in time for the Marriot session next week – See ya.' And she'd disappeared. Ah well, thought Caroline, I just hope it's a man and she's happy – Danae's too much alone, she's too intense. She concentrates on work, and nothing else matters in her life. Everyone deserves a break now and again, she thought, and no one more so than their very own 'ace' photographer.

'Caroline?' Jessie-Ann stuck her head around the door . . . 'you alone?'

Caroline glanced at her sharply. 'You look awfully pale, what ever is the matter?'

'I just had a telephone call from Rachel Royle,' explained Jessie-Ann miserably. 'She wanted to know if I'd heard the rumours about Harrison and Merry McCall. *Harrison and Merry McCall*, Caroline! She told me that there are pictures of the two of them all over the place, in every mag and gossip column . . .'

'Well of course there are,' interjected Caroline, 'Merry is the Royle Girl and Harrison is always off doing PR for the line . . .' She glanced at Jessie-Ann's hurt face, wishing she could believe what she'd just said.

'I told her I hadn't read anything like that, and that things are just great between Harrison and me . . .'

'She just wants to get back at you for the catalogue, that's all,' cried Caroline indignantly, 'trying to mix up things in your personal life . . .'

'The truth is, Caroline,' said Jessie-Ann sadly, 'that until last weekend, things have been going really wrong between us. Oh I know it's all my fault, I should have spent more time at home and not been so caught up in getting *Images* on its feet, not been in so much of a hurry to satisfy my *own* ambitions . . . and apparently, I was too busy to read the gossip about my own husband! He *has* been away so much, on the road with Merry . . .'

'I'm sure it was all in the line of business,' replied Caroline, loyally. 'Didn't you tell me yourself, how happy you were, last weekend?'

'That's true,' she admitted, brightening. 'Perhaps I'm just imagining things now that Rachel's opened my eyes to the gossip.'

'You know how great you and Harrison have always been together,' exclaimed Caroline. 'I always envied you . . .'

'Until you met Calvin,' finished Jessie-Ann, with a laugh.

'Agreed.'

They grinned at each other, understandingly. 'OK, I'll get back to work,' said Jessie-Ann. 'I have a meeting with Brodie Flyte in half an hour, though I guess it was really Danae he was hoping to see. By the way, where is Danae?'

Caroline shrugged. 'All we know is she'll be back next week.'

Jessie-Ann raised her eyebrows to heaven. 'A secret lover? Or has she gone off alone with her cameras? My bet is the latter. Brodie Flyte is going to have a tough time with our Danae. See ya.' She flitted across Caroline's dove-grey carpet, turning at the door with a grin. 'You know what? I think I like your office more than mine! I'm just gonna have to change that red and blue . . .'

'Then wait till we get paid!' yelled Caroline, laughing. But her smile faded as the door closed; there was no doubt Rachel Royle was aiming for the heart – and with a poisoned dagger. She just hoped that Harrison had come to his senses, and she thanked God that Calvin wasn't a human dynamo like Harrison. She just couldn't imagine Calvin rushing across continents after any girl; he was too comfortable in their relationship and their home to bother chasing girls, and Caroline knew that, when he wasn't travelling on a job, he would always be waiting for her when she arrived home from work. He'd be lying across the sofa, barefoot, with his blond hair rumpled, and with Cosmo Steel, the silver cat, lying along the furrow of his legs. There would be a bottle of their favourite champagne chilling in the refrigerator, and maybe they'd make love before dinner – or after – or maybe even both depending on how the mood took them. Filled with happiness, she laughed out loud, she wanted to throw her arms around Calvin right now and just thank him for making her so *very* – so *supremely* happy.

28

Caroline watched in astonishment as Danae stormed out of the studio, yelling over her shoulder at her assistant Frostie, 'For God's sake, get your act together!' Ever since she'd gotten back from Washington a month ago, after those disastrous cancellations which had cost *Images* a new client, Danae had seemed on edge. *More* than on edge, thought Caroline, she was like a woman possessed. Make-up artists and hairdressers sulked in silence over the long hours they were now forced to put in, while the models bickered wearily with each other, glaring balefully at Danae and muttering behind her back that she was a bitch to work for. Monica, the stylist, was reduced to eating endless candy bars from sheer nervousness, and poor Frostie slammed equipment around holding her temper in check like a rumbling volcano.

It really was so *unfair* of Danae to treat people that way, thought Caroline. She wouldn't have blamed them one little bit if they'd simply walked out on her. But Danae's photographs were fantastic; her work was in demand in every top magazine, and she was the darling of the fashion editors and account executives. If you worked with Danae then you basked in her reflected glory, and so of course, no one ever walked out. But the atmosphere at *Images* had changed drastically; Caroline had always liked to think it was like an amiable theatrical club, where everyone knew everyone else and respected their particular talent, but now it felt more like an out-of-town show with a disaster on its hands! 'Danae the despot', was the name she'd heard bandied around behind Danae's back, and she was very much afraid they were right.

Naturally, there was a man involved – wasn't there always? she thought gloomily, making her way down the stairs to Studio 3 to find out what the hell was wrong this time. Gala had told her that the 'trouble' was Vic Lombardi, the TV news reporter, whom Danae had met on that Harbour Island shoot. And of course it was with him Danae had run off to Washington, leaving them in the lurch and at the mercy of a bunch of irate clients for whom they'd had no excuses. Well, if this were Danae's way of making up for her transgressions, she was surely going off the deep end.

She paused outside the door of Studio 3 to eavesdrop, trying to get a line onto what was going on but there was only silence. No music, no loud voices, no sobs . . . and no laughter. 'The Three Musketeers' Danae had dubbed them in the beginning . . . but it was no longer 'one for all and all for one'. Both Jessie-Ann and Danae were involved in their own personal problems at the expense of *Images*. And it was *men* who were at the bottom of it all.

Pushing open the door Caroline took in the ominously silent scene; Gala, in a short, tight black-silk dress, drooped against the white wall, her spindly-heeled suede shoes kicked to one side, a look of exhaustion on her exquisitely made-up face. Even when she was tired, the girl had a magical kind of beauty, thought Caroline smiling at her reassuringly. Frostie was tilted back precariously in her chair, swigging a can of cola and looking pale but stoical. Monica was chewing the last bite of a Mounds candy bar, the wrappers of the two previous ones crumpled into little balls at her feet. Hector smoked silently in a corner, although there was a strict 'no smoking' rule at *Images*; while Isobel leaned on the littered counter in the dressing room, her head in her hands, staring at her own glum reflection in the mirror. A rail of exquisite garments from several of America's top couturiers awaited Danae's attentions, alongside open suitcases full of accessories . . . shoes, belts, bags, jewellery, ribbons, scarves . . .

'I suppose it's no use asking what's wrong?' enquired Caroline, with a sigh.

'Just the usual, that's all,' mumbled Monica. 'A typical Danae tantrum.'

'Not *quite* typical,' corrected Gala wearily, 'it's just that she's spent four solid hours shooting this dress and she's not happy with any of it . . . she's blaming Monica for not getting the right "look" with the accessories, she's screaming at Hector because my hair's not right – but we've tried it half a dozen different ways and she hated them all. Isobel changed the make-up colours from gold and bronze to purpley-pinks, she tried a sophisticated look and an innocent look – neither of which satisfied Danae. And poor Frostie can simply do nothing right.'

'And she blames *Gala* for all of it!' added Hector. 'Danae's had the poor kid under those hot lights since eleven o'clock this morning – she wouldn't even let her sit down because the dress is so tight it'll crease . . . Monica practically has to peel it off every time Isobel has to re-do the make-up . . . It's bad enough for the rest of us, but *God knows* how Gala takes the abuse! Y'know, kid,' he said turning to Gala, 'you're the "number one" face in the US. You don't have to take this shit – you can choose any job you want, *and* any photographer.'

Gala stared at her swollen feet where the high-heeled shoes, half a size too small, had pinched them. 'I'm sure Danae doesn't mean to upset us,' she murmured. 'It's just that she's not seeing what she's searching for in the lens . . . *it's just not happening for her*. And she's frustrated! Can't you understand?'

'Frankly, I can't,' retorted Frostie icily, 'she knows as well as I do that both you and that dress look great . . . she really doesn't have to do much to keep the customers happy except get a decent angle and good lighting, and we've surely got that.'

'She's acting like she's a fucking Rembrandt, or something,' added Hector plaintively, 'and she's driving us all crazy.'

Standing in the doorway Danae surveyed them coldly. 'Is that right, Hector? Well, if I get you too crazy then you might as well quit – before I fire you.'

'Suits me!' snarled Hector, glaring at her.

'Now come on you two,' cried Caroline hastily, 'surely there's no need to carry things this far. OK, so Danae's having an off-day. We're all entitled to those, you included, Hector. You're all creative people, you know how it feels when things are going great – and what a downer it is when no matter what you do it just lacks that special sizzle. Give Danae a break will you, she's trying hard to achieve something special.'

'I *was* trying hard,' Danae corrected her, 'but no more, *I just quit*!'

They stared at her, stunned. 'You did what?' demanded Caroline.

'I quit.' Danae flung herself into a chair, leaning back and running her hands through her tangled red hair that already looked as though it had been attacked by a cyclone. 'I called the editor of *Vogue* and told her there was nothing new to add to these clothes. I've got the top model, and I'm the best photographer there is – and I just hated what we were doing.'

'You called the *editor* of *Vogue* and told her that?'

'Sure did.' Danae stared intently at the ceiling as though it were Michelangelo's masterwork in the Sistine Chapel, a slight frown creasing her brow. She looked like a child who knew she'd been naughty, thought Caroline, angrily, but also who knew she had the grown-ups in her pocket.

'And are we permitted to know what the editor of *Vogue*'s reply was?' she asked icily.

'Sure. She agreed with my new idea.' Danae's gaze shifted to Gala, still leaning against the wall, still afraid to sit down and crease the dress, one aching foot clasped in her hand.

They waited in silence for Danae to go on, but she said nothing. 'Well?' prompted Caroline, 'what was your new idea?'

'I simply told her that these clothes were too much the same, there was nothing new about them, and she agreed with me. I told her what these rags need is true old-fashioned glamour – the kind you used to find in the twenties and thirties. They need gorgeous locations and daring deeds to turn them into magical frocks for sensational women . . . the kind of women men find a challenge. Think you're up to that, Gala-Rose?' she called mockingly.

Gala shrugged, 'I'll do what ever you want me to do, Danae.'

Hector stared at her in disgust. 'Why don't you stand up for yourself?' he demanded, 'what's *wrong* with you, Gala-Rose?'

'Gala-Rose is smart, that's all,' retorted Danae, 'she knows no one but me can make her look the way she does. Without me Gala-Rose doesn't exist.'

Hector glared at Gala, expecting a response, but she merely stared at the floor her cheeks flushed crimson, biting her lip. 'It's worse than I thought!' he exclaimed, disgustedly. 'You don't only think you're Rembrandt, Danae – now you think you're God!'

'And so I am – in my own small world,' retorted Danae. 'And those who don't like it can quit right now.'

'That means me, all right!' Without a backward glance, Hector stalked into the dressing room and noisily began flinging hair-dryers and brushes and bottles of shampoo into his bag, muttering under his breath about 'the bitch goddess'.

'Wait, Hector, *please*.' Gala stood in the doorway, her grey eyes pleading with him. 'She doesn't know what she said, she's just very . . . very *upset* right now. It's this guy she knows, I think he's hurt her pretty badly and she's just taking it out on herself. We're only getting the fallout of what she's going through person-ally.'

Hector paused. 'She tell you that?'he demanded, his voice still angry.

'Yes . . . no. Well, partly.' Gala didn't want to tell Hector the details, but the night she'd got back from Washington, Danae had called her and asked her to come at once. Gala had gone and found Danae tearful and angry – with herself and with Vic Lombardi. She'd seemed determined to plough her way through as many bottles of champagne as she could, drowning her sorrows in her own way because she hated the taste of spirits. After the second bottle was empty, the story of what Vic had said began to emerge. She hadn't asked Gala for her comments, or her sym-pathy, she simply wanted her to be there to listen while she argued first *her* case, claiming she was right and he was just running down her work, her talent – her *persona*, for Christ's sake. Then she'd switched to Vic's point of view, sobbing that of course he was right, her work was trivial, it was just technical expertise and that she hadn't yet learned how to put it to good use. 'He *admits* that I have talent,' she'd wailed, 'but now I'm beginning to wonder. I've never doubted myself before, Gala, and it's terrible, it's undermining my whole security – everything I've learned, every-thing I've built my career on . . .'

'Believe me,' Gala told Hector quietly, 'Danae didn't mean what she said. She's angry with herself, not you or me or any of us. Don't quit on her, Hector.'

Her pleading expression was irresistible and despite his anger, Hector relaxed. 'OK, maybe I went a bit over the top too,' he admitted, 'but Jesus, Gala, you shouldn't let her talk to you like that. It's not right – and it's not true!'

'Maybe . . .' replied Gala vaguely, but in her heart she thought it was. Without Danae, Gala-Rose, the model, didn't exist.

'Please,' begged Caroline as Hector and Gala emerged from the dressing room, 'let's not fall out. *Images needs you all.* Come on now, Danae, you know you'll never find a hair stylist you admire more than Hector, and Hector you know that Danae is the best photographer there is in New York . . .'

'OK. I'm sorry, folks,' said Danae, her face suddenly losing its cast-iron mould. 'I admit that I've been a bitch today, but now it's over. I'm apologising, aren't I? Listen, I'm gonna buy you all a drink – champagne! And make it *Images*' best, please Caroline, for my team – because we are still a team, aren't we?' Her yellow headband was pulled down to eyebrow level over her rumpled coppery hair and her white satin sleeves were rolled to the elbow and Gala thought she looked like an eccentric, too thin tennis player. But it seemed only she could discern the strain behind Danae's dazzling smile and the flicker of anxiety in her eyes . . . Danae was more fragile than any of them suspected.

'OK then,' agreed Hector, walking over and giving Danae a kiss.

'Oh for Christ's sake bring on the champagne,' moaned Frostie wearily, as the others hugged and kissed Danae tearfully, 'and let's get this show on the road!'

Sitting in the back of a too-hot yellow cab on her way home, Gala wondered how she was going to tell Marcus that she was leaving this weekend for extended location work . . . Danae didn't know how long a trip it would be – three weeks – four or five, she'd said vaguely. 'This isn't just a fashion shoot, it's a photo-essay on fashion, *Vogue* plans to run it in three consecutive issues. It will be a triumph, Gala, the peak of my career. So far.'

It was the 'so far' that worried Gala. What else was she going to strive for? And the fact was that Danae, with all her frantic energy, was exhausting! She slumped back wearily against the worn taxi seat. She couldn't blame the others for wondering why she took so much abuse from her. She knew they thought she was under some sort of magic spell cast by Danae and that she was too weak to struggle against, and maybe she was. She stared down at her feet in the white and grey Fratelli Rossetti co-respondent loafers bought just a few days ago from their smart and expensive Madison Avenue store, remembering how she used to gaze longingly in their window on Bond Street, and she remembered the cheap copies that had fallen to pieces after a few weeks of tramping London's rainy streets, searching for a job. Now she had a dozen pairs of Rossetti shoes; she had Valentino cocktail dresses and Ralph Lauren casual wear, and if she'd wanted to wear furs she could afford to buy them. She owned her own apartment and had what seemed to her a great deal of money in the bank. She was recognised wherever she went as a successful model with a lucrative career in front of her. And, best of all, she had Marcus's love. And the truth was if it weren't for Danae Lawrence, she would have none of these things.

Paying off the cab, she swung through the revolving doors, hurrying through the discreetly elegant foyer that was bigger than all the rooms in the old terraced cottage in Yorkshire put together. The immense flower displays were replaced every couple of days with quantities of fresh roses and carnations and lilies and the lift, panelled in pale, bleached wood, was just about the size of her old bedroom in Garthwaite. Turning the key she opened the door to her beautiful, all-white apartment . . . the home that was all hers, where everything was new and unused by any other person. She kept it spick and span herself, wearing jeans and her hair bound in a scarf, vacuuming, dusting, scrubbing out sinks and bathtubs with the peculiar pleasure of absolute possession. At first she had really been afraid of living on the twentieth floor – she'd thought she'd never get used to Manhattan's vertical buildings – they'd brought back the old fears and nightmares about Wayne Bracewell – tottering on that roof with the ground so far below . . . but by now she'd gotten more used to it and had managed to put it out of her mind.

Slipping off her beautiful shoes, she walked, barefoot, across the soft white carpet to the telephone and dialled her answering service. But there was no message from Marcus; and drifting into the bedroom she undressed and hung her clothes away tidily. As she stood beneath the harsh spray of the multi-jet shower the weariness began to ease from her aching bones, and she tilted her head, letting the water flow over her face and through her hair, washing away all the gel and the hair spray and the tensions of the day's work.

What no one realised was that she loved Danae. *Danae was her true friend*. It had come as a shock to Gala to realise that you didn't need to be poor to be lonely – and Danae, successful, was as lonely now as she had been in London. All Danae lived for was work – and all the PR parties and fashion launches she attended could never take the place of a private, personal life. When Danae went home at night it was to an empty apartment and a phone that would ring with calls eager for her services or her presence at an opening or a fashion show, but not with anyone wanting just to say 'Hi, Danae' and to gossip and laugh together. Gala knew that Brodie Flyte had been eased out of Danae's life and he no longer called, because what man would be willing just to hang around on the off-chance that Danae would change her mind? And now this disaster had happened with Vic Lombardi . . . and this time the wound had gone deep.

She would help Danae through the difficult times, just the way Danae had helped her, vowed Gala, stepping from the shower and towelling herself dry, because that's what friends were for. If she refused to go on location with Danae now, then that brittle, high-strung 'don't care' façade might just crack – and Danae would be destroyed. She just hoped that Marcus would understand, that's all!

29

As she did her routine rounds of *Images'* studios, Jessie-Ann wondered wistfully where the thrill had gone? Business was booming and *Images'* name was the buzz-word around town – even though they still seemed to be teetering on the red/black borderline at the bank. Hadn't she achieved success in everything she'd attempted? In her job as a model? In *Images*, and in her marriage and motherhood? What more, she wondered, could any woman ask. Then why was there this small, niggling doubt in her mind? Why, just when *Images* needed her most, was she beginning to question whether *she* needed *Images*?

She would tell Caroline that she was going to cut back on her work, she decided as she walked back to her office, and then she'd try to persuade Harrison to do the same. There was just too much polite distance between them these days. He'd been in Japan for two weeks now and she was missing him like crazy.

Her office door was open and Laurinda was placing a batch of papers on her desk. 'Hi, Laurinda,' she called, 'more work for me?'

'Just some bills I'd like you to approve before I pay them,' replied Laurinda, averting her eyes from the large brown jiffy-envelope she'd just placed in Jessie-Ann's in-tray. It was the one with the clippings – re-packaged so Jessie-Ann wouldn't recognise it.

Sitting in her big blue leather chair, Jessie-Ann picked up the sheaf of bills, adding her initials at the bottom of some so that Laurinda would know to pay them, and passing others on for Caroline to inspect. As she handed them back to Laurinda she caught sight of the large brown envelope. 'What's this?' she asked, smiling, 'not more bills I hope?'

'I don't know,' mumbled Laurinda making for the door, 'it was there when I came in . . . well, thanks, Jessie-Ann . . .'

Laurinda was a bit abrupt today, she thought, slitting open the

317

envelope, and she was in a hell of a hurry. Maybe they were working the girl too hard? She'd better speak to Caroline about it later. Much as she disliked her, the girl was good at her job and she'd hate to lose her. A large bundle of clippings tumbled from the envelope and she sorted them, assuming they must be from the weekly service who sent them copies of every word that was printed in the press about *Images*. She stared in bewilderment at the large photograph of Harrison and Merry, 'dancing, cheek to cheek in a San Francisco nitery . . .' and then another of them 'laughing together over lunch' at a Washington restaurant; and another of them by an elegant pool at Palm Beach, Florida. She sifted unbelievingly through the pile of photographs, and gossip column quotes, pausing at the picture of Merry and Harrison at a Japanese dinner table. Merry was wearing a loosely-wrapped silk obi and she had her arms around Harrison's neck and her cheek against his in a pose of such intimacy that it left no doubt in Jessie-Ann's mind that Merry knew her husband as well as she did . . . and maybe even better , . .

The lurking uneasiness she'd felt earlier surfaced into trembling panic. *So Rachel had been right after all!* Was it Rachel who'd sent this? Could Rachel be *that* cruel, *that vindictive*? Scattering the clippings across her desk, she saw the note and with a sinking feeling in her heart, she recognised the familiar red lettering. 'You should wash your mouth out with soap,' she whispered, reading the piece of paper, 'you terrible, cruel, crazy person.' And then the reality hit her and a sob welled in her throat. Hot tears spilled from her pretty blue eyes as she wailed, 'Oh God, make it not true, please . . . make it not true.' But she knew it was and she didn't even want to think about it because it hurt too much; she didn't want to think of Merry and how pretty she was, and how charming – and how *available*. And she didn't want to think of Harrison, alone with Merry in Japan. The pain of lost love ripped through her, and she pushed the clippings into the waste basket with a sweep of her arm. In an instant she was through *Images*' blue door, into a cab and on her way home. Home? Had the apartment ever really been that? She remembered the suburban 'ranch-style' comfort of her childhood – the house always awash beneath a cheerful litter of books, magazines, clothes, records; the phone always ringing; the good smells coming from the kitchen; the friends dropping by. It had been ordinary, a little shabby, cheerful. A proper home . . .

Tears coursed down her face as the taxi threaded its way through the traffic, and she dabbed futilely at them with a soaked handkerchief.

'Don't take it too badly, Jessie-Ann,' called the cab driver, recognising her, 'there's always plenty of other guys around!' He'd guessed right first time, she thought miserably.

As she waited for the elevator in the elegant foyer her hurt turned to anger. How could Harrison do this to her, she thought furiously? How *dare* he? Had he ever considered Jon's welfare when he was flying across continents to be with Merry McCall? Trembling with accumulated fury, she swept into the apartment, and up to the top floor nursery, calling to Nanny Maitland impatiently.

Jon was just finishing his supper, fingers crunching happily through a mess of red jello that covered his tray. Nanny Maitland looked up in surprise at Jessie-Ann's tear-blotched face.

'Pack everything, Nanny,' commanded Jessie-Ann, kissing Jon and wiping the jello from his face, 'we're leaving.'

Nanny Maitland eyed her warily. Mrs Royle looked very upset and not at all like herself . . . something had gone terribly wrong, she knew it. 'But Mrs Royle,' she said, 'are we going on holiday?'

'No holiday, Nanny. Just pack all Jon's clothes, his toys . . . everything. We are leaving here for good!'

Nanny Maitland could almost feel herself turning pale. 'But, Mrs Royle, this is too sudden, I just can't get everything together like that. And shouldn't we wait and speak to Mr Royle?'

'We should *not* speak to Mr Royle,' replied Jessie-Ann coldly.

'I'll need time,' protested Nanny Maitland, knowing that her worst fears about young Mrs Royle were well-founded. The girl was erratic, unstable, flitting between her responsibilities at home and that dreadful *Images*, with young Jon rattling between the two like a yo-yo. No, she decided, this was no good . . .

'Get the maids to help you,' said Jessie-Ann, picking up the phone and dialling the number of the Carlyle Hotel.

'But, Madam, I do think we should speak to Mr Royle first.'

Nanny's voice faltered as Jessie-Ann glared at her . . . 'or at least speak to Mrs Rachel Royle . . .'

'We shall be leaving here in one hour, Nanny, and I expect you to be ready,' said Jessie-Ann.

An hour and a half later she and Jon, with a dozen suitcases and quantities of cardboard boxes of toys, plus a reluctant Nanny Maitland, moved into one of the Carlyle Hotel's best suites.

Jon trotted excitedly from room to room, pulling open cupboards and drawers, and turning on the tap in the bidet in the bathroom until it gushed so high it almost hit the ceiling. Nanny looked miserable and had to be given tea to soothe her English nerves. And Jessie-Ann faced the result of her precipitate action alone, locking herself in the luxurious, impersonal bedroom and crying her eyes out.

30

Rachel Royle had always found that the world – or her small part
of it – had leapt to do her bidding. She had never had any
trouble getting exactly what she wanted from people, even her
husband, Morris, had bowed to her wishes though sometimes
he'd complained he indulged her too much. And Harrison had
always seemed to follow the course she'd chosen for him – he'd
done well in school and he'd excelled in college. He'd married
the daughter of family friends – a girl she would have chosen
herself – and they had produced a good son – her grandson
Marcus. She had tried very hard to help him that first terrible
year after Michelle's death, but he'd seemed to prefer not to talk
about it. Harrison had dealt with his wife's death the way he had
that of his father. She'd assumed that he'd just accepted it silently,
as he had the fact that he would take over the family business.
Naturally, she'd never asked him if that was what he *wanted* to
do – as her only son it had been his duty to carry on the business,
and of course he had proven her judgement right, especially in
the years after Michelle's death when he'd thrown himself totally
into his work, buying in companies and taking over others,
increasing Royle's profits until they ranked with the major corpor-
ations of America.

In fact Harrison had been the perfect son until he'd suddenly
succumbed to the facile charms of that silly young model, whose
only virtue was that she'd given Rachel a second grandson to
carry on the Royle name and empire.

When Nanny Maitland called to report Jessie-Ann's defection
to the Carlyle, Rachel knew that the moment for a confrontation
had arrived. She would act now, before Harrison heard anything
about it.

'Mrs Rachel Royle is here, Madam,' Nanny Maitland said,
sounding relieved. Perhaps it would all be sorted out now, she
thought, and they could go back now to that lovely apartment. It

simply wasn't right to take a boy away from his home, without his father's knowledge . . . dear me no. People didn't carry on like this in England, not the families she knew anyhow. In England, even if there were 'differences', you'd never know it . . . life would go on smoothly in the drawing room and the nursery and she was sure in the bedroom too.

'Rachel!' Uncurling herself from the depths of a yellow sofa, where she'd been dozing – making up a little for all her sleepless nights, Jessie-Ann immediately felt untidy and crumpled next to her mother-in-law in her impeccable navy and cream Chanel suit.

'I won't waste words – and time – Jessie-Ann. Suffice it to say that I'm here to take my grandson home.'

Her face ashen, Jessie-Ann stared at Rachel disbelievingly. 'What did you say?'

'A hotel is no place for a small child. He should be at home. Since you have now decided – rather arbitrarily and without a thought for anyone else – to move out, I propose to take Jonathan home to his father. And, as Harrison is so busy, I shall stay at the apartment myself and keep an eye on him.'

Taking a deep breath, Jessie-Ann tried to control her anger. 'How did you know I'd left Harrison?' she demanded. 'I only knew myself last night. I haven't even spoken to him yet.'

'Exactly! You simply took matters into your own hands without so much as a discussion. Don't you think Harrison should have been consulted first before you removed his son?' Withdrawing her gloves, Rachel placed them carefully in her purse, swivelling her large diamond and ruby ring into place automatically. 'Thank God there are members of your household staff who have a grain of common sense and who can be trusted to do the right thing,' she commented icily.

'I see,' replied Jessie-Ann quietly. 'Nanny Maitland. Well, she always was in your corner, Rachel.'

Standing her ground in front of the carved marble fireplace, Rachel challenged Jessie-Ann to dare to defy her. 'I shall have Nanny pack Jon's things and take them home with me now,' she said decisively. 'Of course you understand, Jessie-Ann, that what I'm doing is in the boy's best interests. He is a *Royle* you know.'

'A Royle!' shouted Jessie-Ann, 'you silly, meddling old woman!

Just because you've lived like a pampered cat all your life, indulged and allowed to queen it over everybody, it does not give you the right to take my son away from me. And if you dare even to *try* – if you even lay one finger on Jon, I'll have my lawyers over here so fast, *and* the police – *and* the District Attorney – that you'll wonder what hit you! And with the publicity this will get you'll wonder what hit *Royles*! I'll tell the tabloids and the television news and the gossip columns how you tried to snatch away my son; they'll be camping on your doorstep waiting to grab pictures of you as you come out of your apartment . . . I'm warning *you*, Rachel, stay away from us. What has happened is between Harrison and me. It's *our* lives – and Jon is *our* son.'

As Jessie-Ann advanced like an angry Valkyrie, Rachel backed towards the door. 'Don't imagine that you can take *my* grandson,' she threatened, 'because you can't, you'll soon find that out!'

Jessie-Ann watched, trembling, as the door closed behind Rachel. 'Even now,' she thought, 'the woman hadn't *slammed* it!' She walked towards Jon's room, where she knew Nanny was listening. 'Nanny Maitland,' she called, 'pack your things and leave. You're fired!'

Ignoring her outraged gasp, she picked up the telephone with a still trembling hand. She hesitated, wondering who she could call to help her. Of course, she thought with a sudden sense of relief, she'd call Marcus . . . maybe he would know how to deal with his grandmother.

31

Caroline hurried along Third Avenue, keeping to the sunny side of the street because the wind had become suddenly chill, bringing a gust of winter into the autumn air. Ignoring the cruising cabs she walked briskly, her head down, a worried frown punctuating her pretty face.

The financial situation at *Images* had suddenly become drastic and with Jessie-Ann embroiled in her own complex private life, there was no one with whom she could discuss the crisis. Danae was off in Kitzbühel, or Greenland, or Wyoming, shooting the new series of Gala pictures, but anyway, thought Caroline gloomily, she would have been no help. Danae's head was lost in a creative cloud and she'd left all the business decisions to them. To add to everything, Laurinda hadn't been to work for the past two days . . . she hadn't even called to give her a clue as to when she might be back and Caroline supposed she was too ill to get to a pay phone, but it was ridiculous that Laurinda didn't have a phone for emergencies such as this. Scowling, she waited for a large garbage truck to make its way slowly past the intersection, stepping into the path of the oncoming traffic as the light changed and ignoring the shaken fists and loud curses hurled in her direction. What the hell, let them wait, they'd all been trying to jump the light anyway . . .

She wondered if Jessie-Ann would think she were being unsympathetic if she telephoned her at the Carlyle to discuss *Images*' finances? After all, Harrison was a key figure in the current situation and the fact was that the Royle invoice, always presented and paid promptly, was two months overdue, and whenever she called to ask why the delay, she got the runaround. It wasn't like Harrison to be *mean* – and after all he had *technically* been the guilty party, so he wasn't likely to take out his anger on *Images*. She didn't believe it was his doing at all – in fact now she considered it, she suspected the meddling hand of Rachel Royle in the accounts department. Those old guys had been there since her husband's days and were all loyal to Rachel. Still, she thought worriedly, she couldn't call Harrison and tackle him about it, Jessie-Ann would never forgive her.

With the success of the previous catalogue behind her Danae had really gone to town on the current edition, spending a fortune and giving free rein to her imagination. Between those still unpaid expenses and the fees, Royle's owed *Images* hundreds of thousands of dollars. Now interest was mounting daily on their overdraft to some astronomical sum Caroline didn't even want to remember! Oh damn it, she thought, angrily, zipping across the street and heading towards home. At least with Calvin she would be sure of a welcome and a sympathetic ear.

Calvin was on the telephone in the bedroom. 'Hi,' she called flinging her case containing the latest evidence of *Images*' disaster onto a chair, followed by her jacket and her purse. Kicking off her shoes, she trailed to the bedroom door, smiling beguilingly at Calvin, who lay stretched out on the bed, talking softly into the receiver.

'OK, sweetheart, gotta go now,' he said as Caroline turned back into the sitting room, bending to pick up the cat who had followed her, miaowing. 'Cupboard love,' she murmured into his soft grey fur, 'all you want from me is food . . .'

'Hi, babe.' Calvin closed his arms around her, kissing her hair and the cat leapt from Caroline's arms, claws extended and ears back in fright.

'Ouch,' she cried, holding out her arm and examining the long scratch, already oozing blood, 'you startled him, Calvin!'

'Sorry . . . I'm real sorry, sweetheart. Here, let me put some Bactine on it.' Hurrying her into the bathroom, he fished the antiseptic from the cabinet, dabbing it onto her scratch.

Caroline watched him, wondering who he'd been calling 'sweetheart', just now on the telephone . . .

'Right, Courtney, you'll live! Now, how about a bottle of Blanc de Blanc . . . you sure look as though you could use it! What happened? The roof fall in at *Images*?'

'In a manner of speaking,' sighed Caroline, 'or at least, I think it's about to . . .'

Cocking his head to one side, Calvin studied her downcast face. 'Anything I can do to help?'

'Nothing. Thanks. But the champagne sounds wonderful.' Trailing despondently back into the sitting room, she crumpled onto the sofa, tucking her legs beneath her and resting her chin on her hand.

'Champagne's coming right up, sweetheart,' called Calvin, heading into the kitchen.

The phone shrilled and Caroline glared at it balefully, there was no one – absolutely *no one* she wanted to talk to tonight . . . unless of course it were Jessie-Ann? Grabbing the receiver, she growled, 'Hello?'

'Hi, is Calvin there?'

The voice was feminine and not one Caroline knew. 'It's for you,' she called, dropping the receiver onto the sofa.

Calvin walked lazily back across the room, picking up the phone and draping himself over the large chair by the window. 'Yeah?' he said. And then, 'Hey, it's you again! Come on, sweetheart, didn't I ask you not to call . . . yeah, well I know that . . . sure, me too . . .' With the receiver tucked in the crook of his shoulder, he stood up and began pacing the area of floorboards between the rug and the window.

Caroline watched his bare brown feet walking back and forth, no longer pretending she wasn't listening . . . her antennae told her this conversation concerned *her* as well as Calvin and suddenly her secure world trembled . . .

'Sure I do, sweetheart,' said Calvin, 'but well, you know how it is . . . oh come on now, let's not be that way . . . yeah, well me too. Yup. I'm sorry, sweetheart, no hard feelings? Sure. Anytime. 'Bye.' Dropping the receiver in its cradle, he headed back towards the kitchen. The clenched feeling in the pit of Caroline's stomach was really hurting now. Maybe she was just being stupid, and she hoped she was wrong, but to her it sounded as if Calvin were talking to a person he knew *very well*. *Intimately* was the correct word to describe it. Oh God, she thought, clutching her stomach, she just hoped she was wrong . . .

'Here you go, sweetheart,' called Calvin hurrying from the

kitchen with a tray of brimming glasses, 'champagne's the best pick-me-up I know for tired workers.'

'A cup of tea has been known to work wonders too,' she replied distantly, avoiding asking the question that trembled on her lips.

'So? What's new with *Images*?'

He wasn't even going to *mention* those two telephone calls, he was just acting like they hadn't happened . . . Caroline stared into her glass, saying nothing.

'Hey, Courtney, things can't be that bad,' he said, taking her hand and squeezing it, 'it's nothing that can't be worked out.'

'It seems I've got more problems than I bargained for today!' she burst out suddenly. 'Who the hell were you calling "sweetheart" on the telephone, Calvin Jensen?'

He looked at her steadily for a minute, without replying and then he said, 'Come on, Courtney, that doesn't really concern you.'

'Oh? And why doesn't it concern me? Don't I live here with you? Courtney and Calvin . . . the happy duo? So – who is "sweetheart" then?'

'She's no one important, Courtney, just someone I know . . . knew . . .'

'Then she's in the past?' A beam of hope lit her eyes, but Calvin hesitated again. It was ironic, she thought, that one of the things she'd always liked about Calvin was his straight-arrow honesty; Calvin always spoke the truth, always said exactly what was on his mind . . .

'Look, sweetheart, why are we getting into all this?' he replied at last, 'I've told you, it's nothing.'

'*Nothing?* How could it be nothing? She's already called you *twice* tonight! Maybe she wants to come over and stay, the way "old friends" do?' Caroline glared at him, biting her lip to keep the tears from falling. She wished suddenly that she were somewhere else – anywhere else but here, saying these things to the man she loved . . .

'Courtney, look, she's no one, just a girl – a model . . . someone on the Viking shoot in Sweden . . .'

'In Sweden? But that Viking shoot was just two weeks ago, less – maybe ten days.'

'It was nothing, sweetheart, she means nothing . . . she's just a nice girl and I guess tonight she was feeling a bit lonely, so she called me.'

'Just like she did in Sweden?'

Calvin eyed her uneasily. 'I already told you it meant nothing. You know what it's like out on location, it's disorienting, unreal . . . it's *lonesome*, Courtney! Things happen! But no one takes it seriously . . . it's meaningless . . . it's just . . . fun . . .'

Caroline set down her full glass very carefully, keeping her chin high so that the tears wouldn't run down her face. Then she stood up, and walked across the room, retrieving her shoes from the corner where she'd cast them.

'Hey, Courtney . . . sweetheart, I'm *sorry*. But I told you, it was nothing. *Goddamn it, Courtney, why did you have to ask me!*' Calvin stared at her angrily, and she glared back, half-blinded by the tears that now flowed freely.

'*Goddamnit, why did you have to tell me*,' she yelled, 'you could have pretended . . . you could have thought of some excuse . . . oh you *idiot*, Calvin Jensen! *I hate you!*' She kicked him as hard as she could, landing a hefty blow on his shin.

'Jesus!' Calvin leaped backwards, rubbing his bruised leg, 'what d'ya wanna do that for, Courtney? Hey, hey . . . wait a minute now . . .' He edged behind the sofa as she moved towards him menacingly. '*Come on, Courtney*, it's nothing, I *promise* you it was nothing. Sweetheart, I love you . . . now look what you've done to our nice peaceful evening . . .'

'What *I've* done? *My God!*' Seething with frustrated anger and pain, Caroline glared at him, searching for something to throw, but the only object to hand was a delicate porcelain vase filled with the perfect yellow roses he always bought her, and she couldn't bear to throw that . . . but damn it she wanted to hurt him, hurt him as badly as he had hurt her . . . just look at him in his cashmere sweater and white pants . . . God's gift to lonely models . . . *Suddenly she knew what to do* . . . Turning on her heel, she marched into the bedroom. Their walk-in closet was crammed with clothes and sports gear, three-quarters of it Calvin's. Reaching up Caroline unhooked Calvin's Versace leather jacket, his dozen Armani suits and his Gianfranco Ferre trench-coat, ramming them into a large valise and tossing pairs of Gucci loafers on top frenziedly.

With a single sweep of her arm she cleared a shelf of a small fortune in cashmere sweaters, stuffing them in on top of the shoes and forcing the lid closed by sitting on it. Snapping shut the locks she glared triumphantly at Calvin, who stood in the doorway, staring at her in amazement.

'Courtney?' he asked, 'what's going on? What are you doing with my clothes . . . hey, you're not thinking of throwing me out, are you? Because if you are, I warn you I won't go . . .'

Groaning under the weight of the suitcase, Caroline dragged it across the hall. She opened the door and edged the case through and then she turned to face Calvin, glaring at him balefully one last time before she slammed the door in his face. Anger gave her strength as she lugged the heavy case to the elevator, keeping her finger pressed urgently on the button until the doors opened. She knew just what she was going to do, she thought angrily as she dragged the case inside, she knew exactly how to get back at Calvin . . .

'Courtney, wait . . . hey wait . . .' Calvin hurled himself into the elevator as the doors slid closed. 'Sweetheart, what are you doing? Where are you going with my things?'

Caroline stared straight ahead, ignoring him, silently urging the elevator to hurry up! Instead it stopped with a little ping, and a smart middle-aged couple got in. They eyed Caroline's tear-stained face curiously and then the bulging suitcase from which odd sleeves and pants legs protruded. The woman turned her gaze on Calvin, glancing pointedly at his feet and he followed her gaze wondering what was wrong. 'Well now,' he said, attempting a jaunty grin, 'I guess I just forgot to put on my shoes. Never mind, there's plenty in that suitcase – all I have to do is persuade the lady to let me have a pair!'

'Doesn't look as though you'll find that an easy task, son,' declared the man, winking at Caroline as the elevator stopped and they departed.

'Here let me help you with that,' exclaimed Calvin, as Caroline struggled with the heavy case.

'Don't *touch* me! *Get away*,' she yelled.

He stepped back, stunned by her anger. 'Courtney, this isn't like you,' he cried as she pushed her way through the revolving door onto the sidewalk. 'This isn't the quiet, calm, reasonable, logical, beautiful Caroline Courtney that I know.'

'You bet it isn't!' she snarled, flagging down a taxi and heaving the case into the cab.

'Where are we going!' demanded Calvin, holding open the door.

'You Calvin,' replied Caroline, slamming it, 'are going exactly nowhere.'

'Jesus, Courtney, my feet are freezing out here,' he yelled, hopping up and down as a passerby turned to laugh.

'Where to, lady?' The cab-driver's face was blank, he wasn't gonna get involved in no domestic dispute, no siree . . .

'Riverside Drive,' she told him, turning away from Calvin's pleading face at the window.

Calvin watched disbelievingly as the cab pulled away and then quickly flagged down another. 'Follow that cab,' he cried, leaping in and slamming the door.

'You serious?' The cabbie eyed him warily.

'Of course I'm serious goddamnit, my girl's in there – with all my clothes!'

'She could at least have left ya a pair of shoes,' said the cabbie, eyeing his bare feet sympathetically. 'OK, bud, you got it . . . jeez, I always wanted to do this. Ya know, nobody's ever asked me to follow a cab before. Ain't that amazing, in the whole of Manhattan? Y'think nobody ever watched those Bogie and Edward G. movies . . .'

'Move!' bellowed Calvin, leaning forward and scanning the traffic for Caroline's taxi. 'Riverside Drive, that's what she said,' he remembered triumphantly.

'Riverside? OK, that's easy . . . we'll make it before they do . . .' Putting down his foot the cabbie swerved through the traffic, a grin of delight bisecting his face.

Caroline scanned the Drive for a convenient spot. 'Right here, please, driver,' she called imperiously, sounding just like her Aunt Catriona.

The driver pulled into the kerb, and looked at her warily. 'Are y'sure you wanna go through with this now, lady? The poor guy surely looked cut up about things . . .'

'That *poor guy*, as you call him, is a mean, two-timing cheat. I *hate* him,' replied Caroline in a trembling voice.

'In that case,' sighed the cabbie, climbing out, 'let me help you with that valise. It's too big for a kid like you.'

'Thank you. You're very kind.' He placed the case beside her on the sidewalk and Caroline thrust a ten-dollar bill into his hand.

'Hey, lady, what about your change?' he yelled as she picked up the case and lurched back down the street to the chosen spot.

'Keep it – it's yours.'

Shaking his head, he watched alarmed, as she stopped by the parapet overlooking the river . . . the English kid wasn't gonna throw herself in was she?

Calvin's taxi pulled into the kerb with a screech of brakes and he hurled himself out of the rear door. 'Courtney,' he yelled, 'sweetheart, *don't do it*!'

Bending down Caroline opened the suitcase. '*Watch me, Calvin!*' she called. Then picking up an armful of expensive clothing she tossed it across the parapet and into the river. Scooping up a half dozen Gucci shoes she cast them after the others.

Calvin stopped in mid-stride, staring at her in amazement. The two cabbies were watching them both. 'Jeez,' said one, re-lighting his cigar, 'I always thought the English were nice, quiet folk . . . sort of like Her Majesty, y'know . . .'

Caroline launched Calvin's Versace leather jacket over the edge, following it with a half dozen sweaters.

'Will ya look at that?' commented the other driver, 'she's throwing the guy's entire wardrobe into the river – she's even left the poor bastard barefoot.'

Calvin rushed forward, wincing as he stepped on a stone. Hobbling to the river's edge, he looked wide-eyed at Caroline and then down at the river. His Versace jacket floated on the brown water, arms spread like a relaxed swimmer, and his suit and sweaters, sodden lumps of wool, drifted on top of the current heading downstream. One lone Gucci loafer bobbed on the pointed little waves like a miniature kayak ready for the rapids.

Caroline grabbed another armful of clothes, struggling to lift them over the parapet.

'Here, let me,' said Calvin politely. Taking the armload of jackets from her he leaned forward and flung them into the water.

Caroline stared at him, then back at his clothes floating down the river. 'Calvin, that was your very favourite Armani suit you threw in there!'

He nodded, watching the progress of his clothes down the river. 'I know.' He turned to look at her. Her eyes were red and swollen and her brown curls wind-tossed. She was the most beautiful girl he'd ever seen. 'It doesn't matter,' he said. 'None of them ever really mattered to me, Courtney, they're just clothes. The only thing I care about in the world is you and if you ever leave me I think I'd probably want to join my clothes – in the river. Forgive me, Courtney. I didn't mean to hurt you. I love you. And only you.'

'Oh Calvin!' She was in his arms and he was kissing her and all her anger had disappeared, purged like a blood-letting with the gesture of throwing away his most precious possessions – only to find that they didn't really matter after all. *Nothing* mattered any more, not the model in Sweden, not *any* model – they loved each other.

The cab-driver gave a long whistle. 'Did yous ever see Lauren Bacall in that movie with Bogart? Or wait a minute, was it Ingrid Bergman? Y'know, the one where she gets on the plane and leaves him? Well, I wanna tell you, bud, this is better than that movie!' Grinning, the cab-driver called, 'Yous guys goin' home, or what?'

'Are we going home, Courtney?' Calvin asked, still kissing her.

'Where else?' she murmured, her eyes closed.

They turned once more to look at his clothes floating on the tide, and Calvin began to laugh. 'Just look what you did, you crazy woman,' he yelled, gasping with laughter. 'You're *crazy* and I love you! Tell you what,' he cried. 'We may as well start fresh!' In one swift movement he hefted the valise and all the rest of his clothes into the river. Arms around each other, they leaned over the parapet hooting with laughter, as the waiting cabbie scratched his head in amazement.

'Mad,' he commented thoughtfully, 'wasn't it Noël Coward who said the English were mad?'

32

Marcus Royle faced his grandmother across her elegant rose-coloured drawing room, wishing he didn't have to say what he did. Despite her matriarchal manoeuvrings he loved her very much. But Rachel Royle was stronger than most people; she was rich and she was used to getting her own way. She could be a very dangerous woman.

'Well, Marcus, this is a surprise!' exclaimed Rachel. 'I suppose you've heard the news? Yes, that's why you're here of course – when you should be in college.' An expression of deep annoyance crossed her face; 'Jessie-Ann is disrupting all our lives with her stupid actions.'

'Grandmother Royle, I think you are wrong to try to take Jon away from Jessie-Ann,' said Marcus, getting right into battle. 'You should let my father and his wife sort out their own lives, and not try to interfere.'

'You do, do you?' Rachel's voice was heavy with sarcasm, 'and meanwhile my grandson is alone with that silly, emotional girl. God knows what she will do with him. Probably whisk him off to Montana and her family, if she has half a chance.'

'And why shouldn't she? Jon is the Parkers' grandson just as much as he is yours. The only difference between them and you, Gran, is that *you've* got more money.'

'Jonathan is a *Royle*,' she retorted sharply, 'and so are you, Marcus. I'm surprised to hear you saying such things. Don't you have any sense of loyalty to your family?'

'To my family yes. But not to you when you're behaving like this.' Marcus kept his voice even with an effort, he didn't want to upset his grandmother. 'Jessie-Ann is part of our family – only you've never accepted that fact.'

'Nonsense, the girl never fitted in with us. She was never a suitable wife for Harrison. I suppose she'll be happy enough with the lavish settlement he'll no doubt give her; she'll probably pour it all into that silly modelgirl agency, wasting good Royle money! *But the boy is mine.*' Her hawk-like eyes met Marcus's with a gleam of triumph. In Rachel's mind the battle was already over and won.

'Gran,' Marcus said slowly, 'I want you to know that if you try to take Jon from his mother, then you'll lose your other grandson.'

Rachel drew in her breath sharply, clutching the edge of her desk to steady herself. 'You shouldn't say things like that to me, Marcus,' she replied faintly.

'I'm sorry to have to say it, Gran, but after all it's the same way that you are threatening Jessie-Ann . . . you want to take her son from her, for ever.'

Smoothing back her already smooth dark hair with a trembling hand, Rachel sank into the needlepoint chair. 'You mustn't argue with your grandmother, Marcus, you're just a boy . . . you must respect the decisions of people older and wiser than you, people who have had more experience in life . . .'

'That's nonsense, Gran, and you know it!'

'And what do you suggest then?'

'We wait. We let my father and his wife work it out between themselves.'

'Wait!' snorted Rachel. 'Wait – while that girl plans to take not only my grandson, but also the family money.'

Marcus sighed . . . it had always been like that with Gran, the business and the money came first. It would never occur to her that Jessie-Ann might not even care about the Royle money, that she might really love his father and things might have just gotten messed up between them. Jessie-Ann was great, he liked her a lot and he was sure there wasn't a devious thought in her head . . . she just wasn't aware of what she'd done to his father.

'You're very forceful, Marcus,' said Rachel, retreating behind her usual cool mask, 'but that doesn't resolve the problem.'

'*You* can resolve one of the problems and that's why I'm here.' Crossing to her chair he took her hand. 'I love you, Gran, you know that? Remember when I was a little kid and Dad was off in Europe or just plain too busy? It was always *you* I hung out with – despite all those smart nannies and governesses you kept hiring for me. I still remember playing touch-football with you in the drawing room of your big house in Connecticut . . .'

'And breaking the Ming vase!' retorted Rachel. 'You were the strongest little boy, even though you looked like a stick insect then . . .'

'And you took me on picnics to the bottom of the garden – it seemed to me to be miles, and there was a stream that we waded in together . . .'

'And you cut your foot on a stone . . . Oh Marcus, I miss that, I miss it – with Jon . . .'

Her eyes had a lost expression and for the first time Marcus thought his grandmother looked her age. Kneeling on the floor beside her, he kissed her hand gently. 'It'll be all right, Gran, I promise it will,' he said. 'Just give them time. And you know something? I'll bet if you soften up your attitude towards Jessie-Ann, she'll be more than happy to let you share in Jon's life. After all, aren't grandmothers supposed to be there to indulge and spoil their grandchildren? We can't deprive young Jon of that, now can we?'

His brown eyes, so like his grandfather's, demanded her compassion for his father and for Jessie-Ann, and remembering the sweet, small boy he'd been, Rachel felt tears spring to her eyes . . . but she hadn't cried since Morris died and she was certainly not going to cry now, she told herself sternly.

'Come on, Gran, promise me now. No interference?'

'Oh very well,' she said giving in with a sigh, 'but I certainly hope you're right, Marcus. Now, give your grandmother a kiss and a hug, I suddenly feel rather lonely.'

'There's no need to be lonely, Gran, so long as you don't place yourself outside the game,' he whispered, kissing her soft, lightly-powdered cheek. 'You know something – I'm crazy about you . . . you beat any other Gran I know . . .'

'Enough, enough,' she replied, smiling at him, 'now will you stay and have lunch with a lonely old woman?'

'Self-pity?' he asked with a grin.

'Possibly,' Rachel replied.

'The best cure for that is lunch at Le Cirque,' he decided. 'Come on, Gran, put your hat on . . . I can't wait to see the faces

336

at the restaurant . . . they'll all be wondering if Rachel Royle has taken a young lover!'

'Marcus,' she retorted, shocked. But she was laughing and there was a sparkle in her eye that he hadn't seen there in a long time. Maybe his grandmother *was* lonely, Marcus thought with a pang, lonelier than they'd ever thought, because somehow she'd always kept up this façade of indomitable strength and wilfulness. Grandma Royle needed to play a bit more, to get out and about. He'd talk her into booking another cruise over lunch, and what about a villa on the Riviera this summer? Perhaps the whole family could go . . . if he could get them all united in time . . . Rachel and her two grandsons, Gala-Rose, Jessie-Ann and Harrison. His grandmother needed to 'belong' to the family, as much as any of them, and if . . . no, *when* things were worked out, he intended to see that she did.

33

Danae's untidy entourage straggled across the tarmac at Salzburg airport, heading impatiently through passport control and customs and into the waiting limousines that would take them to the international ski-resort of Kitzbühel. This was their fifth – and please God, final – week on the road, thought Frostie, checking the cameras and equipment and watching as the long fibreboard cases containing the precious clothes and furs were loaded into a van before their little cavalcade set off.

Danae's three-part series of photographs was to be called 'Surprises' and – not surprisingly – it featured Gala-Rose. In the past few weeks they had trekked half-way around the world seeking exactly the glamorous settings that Danae wanted. She had photographed Gala in Iceland in elaborate evening dress, heavily bejewelled, all alone and adrift on a pale, chilly northern sea – an exotic shipwrecked beauty in jade chiffon and emeralds; she'd photographed Gala as a smart castaway in tuxedo, black tie and enormous diamonds on a remote archipelago in Finland populated only by matching black and white puffins and screaming gulls; and she'd photographed Gala naked, wrapped in two hundred thousand dollars' worth of sable coat and immense sapphires in a husky-drawn sled in icy Norway. Frostie and the others had been bundled into down-filled parkas and scarves and padded boots and they had felt sorry for Gala on these icy locations. She had managed to look poised and calm but the remote look in her eyes had disguised the fact that she was numb with cold.

Seeking warmth, they'd flown from there to Turkey, and though the sun was far from summer's strength, to them it had felt like heaven after all that ice. They'd watched doubtfully while Danae, in a helicopter, had photographed Gala balancing precariously on the prow of a fast speedboat, looking like some ancient figurehead in Isobel's wild golden make-up, with her eyes narrowed and her hair streaming back in the wind. Gala's whole body had screamed with tension and she'd collapsed, trembling with fear afterwards. But Danae had claimed it was worth it; the photographs were wonderful. And they'd had to admit that they were.

They'd criss-crossed Europe, searching for exactly the right wind-swept moor, finally finding it in Ireland. They'd swathed Gala in priceless old shawls from Kashmir, and the latest Japanese designer's rugged tweeds and, for once, the poor girl had been warm. Frostie thought she'd never seen anyone look more vulnerable than Gala, her slender ankles peeking from beneath the voluminous layers – somehow the pictures had evoked memories of an era when a glimpse of an ankle was considered exquisitely erotic. Next Danae had discovered a forest in France full of wild boar and had commanded that Gala's beautiful naked body be painted to blend into the forest trees. Terrified of the wild boar, Gala had portrayed the spirit of nature . . . her face waif-like in the filtered forest-green twilight, the emeralds around her neck and in her ears glinting with an alien radiance of their own.

Frostie had only seen Gala balk once, and that was when Danae asked her to stand on the edge of a cliff overlooking the sea. Wearing a virginal white silk-tulle balldress, a black cloak billowing behind her, she'd paced towards the edge and then stopped, her face ashen. Shivering with fright, she'd turned imploringly to Danae who'd urged her forward. 'Go on, Gala!' she cried, 'it's no good hanging back like that. Stand right at the very edge!' Frostie had noticed Gala's knuckles showing white through her skin as she gripped her billowing cloak, and then Gala had closed her eyes tightly, edging a little further forward, but still not enough to satisfy Danae. The photographs were a disaster she'd declared that night, they had absolutely zero impact – and it was all Gala's fault. She'd glared angrily at Gala, who had just said quietly, 'I'm sorry, Danae, I just felt a bit dizzy that's all. It won't happen again.' Frostie hoped it wouldn't because it seemed to her that Danae's exploits were becoming more than a little dangerous – for Danae as well as Gala. Since she'd discovered helicopters Danae had found a dozen new angles on a familiar theme and she was like a kid with a new toy. Held back only by the safety straps, she hung from the helicopter as if she were a stuntman on some James Bond movie and they'd watched, their hearts in their mouths as she swooped over the location.

Enough was enough, Frostie decided wearily as the limousines deposited their motley crew at the aptly-named Romantikerhotel Tennerhof at the base of the famous snow-covered Kitzbühler-horn mountain. She could take no more of these trips with Danae; she drove them ever-onwards until they were dropping on their feet, and besides she just didn't like the new element that was creeping into the sessions. It seemed to her that Danae was so immersed in her striving for some idea of 'perfection' that she was unaware of the risks she was taking. This was their final stop and, when they got back to New York Frostie had decided she would quit.

Gala lay back thankfully in the downy pillows of her luxurious bed, feeling relaxed and pampered after a hot bath and a room service tray of delicious soup – which was all she'd felt like eating. Her tired body was warm for once, and it was pleasant to be alone in her lovely wood-panelled suite with the pretty tiled stove in the corner sending out a cheery glow. She wished Marcus could be here to share her luxurious haven. It seemed even cosier when she looked out of her window at the view of snow-covered mountains.

The others had donned their glad-rags and headed for the Casino at the Goldener Greif Hotel, eager for 'a little razzle-dazzle' as Hector had put it, after their previous remote locations. And Danae had gone off on her own, exploring the snowy streets of the small charming twelfth-century walled town. Gala had refused to go along on either expedition, claiming she needed sleep, but really all she'd wanted was to be alone so that she could talk to Marcus. He would be telephoning any minute now, and when he did, she would press the receiver to her ear and close her eyes, and it would almost seem as though she were with him.

Marcus hadn't been angry when she'd told him that she would be leaving on this job with Danae for an unspecified length of time. He'd just looked at her thoughtfully, as she'd run through her quick explanation that she just couldn't let Danae down. 'It's important to me, Marcus,' she'd finished pleadingly.

'Of course it is. Did you think I wouldn't understand that?' he replied. 'I sure hope Danae finds whatever it is she's looking for out there, Gala, but it's you I'm worried about. She drives you into the ground. She monopolises your entire working life, and I don't think it's healthy – either for her or for you. I don't know if you've ever realised this, but when Danae sought *you* out in London, *she needed you* as much as you needed *her*.' He held up his hand as Gala protested, 'Danae's the sort of girl who will go on for ever, searching for her own particular rainbow, and never really finding it.'

'It's true,' Gala had been forced to admit, sadly.

'Promise me that this will be the *last* time, Gala,' he'd said. 'Though she doesn't yet know it, Danae doesn't need you any more – and *you* don't need her. Be her friend, Gala, not her crutch.'

'Haven't you got it the wrong way round?' she'd asked. 'Don't you think Danae is *my* crutch?'

'Not any more, I don't,' he replied firmly. 'I think you are Gala-Rose, a beautiful girl, a good model and my lover.'

Gala listened to the faint patter of snow on the windowpanes and the jingle of sleighbells and horses' hooves from the courtyard outside her cosy room. She knew Marcus had called the situation exactly right; Danae was looking for something she simply couldn't offer; she was only a model, a slender body on which to hang clothes and a pretty face on which to paint expressions. Now Danae's frightening demands made her tremble just thinking about them; the helicopter always sweeping so close, the terrifying speedboat, and, worst of all, that cliff. She mustn't think about it, she told herself, quelling the rising panic; there was just one more week to go – just a few days – and it would all be over.

Danae wandered along the Hinderstadt, sniffing the crackly-cold night air eagerly; it smelled of wood-smoke, and of hot chocolate and apple strudel and a galaxy of delicious pastries from the bakeries and cafés; it smelled of Christmas trees where the freshly-cut pines were for sale by the Church of Saint Katharina,

341

and it smelled of horses whose harnesses jingled like a Christmas melody as the sleighs waited to take some lucky customer on a fairy-tale ride through the little town. Even the sounds here were different, muffled by the heavy early falls of snow . . . the soft woosh of the skis under the sleighs, the ringing of the coachmen's boots on the frosty ground as they stamped their feet to keep warm; the mingling of different languages, French, English, German, carrying clearly on the still air, and the comical sound of an oompah band playing in the terrace café of the Hotel Zur Tenne.

Camera in hand, she admired the thirteenth-century houses and hotels, painted pink and ochre, and blue and green, each window and door embellished with trompe l'oeil architraves and shutters and garlands of flowers – and each one a work of art! Thick walls encircled the old town and decorated archways led into fascinating little alleys. And beyond and around and above were the mountains; vast, encircling and brilliantly snow-capped under an almost-full moon.

Staring up at them, Danae caught her breath. On one side the peak of the Kitsbühlerhorn pierced the night sky, and on the other, loomed the Hahnenkamm, its slopes carved from ice in the moonlight. For the first time she understood what climbers meant by the 'magic of the mountains', why they felt compelled to try to climb them, to conquer their cold, inviolate beauty. Mountains, she thought, were surely the supreme challenge . . .

A crowd of ski instructors looking hard-bodied and bronzed in their smart red ski-jackets brushed past her, heading for a café and supper, and she suddenly felt hungry. It was as she followed them into the café that the idea came to her . . . ski instructors in their red jackets, their virile bronzed good looks – and Gala in the fantastic scarlet Bill Blass evening dress, with the moonlight on the mountains . . . she could visualise it all now! In fact, she knew exactly what she wanted. It might take a few days to get together because Gala had never been on skis in her life, but a couple of days under the tutelage of one of these guys and she'd be coming down these slopes like a pro! *Nothing* was impossible, decided Danae, as she ordered the hot aromatic gluhwein spiced with brandy and cinnamon, and the perfect thing to take the chill from her feet and hands. Absolutely nothing was impossible. Not even the idea of Gala-Rose skiing!

Gala's entire body ached so much, she could barely lift one ski-booted foot in front of the other as she bid goodbye to her coach. Hefting her skis onto her shoulder, she trudged across the nursery slopes at the end of her second day's tuition. Two days was all she had, Danae had informed her, because the moon would be full on the third night, and that's when they would be shooting. 'Just get her functional on those skis,' she'd commanded the ski-instructor, 'I don't want her breaking her leg – not until we've finished at least!' She'd laughed at Gala's indignant face. 'I didn't mean it,' she'd promised. 'I'd hate you to break a leg at any time, Gala. Anyway it would cost you a fortune – there aren't too many jobs for models with legs in plaster!'

Danae had commandeered a café half-way up the mountain as their base; an expert skier herself from years of youthful winter vacations in the Rockies, she'd decided that the winding course of the Hahnenkamm ski-race was exactly the 'challenge' needed for her photographs. 'But it's folly, Madame, to expect a novice to ski that course,' the instructor had told her shocked.

'I don't intend her to *ski* it,' she retorted, 'just to *look* as though she's skiing it. All you have to do is make her look good enough to give that impression.'

'It's risky,' he'd warned her, 'the girl is a good natural athlete, in a week, ten days even, she could manage, but *two days* is asking too much!'

'That's all we've got,' said Danae, determinedly, 'and of course she'll be good enough. Gala never lets me down.'

Gala turned to stare at the slopes of the Hahnenkamm and the distant tiny figures of skiers gliding down its notorious slopes. The mountain looked very beautiful; she could understand exactly what Danae wanted but the idea of herself on that sheer slope, miles above the valley, sent a shiver of terror along her spine. She had refused point blank to go up in one of those terrifying chair-lifts that wafted skiers high over the valley to the top of the slopes, and today her instructor had taken her up the mountain in the cable car instead. She'd clutched the metal rail inside the

343

car closing her eyes tightly to shut out the view of the sheer mountain slopes whizzing by and the sickening drop beneath, only opening them again as the car jolted to a stop. Her knees had trembled and she'd stepped out of the cable car and she could feel the sweat of fear trickle down her spine as she'd gasped mouthfuls of the clean, brittle air like a diver coming up from the ocean. Then she'd looked around and found she was at the top of the world! The valley spread like a miniature tapestry below her, ringed by pointed mountains . . . Gala's head had begun to swim with the old familiar fear . . . it was all right she'd told herself gritting her teeth, there were dozens of people up here. Just look at them skiing off down those slopes with whoops of joy! Of course it was all right . . . it was just the memory of that slippery roof, and Wayne's terrified eyes . . . She had got through the day somehow, but she was glad it was over.

Don't even think of it! she told herself as she plodded towards the hotel's ski-bus. It will be all right tomorrow night. The instructors will be there and it will be dark – you won't even know how high up you are. And besides, Danae wouldn't ask you to do anything too risky; all she wants is for you to pose with the instructors . . . it will be over before you know it. Meanwhile, all she wanted right now was a long soak in a very hot bath!

The weather forecast said that cloud would increase throughout the night and they were in for some snow. Danae scanned the sky anxiously. It was black and starry and lit by an immense perfect moon. It was like a gigantic lantern, she thought, staring at the glittering crystalline mountains.

Wrapped in a vast floor-length silver fox cape, Gala too stared upwards at the moon, wishing it would go away, because it showed how high up they were, and it was even more scary in the moonlight than under the sun. The slopes seemed ominously silent without their gaily-clothed skiers, and the pine trees on the lower slopes sighed eerily in the bitter wind.

'Gala in silver fox and red Salomon ski-boots gazing at the moon!' called Danae, laughing as she invented the caption. 'OK, folks,' she called, 'let's get this show on the road. It's too cold to do polaroids, we don't want Gala to freeze to death, do we? I reckon we've got five minutes at the most.'

Gala slipped her skis into her bindings, forcing herself to be calm, doing as she was asked automatically. With Rudi, her instructor beside her, she followed the others onto the slopes. The instructors lit their torches and held them aloft, illuminating the icy run the way they did for their usual weekly torchlit procession down the mountainside. Danae checked the fastening on Gala's red crash helmet and then removed her fur, handing it to Frostie. The icy night air, well below zero, hit Gala like a blow and she gasped with shock, gripping her ski-poles even tighter.

Danae skied down the slope a way, stopping at her chosen spot. 'OK,' she yelled, 'let's go . . .' With her Rollei at the ready, she watched as, surrounded by her torch-bearing bodyguard, Gala launched herself gallantly down the icy slope. 'Wonderful,' yelled Danae, snatching picture after picture as Gala, her scarlet taffetta ballgown tucked between her thighs, skied down the icy slope. 'That's great,' Danae cried excitedly, 'the best yet . . . just keep on coming . . . we're almost finished . . .'

Gala's long skirt, flying in the wind, tangled between her legs and with a sudden cry, she hurtled forward, her skis spinning off into the air. Danae heard the others scream and she held her breath as the instructor swung around in front of Gala, stopping her icy slide down the run. Helping her up, Rudi checked that she wasn't badly hurt, giving the thumbs up to the others to let them know Gala was OK. Then stripping off his jacket he wrapped it around her and helped her back up the treacherous slope.

Danae let out the breath she'd been holding in a sigh of relief . . . God, for a minute there she'd thought Gala had really been hurt! Rudi bent down to pick something from the snow and then skied to her. 'Here, Madame,' he said scathingly, holding out a priceless ruby earring surrounded with diamonds, 'it's for this that you risk that girl's life, no? Tell me, are you trying to kill her from exposure, or just by breaking her neck? Enough, Madame, I will not participate any further in this madness.'

'But it's not like that at all,' protested Danae as he turned away, 'of course I don't want to hurt Gala!'

Back in the café, Gala was wrapped in her furs, her legs and

345

arms were being massaged by Monica. Hector was feeding her sips of hot mulled wine and Danae smiled in relief as she noted that the colour was already coming back into her face.

'Thank God you're all right!' she exclaimed. 'What happened?'

'My skirt got caught on a ski,' sighed Gala, 'and before I knew it they were flying through the air and I was sliding down the mountain . . .' She smiled tentatively at Danae, 'But it was OK wasn't it? You got what you wanted?'

'Sure did!' Danae hugged her, grinning. 'You're the greatest, you know that don't you?' she whispered. 'My indomitable model. You'll challenge everyone from those magazine pages – you'll look wonderful, Gala.'

'Well, thank God it's all over,' she replied with a relieved smile.

Danae smiled back at her eagerly. 'As a matter of fact, Gala, there is just one more idea I'd like to get on film while we're here.' Gala gazed back at her, anguished, and she added hurriedly, 'Only *one* more, Gala, and I promise you this is the last.'

Gala huddled into her furs trying not to let the fear show in her eyes. She stared into the glass of glühwein, controlling her nervous shivering with an effort. 'Just one more, Danae,' she agreed, 'that's all though. Just one more.'

'Couldn't she just have *faked* it?' demanded Hector, staring up at the roof of the charming wooden chalet, its carved eaves and fretted balconies mantled in a foot or so of snow, and garlanded with icicles the size of stalactites. Silhouetted against a bright, clear blue sky, it looked like a true Christmas card chalet. A huge red, fur-trimmed sack lay on the snowy roof, spilling a pirate's ransom of jewels onto the snow, and Gala, shivering in five thousand dollars worth of white satin and half a million in diamonds, leaned gracefully against the chimney, her red velvet Santa Claus cape pushed back from her beautiful face and shoulders.

'She didn't want to do it you know,' murmured Frostie, 'she told me she's terrified of heights. You saw what happened when Danae wanted her to walk towards the edge of that cliff?'

'Then for Christ's sake, why is she doing this?' Hector exclaimed angrily. 'Danae's crazy – you realise that don't you? When I think of what she's put Gala through to get her goddamn pictures, I have to ask myself if she's in the right business. Maybe she should be making movies . . . at least she'd get the action there that she's craving . . . she's more like a goddamn movie-director than a photographer!'

'Hang on to your hats, folks,' called Frostie, 'here she comes . . .'

The tiny yellow helicopter clattered into view, swinging across the valley before making its turn and zeroing in on the chalet. 'Okay, Gala,' yelled Frostie, 'take it easy up there . . .'

Gritting her teeth, Gala tried very hard not to look down because when she did somehow the whole scene changed, and she was seeing again the concrete school playground and the row of iron railings with their sharp spear-like tips . . . but she'd vowed to herself she wasn't going to think of Wayne Bracewell . . . she mustn't . . . As the helicopter zoomed out of the sky towards her, Gala remembered clinging to the edge of the school roof with Wayne beside her . . . he'd dared her to do it of course, he'd called her a softie and egged her on until all her natural caution and shyness had been lost in anger and her desire *to show them* – all those laughing, jeering kids gathered around her in a circle, taunting her . . . 'Well go on then,' they'd yelled, 'wimpy old Hilda, can't even climb steps . . .' It had been true, she had been an uncoordinated child made even clumsier by her shyness . . . Desperate to prove to them that she was as good as they were, she'd followed Wayne's swaggering progress up the sloping stone buttress and from there onto a window ledge, clinging to it fearfully, her fingers scrabbling in the loose putty between the stones. Then somehow her foot had found a hold and her hands were on the gutter and she was scrambling over the edge and onto the roof. For a minute she'd just sat there, gazing upwards at Wayne who was already perched on the tiled ridge that ran across the summit. His mocking laughter had echoed around the schoolyard. 'Bet you can't get up here to the top then,' he'd taunted.

Gala could feel now the way her breath had seemed to stop as she inched her way crabwise, over the steep slope of the roof . . .

347

and when she'd finally made it, Wayne had pushed his grinning face close to hers. 'Bet you can't do this, scaredy cat!' he'd laughed, standing upright and balancing on the tiled ridge of the roof, arms outstretched like a tight-rope walker. Fear had given her the strength to stand up there and copy him, and she'd walked slowly after him, one hesitant step at a time, towards the grey chimney at the centre, not daring to look down. Just as she'd almost made it, he'd spun around, grinning at her, 'Look out, scaredy cat, you're falling,' he'd taunted, balancing arrogantly, hands on hips. Gala had glanced up at him, panicked, and then down at the playground and the mocking group of children below . . . then suddenly the sky had seemed to be whirling around her and it was mixed up with her view of the playground . . . and there were faces and noises and cries . . . fear had turned her limbs to jelly, as she clung to the chimney. And then there'd been another sound over the voices, a sound from the sky . . . the noise of a plane or a helicopter . . . As if in slow motion she'd watched Wayne's foot slip off the ridge of tiles, and then suddenly he was crashing down the sloping roof past her and his arm was outstretched, reaching for her . . . 'Hilda, Hilda . . .' he'd yelled, his terrified eyes holding hers as her arm reached out for him . . . 'Hilda!' he'd screamed as he disappeared over the edge . . . leaving her clinging to the chimney, her hand still outstretched to the place where he had been . . . There had been a single terrible cry and then a soft, collective moan . . . oooah . . . from the crowd of children in the yard. And that's when she'd looked down and seen Wayne, spreadeagled across the railings with blood pouring from his mouth and his body, and running down his winter-white legs that had suddenly looked so small and childish and helpless . . .

The yellow helicopter swooped closer and Gala glanced up terrified; she'd forgotten where she was, what she was supposed to be doing . . . it was just like it had been with Wayne and the school playground, it was *she* who had let Wayne fall, she had failed to give him her hand . . . she'd known as Wayne slid past her that if she'd taken his hand she would have ended up on those railings too . . . and now it was all happening again . . . As the yellow helicopter zoomed closer it seemed to Gala to block out

348

the sun and all the light was fading and she was back on that other rooftop, sliding, and sliding . . .

'My God, Gala!' screamed Frostie, 'hold on . . .'

But Gala couldn't hold on any longer. Her white satin dress wrapped itself around her like an expensive, elegant shroud as she toppled over the edge of the pretty, picture-postcard chalet.

34

Gala sleeping, thought Caroline, had the face of an innocent child. She was pale with fatigue and shock, the deep curve of her long eyelashes blending with the violet-grey shadows beneath her closed eyes and her soft mouth was slightly open as she breathed with the help of the ventilator in her throat. Marcus sat beside her, holding her limp hand in his, stroking it gently, and gazing at her face as if he could will her to wake just by the strength of his love. But the sad fact was that Gala hadn't awoken since her horrendous fall from the roof of the chalet. Miraculously, the four-foot drift of snow had cushioned her fall and she had suffered no spinal damage, but a broken rib had collapsed one lung and the bones in her left thigh had shattered into several pieces. After a lengthy operation, they were now held together with steel pins. But although a brain scan showed no reason for it, Gala had not emerged from the coma into which she'd plunged at the time of the disaster.

Frostie and Hector's hysterical phone call to New York had woken Caroline in the early hours of the morning, and she'd listened, disbelieving, to their condemnation of Danae . . . Danae had been reckless, she'd been selfish and uncaring, she'd deliberately put Gala in danger to get better photographs . . . They'd told her Gala had been flown to a hospital and was now in the operating room and that Danae was pacing the corridors like a madwoman, demanding that they tell her how Gala was, sobbing that Gala was like her sister, that she loved her, that she knew she'd killed her . . . and it was all her fault . . . 'And believe me, *it was!*' had been Hector's final damning words.

But it wasn't like Danae, thought Caroline worriedly, not the Danae she knew. She was enthusiastic – yes; a workaholic – certainly; and a perfectionist – without doubt. But selfish, reckless, uncaring? What had happened to change the Danae they knew? Right now it was impossible to find out the truth, because

Danae had simply disappeared. No one knew where she was; her answering service in New York picked up her calls and said they hadn't heard from her in a week, and she hadn't contacted *Images* or Jessie-Ann. Caroline had called Danae's mother in California, but she wasn't there either . . . there was simply no trace of her.

Marcus leaned forward, touching Gala's closed eyelids with his fingertip. It was a gesture of such tenderness that it brought tears to Caroline's eyes . . . poor Marcus, poor, poor Gala . . . 'Oh please, *please*,' she prayed, 'let Gala live, just let her be all right . . .' But her eyes were drawn like a magnet across the twilit room to the machines monitoring Gala's brain. The signal that was her heartbeat and pulse flashed silently across another monitor, counting out the rhythm of Gala's life. Such a young life, with so much to look forward to . . . so much in front of her. Oh Danae, thought Caroline helplessly, *Danae how could you do this*?

She looked up, startled, as Marcus's voice broke the silence. 'Caroline, why don't you go back to the hotel and get some rest? I'll stay here with Gala.'

The fatigue that she'd been unwilling to acknowledge engulfed her suddenly, and she thought longingly of bed. 'I'll call you . . . if necessary,' said Marcus quietly, not putting into words what they both feared.

She put her arms around him, and they held each other wordlessly for a moment before she left the quiet room. The hotel was only a few blocks away and after leaving a message at the desk that she was to be awakened at once if a call came from the hospital, Caroline fell wearily into bed. Her last thought before she fell asleep was that if anyone could help Gala, then it was surely Marcus.

'Gala?' Marcus leaned closer so that he could be certain she could hear, 'Gala, my love, I'm here with you, I'm holding your hand . . . you're just sleeping, darling, and when you wake, it will be as though you had a bad dream . . . just a bad dream, baby, that's all . . . and you know what we'll do when you feel better? We'll go away for a holiday – you and me, Gala. What do you think, babe? We'll go to Eleuthera, you'll love it there – the house is on the beach and we'll leave our windows open at night so we can listen to the sound of the sea; and I'll feed you mangoes and melon for breakfast, and we'll catch lobsters for our supper . . . the sun will feel so warm, Gala, and the sea is smooth and soft, just like silk. The birds will be singing when you wake in the morning and at night there'll be cicadas – such soft, warm nights, Gala, nights like you've never felt before . . .'

His voice drifted through the long night, keeping up a gentle conversation with the unconscious girl, stroking her hand, kissing her cheek, humming a tune they both loved, telling her his plans for their future, explaining his ambitions, saying how much he loved his young brother Jon and how they too, one day, would have kids . . . a whole bunch of them, he promised . . .

'Pardon, M'sieur,' the Swiss nurse eyed him sympathetically, 'but I think perhaps you should get some rest; you've been here all day and all night. Look outside, it's already dawn.'

'Open the curtains,' commanded Marcus suddenly, 'and let Gala see the morning sun.'

The nurse glanced at him hesitantly, perhaps the young man was a little mad; he'd talked non-stop for hours and now he believed the poor unconscious girl could see . . .

It was barely dawn and the sun was just a red ball in the gauzy grey sky . . . 'Gala, you've got to see this,' cried Marcus, gripping her hand tightly, 'it's like the creation of the world out there Gala . . . come on, darling, come with me and look at it . . .' He stared at her, urging her to open her eyes but the only sign of life was the soft rise and fall of her chest, and the blink of the machines that told him that – somewhere – Gala was there.

Slumping back in his seat exhausted, Marcus gazed at her sadly.

'Let me get you some coffee, M'sieur,' suggested the nurse, 'and you must eat something. You can't go on like this.'

Accepting only the hot coffee, Marcus stared at the tubes that fed life into Gala; the ventilator tube in her throat that assisted her breathing, expanding her collapsed lung until it could function again on its own; the tube that dripped measured doses of anti-biotics; the tube that fed essential liquids; the electrodes on her skull and her chest . . . Putting down his cup, he took her hand in his again. 'Gala,' he said firmly, *listen to me now*! I'm just never gonna leave you, you know that, so you'd better hurry and wake up because there are lots better places than this to hang out . . . I want to take you home, Gala . . . come on, babe, let's go home . . .'

He was asleep, with Gala's hand still clasped in his, when Caroline returned later that morning. 'He won't leave her side,' whispered the nurse, obviously touched by his devotion, 'he just talks and talks to her, as though she could hear him and answer . . . I've never seen anything like it.' She scanned the monitors again, 'Her pulse rate is down,' she murmured, surprised, 'it's almost at normal resting rate . . . and the heart-beat is steady. This time yesterday it was still very erratic.' She summoned the doctor who came to examine Gala and proclaimed her stronger, and said there was no need any longer for the ventilator, Gala was breathing on her own. There was a glimmer of hope after all, thought Caroline, and yesterday they had thought there was none . . . Sitting quietly by the bed, she watched over Gala while Marcus dozed.

Marcus awoke with a start. Staring at Caroline he said, 'I could swear Gala just pressed my hand!'

'Are you sure, Marcus? You were asleep and maybe you want it so much you just imagined it.'

'No,' he exclaimed vehemently, 'it wasn't a dream . . . I felt her hand move. I'm telling you *Gala moved*, Caroline!'

'Gala,' he murmured, bending to kiss her, 'Gala, sweetheart, I'm here, I felt your hand in mine. Press it again, darling, and then I'll know you are hearing me.' Gala's hand fluttered in his and he stared at Caroline triumphantly. 'Gala, oh Gala,' he said, laughing and crying, 'oh baby . . . at last . . .'

It was late that afternoon that Gala spoke, although she hadn't yet opened her eyes. Her lips moved, soundlessly at first and a galaxy of expressions crossed her pale face, as though she were searching for the right muscles to perform the function of speech and sorting the right words from her jumbled brain to tell him what she needed to say . . .

'Marcus,' she whispered, her voice breathy and faint, 'Marcus . . . where is the sun . . . take me . . . there . . .'

'I'll take you, Gala,' he murmured, 'just as soon as you're

ready. That sun is waiting for you and the house on the beach . . . all you have to do now is get better, baby . . .'

He met Caroline's tearful gaze. 'That's my girl,' he murmured his voice cracking with emotion, 'she's a fighter my Gala – and she's going to win!'

Gala sank back into sleep, but the doctors told them that this time it was a different kind, it was the sleep of healing. But Caroline thought that her face looked troubled and her eyes flickered restlessly beneath her closed lids, as though she were dreaming tortuous dreams. It was at that darkest hour of the night, just before dawn, that she finally opened her eyes and looked at them. 'Must tell . . . you,' she whispered haltingly, 'it's not Danae's fault . . . please don't blame her . . . it was something . . . from my past . . .' Her grey eyes were anxious as she gazed at Caroline, 'my own . . . silly fault.'

'Don't worry, darling,' Caroline told her, smoothing back her hair soothingly, 'it's all over now. Please don't even think about it.'

Gala turned her eyes to Marcus, her face distressed. 'Where is . . . Danae?' she murmured.

'Danae's not here, baby,' he told her, avoiding the issue. 'After she knew you were all right, she left . . .'

'I know she will have . . . run away . . . but she's not guilty . . . must find her . . . tell her . . . it's all right . . . Find Vic . . . Vic will . . . help . . . her . . . you must find Vic . . .' she insisted, her voice a mere breath. 'Danae needs him now . . .' Her eyes closed again and her chest rose and fell rapidly with the effort of speaking . . .

'I'll find her, Gala,' promised Caroline, watching her anxiously.

'Vic,' she murmured again, 'Danae . . .'

'I promise we'll find him,' Caroline said.

'Marcus, don't go away,' breathed Gala, her face peaceful as though she'd unburdened herself of a heavy load. 'I love . . . you.'

Caroline tiptoed tactfully from the room, leaving the two of them alone, their hands clasped across the white sheet, and another new dawn flooding the room with golden light.

Back at the hotel, she placed a series of urgent calls to New

York; to Jessie-Ann who was waiting desperately for news, and to the television news service, to trace Vic Lombardi's whereabouts.

After his conversation with Caroline, over the whoosh and crackle of a terrible international telephone line, Vic made immediately for Delhi airport, stopping at the telex office en route to notify his station of his plans before catching the first plane out. It was heading for London and from there he'd pick up a connecting flight to New York.

As he went over the story endlessly in his mind, he wondered bitterly how much of what had happened was his fault. Had he pushed Danae into trying to prove herself to the world? Trying to show that she could carve new frontiers where they didn't exist? 'Oh Danae, Danae, sweetheart,' he said to himself, 'this wasn't what I meant . . . all I wanted was for you to expand your horizons, to open your eyes to your own potential . . . to free yourself from the small world you were in . . .'

He'd called Danae several times since their fight in Washington, but she had never been home and he'd always put down the phone without leaving a message. What good was a message on an answering service when he was six thousand miles away? How could it possibly repair the rift between them? The only cure was a face to face confrontation . . . a 'but you said . . .' and 'no you said . . .' row . . . and maybe some tears . . . and then his arms around her again. Because Danae Lawrence was part of his life, whether she knew it yet or not. If only he hadn't been sent off to India on an urgent assignment the day after the Washington debacle things might never have gotten to this point. He'd thought it would only be for a week and then he'd get back to New York and sort it out, but he should have known better. *Nothing* was ever for a week in his business – it might be twenty-four hours or maybe six weeks – or even several months. That was the nature of his job.

But this time nothing – not even his job – would stand in his way. Caroline had said that Danae was in trouble; she was *desperate* . . . Danae thought she'd killed Gala, and God only knew where she was, or what she might do.

It was over a lonely beer in the transit lounge at Heathrow airport, London, that Vic realised where he would find her . . . because Danae had nowhere else to run to – but home.

Danae was dozing fitfully in her black leather chair, the television screen flickering silently into the darkness, when the telephone rang. She shot upright, as the phone shrilled imperiously. There was no way she could answer it, no way she could pick it up and hear the terrible news . . . that Gala was dead. Because that was the only reason anyone was calling her, she was sure of it. The ringing stopped abruptly and the room lapsed back into a silence so dense she could hear herself breathing.

She switched off the television and wandered barefoot to the window, opening the curtains onto another day. New York lay spread out before her, its ranks of steel and glass canyons and towers looking like the battlements of a fortress that everyone who came to this city felt compelled to storm. What had happened, she wondered, to the bright-eyed kid from California, with the camera in her hand and her high ideals and ambitions shining like a beacon before her? Where had she gone, that nice girl, with the red hair and the cheerful grin? 'I'm lost,' she murmured despairingly to herself, 'I'm just another statistic in New York's list of casualties . . . I've destroyed myself like so many others, caught on the merry-go-round of success . . .'

Turning from the window, she made her way into the bathroom, switching on the light over the mirror and staring at her reflection. Her long red hair straggled around her pale face and her eyes were swollen from endless crying. She ran a finger across her chapped lips and then turned on the tap, cupping the cold water in her palm and splashing it over her face. She looked terrible – but what did it matter. Who was there to care? Who was there who would even want to speak to her again . . .?

The doorbell rang suddenly, and she peered cautiously around the bathroom door, as though whoever it was could see inside her apartment. No one knew she was here, she hadn't answered her telephone and she hadn't been out since she'd arrived home. Such food as she'd eaten had been delivered. Perhaps this was a deliveryman? Had she ordered something and forgotten? Milk or juice from the little market across the street? She couldn't remember – the days were just a jumble.

The bell rang again, this time without stopping . . . whoever it was had left their finger on the button! Danae tiptoed across the room and put her eye to the peephole in the door. She stepped back with a gasp. It couldn't be! She put her eye to the peephole again. It was Vic! Oh no! not now . . . she looked awful . . . she was a mess . . . she didn't want to see Vic, not ever again . . . and he would hate her anyway, just like all the others . . .

'Danae, open the door!' ordered Vic.

She hesitated a moment then obeyed his command, opening the door slowly and standing back, her head bowed like a convicted criminal awaiting her sentence.

'Danae, love,' he cried, shocked by her appearance, 'what are you doing to yourself? Oh Jesus, Danae, why are you putting yourself through all this . . . ?'

He moved to put his arms around her but she stepped back from him, quickly. 'You won't want to stay when you find out what's happened,' she said, 'so I may as well tell you now and get it over with.'

'No need,' he said shaking his head. 'I know it all – and more. I have a message for you – from Gala-Rose.' Her head shot up and her frightened green eyes met his. 'She said to tell you that it was not your fault. *You're* not to blame, Danae. It wasn't the helicopter that frightened her, it was an incident from her past. The circumstances were the same and it was her own remembered fear that caused her to fall.' He stepped closer as she gazed at him disbelievingly. 'I promised her I'd tell you,' he said. 'Gala won't rest until she knows that you know. Can I tell her you've forgiven her, Danae?'

'*Forgiven Gala?* For almost *killing* her? Oh God,' moaned Danae burying her face in her hands, 'I thought she must be dead by now . . .'

'Gala-Rose is very much alive, and she's waiting right now for you to telephone her.' He came closer, placing his hands on her shoulders. 'You're much too hard on yourself, Danae. And you know something? You try too hard. Come here, my little love,

357

come to me. Let me hold you, let me tell you that it will be all right . . . that I never want to let go of you . . .'

Danae sobbed noisily against his chest and he let her expend her pent-up emotions, waiting until she had quietened a little. 'OK, Danae Lawrence,' he said gently, 'now go wash your face while I fix some coffee in that too-clean kitchen of yours, and then you and I have a bit of straight talking to do. OK?'

'OK,' she replied, looking like a solemn tear-stained child. She turned at the bathroom door. 'Vic?'

'Yeah?'

'Are you sure Gala's all right?'

'She's gonna be just fine,' he told her, 'it's *you* we're all worried about now. Your friends care about you, Danae . . . Jessie-Ann, Caroline, Gala . . .'

Danae's face lit with a small hopeful smile. 'We're still friends then, despite what I've done?'

'You've done nothing, except be very foolish,' he replied, 'now go wash your face and comb your hair . . .'

'Vic?'

'Yeah?'

'Why are you here?'

'*Why am I here?* Why do you think I'm here? Because I love you, of course. Now, get yourself together, Danae Lawrence – then we'll talk.'

She drifted into the bathroom feeling as though the burdens of the world had suddenly been lifted from her shoulders. Gala-Rose was going to be all right – and Vic was here. And he loved her . . . Her face in the bathroom mirror was still swollen and red, but her eyes showed her a different person from before . . . This was a woman who had come to terms with life suddenly, and with love.

35

Jessie-Ann was glad to be in the office because she and Jon seemed to rattle around in that lonely, too-quiet suite at the Carlyle. The Domestic Agency was searching for a new Nanny but this time she knew what sort of girl she wanted and she would settle for nothing less. Meanwhile, she was making sure Rachel Royle wouldn't get near Jon, she wasn't letting the boy out of her sight. He was here with her right now playing with a box of coloured paper clips and happily ripping sheets out of an order book, ignoring all the expensive new toys she'd rushed out and bought him. Of course she knew *Images* wasn't a suitable place for a child, but it would only be for a little while.

Laurinda hovered in the doorway of Jessie-Ann's office, a sympathetic smile on her face.

'Come in,' called Jessie-Ann, glancing up from the schedules of the week's bookings.

'I just wanted to say . . . well, if there's anything I can do, I'd surely like to help, Jessie-Ann. Anything at all . . . You helped me once and I'd like to repay the favour . . .'

'Thanks, Laurinda.' Jessie-Ann managed a smile, wishing the girl didn't always rub her the wrong way . . . she felt prickles down her spine every time Laurinda smiled . . .

'I'll do *anything*,' repeated Laurinda, her small black eyes fixed on Jon. 'I'll baby-sit for you anytime you like, just the way I did in Spring Falls. I know you'll be busy with . . .' and glanced away looking embarrassed, 'lawyers and things, and I guess you can't take a little kid places like that.'

Jessie-Ann told herself that after all the girl was only trying to be kind. 'Thanks anyway, but I want to keep Jon here with me right now.' She wasn't about to go into detail about her reasons though no doubt Laurinda had heard it all on the gossip grapevine by now . . .

'Well . . .' Laurinda shifted her bulk from one foot to the other anxiously, 'I just thought it's kind of a long day for a little kid like that to be cooped up indoors. I mean there's not that much for him to do at *Images*, he'll surely get bored. How about if I take him for a walk? You know . . . to the park, or along the street to the toy store . . . or maybe I could take Jon to the Zoo?'

'Thanks again,' Jessie-Ann replied, 'I appreciate your offer, I'll surely keep it in mind.'

Laurinda's smile disappeared as she closed the door behind her, leaving her face a livid mask of rage and frustration. She didn't notice Caroline coming out of her office until she bumped into her. 'Excuse me,' she muttered, averting her eyes.

Caroline stared after her in astonishment wondering what ever could have happened? Had there been a row? But over what? The accounts? Was Laurinda in some sort of trouble with Jessie-Ann? She hesitated, looking at Jessie-Ann's closed office door wondering whether to go in and find out what was going on, but a glance at her watch confirmed she was already late for her appointment at the Nicholls Marshall ad agency and whatever it was would have to wait.

Laurinda slammed the door of the ladies' room behind her and stalked over to the row of wash basins. Flinging her bag onto a chair, she stared at her angry face reflected in the long mirror, smoothing out the frown lines and the bitter downward curves of her mouth with a trembling finger. *She'd thought it would be so easy!* When she'd heard that Nanny Maitland had been fired and Jessie-Ann was looking after Jon by herself until the replacement came, she'd known that at last here was the moment she'd been waiting for. It was the perfect set-up – *and if she were clever Jessie-Ann would even hand over the boy to her!* The new apartment was ready, with a cot for Jon to sleep on and some toys to keep him amused – she'd even stocked her freezer with the kinds of things that she guessed kids ate. She intended to keep him safe until she had her revenge on Jessie-Ann and she could return him to Harrison – along with herself as his new guardian angel. Of course, should anything go wrong – and as a mathematician she'd assessed the law of averages, admitting that something *might* disturb the careful symmetry of her scheme – then young Jon might have to be sacrificed. But she really didn't want to hurt Harrison by doing that. You mustn't be sentimental about this, she warned herself, her dark eyes staring fixedly into the mirror, *just because you love Harrison Royle!* Remember, Jon is Jessie-Ann's child too, and that same law of averages pointed to the fact that he would have a percentage of her evil inheritance . . .

'Oh hi, Laurinda.' The door swung open as Anabelle, Hector's original model and now one of *Images'* stars, hurried into the room. 'God,' she gasped, 'I've just got to have a cigarette and this is the only place I can come for a quiet drag without Jessie-Ann catching me!' Propping herself against the washbasins, she pulled a package of Marlboro's from her pocket and lit one wafting away the smoke with an elegantly manicured hand. 'You OK, Laurinda?' she asked, staring at the girl in surprise, thinking she looked extraordinarily pale and . . . well . . . *strange* . . .

Laurinda thrust her hands into the pockets of her sweater, turning away from the mirror. 'I'm OK, a bit tired that's all,' she replied abruptly.

'Too many late nights huh?' teased Anabelle, 'you'll have to cut that out now, Laurinda, it's naughty!' Puffing on her cigarette, she coughed, wafting away the smoke again . . . 'God, I should give these things up, I know I should . . . they're killing me . . .'

Laurinda's hand closed around the cold metal keys in her pocket – the keys to her apartment. By tomorrow Jessie-Ann might have found a new Nanny and it would be too late . . . she could wait no longer. *She had to get Jon today.* Without speaking, she strode past Anabelle, her face rigid with contempt.

'Hey I'm sorry,' Anabelle called after her, 'I was only *teasing*, I didn't mean it, Laurinda . . .' She stared in astonishment as the door closed firmly after the departing girl. 'Jeez,' she muttered nervously, 'it was only a *joke!*'

It had been a hell of a day! thought Jessie-Ann, as she sank, exhausted, into her chair; it was six o'clock and the pressure hadn't let up for a minute. Every studio had been booked and *Images* was bursting at the seams with models and photographers and delivery people. It was worse than if Danae had been here, and that was saying something the way Danae had been behaving before the accident . . . sort of like a cross between the mad woman of Chaillot and Orson Welles, stalking round the studios declaring that nothing was right and that no one lived up to her expectations. '*Expectations*,' thought Jessie-Ann, now there was a word that everyone interpreted differently. What had been her expectations when she married Harrison? Had she had any – other than the expectation that their love would last? And hers had, because she still loved Harrison like crazy and she almost wished she didn't because then it wouldn't hurt so much. If she'd thought that working flat out all day at *Images* was going to ease the pain any, or even take her mind off things, then she'd been wrong. Because it was there, lurking at the back of her mind, even while she was talking positively about bookings and accounts, and checking things in each studio. And every time she looked at little Jon, with his frank blue gaze and his dark hair, he reminded her so much of Harrison that it caused a truly *physical* pain in her heart.

Her son was sleeping on the white tweed sofa, his thin little legs with their bony knees sticking straight out in front of him and his small hand curled under his slender cheek. Nobody could know how much she loved that kid . . . he'd brought her nothing but joy since the day he was born, and now, at almost two years old, he was her buddy as well as her child. Jon was an intelligent boy, full of curiosity in the world around him; he seemed to understand things small children were usually unaware of. He always sensed her mood, even when she'd thought she was doing a great job of faking being 'up' and 'happy', and whenever she let her true emotions show he would watch her quietly, holding out a small comforting hand and saying 'I love you, Mommy.' But just look at him now she thought sadly, in normal times he'd have been taken by Nanny to play with other children on the 'nanny circuit', and instead he was having to play all by himself in her lonely office. Jon had adapted to the change in his routine like a trouper, following her on her rounds of the studios, fascinated by the phones and the word processor. But earlier this afternoon he'd asked her when he was going to see Daddy and if he could write him a letter, and she had held his hand clutching the red crayon, drawing the letters . . . 'Darling Daddy, I miss you, love Jon' . . . adding any amount of 'xxxxxxxx's' and 'ooooo's'. Filled with pride, Jon had watched solemnly while she'd placed his smudged letter in an envelope, sealing it down and letting him stick on the stamp. We'll post it on the way home tonight, she'd promised him, but now it looked as if home-going would be a bit delayed. There were problems in Studio 3 and with Danae away and Caroline out all afternoon, it was left to her to sort things out. She glanced at Jon worriedly, she didn't want to wake him, yet she really should get down there and take care of business.

'Jessie-Ann.' Laurinda was at the door again, a sheaf of papers in her hand. 'I just wanted to give you these before I left.' Her cold, brooding eyes swung to Jon, asleep on the sofa.

'Oh Laurinda,' Jessie-Ann cried relieved, 'could you do me a favour? I have to go down to Studio 3 – I'll only be five or ten minutes – fifteen max . . . I hate to wake Jon when he's sleeping so soundly. Could you just wait here with him for me? I *promise* I won't be long.'

Laurinda's usually pallid face was flushed as she deposited the papers on Jessie-Ann's desk and took a seat on the sofa beside Jon. 'Don't you worry about a thing,' she said easily, 'just take your time, Jessie-Ann.'

'Laurinda, you're an angel,' she cried, already half-way through the door, 'I'll just be as long as it takes to sort things out in the studio. Model problems – that's all I need today! Thanks a million, Laurinda.'

Laurinda waited until she heard Jessie-Ann's footsteps disappear down the stairs and then she walked along the corridor, peering down the stairwell cautiously. She caught a snatch of music as the studio door opened and then closed, and she waited another few seconds, listening to see who else might be around. There was no sound from any of the other offices, it was almost five thirty and the receptionist and secretaries had left. Back in Jessie-Ann's office, she gazed for a moment at the sleeping child. He really looked cute, she thought, and so innocent, just the way he had that night in Spring Falls when he'd cried and she'd held him on her lap until they'd both fallen asleep. 'Wake up, Jon,' she whispered, bending over him, 'it's time to go.'

363

Jon's blue eyes flew open instantly, startling her. 'Going home?' he asked eagerly. 'Daddy home?'

'Sure,' replied Laurinda, 'Daddy's home. Come on, let's go.'

Jon's eyes regarded her cautiously. 'I want Mommy,' he declared loudly.

'Sure you do,' replied Laurinda, pulling his sweater over his reluctant, awkward arms. 'Mommy's waiting for you outside. She said to tell you to hurry.'

'OK,' he replied, his small face brightening, as she buttoned his sweater.

Laurinda hurried along the corridor and down the stairs with the child in her arms. The hall was quiet and she unlocked the door with one hand, letting them out into the street and closing it behind them quietly. With her heart racing, she hurried down the sidewalk, clutching Jon to her bosom, walking so fast that his head bounced. *She'd done it!*

'Where's Mommy?' Jon cried, holding tightly to her arm. 'Where's my Mommy?'

'Home,' she replied curtly, 'she's at home with Daddy.'

'No,' he cried, kicking hard with his little red sneakers, *'Mommy, I want Mommy!'*

'Be quiet!' hissed Laurinda, conscious of people staring as they hurried by. It wasn't until she'd turned the corner and was searching Third Avenue for a taxi that she'd realised she'd left her purse behind. *Goddamnit, she had no money!* Panic flooded hotly up her spine and setting Jon down on the sidewalk, she gripped him tightly by the hand, searching her pockets with the other. Her keys were there and a few coins that she usually kept handy for her frequent trips to that machine that dispensed snacks for a quarter. For once her addiction to sweet things was paying dividends – she had enough for the subway! Gripping Jon's hand she hauled him along the street.

'Ouch,' he cried, 'ouch, that hurts . . .'

Laurinda's steely grasp tightened as she urged him along. *'Come on now,'* she said, managing a grim smile, 'you want to see your Mommy and your Daddy, don't you?' It was a chilly night and she had forgotten Jon's coat and she was uncomfortably aware of how conspicuous they looked as he burst into tears.

Picking him up, she wiped his face with her hand. 'Come on now, we're going to the subway,' she told him. 'You ever been on the subway before? Well, you're sure gonna like it, Jon.' Hurrying through the steel barriers she kept up a barrage of chat, trying to divert him in case he caused a scene on the train, and as he became interested in the strange new world and the flashing trains he forgot about his Mommy. Sitting with him on her lap, Laurinda felt like a real mother, taking her kid home for his supper and she smiled suddenly at Jon. The pressure was off, she was home free.

Caroline let herself into *Images*, pausing for a minute in the hall listening to see who was still around, but apart from some activity in Studio 3, all was quiet. Running lightly up the stairs, she peered into Jessie-Ann's office but it was empty. She must have gone home already . . . or at least, she corrected herself sadly, gone back to the Carlyle Hotel. It was really because of Jessie-Ann that Caroline had returned to *Images* tonight. She should have gone straight home from her meeting . . . after all Calvin would be waiting, but Jessie-Ann was her friend and she was worried about her. She'd wanted to ask her and Jon back for supper but she guessed now it was too late.

Still, she'd call Jessie-Ann later to make sure she was OK, she decided, making for the powder room. Switching on the light, she flung her purse carelessly onto the chair, turning around exasperated as it fell to the floor, knocking over someone else's purse and strewing its contents across the carpet. She picked up the scattered possessions, stuffing them into the black leather bag, wondering whose it could be. There was a powder compact, a tube of panstick make-up in a very pale shade, a 'Cerise Gloss' lipstick . . . this purse surely didn't belong to one of the models, she thought with a grin, as she thrust a tough, wide-toothed metal comb into the bag. She picked up the small bottle of perfume, wrinkling her nose as she recognised it. Of course, the bag belonged to Laurinda! She was probably working late and had forgotten it. She picked up a white envelope from the carpet and was just about to thrust it inside along with Laurinda's other belongings, when her eye caught a flash of red type. Caroline paused, she hated to pry into another person's things, but there was just something about that envelope . . . something eerily familiar. She withdrew it slowly from the purse, turning it face up. The bold red type seemed to leap out at her . . . it was addressed to 'Jessie-Ann Parker' at *Images*, just the way all those other letters had been; *all those filthy, obscene, threatening letters to Jessie-Ann!*

She stared at the envelope, with a sick feeling in her stomach. It couldn't be true! *Not Laurinda!* Not sullen, small-town *Laurinda* who Jessie-Ann had helped? Caroline recalled the 'uncomfortable' feeling she'd had whenever Laurinda was around, remembering Jessie-Ann's story of Laurinda's disturbed family life, and suddenly everything slotted into place. Laurinda had always been *jealous* of Jessie-Ann! Staring at the obscene letter, there wasn't a shadow of a doubt in Caroline's mind that Laurinda was the culprit and that she was completely mad.

Leaving Laurinda's bag lying on the chair, she hurried from the powder room suddenly afraid that maybe Laurinda might come in search of it. She'd grab a cab right now, and be home in fifteen minutes, and then she'd call Jessie-Ann at the Carlyle.

'OK, you guys,' called Jessie-Ann, wishing she felt as 'up' as she sounded, 'see you all later.' She waved cheerily at the departing figures, closing *Images*' door behind them with a sigh of relief and checking her watch. Of course it had taken her twice – no *three times* as long as she'd expected and she'd kept poor Laurinda waiting!

She raced guiltily back up the stairs and along the corridor, calling 'Here I am!' as she swooped through the door, stopping abruptly as she saw the empty office. 'Laurinda?' she called, stepping back into the corridor and glancing up and down, 'Laurinda? Jon? I'm finished now.' There was no response and Jessie-Ann walked down the corridor towards Laurinda's office, her soft, flat leather boots making almost no sound. *Images*' offices were eerily silent. The Studio 3 group had decided to call it a night earlier than planned, and for once, all the other studios were empty too. She pushed open Laurinda's door eagerly, assuming that she must have taken Jon into her own office to try to keep him amused. 'Hey there,' she called. The office was in darkness and puzzled, Jessie-Ann let the door swing shut, staring blankly along the empty corridor. Perhaps Jon had been hungry and Laurinda had taken him out to get something to eat . . . but damn, she shouldn't have done that! Not without *asking* her – besides, she didn't want Jon eating any old junk food . . . Surely Laurinda must have left her a note. She ran back along the corridor, and sifted anxiously through the mess of papers on her desk. But there was no note.

She clutched the edge of her desk, telling herself not to panic, that there must be a logical explanation for all this. Everything was OK . . . Jon was with Laurinda, a friend of the family, so no harm could have come to him. The girl had just been thoughtless and not left a message, that's all, but *surely* she would be back soon . . .

The telephone rang, and she grabbed it thankfully. 'Laurinda?'

'Jessie-Ann, there you are!' exclaimed Caroline. 'I've been calling you and calling you at the Carlyle. Listen, I must see you, right now. It's urgent! *Vital!*'

Urgent? Vital? Jessie-Ann clutched the telephone, her face ashen . . . 'Jon, is it Jon . . . ?' she croaked, her voice failing her.

'Jon? Of course not.' Caroline hesitated and she breathed a sigh of relief. 'Look, Jess, it's about those letters you've been getting . . .'

'Letters?' She repeated Caroline's words, bewildered.

'Jessie-Ann . . . you're not going to believe it but it's Laurinda who's been writing those terrible letters.'

Jessie-Ann's knees collapsed from under her and she sank limply into the chair. 'Laurinda,' she whispered, 'did you say *Laurinda* wrote those letters?'

'I found one today in her bag – addressed to you. It's Laurinda all right; she must have been jealous of you since you were kids. She's crazy, Jess, *Laurinda is mad!*'

Caroline's precise English voice reverberated in Jessie-Ann's head, echoing over and over in her brain . . . mad . . . mad . . . mad . . . Laurinda is mad . . .

'Caroline,' she quavered at last, 'oh Caroline . . . something terrible has happened . . . *Laurinda has got Jon* . . .'

'What do you mean, she's got Jon?' demanded Caroline. 'Jessie-Ann, answer me . . . *speak to me, Jess*! Oh my God, look, darling, stay right where you are, we'll be there in ten minutes.'

Jessie-Ann placed the receiver back on its rest as precisely as if she were fitting the final piece into a jigsaw puzzle, staring at it numbly. Jon was with Laurinda and Laurinda was crazy . . . Laurinda had been sending her those letters – *all those years* – calling her all those terrible names . . . *And it was Laurinda who had threatened to kill her!* She was suddenly engulfed by a fear so powerful that it left her shaking . . . she wanted to scream out her fear, to tear it from her so that it would no longer be true . . . *the fear that Laurinda might have killed Jon*. Oblivious to the minutes ticking by Jessie-Ann sat in shivering silence, waiting for Caroline. Caroline would know what to do . . . she was the capable one, she would cope with this . . . she'd find Laurinda and Jon . . .

'Jessie-Ann!' Caroline hurled across the room, and flung herself onto her knees beside her friend, wrapping her arms round her comfortingly. 'It's OK, Jessie-Ann,' she murmured, 'everything's going to be fine. Just tell me what's happened and then we'll soon have Jon back.'

Calvin waited in the background as Jessie-Ann spilled out the simple story . . . 'You see,' she whispered finally, '*I gave Jon to Laurinda. It was me, Caroline, me! I'm responsible for handing over my child to a madwoman!* Oh my God, my God . . .' She covered her ashen face with her hands, moaning softly, as the tears trickled between her fingers.

'We must call the police!' exclaimed Caroline reaching for the phone.

'Hold it,' Calvin said quickly, 'if Laurinda's kidnapped Jessie-Ann's kid then she's not gonna like it if we go to the police. Her next move should be to contact Jess and ask for a ransom. What you've got to do now is call Harrison.'

Jessie-Ann took her hands away from her eyes, and stared at them aghast. 'Harrison?' she whispered, 'oh my God, Caroline, he'll go crazy, he *adores* Jon . . .'

'Where is Harrison?' asked Calvin. He repeated his question a second time when she made no reply. '*Come on*, Jessie-Ann, you must know where he is.'

'I don't know . . . I haven't seen him. I don't even know if he's in New York because he hasn't called me. I thought he would, you see,' she added looking at them piteously, 'even though I'd left him, I still thought he'd call me.'

'I'll call,' decided Caroline, 'Warren usually knows Harrison's whereabouts.' She dialled the home number, drumming her fingers nervously on the blue lucite desk until they answered. 'Caroline Courtney here,' she said quickly, 'is Mr Royle home? He isn't. Then could you please give me a number where he can be reached?' She listened a moment and then shouted, 'Damn it, Warren, don't give me any of that English butler nonsense, this is a matter of life and death! *Life and death* I tell you! Now, give me Harrison's number.' Slamming down the phone she scribbled the number rapidly. 'Washington,' she told them, looking at Jessie-Ann as she dialled.

'Mr Royle, please,' she said, 'Caroline Courtney calling.' She listened and then said angrily, 'Then please interrupt that meeting, this may be the most important call Mr Royle ever took in his life!'

Their eyes were fixed on her as she waited, fingers drumming on the desk again . . . 'Harrison,' she cried relieved, 'thank God! No . . . no it's not Jessie-Ann, she's here with me now. Harrison, it's Jon . . . he's . . . well, he's been abducted . . . Wait Harrison, first I've got to tell you that Jessie-Ann has been receiving terrible, obscene letters, threatening to kill her . . . she didn't want to worry you with them . . . but, Harrison, we know now that it was *Laurinda* who was writing them, *and it's Laurinda who has taken Jon!* Right,' she said, nodding her head, 'OK, we'll go back to your apartment and wait. Very well, no police . . . You're flying out right now? Yes, of course we'll wait. And Harrison . . . I'm so terribly sorry.'

She put down the receiver wearily. 'He's on his way. He had someone else call his pilot to ready the plane while he was talking to me. And we are to wait at your apartment, Jessie-Ann.' She glanced helplessly at Calvin as Jessie-Ann remained inert in her chair, her face in her hands.

'Come on, sweetheart,' Calvin said, putting his arms around Jessie-Ann tenderly. 'It's gonna be all right, Harrison'll be home before you know it. And I bet you, so will Jon.'

36

Laurinda had been watching the entrance to the Carlyle for over
an hour, walking up and down the block, keeping an eye out for
police cars and checking everyone entering or leaving to see if
they looked like plain-clothes cops. She knew it was risky but she
had to get that letter to Jessie-Ann tonight, and that meant she
had to deliver it herself. She waited until the lobby looked busy
and then darted in meaning simply to leave the letter on the
reception desk and rush out again, but the desk clerk spotted her
immediately. 'Just a minute,' he called loudly. Laurinda tried to
edge away as people turned to stare. 'What is this?' he demanded.

Averting her face Laurinda muttered, 'It's a letter for Mrs
Royle, she's expecting it.' And then she dashed through the door
and down the steps, running and running until her lungs felt as
though they were bursting. She stopped in a shop doorway to
catch her breath. Then spotting a passing cab she hailed it on the
spur of the moment, eager to get away. The driver dropped her
at a busy shopping centre in Queens and from there she walked
the two blocks to her new apartment, her steps quickening as she
approached the door.

The law of averages had gone against her more quickly than
she'd imagined – and from a completely unexpected quarter.
She'd always believed the riskiest part would be getting Jon away
from Jessie-Ann, but that had turned out to be easy. The real
trouble had come when she'd gotten Jon home. He'd started
screaming and yelling as soon as they'd left the subway and as
people turned to stare, Laurinda had had to pretend to be an
irate mother, threatening her child with a slap if he didn't behave
himself. But the threat had failed to quieten him and as she'd
rushed him through the hall of her apartment building, she'd been
forced to hold her hand over his mouth to drown his screams. It
hadn't been easy, fumbling with her keys, trying to get the door
open and at the same time trying to stop the damned kid from

yelling. When she'd finally slammed the door behind them, she'd pushed Jon into the new cot in her bedroom, shaking with anger and fear.

Jon had been crying uncontrollably, and Laurinda had stared at him frantically, wondering how she was going to keep him quiet. The sleeping pills had been the perfect answer, though of course she'd been real careful, crushing the pill first and giving him only a small amount. She'd stirred it with mashed banana and thrust the mixture into Jon's reluctant mouth, holding his jaws shut until he was forced to swallow. It had worked like a charm and Jon had been asleep within minutes. Trembling and covered with sweat, Laurinda had sunk into a chair wondering how she was gonna keep him quiet over the next few days, because he sure as hell would start screaming for his Mom as soon as he woke up. Maybe she just wouldn't let him wake – not properly that is. She'd just keep him 'sedated' like in a hospital, until she'd done what she had to do. But that meant Jon wouldn't be able to eat, and a little kid like that might die if he didn't have food for a few days . . . ?

Laurinda had sat there pondering her problem for an hour, and then she'd made her decision. She'd have to speed things up and take a few risks – like delivering the letter instead of mailing it as she'd meant to – but now she couldn't afford to waste any time. *She had to take care of Jessie-Ann tonight.* Her heart had leaped at the thought. All she had to do was compose the letter and Jessie-Ann would come running, anxious to do her bidding. And then *Laurinda* would be in control!

Jon was still sleeping when she returned from delivering her letter, and she bent over his cot, checking his pulse nervously to see if he was still alive – even though she was sure she'd given him just the smallest amount. Jon's pulse fluttered like a butterfly's wing under her fingers and she smiled thinking how peaceful he looked.

With a sigh of relief, she took a can of Coke from the refrigerator and pulling off the metal ring she deposited it carefully in the garbage pail. She drank thirstily and wiped her lips on a paper napkin. Then she took a plastic gadget from the drawer and placed it over the can to close it. Picking up a cloth she wiped clean the mottled-grey plastic counter where the Coke can had stood, looking around in satisfaction. Her kitchen gleamed from constant scrubbing and its two chairs were covered neatly in transparent plastic, as were the sofa and chair in the other room. Like her mother, Laurinda kept things clean.

Returning to the bedroom, she rummaged eagerly in the closet. This was a special occasion, the greatest night of her life and she would need to look her best. She'd bought the dress a few months ago on an impulse and it was quite different from anything she'd ever worn before. It was black and shiny, a tube of shimmering dark sequins that glittered under the light like the scaly skin of a dangerous snake.

It had been in the window of a small off-beat boutique in Third Avenue and it had drawn Laurinda's eyes like a magnet, the large shiny scales luring her as she lingered day after day, fascinated by its shiny glamour, imagining herself clothed in its reptilian skin. She'd finally succumbed to it one Friday lunchtime with her pay-cheque in her purse, even though it had cost her more than her week's salary. She hadn't tried it on, just told the girl what size she wanted and then paid. It hadn't mattered to her that she never, ever had any occasion to wear such a dress, just *possessing* it had given her a strange kind of pleasure. But now, she thought, lifting it triumphantly from the tissue paper, now she knew she must have had this night in mind when she bought it. The snake dress was exactly right for celebrating Jessie-Ann's death.

Casting off her skirt and blouse, she searched her dresser for a pair of black tights, pulling them on, frowning as she caught them on her sharp nails. Standing in front of the mirror she slid the black dress over her head, smoothing it over her heavy breasts and hips. The dress clung to her lumpy figure, gleaming under the lamplight, and Laurinda felt as though she had become the image of the dress, she felt snake-like and sinuous . . . quite different from her usual plain self. The dress had a high round neck and long sleeves and it covered her from neck to below the knee . . . Laurinda was no whore like Jessie-Ann, showing her breasts in low-cut gowns and her thighs in split skirts, displaying herself to men . . . Laurinda was pure and powerful . . . and this glittering black dress proclaimed her status.

373

She brushed her coarse hair, subduing it with a few heavy strokes and anchoring it securely with strong metal barrettes. Then she shined her already flushed cheeks with a scarlet blusher and smeared on the cerise lipstick, standing back to admire the effect with a satisfied smile. A few lavish sprays from a new bottle of her favourite musky perfume, and then the new black-patent high-heeled shoes that matched her shiny dress, and she was ready. She teetered happily across the room to put on her coat. Of course it should have been black mink to go with this splendid dress, but for now brown tweed would have to do. Later, when Harrison realised, gratefully, that it was she who had saved him from Jessie-Ann's evil influence, then there would be mink.

Laurinda checked her watch. It was nine o'clock – almost time to telephone Jessie-Ann for the rendezvous. She exhaled slowly, savouring the moment, feeling truly happy for the first time in her life. Soon, her past would be obliterated. Just one swoop of the knife and she would be a girl again, able to relive her youth. She would be like everyone else. *She would be free!*

The little boy moved restlessly on his cot and she stared at him in alarm; he couldn't wake up yet! She hadn't finished . . . Quickly she ran into the bathroom and shook another pill from the bottle. In the kitchen she crushed it, scraping a small amount into a cup and mixing it with a little water. Lifting Jon's head, she forced open his mouth and poured in the drug drop by drop, until the cup was empty. Then she laid him back against the pillows, covering him with a sheet, smiling happily . . . after all, if he lived, this boy would soon be her own son . . .

The streets were dark and empty as Laurinda hurried through the now-silent neighbourhood, her high-heels ringing on the frosty sidewalk. She hesitated at the entrance to the subway; there might be a long wait for a train and she was in a hurry, but the subway was anonymous – nobody would notice an ordinary girl like her . . . unless of course, she thought with a wild giggle, she took off her coat and revealed *the new* Laurinda! There was no need to hide any more, she realised suddenly, she could hold her head high, her past was almost behind her. Tonight she would be free for all the world to see.

Hailing a passing cab, she climbed in, settling into the seat with a rattle of black sequins. 'Third Avenue,' she snapped, 'and make it fast. I'm in a hurry.'

37

Harrison strode into the quiet apartment, handing his briefcase to Warren, who told him that they were waiting in the library. Throwing open the door, Harrison's eyes sought Jessie-Ann, but the woman slumped in the green silk wing chair seemed light-years away from the vital, eager girl he knew. Her usually smooth and silken blonde hair was in disarray, and her face looked haunted by fear.

'It'll be all right, darling,' he said reassuringly, 'I promise you everything's going to be all right. I've already called in a top private investigator and he'll be here within the hour. But first I want to talk to you.' Caroline and Calvin stood up to leave. 'Please don't go,' he said, his eyes revealing his tension, 'you know as much about this as Jessie-Ann; I'm going to need your help too.' Uncurling Jessie-Ann's rigid fingers from the chair-arm, he helped her to her feet, and took her to sit beside him on the big green silk sofa. 'All right, darling,' he said quietly, 'first we have to establish a few facts. It'll be easier for you to tell them to me, and then I can speak to the detective.'

Holding her hand, he extracted the story of how Laurinda had offered to help and how she'd left her with Jon at around five thirty that afternoon. 'It's all my fault,' Jessie-Ann said desperately, 'I gave Jon to a madwoman . . .'

'*Nothing* is your fault,' he told her firmly, 'you did a perfectly reasonable thing; you asked a girl whom you've known most of your life to stay with your child for a few minutes; a person who was a friend of your family and who was employed by you. Any of us, myself, Caroline, your mother or father, would have done exactly the same thing.'

'*But I shouldn't have! I should never have left him, Harrison . . . he should have been at home where he belonged.*' Her head drooped as she began to sob and Harrison stroked her hair back gently. 'Try not to cry,' he murmured, 'we are going to need all our strength to get through this ordeal.' He watched her sadly for a few more minutes, and then went over to Caroline and Calvin, who were waiting discreetly at the far end of the room.

'I need to know the facts, Caroline,' he said. 'I want to know how long she's been getting these letters and how often, and exactly what they said – or threatened . . . Oh God,' he cried despairingly, *why* didn't she tell me?'

'She didn't want to bother you, she wanted to work it out herself,' Caroline explained quickly. 'Jessie-Ann employed detectives and for a while she had a daily bodyguard, but there hadn't been any letters in ages, so she got rid of him. I realise now,' she cried, her eyes wide with sudden horror, 'that of course she hasn't received any letters since Laurinda came to work at *Images*!'

'Let's begin at the beginning,' suggested Harrison, with a glance at his watch. 'Matt Barclay will be here in a few minutes and I'd like to spare Jessie-Ann as much questioning as possible.'

Pulling the envelope from her bag, Caroline offered it to him. 'I found this letter by accident today. It was in Laurinda's purse. That's how I knew. And then, of course, all the pieces fitted perfectly. I haven't opened it,' she added.

Harrison opened the envelope and read the note rapidly, a frown between his brows. 'My God!' he whispered, horrified, *this is terrible!*'

'She's been getting them ever since she first won the model girl contest,' Caroline told him, filling in the details for Harrison while he made notes of dates and times and places.

Impulsively she took his hand. 'Please don't blame Jessie-Ann,' she begged, 'she left you because she didn't know what else to do. I know she hated herself once she'd done it; she felt she should have stayed and sorted it out. You *know* that what you have going is too good to just throw onto the marriage garbage-heap. And now this happens. She'll never forgive herself, Harrison – but I'm hoping *you* can forgive *her*.'

Harrison knew there was nothing to forgive, it was his fault as much as Jessie-Ann's. 'If we can get our son back, alive and well,' he said, 'then everything else will be all right.'

'Mr Barclay is here, sir,' announced Warren.

Matt Barclay was fifty years old, short and balding. He wore a smart dark-blue pinstripe suit with a custom-made monogrammed silk shirt that showed too much cuff, a pair of five-hundred-dollar alligator shoes and a very large diamond ring on his pinkie finger. His rugged face was smoothly shaven and Caroline could smell his cologne from across the room.

He looked, thought Caroline, like a very shady lawyer, or a very rich hairdresser, she couldn't decide which. But Matt Barclay's reputation preceded him; he was quite simply the best in his profession, running his multi-million dollar investigation company from a sprawling ranch in Texas that was built like a fortress and guarded like Fort Knox – in order to preserve him from the revenge of those who considered that Barclay had wrecked their lives because of his intrusive investigations. Marriage – or rather divorce – along with a lucrative line in industrial espionage, formed the mainstay of Matt's business, and his massive fees had made him a millionaire many times over. It was miraculous that Harrison had been able to get hold of Matt Barclay this quickly, because he was based in Texas. He must have tracked him down in New York.

Shaking Harrison's hand firmly, Matt listened to the story. 'OK, Jessie-Ann,' he said, standing in front of her, his hands clasped behind his back, 'get a hold of yourself here, because we've got to talk. Harrison's given me the facts and now I need you to fill in between the lines. I want to know *where* Laurinda lived – and *how* she lived – and *who* she lived with? You've known the girl since you were kids at school, your family knows her well. I'm gonna ask you to tell me what she was like, where she used to hang out, where she ate – who her friends were, what she did when she went home nights. I want you to think hard about Laurinda now, Jessie-Ann, because I want to get into that girl's *soul*.'

Jessie-Ann's blue eyes assessed the small, strange, dapper little man. 'Will you find Jon?' she asked finally.

'With your help, I will,' he promised.

A small sigh of relief escaped her lips as their eyes met; she knew she could trust Matt Barclay.

Prompted by Matt, Jessie-Ann described the Laurinda she'd known in school, the girl who'd worked for her father and whom her mother had helped. She drew a picture of a deprived, lonely child whose life was dominated by the mother's alcoholism to the point where Laurinda had been frustrated in her ambition to go to college and pursue the one talent she possessed.

'Where are the letters?' Matt asked.

She shook her head. 'I always destroyed them.'

'Here's the one Caroline found today,' said Harrison, handing it over.

Matt's eyebrows rose in surprise as he read it. 'There's more here than just jealousy and frustration,' he commented, folding the letter and putting it in his pocket, 'but no doubt later we'll find out exactly what. OK now, Caroline, you are the one who can tell us where Laurinda lives.'

'I'm afraid I can't . . . I mean I know where she *lived*, but she told me she was moving and she never told me where.'

Matt nodded calmly; these folks certainly weren't making it easy, but then *nothing* was ever easy . . . 'And there's been no communication from her yet?'

'None,' confirmed Caroline, remembering suddenly that Jessie-Ann had been staying at the Carlyle . . . 'Unless Laurinda has tried to contact Jessie-Ann at the Carlyle.'

'The Carlyle?' His bushy eyebrows rose questioningly.

'Jessie-Ann was staying there with Jon,' replied Harrison.

Matt's face was impassive as he nodded. 'Right, then I guess we'll call the Carlyle and see if there have been any messages.'

'I'll do it,' said Caroline, leaping to the phone, eager for action. 'This is Caroline Courtney,' she said when they replied. 'Mrs Royle would like to know if there have been any telephone messages for her? None? I see, thank you. Oh, but there is a letter in her box . . . hand delivered?'

Matt grabbed the receiver from her quickly. 'Yeah,' he said, 'Matt Barclay here. That letter – just take a look at it for me. OK, describe it. Right. About what time was that delivered. An hour ago! Shit! And who handed it in? Got it. I'll be right there, fella, you just hold that letter for me and Mrs Royle, OK? There's bucks in it for you, boy . . . '

Slamming down the phone he turned to them, his face impassive. 'Looks like we got ourselves another of those letters – in red and all – and from the description, it was delivered by Laurinda herself. I'm gonna go over there to talk to this desk clerk and try to get a line on what sort of state she was in and how she was behaving, and then we'll take a look at that letter.'

'It must be a ransom note!' exclaimed Harrison. 'We'll pay anything, *anything* to get our boy back.'

'I wouldn't bet on it,' Matt said thoughtfully, 'I just wouldn't bet that it's only *money* this girl wants.' He walked briskly to the door. 'I'll see you folks in about an hour. I have a feeling we may get some fast action on this one. Meanwhile,' he glanced at Harrison warningly, 'no police – yet. OK? And don't let Mrs Royle out of your sight.'

38

At the Carlyle Matt examined the envelope carefully. It was identical with the one in his pocket, typed on an electric typewriter using a new red ribbon that left a dense imprint, and it was addressed to 'Mrs Royle, Carlyle Hotel'. The message was a brief two lines: 'Jessie-Ann,' it said, 'stay by your telephone and do not contact Harrison or the police – if you value your boy's life.'

Goddamn, thought Matt, he'd expected more than this. The woman was a psychopath, he'd hoped she would act on impulse, pouring out her demands in a rambling letter that would give him some clue as to where she was at and what she *really* wanted, though he was afraid he knew that only too well. *Revenge* not money, was the name of Laurinda's game. It was an eye for an eye . . . a tooth for a tooth. Laurinda wanted Jessie-Ann. The only question was revenge for what? A plain girl and a beautiful one? A happy family life and a miserable one? A successful woman and a frustrated one? A mother and a childless woman? You could take your pick and still not come up with the right answer, because there was one other element that had emerged strongly from those letters. Sex. And how sex and Laurinda and Jessie-Ann tied together, he still didn't know. One thing was certain though, Jessie-Ann was in danger and so was her son.

Thrusting the letter into his pocket, he slid a fifty-dollar bill across the counter, listening as the desk clerk gave him an accurate description of Laurinda, telling him that the letter had been dropped off at around seven thirty.

Matt glanced at his watch; it was now nine o'clock and there had been no telephone calls yet for Mrs Royle. Collecting the keys to Jessie-Ann's suite, he walked over to the pay-phone and made a few quick calls, marshalling his forces. Within the next fifteen minutes there would be four men guarding the Royles' apartment, one in the front lobby, one outside their door, one inside the apartment, and one at the tradesman's entrance at the rear of the building. A 'bugging' specialist was on his way over and within minutes he would have the Royles' phones tapped and monitored. Meanwhile, Matt would wait upstairs for the telephone call that he expected would come sooner rather than later; Laurinda had risked capture in delivering the letter herself, and to Matt that meant she was desperate for action.

Jessie-Ann lay in her darkened bedroom, a cold cloth draped over her aching head and an untouched glass containing a sedative on the bed table. How could she sleep, or even relax – as they'd told her to do – when Jon was in danger? She tossed restlessly, determined not to allow the thought that Jon might be hurt – or even worse – to creep into the corners of her mind . . . and yet somehow it still did. He's just a little boy, she told herself desperately, he's only two years old . . . a baby . . . *no one* would want to harm a child like that, would they? *But Laurinda was crazy* – and crazy people did whatever they felt like doing, Laurinda's sense of right and wrong had been conveniently eliminated to suit her other needs . . . *Laurinda was capable of anything!* Jessie-Ann sat up suddenly in bed shaking with rage; her anger was so deep and consuming that had Laurinda been in the room she would have attacked her with her bare hands . . . she would have killed her.

The hot rage passed, leaving her clammy and chilled. But the anger was still there, only now it became suddenly calm and calculating, as though a computer had taken the place of her emotions, telling her what to do. With her head in her hands, Jessie-Ann tried to put herself in Laurinda's place, trying to imagine what she might do next? Of course she must have taken Jon to a hideout – this was a long-term plan and not a spur of the moment move. She would have had somewhere ready – that's why she'd moved from her old apartment. But Laurinda could be anywhere out there in New York . . . just anywhere, she thought helplessly. Still she would have to get in touch with her – maybe that letter left at the Carlyle had told them Laurinda's next move? It might even have set a rendezvous where she could hand over the ransom money and get her baby back . . . But Matt Barclay was saying nothing. 'Just tell Jessie-Ann to stay quiet and calm until we need her,' he'd told Harrison on the telephone. Then those men had come, bugging the phones to try to intercept Laurinda's calls, and now there were guards all over the place.

She realised suddenly that no one intended to tell her anything that was going on. They were trying to keep her quiet while they searched for Laurinda and Jon. It wasn't right . . . Jon was her son, it was up to her to protect him, to find him . . . to cherish him. She couldn't just sit here any longer . . . she must act! But how? What? Where? Burying her head in her hands again, Jessie-Ann moaned in despair. She must *think*! There had to be an answer somewhere – a clue to Laurinda's movements, if only she could keep her head and figure it out.

She went over the questions Matt Barclay had asked her and for which she'd had no answers. As far as she knew, Laurinda had no friends; she never spoke, as the other girls at *Images* did, of where she'd been the previous night . . . Laurinda always seemed to search out extra work, even taking it home on weekends – and yet once she'd gotten to New York, she'd never pursued her ambition to go to college at night and study for the accountancy exams. It came to her suddenly that there was only one place Laurinda would choose for their meeting. Of course, thought Jessie-Ann, it was all so clear now. She knew where Laurinda would be!

The telephone rang suddenly and she stared at the instrument, wanting desperately to pick it up, but they had forbidden her to do so. It might be Laurinda, trying to get in touch . . . her hand reached towards it – and then there was a tiny click as the call was picked up elsewhere in the apartment. Rigid with tension she waited for the faint trill of the bell that told her the caller had rung off. When it came, she waited for someone to come and tell her what was happening, but no one did. She tiptoed across the room, opened the door and peered out. The corridor was quiet. She would work this out herself. She knew where Laurinda was and she would wait no longer.

Pulling on a pair of jeans she added a warm sweater and a black woollen jacket. She thrust her feet into a pair of sneakers lacing them with trembling fingers, cursing herself for being so slow. Pushing aside a row of Harrison's suits at the back of the closet, she removed the panel concealing a small safe, spinning the dials quickly, waiting for the click that told her that bolts were unlocked. Inside the safe were piles of neatly stacked soft suede boxes containing a fortune in sapphires and diamonds and pearls. She had always refused to keep her jewels in the bank because she enjoyed wearing them. Jessie-Ann would have given them away willingly, along with this beautiful apartment and all the priceless works of art hanging on its silken walls; she would have traded *Images* and her entire future, just to know that Jon was safe, and that she would soon hold him in her arms again. And to know that Harrison still loved her.

Taking a small, chamois-wrapped parcel from the safe, she opened it carefully. The gun lay on its bed of soft cream leather, neat, precise and gleaming – pretending to be an innocuous piece of metal. It was only when it was held in the hand of a human that it became lethal, she thought as she checked the Beretta to see that it was loaded. Jessie-Ann was no stranger to guns, she'd gone skeet-shooting as a kid with her father, and had spent many hours with him on the rifle range in Spring Falls, practising her skills until she was an expert shot.

Tucking the Beretta into her pocket, she walked to the door and checked the corridor. Voices came distantly from the library located on the far right and she hesitated, biting her lip anxiously; it was going to be very difficult to get out without being seen, but surely if she were clever, it could be done. At right angles to the library door lay the wide corridor leading to the dining room and the kitchen. And outside the kitchen door was Jessie-Ann's goal – the emergency stairs leading from the penthouse to ground-floor level. There was also a service elevator . . . but taking the elevator exposed her to risk of capture.

Her sneakered feet made no sound on the thick carpet as she walked along the corridor, pausing as she came to the splash of bright light from the half-open library door. She hesitated a moment, then edged past and hurried along the corridor, past the dining room and into the kitchen. If Warren or any of the servants had been there she would have had to make some quick excuse, but the brightly-lit efficient kitchen was empty. The staff had their own sitting-room and she had guessed rightly that that was where they would be, discussing the crisis and prepared to sit out the terrible vigil with their employers. She noticed a couple of Jon's toy cars, forgotten on the kitchen counter, and still clipped onto the refrigerator door were the magnetic alphabet letters that only days ago she had helped him arrange into his name. 'Jon Royle', they said in bright red and yellow and blue . . .

Forbidding herself to cry, she peered through the glass panel in the service door. No one was there and she slipped through . . . then she was running down the first flight, gripping the metal banister as she swung around the landing and onto the next flight . . . running and running. After ten flights, she sank, gasping, onto a step trying to catch her breath, and wondering whether it would be safe to take the elevator now. If Barclay's guard were waiting at the bottom he'd be certain to notice the elevator stop, but if she took it only as far as the second floor, then crept quietly down the last flight she would be safe.

The service elevator was always empty at night and she leaned against the wall, breathing deeply and analysing her chances. If the guard spotted her, she would just run for it, she decided. The elevator bounced to a stop and as the door slid open she glanced cautiously from side to side, but the hallway was empty and she eased around the corner and down the stairs, walking quickly this time . . . one flight, two, three, four – and she was down.

Through the glass panel of the exit door, she saw the shadow of a man. The guard was right there, just where Matt had placed him! Oh damn it, goddamnit! Tears of frustration pricked her eyelids as she stared angrily at the silhouette that cut her off from her rendezvous with Laurinda – and her chance to save her child. A man's voice shouted across the silence, freezing her. 'Hey,' he yelled, 'hey, Bill . . .'

The silhouetted head swung around. 'Yeah!' he answered.

'Ambrose wants you upstairs right away, Brad's off to the Carlyle' . . . Now there were two heads outlined against the window and Jessie-Ann held her breath, listening. 'So who's taking over here?' demanded Bill, 'I can't just leave this entrance unguarded!'

'OK, OK, but like I told you Matt wants Brad and me *right*

now. He has to cover the Carlyle, and I'm to go with Matt. We're short a man until a replacement gets here. Look, by the time we get to the corner of the block, Ambrose'll be down here to meet you and he'll cover until we get the replacement. There'll be two extra guys over within half an hour, meantime we've just gotta do the best we can.'

Grumbling and cursing, they moved out of Jessie-Ann's view, and she allowed a few seconds to pass before unlatching the door. They were already fifty yards away, walking quickly and still talking loudly . . . she had maybe ten seconds. Closing the big metal door softly behind her, she slid into the alley, running silently close to the wall, shrinking lower as the lights from a street lamp illuminated her and praying all the while that they wouldn't turn round to check.

It took her less than a minute to reach the bright, crowded street, but it felt like an eternity. Out on frosty Park Avenue life was going on as normal and Jessie-Ann stared in bewilderment at the people dressed smartly, heading for restaurants and nightclubs when she was on a mission of life or death.

She hailed a cab at the corner of Park and Fifty-eighth, peering over her shoulder to see if she had been followed as the cab pulled away from the kerb, but there was no sign of the guards and she breathed a sigh of relief. She wanted no one to endanger her plan because she knew that only she could deal with Laurinda. And if she failed, then Laurinda would kill her and kill Jon too.

'Where to, lady?' the cab driver demanded impatiently.

'Where to?' she repeated, jolted from her thoughts . . . 'why, *Images*, of course.'

39

Matt picked up the phone on the first ring. 'The Carlyle,' he said crisply.

'But . . . I mean . . . I asked to speak to Mrs Royle.'

She had obviously expected Jessie-Ann to answer and she was stammering nervously and he knew he had her . . . this was Laurinda Mendosa coming in for the kill. 'Mrs Royle is out right now, Madam, would you care to leave a message where you can be reached . . . ?'

'No . . . oh no . . .'

She sounded panicked and Matt spoke quickly. 'If it's urgent, Madam, you can reach her at her home number.' She rang off without answering and Matt dialled his man at the Royles'. 'She'll be calling any minute,' he told Ambrose, 'get moving.'

'Right.'

The phone clicked off instantly and Matt knew that the recorder would be waiting to tape Laurinda's call. He just hoped Harrison could keep her talking long enough for them to trace it. Meanwhile, he was pulling out all stops and using his contacts to trace Laurinda's new home. The nugget of information that Laurinda kept an account at the same bank *Images* used had been his one clue to finding her. Methodical Laurinda had told Caroline it was so much easier to 'keep all her transactions under one roof'. It just so happened that Matt had once done a job for the Chairman of that bank and, he thought, rubbing his hands together and admiring his diamond pinkie ring in passing, a favour earned was a favour returned. The Chairman had been in touch with a Vice President who was at the bank now, personally checking their records. It seemed to Matt that a girl like Laurinda – who worked in accounts – would be sure to keep all her records straight with her bank. He'd bet his five-hundred-dollar boots that she'd informed them of her change of address. He'd also bet that she'd telephoned the Royles' apartment right after she'd put

387

the phone down on him. He leapt to answer as it rang. 'Yeah?'

'Matt? She called all right, and Harrison spoke to her, but she put the phone down on him. There was no chance to trace the call.'

'Jesus!' exclaimed Matt, frustrated, there sure as hell weren't too many leads on this broad . . . 'I'll call you back,' he said, slamming down the receiver.

He prowled the elegant hotel suite impatiently, checking his 18ct gold Rolex watch every couple of minutes, waiting for the call. When the phone finally rang, ten minutes later, he pounced on it like a hungry panther leaping on his prey. 'Barclay,' he snarled into the receiver.

'Oh Mr Barclay, James Waltham here. Our Chairman and mutual friend, Edwin Green asked me to remit some information.'

'Yeah, yeah,' growled Matt, wafting away the banker's pedantic chat, 'you got the address?'

'We have an address for Miss Laurinda Mendosa, yes. Of course, strictly speaking, I shouldn't be giving you this information . . .'

'D'you speak with your Chairman earlier?' demanded Matt, brusquely. 'Yeah? Well just give me that address then, there's a good boy . . . OK, fella,' he said writing busily on the notepad beside the phone. 'Right, gotcha. Thanks, Mr Waltham. And don't worry about the rules y'know . . . old Ed Green owes me!' Slamming down the phone he simultaneously ripped the sheet of paper with the address from the pad, and dialled the Royles' number.

Harrison answered, sounding nervy and on edge. 'OK, Harrison, it's Matt. I've got Laurinda's address. I'll be with you in ten minutes. Tell Jessie-Ann to be ready – we'll need her there if we're gonna bargain for your kid.' Tossing down the receiver he raced for the door. His driver was waiting and if he dodged through Manhattan's traffic the way he usually did, they'd be there in less than ten.

They were waiting for him at the door. Caroline was in tears and Harrison looked distraught.

'Jessie-Ann's disappeared,' said Calvin.

'She's not in the apartment,' added Caroline, 'we've searched from end to end . . .'

'I thought your men were guarding this place,' said Harrison tersely, 'how the hell could she just disappear?'

'That's something I intend to find out right now,' replied Matt, heading towards the two guards patrolling in the corridor. They explained that the only time it could have happened was when Bill left the service entrance unguarded for a moment as they changed over. There was no sign of a disturbance in Jessie-Ann's room, but she'd obviously changed her clothes . . . Harrison thought she must be wearing jeans and sneakers . . .

'OK both of you,' yelled Matt, 'you're fired. As of now!' Turning his back on them he returned to the group in the library. 'You're sure Jessie-Ann didn't know Laurinda's home address?'

'No . . . at least she said she didn't and I had no reason then to disbelieve that,' Caroline told him.

Matt frowned, he was getting nowhere on this, and fast . . . and he didn't like to be beat . . . especially with a kid's life at stake. 'Grab your coats,' he said, 'we're off to Laurinda's. I think I know where your wife and your boy are Harrison.'

Jessie-Ann closed *Images*' bright blue door behind her, flinching as the lock clicked loudly. The little noise sounded like a pistol shot in the quiet hall. Her heart pounding, she stared down the brightly-lit corridor, expecting Laurinda to come hurtling towards her any minute. She strained her ears into the silence, every sense alert . . . but there was no sound.

She took the small black gun from her pocket. It fitted into her palm as easily as a small calculator and she flicked off the safety catch, wincing at the sound of the bullet clicking into the chamber. Then, her finger on the trigger, she walked soundlessly through the hall and along the corridor. For the first time she wished that *Images* hadn't grown so rapidly. In the early days there would have been only two rooms and a studio to search, but now the studio-complex sprawled uninvitingly before her, hiding Laurinda – and danger.

Keeping her back against the wall, Jessie-Ann mounted the stairs, switching on the light in the first office she came to, Danae's room. It was empty. Caroline's office was next – and it too was empty. She stood outside the closed door that led into her own office, breathing deeply. She mustn't be afraid now . . . she had to find Laurinda in order to get Jon back . . . hurling herself forward she kicked open the door. She huddled back against the corridor wall, terrified . . . if she hadn't been so frightened she told herself, easing her hand along the wall towards the light switch, she would have felt ridiculous, like a lady detective in a losing TV series. Her finger found the switch and suddenly her familiar office was flooded with light. It was empty.

She sank into the chair by her desk, her heart thudding, wondering what to do next. There were other offices in this part of the building, but somehow she didn't think Laurinda was lurking in the accounts department or the powder room . . . And yet she was sure she was here – she *sensed* it. She reminded herself that she wasn't dealing with the plain, methodical, accountant Laurinda now, she was here to meet the crazy Laurinda who had stolen her boy, the crazy woman who had written those vile letters for years . . . and *that* Laurinda would surely want a suitably theatrical location for her final scene. Of course, she would be in the studios! But which one? It would be foolish just to go around switching on lights, she'd be a standing target for whatever Laurinda chose to do. The knowledge that Laurinda was there, waiting for her in the darkened studio made her nerves crawl and sweat trickled clammily down her spine. With an effort she forced herself to analyse the situation. Studio 1 was the oldest and the smallest, Studio 2 had been cleaned out just today, ready for the painters later this week. The photographer who'd been using Studio 4 had left all his own valuable cameras in there and had locked it when he left. That left Studio 3, which was the largest, and still had the props in place they'd been using this afternoon. It was a futuristic set with burnished steel chairs and tables and a stark black and white backdrop . . . one of Danae's ideas for the new catalogue. A gallery ran along one wall of Studio 3, jutting out like a stage. Of course, thought Jessie-Ann, that's where Laurinda would be!

She thought of Jon, alone and frightened, and then with her gun gripped tightly in her nervous hand, Jessie-Ann walked quietly back along the corridor, down the stairs and into the hall. Studio 3 was at the very end and its heavy steel double-doors were closed. No sound came from within, and as she tiptoed towards the doors Jessie-Ann could hear her own heart beating. *If she were ever to get Jon back then she must be brave.* And there was something else too . . . she needed to know why Laurinda hated her enough to want to kill her.

The door swung open silently under her hand. It was black as pitch and she waited for her eyes to adjust to the dark. She'd thought she knew this studio like the palm of her hand but now the proportions and dimensions seemed to have altered. She searched desperately for the light switch, but she couldn't find it . . . it was ridiculous because she *knew* it was there on the left side! She stopped for a moment, holding her breath and listening. Empty silence was quite different from this, she thought. There was an extra, tangible dimension here. She could *feel* Laurinda's presence, the way she would have sensed there was an animal in the room . . .

Holding the small pistol out in front of her, Jessie-Ann edged along the studio wall, making for the stairs that ran up to the gallery. The darkness pressed against her eyelids and she stopped suddenly, realising in horror that Laurinda might be standing right in front of her . . . now! A sob of terror rose in her throat . . . the only comfort of the darkness was that Laurinda couldn't see her either.

Jessie-Ann had forgotten the complicated set and she stumbled heavily as she walked straight into a steel table, sending it crashing to the ground. She froze in horror, as the noise echoed around the black room.

Up in the gallery, Laurinda smiled happily. So, the fly had walked into the trap without even asking. She flicked a switch, turning on the powerful halogen spotlights, lighting up the studio like an operating room, trapping Jessie-Ann in their beams. She just stood there, transfixed. Laurinda thought contemptuously that she could have killed her easily. And then she noticed that Jessie-Ann was holding a gun in her hand!

She hadn't anticipated a weapon and she frowned. But no matter, it would just add a little spice to her game of torture. She frowned again . . . Jessie-Ann wasn't dressed the way she'd wanted her . . . if she'd been able to reach her by telephone she would have instructed her what to wear. She would have told her to put on her whore's costume . . . a red dress, clinging and slinky to show off the body her father had desired so much. No matter, she thought briskly, jeans had always been the way her Pa saw Jessie-Ann anyway. Even at fourteen she hadn't needed scarlet dresses to look sinful.

Laurinda sat at the little table with its bowl of pretty blue and white flowers, contemplating Jessie-Ann in silence, savouring her moments of power the way she had always promised herself she would. The short, stubby-handled knife, its blade honed, gleamed on the clean white cloth in front of her.

Shading her eyes with her arm, Jessie-Ann stared upwards but the banked halogens bounced light back onto the set, leaving the gallery in shadow. Laurinda must have dragged in all the lights from the other studios to set up this battery, she thought. Now the moment was here she felt calm and unafraid. She was going to kill Laurinda in order to get Jon back, it was as simple as that. All she had to do was be cleverer than her . . . and surely it couldn't be too hard to outsmart Laurinda . . . 'Hi,' she called, 'are you there, Laurinda?'

Laurinda watched her, the little smile still curving her lips, thinking that Jessie-Ann looked like a moth caught in the heat of the lamps . . .

'Laurinda,' called Jessie-Ann cajolingly, 'I know you're there and we must talk. Don't you agree, Laurinda? I know my father would want to hear what you have to say about taking Jon away without telling me.'

Laurinda's eyes blazed. 'Don't you talk about your father!' she screamed. She lapsed back into silence . . . Jessie-Ann had tricked her into giving away her position . . . but she wasn't gonna talk about Mr Parker, no way . . . nor Mrs Parker . . . they didn't belong in the same world as Jessie-Ann.

'OK, OK, we won't talk about him,' promised Jessie-Ann, edging slowly towards the stairs on the right-hand side of the room. 'But I want you to know, Laurinda, I really appreciate your baby-sitting Jon for me. I could tell right away you were real fond of him . . . just the way you were hugging him holding him close that night in Spring Falls when we got home from the Old Mill Restaurant, remember? You didn't just leave him to cry, you held him until he went back to sleep . . .' Jessie-Ann had no idea of how she was keeping control and just talking when all she wanted to do was rush up those stairs and fire bullets into Laurinda, but she wasn't afraid of her any more. She was here to fight for her child and for her own life. 'Come on, Laurinda, let's talk about it, shall we?' she coaxed, wishing she could get away from those goddamn lights . . . 'Harrison's on his way over,' she added, 'he'll be here any minute.'

'No! *No! Harrison can't come here!*' That wasn't part of the plan, thought Laurinda wildly . . . he couldn't come here – not until she'd finished . . .

Jessie-Ann ran the last few feet to the stairs, swinging around the newel post and onto the bottom step pressing back against the wall, her gun aimed up at the gallery.

Snatching up her knife, Laurinda ran to the top of the stairs, pausing as her eyes met her enemy's. Only a dozen steps separated them now.

Jessie-Ann stared at Laurinda, stunned. The girl looked incredible . . . grotesque . . . that dreadful dress with the enormous glistening sequins . . . a dress for a cheap nightclub singer on the downward path of show-business or a floosie on the make on Forty-second street . . . and Laurinda's face was plastered with wild colour, she must have raided Isobel's make-up box, piling on everything she could find . . . black circles around her eyes, vivid scarlet cheeks, and her mouth looked like a great, glistening, bloodstained gash. Jessie-Ann levelled the gun at her. 'OK, Laurinda,' she said clearly, 'I want you to tell me what this is all about. Just tell me where Jon is and then I'm sure we can straighten everything out and no harm done. We can still be friends, Laurinda, can't we? After all, you and I go back a long time . . .'

'A *long* time,' muttered Laurinda, edging down a step, 'but you were never my friend, Jessie-Ann. You were always laughing at me, mocking me . . .'

'*Never*,' retorted Jessie-Ann. '*I never did that*, you're imagining things . . .'

'You and your friends, such a tight little circle,' sneered Laurinda, 'always together, always sniggering behind everybody else's back, it was always *you* who were the ringleader, egging them on . . . and it was *you* who . . .'

She stopped suddenly and Jessie-Ann eyed the gleaming knife in Laurinda's hand . . . the girl might fly at her any minute *but she couldn't shoot until she knew where Jon was . . . and she had to find out why . . . ?*

'I'm sorry you felt left out, Laurinda,' she said hastily, 'but you never seemed to want to hang out with the rest of us. I mean, your father always came to get you from school and all . . .'

'Whore!' screamed Laurinda rushing wildly down the stairs. She stopped just two steps above her, the knife glinting under the lights. Jessie-Ann's finger tightened on the trigger but she still couldn't shoot. Laurinda seemed unaware of the gun . . . she was lost in a torrent of accusations.

. . . 'leading him on . . . exciting him . . . he watched you twitching your little ass all the way home from school . . . oh you knew even then how to turn men on . . . I saw how you'd glance back at him over your shoulder with that sly little smile . . . and then . . . and then it would be *me* he'd take it out on . . .' her voice dropped to a whisper, 'it would be *me* he'd take into that back bedroom, *me* he'd touch . . . pretending it was you . . .' Her head lifted suddenly and she glared at Jessie-Ann with her grotesquely blackrimmed eyes looking like a musical-comedy witch. 'It was *you* he was dreaming of fucking . . .' Laughter gurgled from her as she hurled the ugly word at her enemy . . . 'Yes. It was *you*, *Jessie-Ann* . . . when he was defiling me in that nice clean suburban bedroom, every afternoon after school . . . He stabbed me with his body until I bled, and you know what? My mother didn't even ask what the blood was on my sheets . . . she just changed the linen and drank another bottle of Southern Comfort . . .'

'My God!' whispered Jessie-Ann, her eyes fixed on Laurinda's bitter contorted face . . . 'I'm so terribly sorry . . . how could he do that to you . . . your own father . . .'

'It wasn't *his* fault,' screamed Laurinda, 'it was *yours, Jessie-Ann . . . it was you! You* made him do it!' Her voice dropped and she looked at Jessie-Ann calmly. 'And now I'm going to kill you,' she said matter-of-factly.

'My father would have killed your Dad if he'd known,' cried Jessie-Ann desperately, 'it's dreadful, terrible . . . I'm so *sorry* Laurinda.'

'*Your father must never know!*' cried Laurinda, panicked. 'No one will know. Only you.' She ran a finger along the knife's wicked edge, a garish smile lighting her face. 'My Pa used this to prune roses,' she said conversationally, as though they were having afternoon tea and discussing the progress of their gardens. 'Funny though, he was always so tender with plants. He told me he hated to cut off strong shoots but he had to do it in order to allow others to live. *And then he'd beat me with his belt until the welts bled.*' She moved a step nearer and Jessie-Ann's finger tensed on the trigger, but with Laurinda's terrible story her anger had evaporated. All she wanted now was Jon back . . . and Laurinda *had* to tell her where he was . . .

'Where is Jon?' she asked quietly, '*please* tell me, he's too little to be left all alone like this . . . he needs us, Laurinda, we must go back and get Jon . . .'

'Jon?' Laurinda's crazy smile reappeared suddenly. 'Jon is mine now . . . and when you are gone, I'll stay with Harrison and look after him. I shall care for both of them.'

'But where is he *now*, Laurinda? Harrison will be here any minute,' Jessie-Ann lied desperately, 'he'll want to know. Maybe you and I can go there right now, together . . .?'

'You think I'm a fool don't you?' said Laurinda softly, still playing with the knife, running her finger back and forth against the sharp edge until the blood ran, 'but I'm not.' She moved down another step and Jessie-Ann held her breath, trembling, but she knew she couldn't shoot Laurinda because if she did she might never find Jon . . .

'Look, I'm sorry about your father,' she said quickly, 'let us

help you. I'm sure Harrison will pay for anything you might need
. . . just look how much he's helped you already . . .'

'Helped?' Laurinda's black, boot-button eyes glinted ma-
liciously as she crouched just two steps above her. 'I don't need
your help, Jessie-Ann . . . I just need you *dead*.' Her face contorted with insane rage as she launched herself, screaming, at
Jessie-Ann.

As the gun clattered to the floor, Jessie-Ann smelt the girl's
sickeningly sweet perfume and felt the blood trickling warmly
down her face. Laurinda's left arm grasped her long hair like a
vice as she lashed at her with the knife and Jessie-Ann screamed
in pain and terror as the knife caught her again and again, ripping
her arms, her shoulders, her hands, as she fought her attacker
. . . kicking and twisting and turning.

'No, no, Laurinda . . .' she screamed, as they crashed together
down the stairs. Pressing the arm with the knife up and away
from her, she lay, panting with fear, beneath the crazed girl . . .

'Now!' cried Laurinda holding the knife aloft, savouring the
moment, the culmination of all her years of guilt and pain, '*now*
I've got you, Jessie-Ann . . . and you'd better pray to God to
forgive you – *because I never will* . . .'

The door to the studio crashed open, and Laurinda swung
around, screaming as Matt Barclay, Brad and Harrison hurtled
across the studio. Grabbing her upraised arm, Matt forced it backwards, twisting it behind her as she shrieked with pain and anger.
'OK, babe,' he snarled grabbing the knife and thrusting her roughly
to the floor, 'it's all over now so you can quit screaming. Never did
like loud noise,' he added, as he pulled Laurinda's hands behind
her back while Brad slipped on the cuffs and locked them.
'Someone call an ambulance,' he said, looking at Jessie-Ann,
'and the cops . . .'

'Jessie-Ann, oh Jessie-Ann, my love,' groaned Harrison, wiping
her bleeding face with his handkerchief, 'what has she done to
you . . . ?'

She stared bewildered, at the blood. 'Jon?' she whispered . . .
'Laurinda must tell us where Jon is.'

'Jon's outside in the car with Caroline . . . he's all right, love,
Jon is all right . . .'

With a sigh of relief Jessie-Ann closed her eyes. Jon was safe, and Harrison was here . . . and he still loved her . . .

'Laurinda,' she murmured as blackness closed over her, 'poor Laurinda.'

40

Jessie-Ann was coming home from hospital and Harrison had filled the apartment with flowers. Peach-coloured roses that looked freshly-picked from an English cottage garden drooped their heavy heads from low silver bowls, filling the rooms with their delicate scent and exotic tawny lilies dripped saffron pollen onto satin-polished antique tables. The violets that Jon had chosen for his mother were arranged in little crystal vases on a table by her bed along with a picture he'd drawn. A bottle of her favourite Krug '76 Champagne was chilling in an ornate turn-of-the-century silver ice-bucket, from Christofle in Paris, and an exquisite lace-trimmed nightdress and negligée in a shade that the salesgirl had told Harrison was called 'oyster' but looked to him more like pearl – was draped over the turned-back bed.

Jon ran excitedly from room to room, chased by his new Nanny, a twenty-two-year-old fresh from the Norland Nanny School in England and full of practical wisdom, as well as a generous helping of joie-de-vivre that matched Jon's own. Warren stood by the door prepared to fling it open and express his happiness to Mrs Royle on behalf of all the staff that she was safe and well – and home again. The cook-housekeeper and the two maids hovered in the background ready to add their own welcoming words, and a pint-sized Jack Russell terrier pup – Jon's very own dog – got under all their feet.

'Here she is,' called Warren as Jon shot towards the door like an arrow released from a crossbow, hurling himself into his mother's arms before anyone had time to say a word.

Jessie-Ann picked up her son, laughing and hugging him while Warren said how pleased he was that she was home, and the cook and the maids came hurrying forward, tripping over the barking puppy, exclaiming how well she looked and how glad they were to see her again.

With Jon's small hands clasped tightly around her neck, Jessie-

Ann gazed at them all, and then back at Harrison. 'You know what?' she said smiling, 'this really is "coming home".'

It was true, thought Harrison, his arm around her shoulder as they walked through the lovely rooms. Whatever it was that made a place 'a home', had finally happened. In Jessie-Ann's weeks in hospital, it seemed their relationship had healed along with her wounds.

'How beautiful!' marvelled Jessie-Ann, touching the roses, 'and a wonderful bouquet from Rachel too . . .' She read the little card with a smile, 'To my dear daughter-in-law, wishing you a happy homecoming, with love, Rachel . . .'

'She's trying!' Harrison commented, with a smile.

'Daddy has a present for you,' cried Jon, tugging her long blonde hair to get her attention.

'Ouch, you bully, Jon Royle,' she exclaimed. 'A present for me? How exciting.'

'*Two* presents,' cried Jon, wriggling from her arms, 'come and see.'

Standing at the door to their room, she laughed at the sight of so many flowers. 'It's a conservatory!' she exclaimed, her blue eyes sparkling with happiness.

'Here, Mommy, look . . .' Jon pointed to the nightdress on the bed, 'and this too . . .'

'Jon . . . one thing at a time . . .' protested Harrison as the boy pushed the parcel eagerly into her hands.

'Do I open it now?' she asked, smiling.

'Yes, yes,' he cried, 'now, Mommy!'

Pulling off the gold ribbons, Jessie-Ann unwrapped the flat parcel carefully. 'It's a book?' she guessed, pulling out the tissue-wrapped contents.

'No, no . . .' yelled Jon, squirming with excitement . . . 'it's *special*, Mommy . . .'

Jessie-Ann stared at the documents in surprise, they looked so legal, with red tape and seals . . . 'Title Deeds', to the parcel of land known as 'The Framingham Farm and Stud . . .' Her blue eyes grew round with astonishment as she gazed first at the deeds and then at Harrison. 'It's the ranch,' she whispered, 'in bluegrass country . . .'

'The one you always wanted,' he replied. 'I bought it two years ago, for your birthday, but then you wanted something else.'

'Horses, Mommy, lots of horses,' cried Jon, excitedly, 'a special pony for me . . .'

'Of course, darling,' she replied, so brimful of happiness, she wanted to cry. 'And we'll go and see it very soon.'

'When?' he cried hopping from one foot to the other as Nanny appeared at the doorway in search of him.

'As soon as Mommy is well enough,' Harrison assured him, laughing.

'Meanwhile, Mommy has to get some rest,' said Nanny whisking him into her arms and carrying him off. 'And how about supper, young man?'

Jon looked back at them happily. 'Soon,' he called, 'promise!'

'We promise,' they called, smiling.

As the door closed behind him, Jessie-Ann and Harrison gazed solemnly at each other, and then he put his arms around her and she leaned her cheek against his. 'I love you,' she whispered.

Harrison ran a tender finger down the thin red scar that crossed from cheekbone to mouth, 'I love you too,' he murmured. 'I just wish I could have saved you from this.' He thought of the criss-cross of scars that marred her beautiful body – Laurinda's legacy . . .

'It wasn't your fault,' she replied softly, 'it wasn't even Laurinda's. I can only pity the poor girl . . . at least now she will be taken care of.'

It seemed as though with the stabbing, Laurinda had finally purged herself of all her pent-up anger against Jessie-Ann, and she'd simply waited obediently in her jail cell for whatever might happen to her. In the end Jessie-Ann had refused to press charges against her and the psychiatrists had told them that Laurinda had reverted completely to childhood – probably to a time before her father had begun to abuse her. Laurinda now lived, like a happy child, in a beautiful old house set in wonderful gardens, where she was cared for by specialists at Harrison's expense, and where they were assured she would be happy.

'*My* scars will heal,' Jessie-Ann told Harrison. 'I'm the lucky one.' And she knew it was true.

41

Gala lay on a cushioned chaise-longue on the verandah of Framlingham Farm House, her long legs stretched out in front of her and her eyes closed. She wasn't sleeping – she was much too happy to waste a wonderful afternoon like this on sleep. She could hear Jon's excited voice from the paddock as Harrison and Marcus gave him a riding lesson on his brand-new pony, Jolly; and she could smell something delicious baking in the kitchen.

She had been here for two months recuperating from her accident and with her leg finally out of plaster, she was beginning to feel like her old self again. Not *quite* her old self, she corrected. She felt like the *new* Gala, the person she had become.

With her eyes closed she conjured up a faded picture of Garthwaite, its grim grey narrow terraces and the eternal backdrop of ugly man-made hills of shale and slag that were the signature of a coal-mining town. She thought with sadness of her mother who she realised now had been tied down too young by the strange, introverted child she had been . . . and she remembered again the scene on the school rooftop with Wayne. It had all been exorcised now, all the guilt was gone. The guilt at not being what her mother wanted, of not catching Wayne's hand as he fell, of her bewildered search for an identity because in her formative years those around her had failed to show her her own qualities. She was done with the past. She was who she was whether she was called Hilda or Gala, or the future Mrs Marcus Royle.

Opening her eyes she gazed across the flower-filled garden at the wonderful old Italian fountain that Harrison and Jessie-Ann had bought in Italy on what they laughingly called their 'second honeymoon'. It was a sensual sculpture of entwined lovers and mermaids and sea shells that sent forth delicate sprays of water with the refreshing sound of cooling rain on a hot afternoon. In the paddock beyond, she could see Marcus astride an elegant Arabian mare, one of the prizes of Jessie-Ann's brood, and Jon in a special little basket-seat perched on top of his pony, his helmet slammed proudly onto his head and his bare feet thrust into his special new tooled-leather *real* cowboy boots from which he wouldn't be parted.

Thank God no harm had come to Jon in that terrible ordeal with Laurinda; but she would never get used to the long scar that marred Jessie-Ann's beautiful face, though neither she nor Harrison even seemed to notice it any more. Gala knew that eventually it would fade into a thin pale line, and anyhow Jessie-Ann's happiness certainly didn't spring from the knowledge of her own beauty, but from her love for Harrison and her son – and the new baby on the way.

This was her new family, thought Gala, contentedly; these were the people who loved her and whom she loved; they accepted her as the person she was.

It was Jessie-Ann, her childhood role-model, who had given her her first ambition; and it was Caroline who had helped give her a sense of her own value; and it was Danae – dear, wonderful Danae, who had truly *created* Gala-Rose, the model, whose photograph would adorn the covers of no less than six major magazines this year . . . though none of them would be taken by Danae. *She* was half-way across the world, keeping one step ahead of the news with her camera, and Vic Lombardi. Danae's 'Surprises', the pictures of Gala, taken on their whirlwind tour of strange locations, had been an outstanding success, winning praise from fellow-photographers, art critics and the public alike. Eventually an exhibition had toured major cities, drawing unprecedented crowds. But Danae hadn't stayed around to see it all happen. She'd come with Vic to see Gala in the hospital and she and Gala had cried on each other's shoulders, each telling the other it was *her* fault and claiming responsibility for the accident, until it hadn't seemed to matter any more. And then she'd disappeared to find her happiness elsewhere.

'Hi there, sleepyhead,' called Marcus tugging lightly at her blonde hair. 'Mmn, do I smell something good!'

'Me too,' exclaimed Harrison, following him.

'Me too,' cried young Jon, tearing past them along the verandah.

'Is it my imagination, or is something burning?' asked Harrison, as the screen door flew open and Jessie-Ann stared at them shamefacedly. An apron flung over her blue jeans emphasised the curve of her new pregnancy and her cheeks were flushed and her hair was in wild disarray. 'About that apple pie,' she said to them, as the smell of burning became more prominent. 'I forgot to tell you, I never baked one before . . .'

The laughter of her family, thought Gala, was the very nicest sound she could ever wish to hear.

42

'You know what?' said Vic to Danae over Singapore Slings at the bar of Raffles Hotel in Singapore, 'life ain't like in the movies.'

She glanced around the smart hotel, an anonymous modern version of the one whose name evoked memories of wonderful old movies full of international intrigue, a venue for spymasters and double agents and glamorous, dangerous women wielding tiny pearl-handled pistols and bargaining with 'love' . . . a place where you might expect to meet Humphrey Bogart and Sidney Greenstreet or Lauren Bacall and Ingrid Bergman . . .

'Don't I bring you to all the best places?' demanded Vic grinning.

'Well,' Danae admitted, 'it's surely better than the last place . . . a brothel, if I remember?'

'A minor error,' he shrugged nonchalantly, 'though maybe the scarlet and gold decor and the naked ladies in the salon should have given us a clue. But you've got to admit that those beds were a lot more comfortable than the hammock, two trees and a mosquito net you've been used to lately.'

'I'll settle for comfort,' she replied feelingly, 'air conditioning, a real bed, a hot bath . . .'

'Dinner by candlelight, a good bottle of wine, or maybe even two . . .'

'Silk next to my skin, perfume, high-heeled shoes . . .' she continued their dream, smiling.

'You still look pretty good to me,' he said. 'And I like that new haircut. I'll take you any way you come, Danae Lawrence, long hair or short, satin dresses or the latest in safari-wear . . . I love you anyway.'

Danae grinned at him, ruffling her newly-cropped hair self-consciously. 'When I think how easily I used to command the models to cut off their hair – and it took me a month of agonising before I could bring myself to do it. Even then, the only thing that forced me into it was that I couldn't bear the heat any longer.'

'Make the most of this, Danae,' Vic told her, suddenly serious, 'like in Harbour Island I'm never sure how long it will last.'

'Like my hair,' she replied taking his hand, 'long or short, I'll take it any way it comes. And besides, this time I'm coming with you.'

Vic gazed at her seriously. 'Look, Danae, are you certain you want to come along? Surely you've got things out of your system by now? Your photographs are magnificent; but it *is* risky – and you have that whole other *successful* life back in New York.'

Looking into his anxious brown eyes, Danae sighed. 'First you talk me out of that successful New York life,' she said, 'and now you're trying to talk me back into it.'

'Only because I don't like the idea of you being in danger. I'm being selfish, Danae.'

'Then that's the way I like you, Vic Lombardi,' she replied. 'Let's be like they were in the old movies,' she said, touching glasses in a toast, 'let's "live for the moment, and let the future take care of itself". Somehow I seem to have spent years making plans to manipulate my future . . . now I just want to take it as it comes. As long as you are part of it.'

'It's a deal,' Vic promised as her eyes met his over the rim of the glass.

43

Danae's latest batch of photographs from the hot-spots and war-zones of the Middle East, Africa and India were strewn across Caroline's desk, as she circled it yet again, transfixed by what Danae's searching camera had revealed . . . sad sagas of human wasteland; shattered townships where civilised people had once lived together in an ancient, cultured society; bursts of humour in the middle of strife; and portraits of people – bruised by war, with the pathos of loss expressed in their patient, ageless, dignified faces. Men, women, children . . . Danae's camera had caught them lovingly, admiring their bravery and stoicism. The photographs were brilliant, thought Caroline, and they were beautiful, and touching. Danae, dodging bullets, was seeking redemption from her mistakes – and finding it. These photographs would appear in newspapers and journals around the world; they'd been clamouring for more ever since her first pictures had surfaced a month ago.

Caroline slowly reassembled the photographs, replacing them carefully in their folder. It wasn't hard to deduce where Danae was at any given moment; all they needed to do was watch the TV news reports with Vic Lombardi. Where he was – so was Danae. And it seemed that now she understood *why* he was there. Danae had finally found what she wanted, thought Caroline, though it had been a strange and curving path.

The door to her office stood open and she leaned back in her dove-grey leather chair, her eyes closed, secure in her theatre-world of *Images*. She could hear the clack of typewriters from the back room and the constant purr of the telephone, and the voice of the receptionist downstairs as she answered it.

A studio door slammed and she caught a burst of laughter over the strains of Beethoven's Choral Symphony – Mark Ellis was in Studio 3 and he always worked to Beethoven regardless of the fact that his models wanted Bruce Springsteen! The sound of raised voices came from Studio 1 where Frostie White was trying to sort out which model was to wear what in the Avlon ad – and losing by the sound of it; and there was the rattle of metal dress-racks being trundled into Studio 2 for the *Vogue* shoot on Brodie Flyte's new winter collection. Only Studio 4 was silent, and not for long . . . Mort Freeman was expected at six o'clock to take over where Danae had left off on the Royle catalogue. Mort was twenty-four, a New Yorker and, according to Danae, the best talent to come out of this city – apart from herself – in twenty years! And before she went shooting off to points East, she'd promised Harrison that Mort would give Royle's a brilliant new catalogue.

Caroline's office was too far away to catch the smells coming from the kitchen were the chef was preparing a buffet supper for the forty people who would be working at *Images* until late that night, but she knew it would be superb.

Opening her eyes, she looked around her office, enjoying its sense of purpose; it was neat and businesslike with everything in its proper place. Sunlight slanted through the frivolous lilac-swagged curtains she'd been unable to resist, and in a crystal bowl on her desk the magnificent double-petalled rose and cream peonies Calvin had sent her had opened out into the peak of their blowsy glory. Their faint, insidious scent was a constant reminder of his presence in her life, and she smiled.

She lay back in her chair, her legs stretched out in front of her, arms behind her head, contemplating how good life was. She had just that morning seen *Images'* latest bank statements – and there was not a single line of red in them! The studios were booked up for months ahead and their models and stylists, hairdressers and make-up artists were in constant demand. Her concept, conceived over champagne cocktails in the Plaza with Jessie-Ann, was a proven success. So much so that it was already being copied down by others. No matter, thought Caroline, *Images* is unique, because it's real. Its people were hand-picked to suit their style and temperament . . . and of course, *Images* had Jessie-Ann, and Danae – and herself – to offer. As well, of course as Gala-Rose and Calvin, New York's two top models.

Calvin . . . she thought dreamily, her lover and the love of her life. Calvin would always be there, waiting for her, she was sure of that now. When he wasn't away working, of course . . . oh he loved her, but Calvin was a lot like Cosmo Steel, the cat, who ran to greet her joyfully when she arrived home, rubbing against her hand and purring in an ecstasy of love and happiness, and at the same time snatching tiny painful, loving bites at her fingers. The old clichés about love were right after all, thought Caroline, you had to take the rough with the smooth, the good times and the bad, the kisses and the hugs – and sometimes the little bites too.

The petals of the beautiful overblown cream peony fell with a soft taffeta rustle onto her desk and she touched them, smiling. Fate had been kind to her – she had so much to be grateful for now . . . *Images* and Calvin. And anyway, she'd never really expected it *all* on that gold platter, had she?

ELIZABETH ADLER

INDISCRETIONS

Jenny Haven is a Hollywood legend, a movie star living in a world of blue skies and perpetual sunshine. But neither stardom nor money nor beauty can save her from a tragic death. Her lover has something to hide, so do her lawyer and agent. And what of Jenny's daughters – legacy of three grand and passionate affairs?

Paris A long-legged and beautiful fashion designer, struggling for success in a harsh world, sacrificing her ideas and principles to prove herself to Jenny.

India Smaller, rounder, the 'ordinary sister'. Only her sense of humour saves her from a series of disastrous love affairs.

Venetia The product of an expensive English education, she is nineteen and hungry for her first taste of 'real life'. She is the very image of her mother . . .

Born into a world so different from Jenny's, the Haven girls make what fortunes they can – at whatever cost . . .

HODDER AND STOUGHTON PAPERBACKS

ELIZABETH ADLER

THE RICH SHALL INHERIT

'She was the mysterious, elegant woman travelling first class on the liner Ile de France on her way to New York; she was the beautiful, aloof stranger dining alone on the Orient Express . . . the slender wary-eyed chic woman who spoke to no one on the cruise from Cairo to Luxor . . .'

Poppy Mallory: hauntingly lovely and unapproachable. Her whole life had been marked by passion, tragedy, scandal — and mystery.

But now that mystery was to be unravelled for Poppy had died rich; very, very rich. And the scramble was on to lay claim to her fortune.

Claudia, greedy for yet more luxury; Pierluigi, desperate to save his financial empire; Orlando, his artistic genius held back by poverty; Aria, enchanting innocent on the brink of life; and Lauren, who has sacrificed herself to care for a child — all were obsessed with the need to discover the truth about Poppy's life . . .

HODDER AND STOUGHTON PAPERBACKS

ELIZABETH ADLER

PRIVATE DESIRES

Set against a glittering international backdrop that sweeps from the South of France and Paris to Brazil, New York, Cuba and Egypt – the enthralling story of a passion that leads to heartbreak and tragedy.

Half-Egyptian, half-French, Leonie is born into poverty and hardship. Exotic good looks and a fierce fighting spirit lead her to a very different life of wealth and luxury in turn-of-the century Paris – until her fateful encounter with a cruel and powerful man whose obsession becomes her destiny . . .

HODDER AND STOUGHTON PAPERBACKS

ELIZABETH ADLER

PEACH

Peach de Courmont: Born into a world of wealth and luxury, she was heiress to one of the world's great car-making dynasties. Adored granddaughter of the exotic Leonie, and doting half-sister of Lais and Leonore, Peach grew up surrounded by love. She was a child of privilege.

Noel Maddox: His circumstances were very different: born illegitimate, a charity-child who grew up in an Iowa orphanage. Grew up determined to fight his way to the very pinnacle of power — whatever the cost.

Two people born on opposite sides of the world, at opposite ends of the scale of fortune. — Two people who were destined to meet — and destined to love each other . . .

Moving from the slums of Detroit to residential Boston, from the glamorous Riviera to Paris and the peaceful English countryside, PEACH is the enthralling, heartstopping story of their love.

'A long, romantic read . . . one of the best'
The Mail on Sunday

HODDER AND STOUGHTON PAPERBACKS

ELIZABETH ADLER

PRESENT OF THE PAST

Sprightly, aristocratic Maudie Molyneux is an eighty-year-old Irish charmer. She and her friend and housekeeper, 'Faithless' Brigid, are all that is left of the old days at Ardnavarnha, the beautiful old house set above the sea in the green hills of Connemara.

Suddenly Shannon Keeffe arrives from New York, distraught about her millionaire father's apparent suicide. Shannon believes he was murdered and that the clue to the killer's identity lies in the past, here at Ardnavarnha.

It is up to Maudie to spin the tale of her own amusing and indiscreet past, as well as that of the impetuous and beautiful Lily Molyneux, who caused chaos in the lives of everyone she ever met and left a legacy of hate.

Lily Molyneux was a wicked woman – or was she? Was Shannon's father really murdered? And if so why? And by whom?

Maudie and Ardnavarnha gradually reveal their secrets, unravelling the intertwined mysteries of Lily Molyneux's tangled life and Shannon's father's death.

'A terrific read'

Woman and Home

HODDER AND STOUGHTON PAPERBACKS

ELIZABETH ADLER

THE PROPERTY OF A LADY

'A large fine emerald, 45 carats, flawless. The property of a lady.'

A simple description in an auction catalogue sends ripples of excitement and fear around the world.

Rumours surround the sale of the fabulous stone:

Romance: what passion has it brought to the lives of those who have come within its thrall?

Fortune: is it the key to the famous Ivanoff treasure lost in the Russian Revolution?

Mystery: what links it to the orphaned princess whose secret is buried in the past?

Only ninety-year-old Missie O'Bryan knows the dangerous truth behind *The Property of a Lady*.

HODDER AND STOUGHTON PAPERBACKS

ELIZABETH ADLER

THE SECRET OF THE VILLA MIMOSA

Set in Hawaii, San Francisco and Provence, Elizabeth Adler's memorable new novel is an enthralling story of two women whose fates are entwined with a flawed and dangerous family.

In San Francisco a young girl is found half-dead, victim of a murderous attack which has left her without a memory. Watching the news report of her plight, famous American doctor Phyl Forster feels a strange attachment to the unknown girl. For in her, Phyl sees a chance to rebuild a precious, lost part of her own life.

Together they construct a new identity for the girl. She begins to rebuild her life and find happiness again as 'Bea French' – until fate draws her to the tragic Villa Mimosa in Provence. There she discovers a letter that holds the key to her deadly past . . . and an ominous warning for the present.

HODDER AND STOUGHTON PAPERBACKS